THE
KEY
IN THE
WILLOW
TREE

Sherri,
Thanks for reading!

Lisa C. Allen

55 Leslie - H+ hosp, family, Stan, mistress, practical

Carrie - divorcing, Bill dies, media,

Sandra - mistress, pregnancy, had pill addiction, Opal

3/3 Laney - restaurant, Bar chef

Mae - housekeeper for Carries

p. 18. 19 - dark + light

Robert - Laney's family friend - matched c̄
       Carrie

Karen

Winds of change - p. 121, p. 345

p. 264 - Brod

THE KEY IN THE WILLOW TREE

A NOVEL

Lisa C. Allen

ISBN print: 978-0-578-39318-6
ISBN ebook: 978-0-578-39319-3

Design and publishing assistance by The Happy Self-Publisher.

"Painful as it may be, a significant emotional event
can be the catalyst for choosing
a direction that serves us –
and those around us - more effectively.
Look for the learning."

— Louisa May Alcott

Chapter One

Leslie Cartwright

LESLIE CARTWRIGHT packed her bags and checked her list twice. Each time she went on a trip, she couldn't help herself; the same familiar things she needed to do came to mind. Her mother always taught her to make a list, and that is something she had incorporated into every aspect of her life. Lists for groceries were normal, lists for goals, that was normal, too, she thought. Lists of heartaches and sorrows were not meant to be accounted for—but she had done so as if it required a certified accountant. She wished she could take an eraser and wipe it away, but it would take a large eraser. Even then, you would still see the evidence the pencil made on her heart, just like a pencil indentation stayed on the page after the lead was erased away. She felt certain the pains and trials had left a mark on her heart in the same way.

She did have a list that always brought a smile to her face. She recalled the suggestions her mother would remind her of before any road trip. The list began when she was a little girl, and her mother added more to it through the years. Standing on the doorstep before she left to go to college, she recalled the words her mother said, "*Always pee before you leave home. Always flush the toilet at filling stations before you go. You never know—it may be broken. Always keep some cash in your pocket. If you lose your wallet, you'll have something to hold you over. Always have on clean underwear in case you get into an accident. Always remember I love you, and always come back safe to me.*" They referred to this list as "Remember the Always." They recited it before she left to go anywhere. Until her mother passed away, she would call her up before trips and say, *"Remember the Always."*

Leslie admitted the advice had come in handy, especially that one day when the toilet didn't flush in the stall at the Stop and Go. She changed stalls. For a moment she stopped dead in her step and pondered the thought and said out loud, *"What if life was like that–if it was not working, change stalls."*

Leslie picked up her bags and meandered through the hall of their farmhouse and stopped by the mudroom to feed Luke, their dog. Then she checked the refrigerator to be sure she put the chicken salad and deviled eggs on the top shelf for Stan to see. She noticed he had a fresh brisket he had picked up from the butcher. She was hoping he would wait to cook that when she returned, but her guess was he was going to feed the farm hands lunch that week. He liked to do that at least once a month, and it had been a while since he had cooked for them. He appreciated their help and liked to remind them of it every now and again.

She went to her Suburban and tossed her Lilly Pulitzer bag in the back. There was a dawning of a smile when she looked at it and remembered when Carrie gave it to her when the brand became so popular. Carrie presented her with the bag loaded with some of Leslie's favorite items, *"You have to have one. I couldn't resist!"*

Leslie loved the bag, but she loved her friend even more for thinking of her. Leslie had to admit, the soft fabric bags were quite pretty, and it came in handy, as she used it often through the years. Carrie was always so thoughtful and clever in her gift giving. The gifts had the intentional meaning of something she knew would make you feel loved. That was just Carrie.

Through the years, Carrie and Leslie had shared thoughts, dreams, and precarious situations with each other that were never shared with anyone else. Leslie always wanted a sister and so did Carrie, so they claimed each other as sister. Carrie went through a rough patch a few years ago, and Leslie reached out to meet for lunch. Their friendship was a bond that each of them treasured. When Leslie experienced a family crisis, Carrie was there for her. It was as if they had been brought together in life for a purpose—they both needed a genuine friend.

Glancing at the time on her watch, she knew she needed to get moving. She reached down to pat Luke and gave him instructions to stay. As she got in the car, she looked at her list of staples, and checked her list a third time. Her friends said if they were ever stranded on a deserted island, they would want it to be with her. Leslie always declared you never knew when you would need something so carry some of everything, just in case. She realized that was what she had been doing with her life. She was carrying everything in her mind and heart like weighted down luggage. One of those hard shell, fifty-pound airline safe clunkers, and it was over packed. Like at the airport when they charge a fee for overweight luggage, Leslie's emotional baggage had cost her some mental peace.

She left her driveway and headed to town. She had one more stop to make and check off her list—the local bread shop to pick up a few treats for the week. Then she would pick up the girls and they would be on their way for a much-deserved beach trip. Their first stop, Emerald Isle for three days, then down the coast to a couple of other beaches. Three beaches for the week. With a little help from Carrie, Leslie had planned a fun-filled week. At first, Leslie thought the trip was a great idea. Now she wasn't so sure, as anxiety crept in about being away for an entire week.

Leslie's husband, Stan, insisted that she enjoy the time. In all their decades of marriage, she had never done such a thing. She felt out of sorts, like she was wearing an ill-fitting pair of shoes. It was a ridiculous feeling that she always got when she left home alone. Being home with family was always important to her. Always be there, always be present, to let them know they were the most important thing to her, always. Come to think of it, she had created her own *Remember the Always,* list and never realized it.

She did admit that being so dedicated to actual presence meant that sometimes her presence was probably not the best. She didn't take much time for herself because she felt that was selfish. In retrospect, there were times a respite would have been beneficial to her demeanor. She realized that one aspect of hyper-focusing on family, was that she had lost contact with most of her dearest friends. She was out of touch with her inner self as well. Where was that person who once pondered dreams, built ideas, and framed them in her mind, then watched them come to fruition?

The month of May was one of the busiest times on the farm. But what was she going to do—get in the field and work? She often admired women that had no issue jumping into the working role on a farm. But that was as far as the thought took her—admiration. She was not one of those farm wives.

After years of looking after children and the business of the farm, she went back to work full-time. It was a change, but one she liked. Her job at the local hospital was a good one, and she enjoyed supporting the human resources department. Leslie enjoyed helping candidates find the right position. She considered her work to be meaningful, and she took immense pride in the role. It suited her attributes well. The candidates became like family as she walked them through the hiring process. She enjoyed following their careers and kept in touch with many of them through the years.

But as a child and teenager, she did spend plenty of time on the family farm and on farms of folks that were like family. Those days had mixed memories for her, and sometimes she would drive by the old homestead to reminisce. But it was not the same anymore, and not in the family anymore, either. There were times it was too painful to think about it. So, she tried not to think about it at all. Often, she wondered about the possibilities for the farm if it had not been sold. She always hoped it would remain in the family. As she was driving down the road, she said to herself in the rear-view mirror, "*Stop it. You are going on a road trip do not go down that road—that is the one you need to drive away from, Leslie.*"

The Bread Basket was not too busy that Friday morning. She noticed Sara had put out new planters full of petunias, verbena, and ivy. It looked lovely. Everything Sara touched seemed to overflow with perfection. Her attention to detail was a deliberate show of love and a healthy amount of attention. Leslie walked in the door to the shop, the bell rang on the door as it slammed shut behind her.

She walked up to the counter and was admiring the pastries and savories. The choices were tempting. While she was admiring them, she did not realize Sara was standing on the other side of the counter.

"Well Leslie Carol, what brings you in here, girl? I haven't seen hide nor hair of you in over a year!" said Sara.

Leslie nearly jumped out of her skin. She was a bundle of nerves already, and Sara had startled her.

"Sara, you just took a decade off my life! You scared the pudding out of me!"

Sara chuckled at her friend, "So what are you so jumpy over this morning? I would offer you some coffee, but I don't think you need it."

Leslie rolled her eyes and gave her a move along gesture with her hand. "Yes I do, just go on and get me a cup of the House dark blend. Wow, it has been a while since I've been in, your menu options are great. Just look at all the things you've added. Mercy, I didn't know."

Sara grinned as she looked at the chalkboard menu. "Yes, it has been going well. Folks seem to like it, so we keep adding new things, see how they fly, and if it sticks, we keep it on the menu. But it's nice to keep it in chalk for now, as I keep playing around with it. What's been keeping you so busy that you can't even come through the drive-thru window?"

Leslie began with her usual, a list. "You know—life. The last bird has flown the coop, so we are empty nesters. You knew

Mark was at NC State now, right? Alex is working in Wilmington with an insurance firm. Then there is work. We have all the new hires for remote work. You know full-time work is no joke, but I am loving it. It's hard to believe I've been there almost eight years now."

Leslie reached for the coffee cup and Sara put a hand on her shoulder and whispered. "You know I was only messing with you, loosen up. You're tight as a tick. You may need a shot of liquor with that coffee."

"I'm sorry," said Leslie. "I'm doing something today that I've done very little of in my life. I'm excited and nervous about it at the same time. I'm heading out for a girls-only beach trip for seven days. It begins as soon as my Suburban leaves your lot."

Sara's mouth flew open wide, and her gasp robbed her of her breath.

"I know, out of character for me, but long overdue," said Leslie.

"Why, I'm impressed. Who all is in this caravan of yours?" asked Sara.

Leslie roll called, "Carrie, Laney, Sandra, and me. Keep your eye out for pics and vids on Facebook. You know Carrie must document everything—all the shenanigans."

"Although this is fun, you didn't come here just to chat. What can I get for you? I know you're ready to get this party started," Sara said, as she nodded to the counter.

Leslie tapped her chin with her finger as she looked at the menu. "Well, start with a loaf of sourdough, sliced please. Some of the apple cinnamon bread, and my goodness, you have pimento cheese now? I should have brought a cooler."

"Don't you worry about that. I have coolers now for take-out. Want some chicken salad too? I have some nice gouda cheese straws, and for sweets, how about I throw in some lady fingers, mama's recipe. Remember how good they were?" Sara winked at Leslie.

"We would love some of those lady fingers. I remember those at every wedding reception or baby shower I ever went to around here. Every good hostess would order those from your mama. Yes, add those in, but let me pay you for them."

Sara smiled at Leslie and said, "Nope, not a chance. I seem to recall you and Carrie doing me a few favors, when I was sick, and I've never forgotten it. It's on me. Here, take it and go now before those girls blow your phone up wondering where you are."

Leslie traded a glance with Sara and shook her head to indicate her refusal. "No way, no, that's too much. We can't do that!" she said.

"You can, and I insist," Sara wiped her brow with the back of her arm. "You and Carrie helped me through cancer. Your support, prayers, and food drop-ins were so appreciated. From your lips to God's ears, I just know it. Please take it and don't be a stranger now you here? I've missed you."

Sara walked Leslie to the door and gave her a hug. "I'll do my best. Now I better run. Those wild gals are waiting on me." Said Leslie.

"Keep 'em in line. The line dance, that is. Do they still do that?" Sarah asked laughing, as she headed back to the kitchen.

"Yes, they do, but I don't! Take care Sara and thank you again."

Chapter Two

Carrie Hargrove

Carrie Hargrove wasn't sure if she was going to be prepared to leave when Leslie arrived. She had an unexpected call from her attorney with yet another legal issue. She thought it would never end. Bill was unreasonable and acted like the backside of a mule these days. This had become the normal expectation, and that indicated her current life status. Dealing with an unreasonable ex-husband was exhausting, and an endless task.

After Carrie met with her attorney, she felt drained and, most of all, shocked. How could he expect her to settle for this new suggested discounted alimony? Alimony was part of their divorce—a judge approved it. How was it that Bill thought he could ask for a revised amount and take her back to court? How was she to earn an adequate living? He had already excommunicated her out of the family business. They built that empire together, but Carrie often thought how it truly was a sort of religion for Bill. He worshipped the place. They had both built the family business. Carrie had put blood, sweat, and tears into building up their brand. She realized the business they developed meant more to her than she had originally thought. She was not stepping down completely from Eastern Media and Communications without a part of that business, at least to leave as a legacy to her sons. After all, they deserved it. They had worked the business as hard as she and Bill had. She thought Bill would intend to leave the legacy to his new fling, Karen, and shortcut the boys. Rumor had it there was talk around town of them marrying. Carrie doubted it, but nonetheless, she wanted to protect the ownership for her sons.

She parked her BMW in the four-car garage. The garage looked empty without Bill's Porsche, restored 1964 Mustang, and his Harley-Davidson motorcycle. According to her attorney, the lease would soon be up on the BMW, and she would have to turn it in. Her attorney just informed her that Bill asked for her to take care of her next automobile lease. If he continued to reduce the alimony and not pay on time, how was she to afford to purchase anything?

When she walked into the house, went through the mail, and opened a letter from Bill's attorney. Her question was answered. It would not end. She had barely resolved one issue, and here was another. What was he thinking? Or this wasn't him; maybe it was Karen? She was a clever girl, Carrie had to give her that. She had created the largest customer base of advertisers locally, regionally, and across the nation for the business. Her striking looks usually got her through a door, but her keen psychological sales technique made the contracts happen. She had gumption—that had always been obvious.

Carrie shook her head to shake those thoughts out and took a cleansing breath. This beach trip was just what she needed; it would give her some time to slow her brain down. Maybe when she returned, she would see everything through fresh and well-rested eyes. She had not been herself lately, and she wanted to find Carrie again. She missed her. A bit of separation from this monumental mountain of troubles, and when she returned, the mountain might not seem so big.

She strolled through the foyer, crossed over the gallery hall, and entered the bedroom suite to throw a few things in a bag. She had already packed most of her clothes, but now she needed to get accessories. Her style was classic and simple, until it came to jewelry. Over the years, Bill had been generous in his gift giving to her. She now suspected that it was more to make him look good, not because it was an actual token of his love and affection for her. She never asked for a piece of jewelry, he would just show up with some trinket and demonstrate how proud he was of himself.

Going into the closet, she went to the safe and selected items to go with her basic day wear, and some for dinners out. No bathing suit would be packed. She gave up on those years ago, although her figure looked much the same as it did when she was in college. Carrie thought when you reached a certain age, some things were best to be covered up. She looked over the closet and thought about how empty it looked. There were some older items on one side that needed to go to Goodwill. Bill left them and she had told him frequently to send someone over for his clothes. A few shirts and suits were the only thing left of Bill's, and he kept procrastinating about sending someone over for them. His style of attire had changed dramatically since he left their home. Obviously, these suits, although quite expensive and tailor made, were not his style anymore. She would send them by one of the boys when she got back. She thought that would be best.

When she turned out the light, she glanced over the master bedroom suite. The room was beautiful. It was the one room in the house Bill allowed her to choose the furnishings, drapes, and accessories. It was her favorite room in the house. But when she learned of his affair, she had barely slept there at all. After he left their home, most nights she chose the master suite on the second floor. She eventually moved her wardrobe to that suite with the help of Mae, her housekeeper. It moved her as far away from the space she shared with him. She used the landing just outside of the suite as a small den, and she had made it her own little haven.

The ring of her cell phone woke her up from her trance. It was Leslie.

"Hello, what's up?" asked Carrie.

"Carrie, I'm outside. Order that front door to open. Didn't you hear my horn beep?"

"I'm so sorry. I thought I turned it off so you could get in. Hang on." Carrie ran to the front door and turned the alarm off.

"Come in, honey, I hate that alarm. This entire security system is on steroids and way over my head," Carrie opened her arms for the big hug they always shared upon greeting.

"I'm so sorry," Carrie said. "Something fried my brain today. Bill is up to his sorry mess again, and my attorney and I are just fed up to the gills." She motioned for Leslie to come into the kitchen.

"No, no, Carrie, we are not starting this week that way. Your divorce was a mess, I get it. I know how frustrated you are but loosen up and have some fun. When we get back home, we can solve all the world's problems. But you need this lady. You are one big mess right now. This is not who you are, Carrie."

"I know, I know," Carrie said, as she grabbed her bag. "Listen, if I don't have it in this bag, we'll get it when we get there. A girl has to shop, right?" as she cracked a smile.

"Well, at least *you* do. But, my darling, did you bring the good jewels? You know you cannot find those just anywhere."

Carrie patted her bag and said, "Right here, girl. I even picked out those diamond and sapphire ones you like so much—the studs. They'll look good on you."

"Carrie, it would scare me to death to wear those things. What if I lose one?" Leslie asked.

"You won't," said Carrie. "But if you do, they're insured. Ugh! I forgot one thing. Let me get my pistol." As she ran back to the closet in the master suite.

Leslie followed her, "Are you kidding me? You know I hate those things."

"No," said Carrie, "I am not kidding. Four women on the road. I think one of us needs to think about our protection. Especially with us staying in those VRBO rentals."

"Whatever. But keep it locked up in that fancy case you have. What do you mean by "staying in those VRBO places?" You trust my judgement, right? You picked out one yourself missy," said Leslie.

"Yes, I do trust your judgement. But still, alive rather than dead is how I prefer to travel. It's just in case there is a case to need it – I'll have it," said Carrie.

As they headed out the door, the housekeeper, Mae, came in the foyer. "Miss Carrie, you left the alarm off. Did you mean to?"

Mae had been with the family for over thirty years. They hired her when the children came along to be a nanny and help with chores. She was a godsend. Carrie often referred to her as their friend of the house. She was the butler, house steward, footman, valet, and amazingly faithful to Carrie. Her eyesight had been failing her in recent years, but they kept her employed all the same. Carrie demanded it from Bill. It was one of the handful of times she put her foot down. He thought she should be let go, but Carrie would not hear of it.

"Mae darling, I did. Now don't fret over that alarm. The plumber is going to come by and check that leak in the sink at the wet bar. I told him to set the alarm on the way out. He knows how. You know, it's Lee. Remember him?" asked Carrie.

Mae shook her head and her teeth beamed white in her large smile and she said, "Oh yes ma'am, I sure do. My goodness, he was always such a handsome young fellow. Glad my eyesight ain't totally gone so I can lay my eyes on him really good one more time."

"Mae, you spunky thing, you may be getting older, but your mind is as good as ever. You're right though, Lee is a hottie. You behave around him, you hear? Just leave the alarm off. He'll take care of it. I trust him—Bill gave him the code years ago. Bill is always so suspicious, so if he trusts him, then I do, too."

Mae snorted through her laughter. "Well, you might not want to leave me here alone with such a fine-looking fellow, you know how the men folk get me hot and bothered. You trust him, but you sure you trust me around him?" asked Mae.

Leslie chimed in, "Mrs. Mae, you haven't changed since the day I met you. Still as crazy and witty as ever. You are one of a kind and we all know you are full of it."

"You never know about me! Yeah, I'm just messing with y'all. You girls have fun and behave. I'll leave the alarm off, and Sonny will pick me up today since I knew you were gonna be gone. Now you enjoy your week, and I'm gonna enjoy mine off as well. I just have a couple of things to do today. I'm going to finish up ironing those tablecloths and napkins from that fancy supper you had last week. The front parlor needs a good dusting, so I think I will take care of that this afternoon. Miss Carrie, will it be alright if I did the ironing in the master bedroom, that way I can watch my soap operas on the big screen TV while I work. I can see 'em better that way."

"Not a problem at all. Don't wear yourself out now. You don't have to work the entire time. Take a catnap. There isn't too much to do here, get on out of here and enjoy the time off," said Carrie as she gave Mae a hug.

"Now, let's get this party started," said Leslie, as she helped Carrie with her bags, and they headed out the door.

In the car, Carrie noticed how fidgety Leslie was. "What is going on with you? You seem agitate," Leslie asked.

"You know me, I hardly ever go anywhere alone. Being away from home for so long seems strange," said Leslie, as her clinched hands gripped the wheel.

"Stop it, you deserve it, and Stan will be fine. He is a grown man for God's sake, and mercy, he has the farm to keep him busy. He's going to be exhausted and just fall asleep after supper. He'll never know you're gone!" said Carrie.

"Well, I hope he'll notice," Leslie gave her friend a smirky smile. "But you know how spoiled he is and yes, that's my fault, I know. I forgot to tell him there was some chicken salad and deviled eggs in the fridge. Remind me to text him when we stop."

"Stop it! He'll find the dang chicken salad and deviled eggs. He'll get used to it. You may find you like it enough so we can do these trips more often," said Carrie.

"Well, for you and Laney, that's a great option. Sandy and I have to keep the men folk happy."

Carrie giggled, "Yeah right, they might find that you are so happy to get home, they won't mind you leaving again, if you know what I mean."

"That may be a thought. The "absence makes the heart grow fonder" theory. We'll see," said Leslie.

Chapter Three

Sandra Summers

Sandra tested negative on another pregnancy test. She was late, and too eager to wait a couple more days to give the timeframe due process. It was negative, again. It was becoming the normal expectation. Which was just a sad way to live, in her opinion.

If it made any sense at all, she conditioned herself for a negative result, hoping to be pleasantly surprised. Just because she was used to it did not mean it was normal to feel like this every month. Mitch might be right; they should give up trying. All the medications, injections, and treatments over the last three years had taken a toll on her.

She really had to respect his instincts. He always led in love and in her best interest. Sandra thought back to how her life was such mayhem before she met Mitch. She was broken in her heart and soul. She admitted she secretly blamed God for letting her misfortune come upon her that dreaded night long ago. For years, she could not forgive God or herself. Then the pills just made it better, made her numb, so much so that she took more than prescribed and that put her job in jeopardy. Few people knew she went away to get clean, just Leslie and her parents. Leslie walked with her through the entire process, even helped her find a discreet facility out of state. Later, eventually, she rid the pills from her life, but her life had been slow to return to normal.

Mitch helped her learn to forgive herself and how God was for her, not against her. She came to realize that God was good, even during the tough times. God had to be good, he brought Mitch to her. Even through her mess, Mitch saw a beautiful message hidden in her. He brought it out of her, and it was like a beautiful song. He was that good for her. He knew some of her darkest moments, but many were too painful to talk about with anyone, including Mitch.

Sometimes when they were at church on Sunday, her guilty conscience would interfere with her paying attention to the sermon. She wondered if it was God or if it was her own mind continuing to self-inflict shame. Whatever it was, it made her feel disconnected and ashamed to be in church. Mitch could always tell when she became overwhelmed when they sat in the sanctuary. He would watch her feet, if she crossed her legs and swung her foot, he would put a hand on her knee and offer to hold her hand. One Sunday, when they got home after service, he asked her about it. Sandra attempted to blow it off by explaining she had a cramp in her foot. Mitch would often remind her the guilty feeling was not coming from God. "That's the devil talking to bring you down," he would say. He would always remind her she was precious in God's sight. It helped when he talked like that to her; it filled up the dark and empty place in her soul with light.

Sandra was closing in on the fourth decade of her life. The proverbial ticking clock made her think how she regretted throwing away two decades. In her twenties, she spent her life going to the clubs where she would dance the night away. She took long weekend cruises, loved Mardi Gras in New Orleans. She had thought it was harmless. She dated—a lot, but never found that love she was looking for that made her feel electricity and totally swept away. That was until Mitch.

Her early thirties were spent recovering from the nightmare that happened to her when she was twenty-eight. A friend set her up with her husband's coworker. The night did not end well for Sandra. Her date had the wrong impression of her from the way her friend's husband described her. The blind date did not go well for Sandra—he raped her. Afterwards, he said he heard she was always up for a good time. She was, but it never included jumping in bed with the men she danced with all night. They were her friends. It was not like that with them. Although there were rumors about her, they were just that—rumors. It was easy for Sandra to be the discussion of envy, rumors, assumptions, and accusations. Everyone could see she was magnetic and possessed an energy of high intensity that captivated those in her company. Her physical appearance only added to the magnificent internal side of Sandra, as her inner beauty was just as mesmerizing. She marched to the beat of her own drum, and it was always amusing to be in her presence.

After the rape, the spiral downfall was a fast descent to a period of life that she called *"the gates of hell."* She was certain she was close, and at any moment she could almost feel the flames. The devil pursued her, and she began to dance with him. It almost ruined her. She was in darkness, and no light was peeking through to any crevice of her heart.

Then Mitchell Summers came into her life. Just like his name, he was warm and bright, and he saw something in her that no other man had. He helped her get her light back. He put the music back in her life and she returned to her old self. But even Mitch did not know about the deepest and darkest holes she still needed to be filled with light and acceptance. She could not bear to tell him of such darkness that had been in her life. She never wanted his opinion of her to be marred by knowledge of her addiction to pills. He knew about the most important bits, but not the pill addiction. That was where she had been selective about her sharing.

Mitchell was born a Southern Baptist Pastor's son. Although he had not gone into ministry, he was a faithful member and served in the congregation back in his hometown. He was a deacon, youth leader, and sometimes the barbecue pit master for their annual fundraiser at their church in Greenway.

When Mitch asked Sandra to church the day they met, she thought he was insane. He was new in town and was having lunch at Wimpie's Cafe. Sandra was on her lunch break from the clinic, where she worked as a nurse. Mitch worked at the bank across the street. He had not been around long enough to hear about her story, her history, the lengthy process of pressing charges, court, the finger pointing. She was thirty-three years old when they met, and she still could not get past the horrible haunting memories that had plagued her for the last few years.

Sandra could remember every detail about the day they met. Mitch had walked up to Sandra sitting at her table and asked if she was local. He had inquired about the best bakeries, golf courses, and churches.

"I would like to find a new church in town. I'm a Pastor's son, so when the old man checks up on me, I better have one I can tell him about. Can you recommend one?" he asked with a sideways smile.

Sandra became nervous immediately. She had not been to church in years. She couldn't bring herself to walk through the doors of a sanctuary. Her shame held her back. It would mean bringing what she believed to be her sin, her uncleanliness into a holy place. She thought God was angry with her, and she was not ready for the punishment she was confident would greet her if she darkened the doors.

Sandra gazed out the window, avoiding the stranger's eyes, and asked, "What denomination are you looking for? We have a Methodist, Baptist, Presbyterian, Episcopalian, and a contemporary church. But if you are looking for a Pentecostal, we do not have one of those around here. Most folks in this town like their church to be done in an orderly fashion. They are conservative in everything around here, even the contemporary church is not that contemporary, I hear. But there is a Pentecostal church about 15 miles in the next town, if that is what you like. The Presbyterian church down on Lewis Street is nice. Some of them go to the country club for lunch after church and have a Bloody Mary, or a mimosa, if you are into that sort of thing," she grinned and found the courage to look into Mitch's kind eyes. Then she realized she just rambled away for quite a long period of time.

Mitch had thrown his head back in a good ole belly roll laugh. "Now that right there is funny," he said. "So, which one do you recommend?" he asked as he sat down at Sandra's table. "Where do you attend services?"

Sandra felt her face flush. She thought the stranger could see her uneasiness, and it embarrassed her. How could she tell him she had not been to church in years? What would he think of her? Everyone around here went to church. That was just what you did.

She looked him square in the eye and said, "Well, here's the thing, I am not used to telling strangers such details about my private life. We have not been properly introduced."

At that moment, Mitch felt like a proper and genuine Southern lady had put him in his place. But she said it with a smile and an accent that was sweeter than the tea he had with his club sandwich.

"Let me introduce myself. Forgive me, ma'am, my name is Mitchell Summers. I am from Spartan, South Carolina. I am pleased to meet you and you are right to put me in my place. My mother would be ashamed of me, but she would fall in love with you," Mitch held out his hand to shake hers.

"Wow," said Sandra. "Thank you for that, and since we are getting to know each other, my name is Sandra Forlines. It's nice to meet you. What brings you to Greenway?"

"That bank across the street scouted me out to come up here and be the Vice President. They thought I would be a good fit," said Mitch as he shrugged his shoulders and winked at her.

Sandra heard the car horn blow, and it broke up her memory lane stroll. Mitch came into the bedroom and caught Sandra grinning.

"What is that smile about? Are you that happy to be ditching me for a few days?" asked Mitch, as he went to her and wrapped his arms around her.

"No, it's quite the opposite. I remembered the day you walked into my life. I have loved you ever since that moment. Listen, I will call you when we get there. Remember, there is a meat loaf for you tonight, and I took out one of those frozen chicken pies that Sara makes down at The Bread Basket. You might like that tomorrow night. The directions to bake it are on the label," said Sandra as she zipped her bag.

"Stop worrying about me, I was a single guy for quite a while. I can fend for myself. I want you to go relax. It seems like you are getting yourself in some dark places and I don't want that for you."

Sandra nodded because she knew he was right. "I will try. These girls make it easy. I love you, and I will miss you though."

"I will miss you more. I plan to get the fence fixed this week while you're away. It will give me something to do at night. Unless I can talk you into replacing it with the vinyl fence?" Mitch tipped her chin up so he could look into her eyes.

Sandra held his cheeks in her hand. "Mitchell, you know how I feel about keeping the authenticity of this historical house. Absolutely not," she said and kissed him and finished packing her bag.

The back door slammed, and they heard Carrie and Leslie coming down the hall. "Hello, by any chance is there some crazy dancing, karaoke singing, line dancing chick in here that wants to come and play with us this week?" Carrie yelled down the hall.

Sandra stepped out into the long hallway and danced down the hall. "There sure enough is."

"Good grief girl, you look like you are doing the Soul Train dance down the aisle, I swear you ain't right," laughed Carrie.

"Soul Train?" asked Sandra, with a raised eyebrow.

"Never mind, I forget I'm ahead of you all on the calendar by a few years," said Carrie.

"Mitch, you think you're going to be alright without her for a week? You know this could be a test to see if we can do this more often. We want to see how you and Stan hold up," Carrie played at a smile and Mitch laughed.

"I'll let Stan speak for himself, but somehow I think he's going to be exhausted this time of year, so no time for him to get into any trouble."

"Yep, that is exactly what Carrie said," remarked Leslie.

"Ladies, are we going to stand here and chat or are we getting this party on the road?" asked Sandra.

"Let's do it," said Carrie.

Mitch gave Sandra one last kiss, and he blew the other ladies a kiss. Then they were off to the next stop to pick up Laney.

Chapter Four

Laney Rich

Laney was in her kitchen and had cooked one more batch of muffins, finished mixing up the redneck blue collard dip, and she was ready to go. Carrie loved that dip and always requested that Laney make it for every occasion. Just a little blue cheese, collards, cream cheese, and she always added the right balance of spices. The muffins were for Leslie—she loved her salted caramel muffins. As for Sandra, she barely ate anything, because she was so afraid of a little weight gain. Laney thought she was as thin as a piece of parchment paper. Laney herself had a few curves and would not starve herself. It would not look good for a chef to be so thin. She always thought that reflected on your cooking skills. She was comfortable in her own skin and was still in the ideal weight bracket for her frame, so she felt good about a couple of little ruffles and curves.

Laney said yes to this trip before she thoroughly thought it out, and now she thought the time could be better spent looking for a job. She saved up through the years, but now without any work at all, she would have to dip into that nest egg. Her modest home in Greenway was vacant most of the time since she stayed on the road. So, through the years she rented out her place on a rent by owner vacation website. Folks liked to come stay in her cottage and visit local southern attractions like the beaches, the wineries, and golf courses located nearby. The renters liked the slow pace of life there. Being close to the coast was also a plus. She had to admit that since she was back home, she liked it, too, and recalled why her parents moved there many years ago. Laney was fortunate to find a place near them, so she could check on them in their older years. However, they had a sudden change of life plan and moved to Oriental, North Carolina, and loved life near their boat. Even when her father passed away, her mother stayed in Oriental. She said it had just been a good fit for her, and she felt close to her dad there.

In the Food and Dining Restaurant arena, Laney Rich was a well-known name. She often dismissed job offers from other companies to stay with the company that believed in her and gave her a start in the beginning. Fresh out of culinary school, she finished her master's degree in business. She was ready to be a traveling restaurant featured chef. It was a trend that she birthed in the company, and the higher executives adopted the concept. Laney did a good job of selling it to them. They believed it could work, and it did. She spent a decade traveling the states and marketed a couple of international gigs as the "Featured Chef." She came, she delivered, the crowds came, and then she would book the next event. It was a fast-paced life and in the restaurant's arena industry, she had taken it by storm. That is, until the last year. When the restaurant economy took a hit, her job did as well.

She hosted cooking competitions on-site, and discovered new talents that were placed in major metropolitan kitchens all over the United States. There were many chefs that owed her a tremendous amount of gratitude. She taught them all her trade secrets, and her Southern specialties, but she was equally equipped to prepare more sophisticated plates of fare. It was not unusual for her to talk a restaurant owner in New York City to include collard greens on the menu but prepared in a new way that differed slightly from the mashed greens from the South. She got the most Southern kitchen to experiment with items like baked brie or baked bean casserole, and hot potato salad. Her proudest moment was when she talked to the chef of Roof Top in New York City and persuaded him to include pimento cheese dip with pork rinds as an appetizer. It was a menu success, and the owners kept it in as a mainstay menu item.

Laney finished packing up the food and went to look at the vegetable garden in her side lot. That was the best concept she had yet, and the only thing she splurged on through the years.

Purchasing the lot beside her cottage was exactly what she never knew she desired so much. Growing her own vegetables and a few flowers for cutting took up her days, and she found genuine joy in taking care of the little two-acre plot.

Laney had just turned thirty-three, and she had been contemplating the probability that it may be a credit to her life to settle down and stop jet setting all over the world. The little garden had helped her decide that she was ready to put down her roots, literally and figuratively. It was amusing jaunt jetting all over the planet, but now she needed to get grounded somewhere. How was she ever going to find the love of her life if the love of her life was an airplane and hotel suite? It was time. She just prayed the right one would come along. There had been too many disappointments. Dating just long enough to be invested in the relationship, and then the breakup. Too many of those had hardened her heart, and she had built a protective wall around her heart.

Once there was a pleasant prospect, and Laney thought he was the one—Jim. The chemistry was there. He was easy on the eyes and said all the right things. He treated her with respect and was in love with her, as she was with him. Just turned out, Jim didn't know how to stay faithful. She was the owner of a broken heart and damaged ego. He later confessed that he wanted more from their relationship. She had made a promise to be true to her pledge she took years ago and save herself for marriage. It was not a trendy idea in dating agendas these days, but it was her personal conviction. Months later, she learned he married the one that took him away from her. But recently, she heard that he couldn't be faithful to his wife, either. They divorced.

Laney learned with Jim that her emotions did not have an order of processing or expiration date. The shelf life of her heartbreak had surprising longevity. There was not a box to check yes or no if they were over, in her heart at least; but then her brain needed to be told. But she knew there was no going back to that relationship. That did not stop the emotions that were still in motion every time she thought of him. It had been over two years. She had to stop thinking about the past and focus on the *what could be* in her life. She had dated a bit, but nothing serious since Jim.

As Laney left the garden, she remembered when she came back home and started this little plot. Some neighbors thought she was a screwball. A little garden in the middle of town seemed odd. But it became a place where folks walked by and stopped to admire the love and attention Laney gave to the garden. The neighbors saw her in the side yard tending to her garden any day that it was not raining. Someone anonymously donated a couple of park benches to set by the sidewalk. There was just enough shade from the oak tree in her yard to offer a quiet reprieve to sit down for a spell. *"It was not a bad idea,"* mumbled Laney as she moved the rotating sprinkler. Her attention diverted when she saw Leslie's bus pull into her drive. That is what Laney called Leslie's Suburban—a bus. It always got Leslie a little riled up since Laney drove a compact car these days, which Leslie, in return, called an egg with wheels.

Leslie, Carrie, and Sandra jumped out of the car. Laney wiped the sweat from her brow as she waved at them on her way to the porch.

"Get out of that garden and come on here!" yelled Carrie.

Laney walked up to the porch and replied, "You won't be in such a big hurry that you let me forget those muffins and blue collard dip now, will you?"

"Mercy, you didn't! The salted caramel ones?" asked Leslie.

"Yes," Laney replied. "Of course I made them."

They all went into the kitchen. Sandra immediately held her head back and took a long dramatic inhale. "It smells divine. The air in here is making me gain weight. It smells like calories."

"Alright, now that's no way to start off a vacation. Thinking that you are going to diet this week is out of the question. We have some fine dining experiences to encounter, ladies, trust me. You are going to eat," said Laney.

Carrie joined in, "You know that's right! We are going to do that, and dance!"

"Carrie, I swear on my life, I don't know where you get your energy from. You need to bottle that stuff and sell it," said Leslie.

Laney burst into laughter, "Ladies, I want every stage of my life to look like what yours at this stage looks like right now."

Carrie's head spun around, her eyes squinted at Laney, and she shouted, "Girl, have you not seen the life I am having right now? This divorce, the adultery! My ex is probably already planning his next marriage to the floozy he left me for."

"I certainly have, Carrie. You very well know I have been here through it with you, and I cannot say enough how proud I am to call you a friend. You have handled it with so much grace. Until now, though. Did you just call Karen a floozy?" asked Laney with a chuckle.

"Yes, it's been a difficult day. I'm not feeling like myself. I probably should not have said that," said Carrie.

"Why not?" Sandra asked. "Doesn't the proverbial shoe fit?"

"Really, y'all, I only tried to keep my integrity intact. Some days I did, some days not so much like now—that was just downright loose lips," said Carrie.

Leslie broke in, "You are just burnt out over all of it right now. That's all. Show yourself some grace, alright?"

"I think so, too, Carrie. Lord knows you had every right to throw a hissy fit anytime you felt like doing it with what Bill put you through, but you didn't. He's thinks he's as slick as pig snot on a radiator," said Sandra.

Everyone belted out a laugh, and Carrie asked, "What did you just say, Sandra? What are we going to do with you, girl?"

"We are something else, aren't we? All of us are so different, but the same in a way. I mean, look at us four ladies, one from each generation, two married, two singles. We are just about as balanced as my fine salted caramel muffins. We are just enough sweet, enough spice, and a tad bit of salt to round it all out. I think we are like a tetradic color scheme!" said Laney.

"We are what?" asked Sandra. "What the hell is tetra ... or tetris whatever you just said? That arcade game?"

"Tetrad–the four colors corners of the color wheel," Laney explained. "Didn't you learn that in school? Art class?"

"I must have been absent that day," said Sandra.

"We all bring something different to the table, just like the four distinct colors in the tetradic color scheme. I visited a restaurant in Australia that used the tetras color scheme, and it was so alive and powerful, just like us."

Carrie joined in, "Yes, we are powerful! I can tell you that if it hadn't been for y'all these last few years, I would have drowned. You rescued me from myself. I know we all said this week was going to be a celebration of many things for us, Leslie turned fifty-five. My divorce is final. Laney is back home more often, and Sandra, we are hopeful for you that any day we get to have a celebration for a new baby. I just know it's going to work out. I'm believing in a miracle for you."

Sandra became quiet, and she was wringing her hands. She did her best to keep tears back, but one slipped from her eye. "Thanks Carrie, I needed to hear that right now. I just had another negative pregnancy test today. I have really become quite numb to it though, so it's all good. Maybe I should stay home and binge watch *Call the Midwife* all week."

Leslie immediately went to hug Sandra and said, "Nonsense, you are coming with us! We're just going to keep on praying on that baby for you. It will happen. I know God will make a way."

Laney looked at all three of her friends with a smile and said, "You know, all my heroes are right here in this room. My mentors, my best and truest friends, this right here is what I'm talking about. I look at each chapter of your lives and learn from you. So, I need for you ladies teach me a thing or two this week. Let the good times roll right out of this town!"

"You got it!" said Carrie.

They loaded up all of Laney's treats, grabbed her bags, and headed out the door.

Chapter Five

Bill and Karen

Bill was in the office at the station mulling over paperwork and contracts with Karen when his phone rang. He pressed the speakerphone button, "Bill Hargrove speaking."

"Bill, this is Natalie with Security Elite Systems, the alarm at your residence is disabled. We are checking to see if there is a problem with your equipment. It looks like it was offline this morning about 9:00. This is a standard courtesy call with your Elite Plan. We alert you if the equipment has not been working for some time. How may we help?" asked the caller on the line.

Bill scratched his beard and looked at Karen with a bamboozled face.

"Did you set the alarm? I thought I turned it on when we left, didn't we?"

Karen nodded, "Yes, we did. Natalie, can you verify the address you are referring to?"

"The address at Hargrove Hill, Greenway," said the caller.

Bill rolled his eyes and threw his pen down. "Ok, I think I see the confusion. That's my damned ex-wife's residence. The contact info must need updating. She's out of town, so I'll go by and check on it," said Bill, and he hit the button to end the call without saying another word.

"Bill, really, you could have at least said thank you," said Karen.

Bill looked at her, leaned back in his chair, and crossed his arms. His wrinkled forehead and frown displayed his frustration.

"What damned good sense does it make for us to spend all this money on a security system. I did the Elite plan because she never remembered to set the damn thing. I swear, sometimes I think that woman does this crap to get under my skin. It's not like she's living in the ghetto, that's a high-end piece of property. And she's not even home, which is more of a reason to be sure the security system is on. All of Facebook knows she's gone because she can't keep her business off social media. I should've kept the house, and this proves it."

Karen shifted to the other side of the desk, plopped down in his lap, and kissed him.

"Easy now. You need to calm down. I need you to save up all that energy for the engagement party tonight. You are getting all frustrated and aggravated, and that is not good for you. Your blood pressure will go through the roof, so calm down. We can check the alarm on our way home."

"No, I'll go. You'll be late getting all dolled up for tonight. I want you looking your best in that hot little dress you picked out. And I know how you love to take a long bath, then do your thing that you do to get all gussied up for events," said Bill as he stood up and helped Karen to her feet.

"You sure?" asked Karen.

"Yes, I'll go by the house. You take your car home and get a head start on looking gorgeous for me," said Bill. He took her hand and gave her a twirl behind the desk, dipped her, and kissed her.

Karen smiled as he raised her back up and she gazed into his eyes. "Bill Hargrove, no matter what they say about you, it isn't true. I know better. I'm so happy. You make me happy; this life makes me happy, and I cannot wait to be your wife."

"Well, I am astonished we have been able to keep the purpose of this event our little secret. A few chosen guests to come for dinner with no explanation why. That was brilliant on your part. You always have that element of surprise, and you know when to use it and that attracted me to you. You know that, right?" asked Bill.

Karen looked disheartened and frowned. She did her signature hair fling with one hand, with her other hand on her hip. "Well, that's nice to know. So, it had nothing to do with my beautiful heart, wonderful personality, and hours in the gym to get this bod?"

"All those attributes are great, darling, and you have the last one to your credit for sure. Nobody holds a candle to that body of yours. But let's be honest, that personality thing, girl, you aren't known for that, and I am fine with it. I know you have a heart deep down in there. I see what others don't understand about you. Always have, always will. But don't let on to anyone that you are a softie. That side of you is for me only," said Bill, and he kissed her cheek.

Karen walked over to the sofa in Bill's office and sat down. "Just so you know, I might not always be arm candy. There is a bit of difference in our age. But one day, Mr. Hargrove, I will catch up to you. Will you still love me when I'm old and gray? When I'm 64, as the song says?" she asked.

Bill bent down and kissed her and said, "Absolutely. I'll see you at home as soon as I set that damned alarm."

For a moment, Karen drifted off in her thoughts. She looked at Bill's desk and remembered her interview for Assistant Vice President of Sales and Marketing. Little did she know that a few years later she would be Vice President of the entire franchise. They were doing well when she came on board, but things got a swift boost when she implemented new strategies in marketing. She had worked hard. She was diligent, and the dividends of her invested time were providing the companies with a steep profit margin.

It had been Karen's idea to keep the engagement announcement low key. She planned it when Carrie would be out of town. A thorough perusing of the office calendar showed Bill had her marked for being out of town. The office chatter supported and verified Carrie's best friends were going as well. That was also helpful. The plan was to make the announcement, have dinner, some dancing and celebrate with their guests. Later, Bill would let Carrie know the news. Karen felt like that was a reasonable and perfect plan.

Karen looked at her watch. She had to get moving. As she jumped up from the sofa, in seconds, the room was spinning around. She felt weak and faint. She landed with a hard knock, up against the office door. For a moment, the room went black. She sat there for a split second to gather her composure. Her vision became clear again, and she sat up. The room still looked grey, but at least it wasn't black anymore. She heard and felt a knock on the door against her back.

"Hey, hey are you alright in there?" asked Debra, the office manager.

"Karen are you in there?" she kept knocking. "I heard something. Did you fall on the door? Karen!"

The vibration of Debra beating on the door made Karen's head throb even more. "Oh, thank you, Debra. I just dropped some files as I was opening the door." Karen put her head in her hands. *What a lame lie*, she thought. She got up and opened the door to find Debra still standing on the other side.

Debra was reading her face like a map and said to her, "Karen, you don't look so good. Let me get you some water. And what files? I don't see any files," and she went to the water cooler. Karen followed her and sat down in the foyer.

"I'm fine, Debra. No worries, I just think I tried to stand up too fast, and I didn't eat lunch today. You know I had that Zoom meeting. I think it is so rude when participants are eating. I hate it when they do that, don't you? I mean, where are their manners?"

Debra handed her some water. "You sure? I can get you a candy bar from my secret stash." She said.

"I'll be fine. But thank you, though."

Karen left the office and walked to the parking lot. Once inside the car, Karen grabbed her phone. She had a text from the caterer. They were running on schedule. The florist already delivered flowers, and the bakery was on the way. It was all coming together. Karen breathed a sigh of relief. *Thank goodness!*

As she drove toward home, she thought about the fainting episode. What in the world was that about? Was it her nerves?

She always got a bit worked up and overwhelmed with mile-stone events. She had not experienced one in so long; she had forgotten how they used to affect her. As a child at her piano recital, she froze, forgot how to play her piece, and dashed off the stage. In school plays, the same thing. She would become a bundle of nerves and run to the restroom to throw up. She thought maybe the fainting episode proved that all of this was extremely important to her.

Karen felt that her life was completely perfect, and her orchestrated plan was in motion. She liked how it felt. All the excitement was giving her nerves a rattle. It would be fine once the engagement dinner was over. The excitement would wane, and she would be back on level ground with her emotions again. Karen was always in control. That motto had served her well for the last few years, and it would continue in years to come. She created her world, and it was perfect. She had a huge smile on her face as she punched the gas of her Jaguar.

Chapter 6

Welcome to Emerald Isle

Leslie took a deep breath of salt air and exhaled as she raised her arms toward the sky to stretch. It had been a long day of preparations and travel to get settled in at the magnificent beach house. They each had their own room, and there were four bathrooms in the house. They had plenty of room to spread out. The top floor had a vast living room that overlooked the ocean on one side, and the sound on the other. Down below was the large deck facing the ocean, a pool, and hot tub. It was the perfect rental, and it was theirs for three nights.

Laney and Carrie were on the other side of the deck in an intense conversation about dinner plans and club hopping. Leslie overheard a few keywords that let her know which direction the night would take. Memories Beach and Shag Club and Big Sammy's Beach Club drifted to her ear, and she smiled as she recalled all the wonderful nights she and her girlfriends had enjoyed there through the years.

"I really want to go by 8:30, don't you? I mean, if we get there early, before the crowd, I think it would be good," said Carrie.

Laney pulled her sunglasses down with her finger and glared over them to look at Carrie. "Honey, it's been a while since you went clubbing, I'm guessing. Did you say 8:30? How about we try for 10:00? That's when all the fun begins—at 10:00."

"Well, Laney, yes, it has been a while since I went clubbing. So, school me. How is it done these days?" asked Carrie.

Leslie waited patiently to hear Laney's answer, as she was curious to hearing what the younger generation did these days when they went out on the town.

Laney replied, "It really has changed very little Carrie, but you have. If you show up early, you are going to be bored out of your mind waiting for the fun. How about we go to the restaurant I was telling y'all about, and then we can hit the clubs."

"Sounds good, I'll tell Leslie," said Carrie. She turned around and almost bumped into Leslie standing right behind her.

Leslie smiled and pretended to know nothing about the conversation. "Tell me what?"

"Let's go clubbing! It could be so fun! But first, Laney says we have to eat at her favorite restaurant," said Carrie.

"How about this—we all go out to eat, then you girls can go clubbing and dance the night away. Sandra and I will call it a night after dinner. She's pretty tuckered out. Something is going on with her. I want to sit and stare at the ocean and share some quality time with her," said Leslie.

"Well, what do you think, Laney? You up for that idea? But are you sure you two will be okay here? How will y'all get back?" asked Carrie.

"No worries," said Leslie. "I'll drive, and y'all can get an Uber to come pick you up and deposit you safely here at the house."

Laney jumped up off the lounge chair, "Put your best dress on ladies, it's time for Island Time Dining. Trust me you will not be disappointed. Now Carrie, you wear some good shoes, because we are going to have all the men on the floor tonight. I have some friends down here we'll meet up with and trust me, we'll have our dance cards filled up!"

Within no time, all four were ready to go, looking very stylish. Carrie was wearing a colorful watercolor print sundress and heels. Sandra's dress was pale blue linen, and she wore slides. Even Laney joined them and donned a dress that was a boho style with her flat sandals. Leslie wore a floral wrap over a navy sundress and sling back espadrilles.

"Leslie, come here. You are wearing these sapphire studs. They will be perfect with that dress. Here, add these pearls too." said Carrie, as she motioned to Leslie to come over to her jewelry case.

Leslie agreed, "Fine, whatever, you will never shut up about it, anyway."

"They look great with that dress," said Carrie.

They all took a second look at each other, made necessary tweaks to hair, and lipstick, then headed to the car. As the sun was setting, it painted the skies with lavender, pink, blue, and orange hues. The sunset reflected how colorful their lives were, and a good omen as to the night that would unfold.

Chapter Seven

A Little Dining and Lots of Dancing

At Island Time Dining, the elegant ensemble agreed that Laney was right—the food was exceptional, and her friends were full of energy. Laney had a uniquely diverse group of friends, and one she wanted Carrie to meet. She had intentionally made sure they sat near his usual designated table. Robert Ryan was a regular customer at this restaurant. He dined there not only because of the exceptional quality of the food, but it kept him from being lonely at an empty dinner table in his studio apartment.

Laney finished her dinner and walked over to the next table where Robert was finishing his meal. She wanted to see if he was going to Memories Beach & Shag Club or Big Sammy's after dinner. Her intentions to get Carrie and Robert talking needed to be executed very carefully if it was going to be successful.

"Laney, how was your meal? Superb, I trust? Chef Scott outdid himself tonight, mine was divine," said Robert.

Laney gave Robert a hug around his neck from behind, as he was still sitting at the table. She leaned over and kissed him on the cheek, "It was fabulous, from one chef to another chef that is an extreme compliment. I was back in the kitchen talking to Chef Scott and letting him know that his crab bisque was the tantalizer at our table. Did you try it?" asked Laney as she sat down in the empty seat beside him.

"I did. It was some of the best I've ever had. I like what he did with the New York strip. The sauce on top was particularly good," said Robert.

"It's bearnaise sauce. I can show you how to whip that up yourself. Say Robert, what are you doing later?" asked Laney.

Robert took one look at Laney and knew that something was occupying her head space, and it must include him.

"Not sure. Depends on what you have planned. What are you up to? It seems like it must involve me."

"Well, I have a friend over there at my table. Carrie—you met her," said Laney as she looked back at their table.

Robert looked over at the table and admired the view. Carrie was lovely and had such an effervescent personality. Her smile would illuminate any room.

He looked back at Laney, "Yes, Carrie is a lovely lady. So how does this involve me? You're not planning any matchmaking, are you, Laney? You know I don't like that kind of thing."

"No matchmaking, but maybe just a little dancing opportunity for her later at the club. She's hasn't done this kind of thing in years. Can you show her a little fun on the dance floor? She's got moves, just lacking a bit of confidence."

Robert rubbed his chin and looked at Laney, "As long as you haven't promised her a setup or blind date kind of thing."

"No, code of honor, I swear on my heart," said Laney with her left hand over her heart and her right hand raised.

Sandra and Leslie walked over to say their goodbyes. Leslie told Laney that she and Sandra would go back to the house soon. Laney informed Leslie that they would hang back with Robert.

"Leslie, Sandra, Carrie, you met Robert earlier remember?" asked Laney.

"Yes, it was nice to meet you, Robert. Now we are calling it a night, Leslie and I are heading back to the beach house," Sandra said.

"It was a pleasure to meet you ladies, I hope you have a great weekend," said Robert as he stood up to wish them goodbye.

"You girls have fun. Robert, you look after them. You're in charge," Leslie said, as she pointed to Carrie and Laney.

"It will be my honor. I'll be sure that an Uber gets them home, too. I'll ride with them myself to make sure they get back safe and sound," said Robert.

"You are a true gentleman, Robert. I appreciate that," Leslie said with a smile.

Sandra and Leslie headed to the car. Robert, Laney, and Carrie watched as they pulled out of the parking lot, then they crossed the street and headed to the club.

It did not take long for the club to come alive once the crowd from Island Time Dining arrived. Along with Laney and her friends, several other patrons crossed the street to the club after dinner. The club filled with dancers shagging, doing the bop, and line dancing. Robert held up his end of the bargain and kept Carrie on the dance floor. As for Laney, nothing ever held her back. She loved to dance and knew many of the regulars, so her opportunities were endless.

The club was small, and, ironically, that magnified the vibe. It kept everyone close, and mingling was easy. This also allowed for an admittance quota, which limited the quantity and quality of those in the club.

The disc jockey stopped the music to take a break, and Sandra and Laney rested their dancing feet for a moment. Robert ordered them a round of drinks, and he waited at the bar as he watched the girls take a seat at a corner table.

When they sat down, Laney was curious to see what Carrie had to say about Robert. But she didn't want to be incredibly obvious.

"Carrie how are those feet of yours holding up?" asked Laney.

"Just fine! You know me—I can hang with the best of them. These heels are great—they are actually some of the most comfortable shoes I own."

Laney nudged Carrie with her elbow. "So, Robert, look at him. He is just about the bee's knees, right?" she asked.

"Stop it! He's a wonderful dancer and so much fun. Don't go pushing an agenda; let's just have fun," replied Carrie.

Robert returned to the table with their beverages. Just as he thought of sitting down and joining them, the disc jockey returned to his booth. The lights grew dim on the dance floor, and the chosen tune was Al Green's "Let's Stay Together." The club was filled with the well-known trumpet and saxophone overture. Couples holding hands progressed to the dance floor, and Robert looked over at Carrie and held out his hand.

"Well, would you care to dance?" asked Robert.

Laney looked at Carrie and nudged her with her knee to go ahead. Laney could see Carrie's cheeks flush pink, even in the dim light of the corner table. But she still offered her hand to Robert.

Robert took Carrie's hand, and they went to the dance floor. Carrie felt awkward. Shagging, bopping, and line dancing were all good and perfectly acceptable. The two of them had been on the floor all night. But a slow dance, cheek-to-cheek? Well, that was another situation all together. She felt her heart race, and she could not decide if it was the heat in the club, or if she was feeling something else. But the feeling shifted as soon as Robert came with a slow hand to spin her softly, then bring her back into a hold.

"That was nice and smooth," said Carrie.

Robert smiled, "I try."

Then there was a long pause. Carrie didn't know what to say. She had not danced like this with a man in years. But as their silence lasted longer, the soft sway along to the melody became the focus and her anxiety vanished. His soft touch and kind demeanor, and the sway that he moved her with so easily, was quite comforting.

"You're awfully quiet. Has the life of the party gotten tired?" asked Robert.

"Oh no, not at all. I'm just enjoying your dance moves and your gentlemanly behavior. Thank you for this dance. To be truthful, I was a tad nervous," said Carrie.

Robert slowly stepped back and gave her a gentle twirl and brought her back into his arms. "No, it is I who should thank you. You have really been a ray of sunshine tonight. I appreciate that. I needed that today."

As they continued to sway, Carrie pondered the significance of the day for Robert. As if he read her mind, he leaned into her ear and whispered.

"Today, would have been my wife's birthday. Beth and I danced to this song many times. It was her favorite. I haven't felt comfortable enough to ask another women to share this dance with me ... until tonight."

"Oh my. I must tell you, though—I'm incredibly honored to be the one to share it with you. Thank you for showing me a little piece of your heart. I know how difficult it is to open up and talk about these things."

As the song ended, Carrie stood on her tiptoes and gave Robert a kiss on the cheek. He looked shocked, and Carrie thought she had overstepped. That may have been a risky move on her part. But somehow, she felt like he needed a touch of something gentle and sweet to end the night. He had been nothing but a gentleman to her, and it was obvious it had been an emotional day for him. It seemed like the thing to do, and she waited for Robert's reaction. Instead of waiting very long, she decided she needed to clarify her intentions.

"I just felt like you needed that. I don't know what came over me. Mercy, now I'm babbling. Just don't pay any attention to me. I'm glad you asked me to share this dance. That's all I meant," said Carrie.

Robert gazed into her eyes. Carrie realized there were tears in his eyes. "That was the sweetest thing ever. Please, don't you apologize. I loved it, but there is just one problem," said Robert.

"What is that?" asked Carrie with a raised brow.

He pointed to his other cheek and laughed. "This side is jealous."

"We can fix that!" said Carrie.

She reached up and kissed him on the other cheek. As she came back down from her tiptoes, Robert pulled her back up, gave her a hug, twirled her around, then led her off the dance floor. He literally swept her off her feet, both figuratively and emotionally. At that moment, Carrie didn't think of anything else, only the feeling of pure joy that washed over her.

They returned to the table to find Laney chatting with a group of friends and smiling like a Cheshire cat. Carrie sat down and Laney nudged her on the arm. Carrie nudged Laney back.

"Well ladies, I promised Leslie I would have you back and that I would go along for the ride. A friend of mine runs a shuttle service. I'll call him now. So hit the floor one more time. This one is a great line dance. Laney, show 'em how it's done," said Robert and he walked away to place a call for the shuttle.

Laney was teaching Carrie the steps to the line dance, and Robert was taking in the view as he stood in the distance on his cell phone. He surprised himself tonight. He felt a bit of peace for the first time in years. He missed his wife more than he let anyone know. But something about Carrie just warmed his heart. Robert had not expected to become so emotional. He watched her and smiled. This was nice, he thought, exceptionally nice ... and long overdue.

Chapter 8

Friday Night at the Beach House

Sandra and Leslie were sitting on the deck watching the full moon rise over the ocean. They found a local station that played classic beach music. The music and the glow of the moon could not have been a better pair. It was as if they placed the order for a perfect atmosphere. It was getting a little chilly, so they grabbed some blankets. The investment of time was good for Sandra to talk, and Leslie was always good at listening. She would offer her thoughts, but never advice. Sandra valued that in their friendship, and the fact that Leslie was never judgmental.

"I didn't want to say anything to Mitch about it, I mean I know, he is my husband, and I should tell him, but he doesn't know about the seriously dark places I have been to in my life, but you do," said Sandra as she wiped a tear away.

Leslie looked over at her friend and knew the last hour and a half of conversation had been tremendously difficult for Sandra. It took courage for her to admit her true feelings, and she tended to bottle them up for exceedingly lengthy periods of time. This usually presented a tumultuous spiral of unstoppable depression. Leslie had witnessed it before and would do anything to help prevent a repeat.

"Honey, listen, you sorted it out for yourself first. Now you can share it with Mitch. He is going to understand. He loves you more than the air he breathes. I understand you are not sure about sharing too many details with him about your past. You decide when the time is right, but I think you are selling him short. He would want to know and to help you process that past life hurdle. It could help you move on from the hauntings of it," said Leslie as handed Sandra another tissue.

"But for him to think I may be back in that black hole of depression—he may think twice about pursuing invitro fertilization. But I really believe most of my depression is coming from not conceiving. Every single month the letdown. I cannot tell you how I have become so weary of it, and I am emotionally drained," said Sandra.

"I understand how that could be the reason; but also, it may be because you've been without your medication while you're trying to get pregnant. You've been off your depression medication for the last two years. Then add the fact that you go through a disappointment every month, which must weigh into some of the root cause, don't you think?"

"Yes, you're right, I have looked at it like that, too. I just don't want Mitch to think I will not be a good parent. If you recall, my depression from years ago was debilitating. But trust me, I am not abusing any meds or pills, I promise," said Sandra, as she put her right hand over her heart.

Leslie leaned her lounge chair back and looked up at the moon. It was if she was searching for the right words to guide Sandra without offending her. "With that circumstance, you just needed time to process a truly horrific thing that had happened to you. You just did. That's all. Things got out of control, and you felt like you were all alone. This is a different time, and a different matter and you have Mitch now. I really think you need to sit down and tell him what is going on. Talk to your doctor about options for treating depression while working on getting a little one here."

Leslie stood up and went over to her friend's lounge chair and sat down beside her. For a moment she embraced her, and she could tell that some of the tension in her arms had decreased from the time they first began the conversation. "As soon as you get back, talk to Mitch. I know he is going to support you in whatever you need from him. He thinks you hung the moon up there in the sky. That is love."

"My friend, I have loved this time with you. It has been exactly what I needed to help me balance the scales. You always do that for me. I think I needed to admit this out loud so I can address it, and not hide it," said Sandra, as she hugged Leslie.

It was getting late, and the full moon was growing more magnificent as the night progressed. The higher the rise, the brighter the glow on the ocean. As they stared out over the deck, admiring the wonder of the world before them, they heard a noise coming from below. They looked down to see a van pull into the drive. They both smiled when they could hear the laughter echoing up to the deck.

"Would you listen to Carrie laughing down there. Gosh, that sounds like pure music to my ears," said Leslie.

Sandra replied, "Music? She sounds like a cackling hen."

They heard Laney laughing too, but there was also another voice. Leslie and Sandra both looked at each other. It was a man's voice, and they looked over the deck railing. They glimpsed the three walking through the front door.

Sandra grabbed Leslie's arm, "Leslie, that's Robert! He kept his promise and brought them back and came along for the ride."

"Hello there, I told you I would see these lovely ladies home and deliver them safe and somewhat sound," Robert said with a grin.

He was standing in the middle of Carrie and Laney with a smile so bright it competed with the moon over his head.

"Well, I see you did just that Robert! We knew you were a gentleman. A man of his word is hard to find these days. You are a keeper," said Leslie.

Carrie's grin matched Robert's very well. It was obvious the two of them hit it off. Carrie offered Robert a seat on the deck, and they sat and talked for a few minutes about the night. Leslie noticed the magnetism between Robert and Carrie while Sandra was still looking at him with a watchful eye. The verdict was still out and pending for Sandra. Laney was happy to be there and share the night with her friends. It had been a great first night at the beach. All of them talked about how they could not have planned a better evening.

Laney and Sandra said their goodnights and went to their rooms. Leslie hung back for just a while, not sure if she should leave Carrie alone with Robert. It wasn't that she didn't trust him, but would Carrie feel awkward? Leslie did what any loyal friend would do and jumped in with a question to test the atmosphere.

"Robert, the Shuttle Bus just left you here? Are you planning on walking back to Atlantic Beach?" asked Leslie as a smile came to her face.

Robert gave her a half-baked smile, and Carrie was the first to speak up. "No, heaven's no. The shuttle is circling back around to pick him up on his way back from another pickup. I asked Robert to come in for a little while," replied Carrie.

"Well, sounds good to me, and if you will excuse me, getting some shut eye sounds superb right now. Carrie don't keep him up all night now, you hear?" said Leslie as she gave Carrie a hug and patted Robert on the back, then headed inside.

The breeze was coming in off the ocean, and it was obvious that Carrie's arms were getting chilled as she kept rubbing them to keep warm.

"Here," said Robert, as he took a blanket from the lounge chair and wrapping it around her shoulders.

"Thank you," said Carrie.

Carrie stood there admiring the view out over the Atlantic Ocean as she took a deep, cleansing breath. Robert was admiring the view, too, but it was not the ocean or the moon. He watched Carrie with her face up to the night sky with the moonlight reflecting in her bright eyes. She was a beauty. The years had been kind to her.

"You know something, Carrie, I don't want to sound all hokey and weird, but tonight was good for me. I mean it; it truly was wonderful," said Robert.

Carrie looked at Robert as a smile adorned on her face. "Me, too. I can't remember the last time I had so much fun. I'll pay for it tomorrow, but for right now, I can say it was totally worth it," said Carrie.

"I'm glad to hear you agree. Now, I hope this next question won't alter your first impression of me, but I would like to do it again sometime. Over dinner? I'd like to know more about you, Carrie."

Carrie's head spun around, and she looked Robert directly in the eye. "Me? There really is more to tell than you could imagine, the last few years have been insane. My life has been anything but normal lately. But there are parts that are wonderful and parts that are just downright pitiful. Sometimes I need duct tape just to keep it all together, and then there are some parts that are as joyful as Christmas morning. You sure you want to hear about things like that? It's the proverbial Pandora's Box you would be opening."

"Absolutely. I want to hear it all. How about we start in small chapters? One lunch or dinner equals one decade. We progress on the chapters as we go. Sound like a plan?" asked Robert.

Carrie was pointing her finger at him and waving it back and forth. "Now that sounded like more than one invitation. You said chapters."

"Yes, I did. No pressure, we will start with Chapter One. You just set the date. If you like, this week we could meet for lunch or dinner. I know a quiet little spot that has the best seafood mac and cheese."

Headlights coming into the drive broke the conversation up. It was the Shuttle service back to pick up Robert.

"Prince Robert, I believe your carriage has arrived sir," said Carrie as she performed a curtsy. "Seafood mac and cheese sounds divine. We're here through Monday."

Robert was walking down the steps as he looked back at her. "Well then, we better do it tomorrow night," he said, as he winked at her.

"Okay, sounds great, but I don't have your number. I don't have my car either," Carrie called back from the deck.

"No worries. Leave the details to me. Good night, Carrie."

Robert opened the shuttle bus door and Carrie waved goodbye from the deck.

She stood on the deck for a moment, then said to herself, "I was just asked on a date. I just accepted a date with a man I just met," she mumbled. The only one she thought was listening was the full moon. She gazed at the bright moon with a soft smile on her face. She felt happy and relaxed. She had not felt that way for a long time, and it felt wonderful. No tightness in the jawline, no nagging throb of a tension induced headache.

She walked inside and attempted to be quiet and not disturb anyone, then the lights came on and it startled her. "Gosh y'all, what are you doing up?" said Carrie. "I thought you went to bed. You scared the mess out of me! How long have you been in here in the dark?"

"Long enough to hear you accept a dinner date for tomorrow night. You go, girl!" said Leslie.

"Robert is a great person, Carrie. I had a feeling the two of you would hit it off. It was great to see him smile and laugh tonight. It's been a while since I've seen him look so happy," said Laney.

Sandra was looking back and forth as if she was watching a tennis match. She stood up and started waving her arms. "Well, I sure hope he *is* a nice man. For God's sake, we hardly know anything about him. I mean, he is handsome in a Sean Connery sort of way. He says all the right things, but Laney is the only one here that knows anything at all about him."

Leslie immediately noticed Sandra's fear. She was thinking of her own blind date many years ago and how it did not go well for her. The rape was still a stab in the gut anytime Sandra heard of blind dates or set-ups. Leslie went over to hold Sandra's hand to help stop her anxiety.

"Sandra, it's simply fine. My gut tells me he's one of the few Southern gentlemen left out there. Some young men could take lessons from him. She's going to be fine," said Leslie as she patted Sandra on the shoulder.

"Sandra, it's okay. Really it is," said Carrie as she smoothed out the wrinkle that bridged Sandra's forehead.

"So, you don't trust my verification skills, do you, Sandra? Gee, really Sandra, come on, you know I wouldn't steer her wrong. It's okay. Robert has been like a dad to me most of my life," said Laney.

"I'm sorry," said Sandra. "Y'all know how I get over situations like this. Just ignore me. That was some knee jerk response. I love y'all, but I think this is my clue that I need to go to bed. I'm sorry, Carrie. My emotions are all over the place today."

"It's okay, really. You get some rest so we can hit the beach in the morning," said Carrie.

They were all exhausted, so they called it a night and went to their respective rooms. They headed to bed with hopes of starting the morning early for their first day on the beach at Emerald Isle.

Chapter 9

Where is Bill?

Karen had called Bill's cell dozens of times. What was he thinking? Where was he? This was getting ridiculous. Everything was ready. The caterers had delivered the food. The flowers were in place. The band was set up on the lawn under a tent with a dance floor. Everyone was going to be surprised, but she did not think that included her, too. It surprised her already that Bill was so late.

What was he doing? "Where on God's green earth are you, Bill?" she yelled out as she walked onto the terrace. She checked with all the waitstaff on the setup of the food. This town was not accustomed to such fine dining and sophisticated entertainment. She wanted everything to be impeccable.

Karen heard a car pull into the driveway, and she ran to the front door to see if it was Bill. It wasn't Bill. She looked again and realized it was the TV station's General Manager, Jerry. The waitstaff greeted him and showed him to the bar. He was always early, and always ready for a drink.

As the minutes slipped by, she realized she had paced the floor so much and so fast that her heel strap had given her a blister.

"*Damn it*," she yelled out. "*Damn, damn, damn. Where are you, Bill?*"

She looked out on the lawn and courtyard as more guests were arriving. "*Bill, when I get my hands on you, I will wring your cotton-picking neck.*" She stomped to the bedroom and grabbed the phone. She called again. Nothing. No answer. Straight to voice mail.

"Bill! Pick up the phone! What the hell are you doing? Guests are arriving. You were supposed to be home two hours ago. This is not funny, Bill, answer the damned phone!" After leaving the voice mail, Karen threw the phone on the bed.

"Miss Karen?" one of the waitstaff, popped her head in the door. "More guests have arrived. Would you like to join them, or should I let them know you're delayed?" she asked.

Karen threw her hands up in the air and said, "Well, of course, I'm delayed. I'm waiting for my slow as molasses fiancé. You tell them whatever and let them start with appetizers. I imagine they have made a huge dent in the open bar by now, so they may need food."

"Yes ma'am, I will. They are enjoying the open bar and the music. It sounds really nice. I never heard a band like that before."

The young woman left, and Karen yelled out, "Mercy, of course, you haven't. You've probably never left this backwoods town in your life," and she slammed the door.

Karen shook her head and opened the door and walked to the kitchen. She paused to get her composure together. She smoothed her hair and flung it back over her shoulder, took a deep breath, then went to the kitchen to find the young lady.

"I'm sorry, that was unnecessary back there. I should not have yelled at you. I'm sorry. I'm glad you like the music." Karen reached her hand out and placed it on the young girl's shoulder as she looked at her name tag. "Sue Ann, please forgive me. I don't know what came over me. It seems I've been having a bit of a rough day."

The young girl nodded her head in acceptance of Karen's apology, then she took the appetizers to the tent on the lawn. Karen looked out over the pool and grounds. It was lovely, this was a plan for a perfect night. The flowers were beautiful, her engagement ring, waiting in the safe, was spectacular. The guest list was perfect, but the rest was not shaping up as she planned. Her perfect plan seemed to be less than stellar if Bill was not going to be there.

Karen realized she needed to make an apology or an explanation for the delay. She walked to the double French doors, placed her hand on the doorknob, and exhaled a breath of air. She had to do this; it was time to address the guests. Karen was good at this type of thing. She put on her sales pitch face. That is what she did. She was good at it, and she really had to do something now. Then she had a thought: Why was Bill late? Was he late because he was showing her up? Did he run into Carrie and change his mind? What was happening? Brushing those thoughts away, Karen shook her head, adjusted her dress, and opened the doors.

She looked fabulous, and every head turned as she stood in the doorway. The light behind her framed her silhouette, and she appeared to be entering a stage for a performance. Karen was comfortable in her own skin and body and wore the latest fashion trends. Her tight black spaghetti strap dress showed off the work she put in at the gym. It had a long hem line, but the slit over her left leg went almost to her hip. The neckline dipped in a low plunge and left nothing much to the imagination about her cleavage. She adjusted her footing to accommodate for the blister. She took one step over the threshold and walked across the patio towards the tent.

"Hello everyone," said Karen as she reached for a glass of champagne. "What a fabulous looking group of people we have gathered here at our home. We are so excited that you came. As you can see, Bill has been delayed. I like to refer to him as my Dollar Bill, always making a deal. Some of you have said the same of him. I am sure he will be home soon. Until then, please, enjoy the appetizers and drinks, and we'll have dinner momentarily, with or without him. His loss, right?" and she laughed as she raised her glass of champagne. "Cheers to you all!"

"They seemed to buy it," she thought, and she walked back into the house. As she crossed the threshold to walk into the living room, Jerry walked in behind her. He already had his share of drinks, and his tongue was as loose as a goose when he drank.

Karen braced herself for the forthcoming conversation and mumbled under her breath, *"What drunken bull crap do I have to hear from him?"*

"Karen, I've been watching your sales pitch for a few years. That right there was a bunch of damned malarky. Where the hell is Bill?"

Suddenly, Karen felt like her head was spinning, and she felt sick. "I don't know! Shut the door and lower your voice." She walked into the living room to sit down for a moment.

Jerry followed her, "What do you mean you don't know? What kind of messed up answer is that, Karen?"

"We were both at the office. He got a call from the security company. They said the alarm wasn't set at Carrie's, and since she was out of town, he made it his business to go over to set it. He said he would be right home—early. He said early, Jerry. He said early so he could get ready for tonight. What the hell?" she dropped her head in her hands.

Jerry laughed and said, "Well, Karen, do you think he got a case of cold feet?" he asked with a smirk on his face.

Karen's head spun around as she looked at Jerry. "What are you talking about, Jerry?"

"Now Karen, it ain't no secret. Bill told me what the actual plan here tonight was all about," Jerry slugged the last of his bourbon and coke. "But I didn't think he would get cold feet. You know I'm just teasing you."

By this time, it was obvious Karen was more than frustrated. Her anger had turned into panic, and frustration had evolved into concern.

"Jerry, cut it out. Seriously, what do I do? I've called his cell phone a million times. If you weren't so drunk, you could go look for him."

Jerry shook his head and put his hands in his pockets. "Guilty as charged. I could never turn down an open bar. You know that. But you don't have to make it sound so disgusting. I recall you could knock 'em down with the best of them until you got on that health kick."

"Jerry, just stop talking and start thinking. Help me here. Now I'm getting worried. What if he was in an accident or had a heart attack? What if he and Carrie got into a fight? I thought she was out of town on her little debutante preppy girl's party week. What if he told her about the engagement announcement? Crap, help me here. I am losing it, Jerry. What if he did get cold feet? What . . ."

Jerry interrupted her, "Stop it. You're just torturing yourself. Slow down. I feel like right about now is when they always slap the irrational woman in the face. You want me to slap you? Like in the movies? Now calm down." Jerry walked over and looked out the window at the guests in the yard.

"The Sheriff is here. He just arrived. Let me see if he can make some calls. Sit tight. There is a reasonable information for this, I mean, sorry . . . I meant explanation. That last bourbon was strong, that was good stuff. How much did y'all pay for all of this? Okay, never mind, sit tight, and let me go see what he can do."

Karen thought if Jerry was her only hope and help, she was in a deep predicament. She couldn't deal with facing the guests, so she stayed inside staring at the landline so long that it startled her when it rang.

"Hello, hello! Bill, is that you?"

"Karen, this is one of Carrie's neighbors," said the voice on the other line. "My name is Kemp. Is Bill home? I got your number from the office earlier today, but just getting around to calling."

Karen looked confused. Why was this man calling for Bill? "No, Bill is not home. Do you know where he is? He's late for an important dinner engagement."

"Well, yes and no. Maybe. Listen, a little earlier this afternoon, I spotted his car flying down the lane at Carrie's house. He was driving crazy and erratically. It just dawned on me that it was odd for Bill. He loved that car. No way he was going to drive it like that. He must have been good and hot about something, huh?"

Karen took a deep breath as she realized it sounded like the neighbor was just nosey and not too concerned about Bill. "Okay, Kemp, thank you for calling, but can you tell me where he went when he left Carrie's house?"

"He headed east and was driving like a bat out of hell. I wished I had thought to call earlier. I just sat down for dinner and remembered that it was strange. I mean, I was out on the main road turning into my drive when I heard him ripping out of the drive. What's got him so riled up, I wonder? It looked like he had someone with him too."

"Thanks for calling," said Karen, and she hung up. She immediately went to find Jerry.

She looked out at the foyer and Jerry was talking to the Sheriff.

"Hey, hey, I have news," said Karen. She told them about the caller and what he witnessed. "Can you check it out? Bill never takes chances with his Porsche and Kemp said it looked like someone was with him. So, I am even more confused now. He wouldn't drive like that, so this seems very odd to me."

"On it," said the Sheriff and he motioned to Jerry, "You want to come along?"

Karen sat down on the bench in the foyer. Her voice trembled and she was clearly on the verge of tears.

"Jerry, do you think this is serious? I need you to stop clowning around and be real for a minute. What if that someone with Bill was Carrie?"

"Nah. Simmer down. Look, I'm the one drinking. You are panicking. Focus here," said Jerry, as he snapped his fingers in her face. "I'll go with the Sheriff, and we'll find out what's going on. You have guests, so go make the rounds and strut your stuff. Go sell that pretty smile you have, babe. Make Bill proud. He'll be here," said Jerry as he popped her on the backside when she walked away.

Karen spent the rest of the night mingling with the guests, explaining that Bill was called away on a business venture unexpectedly. There were a couple of whispers she overheard by guests referencing Bill and Carrie's divorce. Why would someone speak of that in her home? How rude could they be? A few of them whispered about the purpose for the dinner, and she even had one guest ask her if it was an engagement announcement dinner. Karen did her best to blow her off by saying the buffet looked like it needed restocking. The guest looked straight at the buffet and could clearly see that it was amply stocked. Her eyes shifted back to Karen, as if she knew she was not being forthright. Karen headed to the kitchen and poured herself a glass of tea. She was looking for the lemons and couldn't find them. She always had lemon with her unsweetened tea.

"Where are the damned lemons? Can anyone tell me that, please?" She slammed her glass down on the quartz countertop, and the staff in the kitchen jumped when they saw she had shattered the glass. Karen jumped back and looked at her hand to be sure she was not cut. One server brought her another glass of tea with a lemon on the rim.

"Thank you, I'm glad to see that one of you knows how to wait on someone like they should." And with that, she stormed out of the kitchen.

Within seconds, Karen turned around and was back in the kitchen. "I'm sorry, please forgive me. I am so on edge tonight.

You all have done such an excellent job. The food was wonderful, and you kept the buffet stocked so well. You all get an extra tip. Have a splendid night. I want this kitchen spotless when you leave, though."

Once the last guest left, Karen went to the bar and told the bartender to pour her a strong one, clean up, and head out. She sat by the pool reflecting on the evening and how she looked like a fool. Karen's cell phone rang, and she almost dropped it as her hands fumbled to pick it up and answer.

"Hello, Bill?" she asked.

"No Karen, it's Jerry. Listen a deputy and I are going to head back over to your place. Just sit tight for a minute."

"Why, Jerry? What's wrong? A deputy? Where's the Sheriff?"

There was a pause.

"Jerry, what is going on?"

"Just sit tight Karen, we are on the way now. The Sherriff has some business to attend to. Have the guests left?" he asked.

"Yes, Jerry. Tell me what the hell is going on?" Karen screamed.

"We'll be there in five," said Jerry, and he hung up.

Karen threw back her drink in one gulp and winced as she felt the burn down her throat.

Chapter Ten

On the Beach: "That's Where I Wanna Be!"

The dawn of the sun glowed through a filtered misty horizon. After a time, the sun took care of burning the haze away. Leslie was on the deck, having her morning espresso. Her early-to-rise mentality would not let her sleep in. Laney was getting breakfast ready. Carrie had just come in from a stroll on the beach. Sandra was still in bed, as she did not sleep well during the night.

"Morning Sunshine," said Laney as she stepped on the deck with coffee. "As the song declares: "that lucky ole sun has nothing to do but roll around in heaven all day." She sang as she waltzed around the deck. "Sorry, shouldn't try singing this early in the morning. That was just playing on the radio. I love this station y'all found last night. Breakfast is all settled out on the island bar, y'all help yourselves whenever you're ready." She pointed to the kitchen.

Carrie headed to the french doors. "You know you don't have to call me twice. I worked up an appetite on my walk."

Leslie looked over at Laney and said, "I wager that woman didn't sleep a wink last night. I haven't seen her so enthusiastic and content in a long time. She needed last night."

"Precisely, and so did Robert. You realize they could be an ideal couple. I wouldn't mention it to her right now, but I have been pondering about the two of them together for a while. I suppose last night just showed my matchmaking skills are still on point," said Laney as she smiled, leaned back in the lounge chair, and closed her eyes.

Leslie tapped her on the arm and said, "Laney, slow down a bit. The more you say, the further you will shift her away. She's her own woman. I recognize you love Robert, and he has been a valuable friend to you and your family. He seems like a pleasant gentleman. Just let them proceed at their own pace. You are going to have them married before sundown today the way you're carrying on right now."

"Yeah right, you know how passionate I get about these things. I'll put my matchmaking endeavors in neutral. Well, at least I'll try. I'm just pleased to see romance happen for someone. If it can't be me, can I at least enjoy following it?" she asked.

Leslie frowned and said, "Of course you can, honey. Just slow down with those two. Now don't pout, it's not your style. Chin up."

"Yes ma'am," replied Laney.

"I wonder what's keeping Sandra. I heard her get up and down most of the night. I checked on her once when I heard her get up. She walked down the hall to the window, and I saw her staring up at the moon. She has always been a moonchild. We had a wonderful talk last night. But then when Carrie came home with Robert, the dating issue came up. I think it sort of sent her into a PTSD moment of her blind date when she was abused."

Laney nodded her head in agreement and said, "I think you may be right. She went from 0 to 80 in a millisecond for sure. I guessed she recovered, though. She seemed fine when she went to bed."

"Yes, she seemed okay, but she has an undercurrent that is stronger than any of those waves out there," replied Leslie.

Sandra came out to the deck with a cup of coffee, a plate of fruit, a couple of mini muffins, and a one strip of bacon.

"Here, I brought enough to share. The bacon is mine, the rest is for y'all. I love this stuff. I just can't eat too much of it. I am literally gaining weight by looking at it," said Sandra, as she popped a small muffin in her mouth. "Well maybe the bacon and one tiny muffin is mine."

Carrie came up behind her and sat down at the table. "Laney, you did good, girl. This is delicious! And Leslie, thank you for picking up the goodies at Sara's bakery. I can't wait to try her pimento cheese today."

"You are welcome," Leslie said, with a smile. "You know, Sara mentioned you when I was there. She would not take one red cent from me for any of that food. She said she wanted to treat us for helping her out when she had cancer. I told her it was unnecessary, but she insisted."

Carrie gasped, "What? No way! She shouldn't have done that. I know she needs every bit of income she can get. Bless her heart. I just love her."

Laney chimed in, "You know, Sara has about the most perfect small town set up. She is expanding her menu. I love what she is doing over there."

"Me too. We need to support her as often as possible," said Leslie.

"I hate to be the mood killer here about entrepreneurial things and such, but are we going to the beach today, or stay up here like old sitting hens on this porch? Y'all really take life too seriously sometimes. Loosen up," said Sandra as she stood up, jumped up and down, raised her arms over her head and began to wiggle all over. "Shake it off, shake it off, for a while alright?"

"Girl, you need to stop. The folks over on the other deck are staring at you like you are having some sort of conniption fit," said Laney as she turned around to see the other deck across the street and several faces quickly turn away.

"Maybe they liked the show. Folks don't watch what they don't like," replied Sandra.

"Well, I'm ready to hit the beach. I just need to change clothes," said Leslie as she headed to the french doors, they all followed her inside.

They made their way down to the beach, and set up their chairs, towels, and cooler. They brought an umbrella for Carrie and Leslie because they burned in the sun. Sandra and Laney were the sun worshippers in the group. Laney brought her echo and started the beach music playlist. First one on the top – "Everything is Tuesday." They sang along with General Johnson and The Chairman of the Board; they all knew every word.

"I wonder why they used the name Tuesday in this song. Y'all ever wonder about that?" asked Sandra.

"Only you would think of something like that, Sandra," said Carrie. "No, I can't say I ever thought of that before. I've just always liked that song, though."

"Well, leave it to me to do such critical thinking. Thinking deep about minor details keeps my mind from getting preoccupied about major things. It works for me. Most of the time," said Sandra.

"Your coping skills are one of a kind that is for sure. So, what's the plan for tonight, ladies?" asked Laney.

"One of us already has a plan," said Carrie as she grinned and laid back in her lounge chair. "I don't know what you girls are doing, but I have a date. I cannot even believe I am saying this—a date."

Leslie grinned as she looked over at Carrie and winked and said, "I can see you're excited."

"You know what? I am," said Carrie. "I never imagined that someone would ask me out. And then I said yes! That was even more of a surprise. But he made it sound so natural, so easy. Let's just talk, he said."

Laney looked over and noticed that Sandra was not saying a word. She was hoping she was past the notion of it being a bad idea for Carrie and Robert to go out on a date.

"Robert will text me later today with the details for meeting up tonight. He sent me a message earlier saying that he was working on a surprise for you," said Laney.

Laney looked over at Sandra. She was staring at them intently over her sunglasses. Laney met her gaze straight in the eye and told Carrie, "No worries about being alone. He promised you would always be in the company of other people. He doesn't want you to be uncomfortable." Sandra went back to reading her book after that comment.

"Y'all do not have to keep pussy footing around talking about this date and acting like I am some fragile child. Really, it's okay. It just caught me off guard last night," Sandra said and went back to reading.

Laney went for a swim, and it was not long before Sandra jumped in, too. The sun was hot overhead, and Leslie and Carrie sat under the umbrella watching their friends as they jumped the waves.

"Leslie, I can't thank you enough for putting this trip together. It really has gotten off to an epic start," said Carrie, as she watched the girls in the waves.

"It has. Look at those two they are fearless in the ocean. Always have been. They make it seem so easy. I love watching them. You know, Laney had a point earlier today."

"Oh yeah, about what?" asked Carrie.

"She said she was glad someone had a romance going on, and she was happy to watch you and Robert last night. She said that love might as well be working out for someone."

"Yes, it has been a long time since she and Jim split. I have been hoping and praying someone would come into her life. She is such a total package and would make some man incredibly happy. But as for romance with Robert, I'm approaching this as friends."

"Okay, friends—time will tell. But know that Laney may be hoping for something more. She adores that man, and you, too. She may be dreaming up something in her own mind," said Leslie, as she popped the top on a Diet Coke and put it in her koozie.

Sandra and Laney came up from the beach and flopped down on their beach towels. They heard a phone ding with a text alert. All four ladies reached for their phones.

"I don't have any reception down here, so that was not my phone," said Carrie. "I couldn't even post those pics this morning. No bars—nothing –nothing. As much as we paid for this house, you would think they would provide internet. I guess they think people will be on the beach all day and not worried about social media, they don't know me then do they?" said Carrie.

"It's mine, Carrie, your carrier must not have coverage down here, but mine is good," said Laney as she scrolled through, smiling as she read the text.

Leslie looked over at Laney and said, "Girl, that must be something juicy in that text. Look at that grin on you."

"Actually, it's going to make Carrie smile more. It's Robert. He has pulled some strings and has that surprise for you. All of us, as a matter of fact," said Laney.

"Well, are you just going to keep it to yourself?" asked Sandra, as she put down her book. "Well, are you? Stop all that grinning like a possum and talk."

By this time, Carrie, Sandra, and Leslie were staring at Laney. She kept reading the text.

"Dish it out, Laney! What is it? The suspense is killing me," Carrie said.

"Ladies, my friend is very resourceful and clever. A little something you may not know about Robert. He was in sales and marketing for years as an independent yacht wholesaler. He has brokered deals up and down the East Coast," said Laney.

"So?" asked Sandra. "We're not asking about his resume; we're asking what about tonight?"

"Because ... he has secured a yacht for the night and wants to know if we all want to spend the night on the yacht. We'll have our own quarters. He already has a captain and a crew lined up, and he has hired a chef. Although, I do not understand that part, I am totally capable," said Laney as she rolled her eyes and kept scrolling through the text.

Carrie's hand went straight to cover her mouth as she gasped, "You are so full of it, Laney. What does it really say?" asked Carrie.

"That is what it says. Look at it," said Laney, as she handed the phone to Carrie.

Carrie took the phone and scrolled through the text, scrolling up and up. "Well then. Who is up for an overnight excursion? Girls, we are going on a yacht!" screamed Carrie.

Sandra immediately walked over and grabbed the phone from Carrie. "Let me see that text. Uh huh, yes, uh-huh. Shut the front and back door. He's serious!"

After reading the text and the details, the ladies headed back to the beach house. Their excitement was noticeable by other beach dwellers that watched them squeal and laugh like little schoolgirls. When they reached the house, they got showered, packed bags, and met up in the living room to go over the plan.

"So, here's the deal. We'll meet Robert at the marina. He gave me all the details. We'll go out this afternoon. Free time on board until cocktails at 5:00, dinner at 8:00, and we'll return by noon tomorrow. Sound good?" asked Laney.

"Sean Connery, come take us away. It's like a real-life James Bond movie being played out in real time. What is that Carly Simon song again, "You walked into the party like you were walking onto a yacht." And ... we are!" said Sandra with a laugh.

"You're so vain. You probably think this song is about you," Leslie sang, a little off-key.

They all laughed as Sandra danced across the living room holding an imaginary cocktail. They all belted out the lyrics to "You're so Vain."

Then Sandra plopped down on the sofa, "Just what are we supposed to be doing while Carrie and Robert have their date?" she asked while making air quotes with the word *date*.

"No worries. Robert said there would be plenty of time for Carrie and him to talk. He just felt like this would be more comfortable for her and he wanted to treat us all. I'm telling you, he's a keeper," Laney said.

They finished packing their bags, and after a quick bite of pimento cheese sandwiches, they headed toward the marina and ran a couple of errands. The excitement was more than they could bear, and they were eager to get on their way. Laney was the only one who had been on a yacht. The other three were first timers. She enjoyed watching their enthusiasm and knew they were going to be blown away. This wasn't just any yacht. She kept the details to herself so she could see their faces when they boarded. Laney knew exactly which vessel Robert was referring to.

Chapter Eleven

On the Boardwalk

The noon day sun was accompanied by a few clouds that allowed for them to walk down the boardwalk without such scorching heat. They enjoyed dropping in quaint boutiques and picking up a few items. Carrie went into Beaufort Linen Company and picked out a hat to wear on the boat, and a couple of blouses. Laney had them stop at the Trading Post on the way to select spices and a few items for appetizers. No chef on board the yacht was going to completely take over the kitchen. After all, she had her pride.

As they continued down the boardwalk, Carrie stopped in front of a wine shop. "Wait, let's grab a bottle of wine, maybe two. As a thank you." She waved her hand for everyone to come join her in Cru Wine Bar & Coffee Shop, and they found four bottles of wine, one from each of them. Laney helped them pick the perfect wines. She knew Robert was partial to red, and his favorite was in stock at the shop. Laney stopped as she was walking out the door and looked around the wine shop, then looked across the street at the bakery.

"You know what, ladies? I have been looking for a new position. I need to change my way of thinking. I am thinking I would love to have a bakery and wine shop combo kind of thing. Maybe have a few specialty meals to go. That has been all the rage lately, and it seems to hold up. Fresh pasta—I want to include fresh pasta. There truly is nothing like it. Maybe catering for weddings too. Family meals to go. The options are endless!" Laney's eyes twinkled like stars as she revealed her newfound revelation.

All of them shook their head in agreement as they headed out the door. Once again, Laney stopped for a moment, and turned around and looked at the wine shop and glanced around the area. You could tell her mind was churning up something and the other three waited and gave her a moment to think.

"I could make it work in Greenway. Really, I think I could pull off a wine, coffee, bakery thing. Of course, I would depend on Sara at The Bread Basket for some items. I wouldn't want to hurt her business. I'd want to help her grow. I want to do some thinking about this when we get back home. I can dream, right?" asked Laney.

Leslie agreed with a firm headshake, and Carrie chimed in, "I think it would be amazing to have something other than the Burger Box closer to my house."

"Exactly!" said Sandra. "It would be great if you could serve smoothies? If so, I will be there every day."

"Well, maybe I can talk to Mitch about financing options and a business plan. I like this idea ladies. I feel like I have just had an epiphany, and this is exciting! If not Greenway, I could do it in a neighboring town. We'll see. Sorry to bore you with my revelation," said Laney.

"No apologies necessary! I love seeing your fresh perspective and hearing your innovative ideas," said Leslie.

The four headed to the Suburban, gathered a few items together. They brushed their hair and touched up lipstick and mascara. It was time to head down to the marina.

"Well ladies, let's head over to meet Robert. Like they say on *Beat Bobby Flay*: 'Let's do this!'" said Laney.

Carrie started fanning herself with her hands. It was obvious she was overwhelmed.

"I don't know about this. I think I'm a little nervous, like a silly high school girl. Do I look flushed? I feel flushed. I'm going to have a panic attack. Why did I agree to this?" she asked as she started walking around in circles as the others just stared at her.

Sandra walked up to Carrie and put both hands on her shoulders as she looked her square in the face and said, "Put your big girl panties on. We are getting ready to have the best night ever. Besides, you have your friends with you. Nothing is going to go wrong. Just take a deep breath. Nice and slow and focus on your breathing rhythm." Sandra began breathing in and out very dramatically.

Every one of them burst out in laughter at the sight of Sandra counseling someone on methods of calming down.

"What is so dang funny, y'all?" asked Sandra, with raised eyebrows.

Leslie spoke up, "Honey, you are the last one to be schooling someone on ways to calm down. Mercy girl, what are we going to do with you?"

"Just love me. You love me. Y'all love me, and you know it," said Sandra as she started walking down the boardwalk.

"Thank you for this moment. I needed that laugh. I'm ready now. You know what, Sandra, that was actually very helpful. Thank you. Let's go."

Chapter 12

Sail Away

Robert was sitting on the deck, waiting anxiously for his guests to arrive. He smiled as he thought about his bold move with the invitation he extended. He hoped it was not an overstep that would make a bad impression with Carrie. This was the first woman he felt comfortable enough to ask out. Quickly, too, he surprised himself at how easy it had been. It seemed natural. Carrie had such genuine warmth that he quickly discovered how easy it was to talk to her. He had never been this bold, ever. But he had met no one quite like her. He struggled to describe her, but it was difficult to narrow it down when so many words could be used to describe her many attributes.

As he thought back to the conversation the night before, he felt something stir in him he thought was dead. He thought it died with his wife. He had not felt like loving anyone in that way again until he spent a few moments with Carrie.

Robert was standing there, lost in his thoughts, when he heard chatter coming from down the dock. He turned around to see the most beautiful vision of the four of them coming to greet him.

For a moment, he admired the view. What an incredible group of ladies. Carrie, of course, caught his eye first. She was wearing a beautiful blue and white wrap over a magenta sundress. Her soft, flowing curls of black and silver were like sterling silver accessories. Her petite frame was gliding toward him with her wrap flowing in the breeze. It was a sight to behold.

Then he looked over at his friend—smart and beautiful Laney. So much talent and energy. He admired her smile and her laugh as they walked up to him. Knowing her since she was a tot had led to a strong admiration, and he loved her as if she was family. Her chestnut brown flocks flowed over a yellow jumpsuit, and she was glowing as bright as the sun.

Then there was Leslie. What a lovely person, inside and out. She was wearing a pair of emerald colored palazzo pants and a floral blouse. She was the glue in this group, and the sensible one. Robert imagined that she would be the one to go to bed first that night, and the first one to rise.

The last to get his attention was Sandra, a beautiful lady, but she did not shine like the others. She was wrestling with something. Robert made a mental note to be sure she had a good evening. She needed to smile more because when she did, she was gorgeous. She was wearing a long, flowing, floral sundress. The cheerful print complemented her well, but it contrasted with her disposition.

As the ladies drew closer, Robert stood at the dock with open arms. "Welcome to all of you beauties. What a fortunate man I am to be in the company of such amazing women." He greeted each one of them with a cheek-to-cheek embrace.

When Robert got to Carrie, he held her hand and kissed it, and then bowed to her and said, "Welcome aboard, my dear. May I escort you on deck?"

"Why, of course you can. Now stand up and stop being silly," said Carrie as she looked around the deck of the yacht. "Robert, this is awesome. How in the world did you pull this off? I don't think I have ever seen anything like this except in a movie, or at the port when driving by. You can't grasp the massive size from a distance. This yacht is huge!"

"When you were in the business as long as I was, you know a few people and where they dock. I got lucky; a friend helped me out. This magnificent Benetti yacht is from Italy. Their work is superb. The present owners have been working on the rebuild for a while now. The teak deck floors were completed last week," said Robert as he looked over the yacht with an admiration that resembled a lovesick gaze.

A member of the crew greeted the ladies and took their bags below to their respective rooms. When he walked away, Robert laid out some rules and processes that would take place on the yacht while they were on the voyage.

"Just one more thing, once we get out to sea, we will not have consistent cell service. That is part of the new upgrade. In the re-build of this vessel, they will put in all new state-of-the-art internet and satellite equipment. The previous equipment was very outdated, so the owners had it stripped out. For tonight, you may not get service. But no worries, if we have an emergency, we have the proper equipment to get help. Plus, I see this as an opportunity to lose that distraction anyway."

Carrie looked back at the others, and all of them shrugged their shoulders. It did not appear to be an issue.

"We can text anyone we need to now, before we leave to let them know we may be off the grid for a bit," said Leslie, as she picked up her phone to text Stan.

"Yes, I think it will be fine to shut down and get away from that ball and chain cell phone for a little while," said Sandra.

Carrie reached for her purse and started fidgeting inside the compartments. She tossed all the contents around and kept coming up empty-handed. "In all the excitement, I think I left my phone back at the beach house. Oh well, we'll see if I can live without it for a night. But who needs a phone? You're right Robert, look at this beauty all around us, and the weather is amazing. Why would anyone waste a moment of taking it all in by staring at a phone?"

They got settled in their rooms, and Robert asked them to come back up to the deck when they finished.

Carrie and Robert walked over to the bow of the boat as it was maneuvered out of the marina. Carrie lost her balance for a moment, and Robert quickly caught her and steadied her stance. She turned around to thank him, and his soft green eyes had her mesmerized. The sun was shining on his face, and she could see deep into his eyes. They were almost the color of the sea, and his hair was as white as the waves that were rippling under the boat. These features were very flattering with his tan. She hadn't seen all of this in the darkness of the club. The sunlight and water suited him well, and she could see how the boat life was a perfect and well-matched career for him.

"It may take you a while to get your sea legs under you. Until then, stay near to something that you can grab hold of, you hear?" asked Robert.

When he spoke, Carrie hung onto his every word. His accent had a twang that Carrie could not identify. She stared into his eyes and noticed how the sun made them sparkle. She broke out of the trance when she heard a horn blow on a nearby boat.

"You know, this is probably my favorite time of day to be near the ocean, or on the beach," said Carrie as she gazed over the water. "I find the afternoon sun so beautiful, watching it make the descent from high noon to sunset. The sparkling of the water and color reflections. Some like sunrises, but for me it's sunsets."

"Ah, for me it's sunrise. I like a fresh new perspective and the smell of coffee in my cup. Like the old song *Sweet Virginia Breeze.* Have you heard that one?" asked Robert.

Carrie laughed and said, "Yes, that's one of my favorites. Steve Basset, right?"

"Absolutely. The lady knows her beach music, I see. That's impressive."

"My all-time favorite was The Chairman of the Board, way back in the day. I like the Band of Oz, too, and I wouldn't say no to hearing anything by the Tams, The Drifters, or Lou Rawls."

"Yes, I like all of them as well. Speaking of back in the day, let me show you the lounge and dining quarters."

They walked to the lounge area of the yacht. The well-appointed and tastefully decorated room was a retro 70s style living room. It astonished Carrie as she looked at some pieces in the room. As they sat down to talk, Carrie watched Robert pull up a playlist that was saved on an iPad.

"Robert, are these original cushions and furnishings? They look immaculate," said Carrie as she was looking at the sofa. "I swear, I think my family had one just like this when I was growing up with the same color and pattern."

"Some are original, and some are not. The owners did an outstanding job when they upgraded in here. Looks like you walked into a living room from 1970 something, right? It's an older boat and they wanted to keep it classic, so this was a perfect fit. I love an older yacht. today's versions seem a bit too electronic and cold for my taste," said Robert.

"This retro vibe makes me feel young again. You have a playlist saved there; what's on tap for music?"

"I don't know. My collection is so diversified. What would you prefer?"

"Oh, I love anything, especially music to dance to. I think you figured that out last night. Shag, bop, line dance, heck, I even took a square dance class one time," said Carrie and she squinted her eyes as she braced for his reaction.

"What in the world for, may I ask?" asked Robert through intense laughter.

Carrie popped him on the arm. "Stop laughing. They offered it at the local community college, and I thought it sounded like fun. Being newly separated, the nights were boring, so I tried it. Little did I know the music would be the death of me. Gosh, it was horrible! But the class was fun. I learned how to square dance and to dance the reel."

"Oh really? Now that is interesting," said Robert with raised eyebrows.

"Yes, ever since I saw the movie *Titanic* and the dance party they had below on the ship. Then, most recently, the *Downton Abbey* series. There's a part where the staff dances the reel, and I wanted to learn how to do it. It's fun! I just can't tolerate some of the music, but I'll have to teach you sometime."

Robert leaned into her ear, "I will look forward to that, especially if you are the instructor. How about right now?" he asked.

"Well okay, but we need some music and it's just us, so I will show you the basic square dance moves," Carrie said, as she shuffled her feet to get in position.

Robert pulled up a selection that was saved on his iPad. He smiled when he found the one that would suit their purpose.

"Not a problem, I just have something here in my playlist." He put the music on a Celtic play list and offered his arm to Carrie.

Carrie quickly took him up on the offer, and they danced around the lounge. The music was much more sophisticated and an improvement over what she recalled from her class. It was upbeat, classic, and traditional Irish Celtic music. She liked it and they were doing well with making it work for their first try. Robert impressed her with his knowledge of the lyrics as he sang along with the tune.

"Okay, easy, my dear, this boat is moving, and we are going around in circles, let's have a slow down before we fall down," Robert said, as he led her outside to the deck to get a breath of fresh air.

The yacht was well on its way, and the skies had cleared. The water glistened like diamonds. The air was getting a little cooler as they picked up speed. Carrie looked back at land, and it seemed like in minutes they were in open water.

"Robert, how did you know what music to play? That was great, and you were awesome. Are sure you haven't done that before?"

Robert smiled as he slowly blinked his eyes and said, "That's a simple question to answer. My grandmother was Irish and danced a rather good reel and square herself. I grew up watching her and my papa dance, but it was more of a Virginia reel. I have a magnificent collection of contemporary Irish Celtic music since my grandmother loved it, I seem to have grown a fondness for it myself. I still have her old Victrola."

"You just played me there about like a Victrola player; you already knew how. Robert, you sneaky little devil. I think I'd like to hear more of that music. Our music for the class sounded more like country square dance music, like when they wore those ridiculous big fluffy skirts. I actually found it kind of irritating."

Robert leaned in and put his hand on Carrie's shoulder. "You danced that well. My granny would have been proud of you. Maybe some time we can listen to her records. I really like the modern Irish Music. I have one called Celtic Music Voyage. Would you like to hear it?"

"Yes, please."

Robert pulled up the playlist and, in seconds, Celtic Music Voyage filled the lounge with an air of sophistication and relaxation. It was a complementary undertone to conversation, not too loud or overbearing.

"I like it," said Carrie. "So that is the twang I'm hearing in your voice, a little fragment of an Irish accent there."

"Exactly. My Grandmother and Pap raised me. She taught me how to read, write, and dance. Pap taught me how to talk like an Irishman, fish, and to love boats. He was a captain of his own fishing boat. He loved a boat, and he did well in the seafood industry for many years. When he retired, he bought a small sailboat. Not much, but it had a room for him and my grandmother to sleep and eat in a little kitchen. They would play around in the wharf and occasionally, if the sea was calm, he would take it out."

"The way you describe it, seems like they had a wonderful life. I can also see by the way you talk about them, how much they meant to you."

"Oh yes. Yes, indeed."

They walked out to the bar and joined the others. By this time, Leslie, Sandra, and Laney were in a conversation with the bar attendant and it seemed rude to interrupt them. He was prepping everything for the cocktail hour, and Laney was helping. Robert and Carrie walked over to the deck seating and continued their conversation.

"So, this is chapter one. What would you like to tell me about Carrie?" asked Robert

"For heaven's sake, where do I begin? Well, let's see, you know I'm divorced. I have spent most of my career in the broadcasting and media business. I have two incredible sons, John and Jason. So that's a start. Now, you go."

"Well, as you know, I am a widower. I worked in yacht and boat sales for years. I am retired, and I have no children. I live in a studio apartment on the Sound side. I can't cook, I love to play golf and I have an addiction to traveling. Have boat, will travel is my motto." He pointed back at her. "Your turn."

Carrie looked at the sun sparkling on the water and thought for a moment. "Well, I once hosted a TV show," said Carrie.

"Wow, I can see that. You would be a natural for the camera."

As they continued to talk, Laney and the bartender called them over to taste some concoctions. Robert approved the samplings to be served for the cocktail hour.

Carrie and Robert made their way back to the lounge with a glass of lemonade. They spent the rest of the afternoon talking with the group. Robert was a natural at balancing the conversation, so all the ladies felt equally included. He was inquisitive and seemed to be genuinely interested in their lives. It was an innate behavior, or possibly learned. Either way, Carrie found it admirable and endearing. She watched as he interacted with each of her friends in such a unique matter, but never let her feel left out.

The cocktail hour approached quickly as their conversations filled the minutes leading up to the designated time. Drinks were enjoyed as they all watched the sinking sun. By the time dinner was served, the sun was just peeking over the water, and the sky was painted orange, lavender, and shades of blue. They devoured divine creations of Mahi tacos, gumbo, bacon wrapped scallops, and a key lime cheesecake. Laney made her way into the small kitchen and helped spice things up a bit. She was always most at home in any kitchen, especially when she could see how other chefs created their dishes. When she found out that the bartender, Ben, was doing double-duty as chef, she just pushed herself through with him to the kitchen and helped with the gumbo.

After dinner, they all returned to the upper deck. The sun was replaced on the horizon by a beautiful moon rising, and the lights on the yacht reflected in the dark ocean displayed a magical presentation.

As they went to individual chaise loungers, Leslie sat beside Robert. He obviously had some very intriguing stories to tell if he could create a night like this in less than a day. To invite them all was a smart move on his part if he expected to see Carrie again during the weekend. She would have never chosen to go on her own.

"So, Robert," said Leslie. "Tell me more about how you pulled this arrangement off?"

"It really is not that impressive. I know people. My people know people. I just know the right people. Really, a friend docked it here while they went out for a month's cruise out of Europe. Of course, I know quite a few captains, and one of them helped me line everything up. It just fell together. It's a great boat—one of the best in its day. With the final refitting, she is going to be a beauty. Her features make her such a nostalgic vessel and it gives her so much character. All the woodgrain is just magnificent. The newer yachts often seem big on high tech. I like this one's style. I think it draws your attention to the natural beauty; lets the ocean and sky be the backdrop to the stage that glides along," said Robert.

Sandra was hanging on to every word Robert spoke. "You are a genius in my book. I tell you this has been the most wonderful night of my life. Well, of course, except for my wedding night." She laughed and then everyone else joined her after a brief pause to read the reaction everyone had to her unfiltered information.

Robert smiled, "Well, I am sure your husband would be happy to hear that, Sandra."

Leslie spoke up, "I think that quote needs to stay on the yacht, Sandra. Our lips are sealed."

Laney shook her head at Sandra's comments. "She should come with a disclaimer: You never know what is going to come out of her mouth."

They spent the evening talking about dreams, goals, past failures, successes, and no cell phones. No reception for cell phones led to intentional conversation about all things meaningful.

As the hours went on, they realized it was almost midnight. One by one, they retired to their designated quarters. When all the others were gone, only Robert and Carrie were left sitting on the deck.

"Thank you for this evening. It has been a pleasure," Carrie said, as she sat facing Robert on a lounge chair.

Robert leaned over, touched her hand, lifted it to his lips, and he kissed it. Carrie knew that somehow this incredible man might just change her life forever. She didn't know where it would go from here, but she was willing to follow Robert to see where the road would lead them. There was a strong wind blowing on the deck of the yacht, and she felt as if it represented a change of winds for her life.

Robert was releasing her hand when he put both hands on her shoulders and leaned in to kiss her forehead. Carrie was receptive and leaned into his kiss. How was it they only met the day before but felt as if they had known each other for so much longer? It was as if they possessed an inner knowledge of each other along with a healthy dose of comfort.

Robert helped Carrie up from the lounge chair, then he stepped back and gave her a look of admiration. The moon glow was bright on the water, and it reflected on her face. He paused and admired the view for a moment.

"Carrie, you need to be reminded of how amazing you truly are. I would love the opportunity to remind you. Would you be interested in continuing on to Chapter Two?" asked Robert as he turned to look out over the water. Not knowing what her response would be, he thought it best to not look her in the eye, let her answer with no pressure from him.

"Of course, absolutely. I think there is much more about you I would like to know. You intrigue me; you spark my imagination. Not to mention, you are easy on the eyes. That never hurts either," Carrie said with a grin.

Robert repaid the grin with one of his own and said, "I think I see you blushing in this moonlight. I hope you rest well, and plan for an awesome day at sea in the morning with brunch before we head in." He walked her to her door and paused for a moment as he kissed her on the cheek.

Carrie smiled up at him and gave a little salute. "Aye, Aye captain."

Chapter Thirteen

Up in Smoke

Karen kicked her stilettos across the room, and they ricocheted off the bedroom wall. She paced the floor. She knew Jerry had bad news, or he would have told her what he found out over the phone. As she stared at the front door, she noticed headlights flash across the drive. She ran out to find Jerry and a deputy in a patrol car. Both men got out of the car and met her on the porch steps.

"Hey Karen, let's go inside," said Jerry, as he motioned for her to go to the door.

Karen did not move.

"No, tell me what is going on ... now."

Jerry threw both hands in the air in surrender, and he took a seat on the deacon's bench and offered for Karen the spot beside him. He put his hand on her knee. Karen noticed the headlights were shining on his face and she could see tears.

"What happened? Jerry, what is going on? You're scaring me. Tell me now."

Jerry wiped away a tear. He looked her straight in the eye and said three words, "Bill is dead."

Karen started shaking her head then gave him a stare as bitter as vinegar.

"Jerry, that is a messed-up thing to do. Stop it, now, and tell me what's really going on."

Jerry motioned for the deputy to come to the porch. "Sir, can you come up here for a minute? Then we will let you get to your work."

The deputy approached the porch and he knelt beside Karen to give her the news.

"Ma'am, there was an accident. I know this is a lot of information to hear and process. Is there someone you want to call to be with you right now?"

"No. Please go on," answered Karen as her lips trembled.

"Ma'am, it appears that Bill went to check the alarm at his former residence, like you thought. A plumbing crew didn't set the alarm when they left, most likely by intention, so they could go back to rob the place. We got up with the owner, Lee, and he states specific instructions were given to set the alarm when they left. We suspect they came back to rob the place and we believe Bill walked up on said robbery in progress. He suffered a head wound and most likely was unconscious."

"Okay, well, that doesn't mean he's dead. He's just unconscious, right? So, did they take him to the hospital? I have to get there! Take me to the hospital!" cried Karen as she grabbed Jerry's hand to go to the car.

"Once again, are you sure you don't want to call someone to be here with you?" asked the deputy.

Karen stood and faced them both with crossed arms.

"I don't have anyone I can call. Bill is all I have! What are you not telling me?" she asked.

"That's just it, ma'am we *are* telling you. Bill is dead. These crooks were amateurs, they were sloppy, they left clues and evidence all over the place," said the deputy as he motioned for Karen to come back to the porch.

"We just left the house, Karen. The crooks got scared, honey. They left out of there with Bill's Porsche and obviously took it for a joy ride. That's who the neighbor saw driving like a madman. It wasn't Bill. They must have freaked out later, and they wanted to make sure Bill's mouth stayed shut. The sheriff figures they came back and tried to set a fire in the closet, where Bill blacked out. They were dumb asses. It caused a huge smoking mess and barely burned anything, except for some clothes that caught fire and caused a lot of smoke. I put it out with the kitchen fire extinguisher when we got there. They left him to die in that damned closet. I'm so sorry. If we had been a few minutes sooner ..." he couldn't finish; his emotions got the better of him.

Karen grabbed the post of the front porch and sat on the railing. Emotion surged through her, and she couldn't contain her cry of grief. You could hear her screams blocks away, and Jerry was quite certain every neighbor was aware as well, as lights came on one by one down the street. Jerry put his arms around her. He motioned to the deputy to go on and continue with his investigation.

"Karen, we will investigate. We're leaving no stone unturned until we catch these guys. We'll charge them with anything we can throw at them." And the deputy walked to the car.

Jerry walked Karen into the house. He held her up as she walked down the foyer and then to the sofa to sit down. She was shivering, but it was not cold. He took her a blanket and wrapped it around her shoulders. He imagined she must be in shock.

"I'm going to make you some hot tea, or do you want coffee? It may be a long night," said Jerry, as he pulled the tail of his shirt out of his slacks and threw his belt on the chair.

"I just want Bill," Karen whispered. She laid down and cried herself to sleep. Jerry sat in the chair beside the sofa and placed his hand on her head, stroking her hair so she would know that someone was near to comfort her. He admired her beauty as she slept and soon Jerry drifted off to sleep as well.

When the sun rose, Karen sat up, shielding her eyes with her hand. "It was a dream, right Jerry? It was all a bad dream?" she asked, as she tapped him on the knee.

Jerry lifted his head off the side of the chair and rubbed his eyes. "No, it was not a dream. But yes, it sounds like a bad dream. I am so sorry, Karen. I'll make you some coffee." He said as he got up and headed to the kitchen.

Karen laid flat on her back and stared at the ceiling. Tears were streaming down her face. She wiped them away as she stood up and called out to Jerry. "I'm getting a shower and getting dressed."

Jerry peeked out from the kitchen, looking for her, but she had already left the room. He put the coffee on and reached in the fridge for eggs to scramble. He noticed some leftover charcuterie board meat and cheese in the fridge and he put that on the island bar. He found some bread leftover from the night before and made toast, then he sat in the breakfast nook and waited for her to come to the table. As he took his first sip of coffee, his cell phone rang.

"Hello, this is Jerry."

"Jerry, it's Sheriff Johnson. Listen, we have some more information. What we suspected was correct. We have con-firmed they stole Bill's Porsche and abandoned it out on Highway 43, then pushed it into the river. Such fools, the tar river is too low to hide anything right now. We discovered they came back on a pickup truck just before dark. According to witnesses, it was possibly within an hour of their first visit. That is when they set the fire—most likely to cover up any evidence and to keep Bill from talking. The neighbor says he saw a truck leave, but they were eating dinner and didn't get a license number, but they could give a description – so that is helpful. He's the one that called Karen and inquired about Bill's car racing down the road. Listen, these guys were idiots, and I don't think it will be difficult to find them. Just keeping you posted."

"Thank you for the update. Karen is in the shower right now. I'll inform her," said Jerry and he hung up the phone. Jerry rubbed his neck to relieve the kink from sleeping in the chair. Exhaustion was sitting in, and he needed some proper sleep.

He sat at the table, laid his head on his folded arms, and waited. He waited for what seemed like forever. Karen had been in the shower a long time. Jerry got up and walked through the foyer over to the master bedroom and knocked on the door. When she didn't answer, he knocked again. Still no answer.

"Karen, your coffee and your eggs are getting cold. Come on out and eat something."

No response came from the other side of the door. He turned the knob and entered the bedroom. He heard a noise in the closet, and it sounded like something dropped to the floor.

"Karen, are you okay? Come talk to me, please. Don't make me go in there after you."

He saw a suitcase on the bed. It held clothes, jewelry, and a notebook. "Karen, what is all this? What are you doing?"

Karen walked out of the closet with another suitcase and more clothes. She flung it on the bed and turned around to head back to the closet.

Jerry reached out and held onto her arm with a firm grip. "Stop this! What are you doing? Stop it and talk to me. Please. I know this is the worst thing you could have imagined. Your engagement party has turned into a precursor to a funeral for your future husband. Hell, that is some heavy stuff. Sit down, slow down, and do not make any rash decisions."

"Take your hands off me. I don't need or require your pity, and I will not stay around and watch the pity party form around me. I will not stay here and watch his ex-wife and sons come together and mourn him. He was supposed to be my husband! Now leave me alone to do what I need to do," said Karen, as she pushed him out of the way.

Jerry threw his hands up in the air, then he rested them on his hips. He stood there with both hands on his waist and shook his head. "You have got to be insane. You can't leave right now. People are going to want to see you, talk to you, help you. There's an investigation, and they'll need to question you," said Jerry.

Karen walked up to him and put her finger in his face. She paused for a moment to wipe away a tear. "That is what I'm talking about. I'm not having it. Don't ask me where I'm going and don't try to find me. I will come back to get the rest of my things later. Do you really think anyone in this town is going to give a rat's ass about how I feel? No, it will be poor, perfect Carrie. A divorcee and now a divorcee widow—if it's not a thing, she will make it one! Besides, we should blame the whole damned thing on her. Who leaves a plumbing crew in charge of sitting your home alarm – she is to blame here."

Karen had three bags packed, and she picked up two of them and walked to the front door. She yelled out to Jerry, "Well if you want to help me, get that other bag. Don't just stand there."

Jerry took the other bag to the car. "I swear, Karen, if you didn't have an alibi of a crowd of people, I'd think you killed him yourself. They just called and they have more information. Karen, look me in the eye and tell me you had nothing to do with this? Your hauling ass out of town makes me wonder."

Karen reached her car and put her suitcases in the trunk. She slammed the lid after Jerry put in the other one. She stood beside the car and by the way she looked at him, Jerry knew he had crossed a line by simply reading her face.

"Go to hell, Jerry; go straight to hell. How dare you?"

Jerry ran around to the other side of the car to the driver's door as she got into the driver's seat and was fastening her seat belt. "Can you blame me? Your fiancé dies in a stuffed-up robbery by a couple of novice burglars and then they set a fire. Now you're running away like you have something to hide. What are you hiding?"

"I can't explain it, Jerry. I feel broken. That's the only thing I'm hiding. My entire life just got turned upside down. I'm alone. My dreams are shattered, and everyone is going to gloat or feel sorry for me. It's going to be either "she's a home wrecker, serves her right," or "poor thing, she didn't get what she was after, after all," said Karen.

Jerry reached his hand to her in the car, and she unfastened the seat belt and got out. He held out his arms to give her a hug, and she fell into him. He let her cry for what seemed like forever, but he didn't mind. He found he enjoyed holding her in his arms. That was an odd feeling, especially since they usually were at odds with each other. No matter the reason, Jerry liked it.

Karen broke away from his embrace. "See, this is what I mean. I can't do this. I need to go away and do it my way. I will be back, but I don't know when. You can handle work."

Jerry backed up. "Okay, I get it. Do it your way. But what in the hell am I supposed to tell the Sheriff? He is going to want to talk to you."

"Don't worry, I have nothing to hide. I can see how you think this looks suspicious. But really, I just need to go. I feel like a fool right now. I've lost my dream of this life with Bill. The legendary Dollar Bill. Well hell, Bill bought me this car just last month," Karen said, as she got back in the car.

Jerry knocked on the hood. "It is nice, for sure. I love a Jaguar, but unfortunately, I don't get compensated enough for one of these babies."

"Oh my, Jerry. Carrie! Has anyone contacted her?"

"Well, I don't rightly know. Everything is happening so fast. I could call the boys. Someone needs to tell them. Do you want to do that?"

"No," said Karen firmly. "Absolutely not. You tell them."

Jerry rubbed his chin and looked at her. "You are asking me to clean up a real mess here, Karen. I have a station to run now, not to mention the syndicated networks."

"No worries. I'm sure his sons will step right up. Carrie has been wanting to get back in the business. I'm sure you will be in fine shape."

She cranked the car as Jerry leaned over. "Honey, I wish you wouldn't do this, but I understand your reasons. Just keep in touch with me and let me know you're well, and that you arrive wherever it is you are running to. I will keep my lips sealed. Or you could call me and let me hold you in my arms. I'm up for that again."

Karen was looking straight at the steering wheel as she started the car. "Gosh Jerry, really. Stop it. I will have someone come and take care of the house and finish cleaning up the mess from the party. You might see a For Sale sign out front soon."

"Please, keep in touch," said Jerry.

She pulled out of the portico and never looked back. Jerry stood there with his arms crossed, watching her drive away as he attempted to process the happenings in the last 24 hours. He turned around to see the sunrise coming up over Karen and Bill's home. Time waits for nothing, no matter what the situation may be. The sun still comes up faithfully every morning.

How could he get up with Carrie? How could he tell the boys? Maybe the Sheriff's office could do that for him. Jerry realized this was a fluid situation in a fast forward motion, with no option to stop this from cascading.

"I'm left with a trifecta here. Damn," Jerry said aloud.

Chapter Fourteen

Day Two—Sail Away

Leslie felt the warmth of the sun on her face as it beamed through the cabin window. She put her feet on the floor and leaned back to look out the window. The view was mesmerizing. The water looked like diamonds, sapphires, and emeralds. It was as if they were floating on a sea of jewels. The sky was clear, and the ocean was smooth, but Leslie's mind was not. All night she worried about home, and she tossed and turned most of the time. She rolled over and looked up at the cabin ceiling, rubbed her eyes and said out loud, "Rise and shine!"

"Stop," Leslie heard Sandra moan from the other side of the room. "Roll over and go back to sleep. I know that look on your face, and I can tell you're over thinking something. You have those elevens on forehead again. I declare you are going to need Botox for that thinking line." Sandra rolled over to face the wall and to go back to sleep.

"I'm sorry, did I wake you up? I am just wondering about everything at home, that's all. Being without cell reception is a little nice, but simultaneously a tad bit frustrating," said Leslie as she reached for her robe.

"I know, right? Poor Carrie, she loves to journal everything on Facebook and Instagram. She'll have so much to load up when we get back. What time should we be back?" asked Sandra.

"I believe Robert said we would be back at port by noon. Let's grab some coffee and find out." She opened the door to the cabin and almost bumped into Carrie as she was on her way into their cabin.

"Morning ya'll! I brought you a tray. Laney is up there all in the chef's business, but they are having fun. How did y'all sleep last night?" asked Carrie, as she set the tray on the bedside table.

Sandra and Leslie looked at each other as they reached for the coffee cups.

"We slept fine. How about you? I am assuming you had sweet dreams after last night?" said Sandra.

"I truly did. I felt like a queen. Robert is such a gentleman," said Carrie.

"This is the best I have rested in months. My husband needs to up his game and get us a little dinghy to putt around the river. Even Leslie's tossing and turning over there didn't bother me once I fell out," said Sandra.

Carrie sat down on the bed. She was looking at them both with a devious smile.

"I know that look. What are you up to, Carrie?" asked Sandra.

"Well, I have a question for both of you. Robert says we can stay out one more night if we like. Totally up to us. If not, he can get the captain to take us back this morning. But the boat doesn't have to be back until late on Monday. So, what do you say?" asked Carrie.

Leslie was shaking her head *no*, and Sandra was nodding her head *yes*. A *yes* and a *no* meant someone had to be the decision maker.

"Well, Laney is loving it and I think she is getting a bit of attention from that bartender and chef mate up there," said Carrie.

Leslie stood up and threw her hands in the air. "So, I know what you are thinking. You want to stay too, right?"

"Of course, I do. Is it going to be a problem?" asked Carrie.

Leslie shook her head *no*. Carrie liked that *no* response better.

"It's okay, but what in the world are we supposed to do on this boat all day long?" asked Leslie.

"I know what I can do. I can lay on that upper deck and watch the sun roll around in heaven," said Sandra.

Carrie clapped her hands in joy. "We are not going to stay on the boat *all* day. He wants to take us to Charleston if we want to go. If not, you are welcome to stay on the yacht when we dock. Robert said we are already almost halfway there!" said Carrie.

"Get out of here! You are messing with us, right? What about the beach house?" asked Leslie.

Carrie put her hand on Leslie's shoulder. "You worry too much. Remember, we don't have to check out until Tuesday morning."

"Okay. But wait, does everyone have enough clothes for another night?" asked Leslie.

"Mercy woman, what are we going to do with you? We are going to Charleston! I think we can go shopping," mumbled Sandra, as she ate a piece of toast.

"Let's go up to the kitchen," said Carrie. "There is a major spread of food up there, and we don't want those chefs to feel unappreciated."

The three ladies headed to the kitchen. Ben and Laney were comparing notes on how to make bread, pasta, sauces, and, of course, the best shrimp and grits. That was one of Laney's dishes she had perfected, and she always liked to hear the different varieties from each pocket of the coastal towns up and down the east coast.

After breakfast, Robert suggested they prepare for the boat to sail again. He had expected and hoped they would agree, and had the captain ready to set a course for Charleston. They could spend the travel time doing whatever they pleased: sunning, reading, playing cards, or sleeping. All four of them decided on separate agendas.

Leslie decided she would go back to the lounge and read. There were several novels and historical books on plantations that were right up her alley, and she would be content all day. A lazy day of reading would be good, as she had not had time for that in years.

Sandra chose the sun as she said she would. The sound of the waves and the beauty of the vast openness was soothing to her. The wind felt like a massage on her skin. It felt as if it was blowing away the static in her brain, and she felt relaxed. The busy life she was leading trying to conceive a child seemed like a full-time job. She already had a full-time job as a nurse in the medical clinic. She often thought about putting that on hold to see if it would help with their infertility issues. She was too stressed. This was the first time she thought clearly enough about that decision to realize that it might be the right one. She would have to talk that out with Mitch when she returned home. She smiled as she lounged in the sun. It was amazing at how clear her thinking had become in just a couple of days away. It would please Mitch to see a newly rested version of her return home.

As for Laney, she and Ben were whipping up some sauce in the kitchen and tasting the creation. They decided to stay on the boat for dinner that night and have a sort of cooking round. They planned to go into town when they arrived, grab some ingredients, and come back for a little friendly competition. Laney asked Sandra and Leslie to stay and be the judges. Sandra was the first to say *yes* to the offer, which surprised them all.

Carrie was sitting on the deck when Robert walked up to her. She was resting with her sun hat over her face under the yacht's canopy. She felt like she could make out someone walking on the deck between the space of her cheek and the brim of her hat.

"Hello. I hope I am not disturbing you. I am pleased that everyone wanted to continue on this little escapade," said Robert.

Carrie moved her hat and smiled. "Me too? What do you have planned for today?"

Robert sat down in the lounge chair beside her. "Well, I was sort of hoping to let you enjoy your day here however you wish. Then when we dock, I would like to take you to one of my favorite Charleston restaurants. If you can stand to leave the others long enough for me to have your undivided attention."

Carrie sat up in her chair, looked at Robert, and smiled. "You had me at Charleston. I love Charleston. I think I'll just soak up the sound of waves and rest up under this canopy for a fun evening."

"Well, I will leave you to it, then. I think I'll try to catch up with the captain and see if I can talk him into letting me maneuver this vessel for a bit." Robert patted her shoulder and walked away as he whistled a little tune.

As he strolled away, Carrie watched his tall, slim frame head back to the cabin. Sandra was right—he reminded her of Sean Connery. He was charming, handsome, and full of chivalry. She laid back, closed her eyes, and took in the sounds of the yacht cutting through the water. It was like a musical melody, and she drifted off in a sea of theories about where the weekend was taking her, figuratively and emotionally. She never considered dating; the divorce was still a stinging, fresh wound. It was a process of hurt and anger combined, but she had to admit, a bit of relief as well. The last few years with Bill had been brutal. So many nights she was alone and had total knowledge of who he was with. Bill thought he was smarter than her or anyone else and was oblivious to how many colleagues and members of the community knew about his affair. As she processed all these thoughts, she reminded herself that this was what she was sailing away from. She concentrated on the melody of the waves below her, as a wave of peace washed over her. Within minutes, she had drifted off to sleep.

Chapter Fifteen

Charleston

It did not take as long as expected to reach the port in Charleston. Robert mentioned to Carrie that the winds were simply perfect for the voyage. The yacht docked, and in minutes, Laney and Ben were off to pick up supplies for dinner and breakfast the next morning. As they left, you could hear them talking about their favorite Charleston Restaurants. Sandra and Leslie were ready to explore the waterfront shops and had quickly departed to send for an Uber driver. Sandra loved the nostalgia in Charleston and wanted to visit a few of the interior design shops. Leslie was going along for the adventure to witness the elation in Sandra's face as she strolled through the shops and searched out pieces and trinkets for her historical home.

After Sandra and Leslie departed, Carrie ventured out to the deck to look over the marina. She looked at all the vessels docked in the area and imagined where they sailed from. It was an incredible sight to see, and she found herself lost in a trance of thinking about all the different lifestyles of the many occupants on each one.

"Hello there, beautiful," said Robert, as he walked up behind her.

Carrie turned to face him. "Hello handsome. I feel like a celebrity on this yacht. Speaking of celebrities, you were the hot topic of our conversation about your features the other night."

Robert smiled. "I'm almost afraid to ask. Should I be?"

"Absolutely not. The name Sean Connery came up," said Carrie as she leaned her head to the side and braced for his response.

"Wow. I do like all the James Bond actors, but Sean Connery? Really?"

Carrie quickly responded, "Get out of here. You know someone has to have mentioned that to you before."

"Well, funny you say that. You know those apps the kids play with on their phones where they put in your photo, and they tell you which movie star you are? Sean Connery came up. I was always a James Bond fan, and he was my favorite one."

"So, you just shocked me there. I didn't take you for someone that played with apps on their phone," said Carrie, as she attempted to stifle a giggle.

"And you are correct. I do not experiment with such things. Some kids at the marina were doing those one day with some of the staff in the office. They talked me into it."

Robert offered his arm to walk her to the lounge. Carrie looked up at him admiring his smile, his charm, and his calm demeanor. It was refreshing to be around a man so at ease without anger and tension, but with peace and composure. He seemed to have good intentions, not motives. His excellent conversation skills and manners were refreshing.

As she walked beside him, her curiosity got the best of her. "How in the world have you not been snatched up is a mystery to me. I mean, really, you are kind, smart, witty, incredibly handsome, and highly creative. I'm sure losing your wife was difficult for you, and you have been without her for quite a while. You can talk about her anytime with me," said Carrie.

There was no answer. Carrie immediately felt like she stepped onto the edge of the abyss. It was too soon to bring up such intimate conversations about the loss of his wife. But he had mentioned it first that night at the club, so it felt right to bring up the subject. She waited for Robert to respond. It seemed like minutes, but she knew it was only seconds. In the brief time she had known him, she knew he was reserved with his words. He was thoughtful and meditated over being intentional with what he said when he spoke.

"Carrie, my dear, you are already helping me process those feelings. Until now, I would have never had a conversation like this with another woman. You give me an extraordinary level of comfort, and you obviously make me brave," said Robert. He smiled at her. "No worries, this is just new to me. But I like it."

They sat down in the lounge on the sofa, and Robert looked around the yacht and for a moment the silence was awkward. Carrie wondered what was coming next. He said there would be a plan when they arrived in Charleston.

"I have arranged for a very eventful evening. Would you like to hear about the plan?" asked Robert.

Carrie noticed a twinkle in his eye. He was expecting her reaction to be one of delight, and she did not want to disappoint him. It was obvious he had something splendid planned.

"I'm waiting. The suspense is brutal and unusual punishment. There is no telling what you have up your sleeve."

Robert crossed his arms and looked at her with a raised eyebrow.

"My dear, how about a horse-drawn carriage ride to the restaurant I was telling you about? In my opinion, it is Charleston's finest, because my friend owns it. First, we will Uber over to the carriage," said Robert.

Carrie was impressed. She couldn't contain her joy. "That sounds wonderful!" she exclaimed. He had connections in all the right places, and she could not wait to hear more about his life. What an amazing story he had to share. She thought how magical the years must have been for his wife.

"Robert, what should I wear? I have a limited selection in my overnight bag."

"Anything you want. It's a very eclectic place, and anything goes. But I promise you, the food is stellar," he said, as he patted his stomach.

With that last bit of information, he left her to get ready. He went to his quarters to do the same. He gave her one of his dazzling smiles as Carrie waved at him before she entered her cabin. Robert whistled on his way down the hall, and Carrie paused to listen. He was whistling the Celtic song he played the night before. He was even good at whistling!

Chapter Sixteen

Breaking News

Jerry sat at his desk at the television station, contemplating how to coordinate the next step. With Karen and Bill gone, that left him abandoned to resolve many issues in the media empire, and it was much more than he was compliant to take on.

Jerry asked the Sheriff to do his best to keep Bill's death out of the headlines for a day or so. His department agreed to honor his request. As for Carrie, Jerry had to call her, eventually. He would let her determine when and how to share the news with the boys. Jerry sent a fire and restoration company over to take care of the damages in the house. Thankfully, they were minimal. The fire had not spread, and there was the good fortune to have a fire extinguisher nearby. Jerry guessed Bill never had a chance. The burglars had attacked him and left him for dead. *"What a crappy way to die,"* Jerry mumbled.

Jerry couldn't understand Karen's abrupt departure. She should have at least stayed for the funeral. He understood the embarrassment issue. She and Bill had an affair, and now she was the one left standing alone. He speculated on how Carrie would accept the news. Although she and Bill divorced and it had been a bitter and unpleasant experience, they had shared many years together, and had two sons and a business.

Jerry glanced at the phone, but that was all he could do. He stared at it for what seemed like minutes, but it could not have been that long. But it was, he had stared at the phone for over fifteen minutes as he thought of ways to carry on and tidy up. He knew he was the most improbable successor to do so. He was not equipped for this height of management. He was not adept for such contract negotiations; he was not like "Dollar Bill." And there was no way he could pitch a sales campaign like Karen. Even though Carrie had not been a part of the business in some time, he sure could use her help right now. Should he make the call? He paused again staring at the phone and said, *"Bill can't stay at the morgue forever."*

He picked up the phone and placed his thumb on the dial button but slammed the phone down on the desk. How in the hell do you call up your boss's ex-wife and tell her news like this? It should not come over the phone. Jerry knew from looking at the station calendar, that Carrie planned to be gone for a week. They still posted her schedule because Bill preferred to know of her whereabouts. That always rubbed Karen the wrong way, but Bill proceeded to track Carrie's every step. Seemed odd to Jerry since Bill left her for another woman and polluted everything about their marriage by deserting her and leaving her embarrassed and alone. On some level, he felt empathy for Carrie, and he felt the same for Karen. Bill, although a sharp businessperson, was not a good person. He had broken Carrie's spirit. It had been heartbreaking to watch her go through the separation and divorce. For whatever reason, Karen wanted the cold and rough façade Bill exhibited. The two of them together seemed to bring out the best and the worst of each other.

Jerry rubbed his eyes; the exhaustion was relentless. Sleep was not a possibility. Every time he closed his eyes, he saw Bill's lifeless body in the closet. As the light illuminated the darkness of the closet, he peered through the smoke and saw Bill lying there. That vision was on a repeat reel in his mind.

Most of the staff were off for the weekend. A skeleton reporting crew and news staff were on hand. Soon they would knock on his door asking about headlines and story lines that would need approval. Bill was always there first thing in the morning on the weekends. The staff depended on Bill's direction for stories to cover. They had a fearful respect for him and would always want to clear their reporting with him. Jerry knew he could not hold them off for very long. The truth needed to be told. They would be coming down the hall and asking for Bill at any moment.

The silence in his office was deafening. As he mulled over the myriad of scenarios to carry out, he knew that any one of them would end poorly. For a moment, he thought about stepping away. Why should he have to deal with this drama? Hell, if he was totally honest, he had been hoping for a new position with another network for a while. He loved his job, but Bill was stingy at rewarding and recognizing good people. He managed the station well, but could he manage even more duties now and be happy? That was something he was going to have to address with whoever would be in charge now.

He picked up the phone again, and this time he dialed Carrie's number. There was no answer. It went to voice mail. He dialed again. No answer, only voice mail. He slammed the phone down and walked around the desk. He was on the way out the door, but then as he grabbed the doorknob he stopped. He called Carrie's number again. This time, he left a message.

"Carrie, hey, well, hi, um, this is Jerry at the station. I mean, I hope you are well. Listen, Carrie, I need you to call me. Can you do that as soon as you can, please? I look forward to hearing from you soon. You hear? Call me. Please. Call me as soon as you can, Carrie. Thanks."

Chapter 17

Docked in Charleston

The marina was a lovely chaotic mixture of activity. People and boats were constantly coming and going. If you paused to listen, you could hear the melody of life all around. Leslie, Sandra, and Laney were in the kitchen with Ben. Whatever they were cooking smelled marvelous. The girls were enjoying the competitive mood between Ben and Laney, but Leslie saw more than competitiveness. She could see a spark in Laney that had not lit up in some time.

Leslie watched from a distance as Sandra licked her lips, while watching Ben concoct the beginning of what looked to be a sinfully delicious desert. She was practically drooling, no doubt she would taste test that one. Leslie thought about Carrie and Robert and the way they took to each other. A natural, and genuine relationship was emerging. She expected this might be the beginning of something new for Carrie, and now, perhaps for Laney, too.

Sandra came and sat beside Leslie. "What are you over here daydreaming about?" she asked.

Leslie shook her head, not even realizing she was lost in thought. "Just thinking of Carrie and Robert and the fireworks

I see igniting. It's sweet to watch Carrie smile and be treated so well."

"It really is. I know I was cautious and acted like a bit of a freak about this thing. I was misguided. My instincts just get a bit off sometimes because of circumstances—well, you know that. Hey, I think Ben has his sights set on Laney," said Sandra as she turned to look at them in the kitchen. "I think they're cooking up more than food. You know what I mean?"

Laney suddenly appeared behind them. "Here, taste this, please. What are you talking about?"

Sandra stood up to take a sampling from the spoon and pointed to Leslie. "Ask her. I am sworn to secrecy."

"Ask me what?" asked Laney, with a hand on her hip. You could tell that the word secrecy made her a bit more curious. "Secrets? We don't have secrets. Remember, we may tell little white lies to others, but we never lie to each other."

Leslie chuckled and said, "Since the day you heard my mother say that, you have never forgotten it. God rest her soul."

"I know, right? The organist and circle meeting, choir singing, pillar of the church. Then when she explained what a white lie was, I was in stitches," said Laney, with a sneaky grin.

"I wasn't there, so what are you talking about?" asked Sandra. "Sounds like some information I need to know."

Leslie was waving her hands in a motion to get Laney to stop. "Don't even, please, don't."

"No, that was classic. She said a white lie was when you told someone the cake they brought over when you had surgery was good, even if it was not," said Laney.

Sandra laughed, "No, that's just being polite, in my opinion."

"That's not the funny part. Then she elaborated. The same goes when your husband asks was that good for you? You tell a little white lie and say yes, even if it wasn't," said Laney as she bent over in intense laughter.

By this time, Leslie was more than embarrassed, and her cheeks turned red. "Sandra, you and my mother could have been kin. You could never perceive what was going to come out of her mouth, either."

"It was one of the best memories I have of your mother. What gives? What are you two talking about?" asked Laney.

"We think Ben may be sweet on you. I think I need to learn a bit more about him," said Leslie and she got up and walked to the kitchen.

Leslie walked over to Ben at the counter, leaving Sandra and Laney standing to watch. Ben wiped his hands off and poured a glass of lemonade for her. She took the glass and he looked at her with a grin. Laney noticed it, and so did Sandra. He obviously wanted to share something and was holding back. All of them studied his face and tried to determine what he was hiding behind the devilish smile.

Sandra could not stand it any longer. "What the heck is all that grinning over there about?"

"I'm just in awe of your presence, ladies. That's all," said Ben as he tried to stifle a laugh.

Laney walked over, took the towel from the counter, and popped him with it. "We don't play like that fellow. The three of us can take you, torment you to death, and get it out of you. Sandra is a natural at interrogation. You don't want to encourage her."

Ben looked at Laney and said, "I was just thinking about how I'm getting ready to show Laney up tonight with some mad cooking skills. I hope she's tough enough to take the heat, no pun intended. This is getting ready to be a rendition of Hell's Kitchen TV for real." He popped Laney with the dish towel as she smirked back at him.

"Ben, tell us a little about you. What does Ben do other than cook and enjoy a bit of competition?" asked Leslie.

Ben rubbed the top of his head in a nervous reaction to Leslie's question. "Well, I wrote a book. Actually, two books," said Ben and he waited for their reaction.

"Well, I'll be. How about that! Is it one of those romance novels that features you as the main character? If so, I'm reading that. Seriously, what kind of book?" asked Sandra.

"The first book - that is the even more surprising part . . . it's a children's book." He looked at them and waited for their second response. "I wrote a cookbook, too, but I'm pretty stoked about the children's book."

Sandra's hands flew to her cheeks, and it only popped her mouth wide open. Laney was looking at Ben with her hand over her heart. Leslie smiled. All three of them were speechless.

"You don't believe me, do you?" asked Ben, as he went back to working on his creation at the stove.

Laney leaned over the counter. "Well of course we do. We just didn't expect that."

"I think it's the sweetest thing ever. What is the book about?" asked Sandra.

Ben set his spoon down, turned the heat down on the stove and turned back to give them his full attention. "It's about a princess that cooks for her kingdom."

"You've got to be kidding, right? That is the coolest story line! How did you come up with the concept?" asked Laney.

Ben smiled so wide that his face looked as if it would crack. He pulled out his wallet and fingered through to a picture.

"She did." he said, as he pointed to the child in the picture. "It was all her. Her name is Charlotte, she's my niece. She likes to cook with me."

All three of them loved the picture of a sweet little girl dressed up as Disney Princess, Elsa. The child was beautiful. In her smile, you could see a little resemblance to her uncle.

"I'm Uncle Ben. I know, right—hysterical, huh? I'm a mahatma guy."

Leslie laughed hysterically, and Sandra looked puzzled.

"Seriously Sandra, you haven't heard of Uncle Ben's rice?' asked Leslie.

"Oh that. I don't buy rice—too many carbs, so how was I to know? What's mahatma?" asked Sandra.

"That would be rice too," said Laney with a smirk as she shook her head at Sandra.

Ben continued, "Charlotte loves to cook with me, and one day she dressed up as Princess Belle. Sometimes, it's Elsa, and occasionally it's Cinderella. But anyhow, we started chatting about how the princess was cooking for her kingdom, a.k.a. family."

"That is adorable. What a neat story," said Leslie.

"It really was her idea. She said all the kingdom had a terrible year for their harvest and she needed to provide food for them. Like her mom and dad did at the homeless shelter for people who were hungry. I took the concept and ran with it. A friend of mine did the illustrations, and I self-published. I sold it on Amazon, at Barnes and Noble, and other outlets."

"Some child is going to have themselves the Dad of the Year in you," said Sandra, as she sat back on her bar stool and looked at him intently.

"Absolutely!" said Laney as she gazed at Ben.

Just then, Robert and Carrie walked into the lounge together, dressed for their evening on the town. Robert looked sharp in a white pressed shirt with a blue and white seersucker dinner jacket, khaki trousers, and tasseled tan loafers. Carrie was wearing a lavender linen blouse she purchased at Beaufort Linen Company, with white capris and a floral wrap. Her hair was in an over the shoulder ponytail that allowed for her pearl and diamond stud earrings to show.

"Look at the young kids all dressed up to go out for the evening. You two know you have a curfew and need to be home before that carriage turns into a pumpkin, right?" asked Sandra, as she took a sip of her lemonade.

Leslie watched as Robert took Carrie's hand and wrapped it in the crook of his arm. Carrie looked at him with adoration. Her cheeks glowed with a special radiance. None of them had ever seen her look so delighted and at ease. Even if it was short-lived for a weekend, it was at least lived and worth every moment.

"We promise to be home early enough so we can pull out and set sail back to Beaufort." said Robert.

They said their goodbyes and headed to the dock. Carrie blew them a kiss when they reached the boardwalk. Leslie, Sandra, and Laney waved at her from the yacht's deck and then returned inside to the kitchen and dining area.

"It smells so good in here," said Sandra. "Just breathing the air is going make me gain weight, why are y'all always doing this to me? I'm going to change clothes before dinner. We walked up a sweat going down the streets of Charleston. Will y'all excuse me for a few moments? I'll be back when it's time for cocktails." Sandra exited the kitchen and winked at Leslie on the way out as she motioned for Leslie to join her with a head nod. She really was giving Laney some time together with Ben.

"Of course, go get changed. I'm going to go back to reading my book and leave these two chefs to ring the dinner bell," said Leslie.

"We'll give you a shout out when it's cocktail hour. I promise," said Laney, as she returned to the stove, beside Ben. Then she turned back around to mouth the words "thank you" to Leslie.

Leslie smiled when she thought of romance in the air as if it were a vapor being breathed in and out. It was sweet and quite unexpected, but it was all around them right now. That's what made it so unique; it was happening so naturally. As for Laney, it sure looked like something could be brewing. It was just a weekend, but it was turning out to be a special one for them. Eventually, they would return home and back to their lives. So, for now, it was good to ride the winds of change that wafted through their moment in time.

Chapter Eighteen

Charleston with Robert and Carrie

Carrie thought nothing else would surprise her about the weekend. Her life had become so lackadaisical that everything surprised her now. She also realized her excitement over everything might appear to be put-on or a fake sentiment to Robert.

As the carriage made its way down the street, she took in all the sights and sounds of the city. Rainbow Row and the historical mansions—Charleston featured architecture that drew her in, and she instantly fell in love with the area. Their coachman held a wealth of knowledge, and he described the destinations, boutiques, and shops that made Charleston famous. They rode down Bay Street and on cobblestone paths. As they passed the Battery, he explained about the rich history of the sea wall that was there for protection during the storms. He showed them water level lines from years of hurricane flooding.

The smells floating in the air from each restaurant gave a sense of the variety the city offered. As they traveled down palm tree lined streets, he pointed out St. Phillips's Church, standing tall in the glow of the sunset on the horizon. As they pulled up to their destination and the carriage came to a stop, Carrie noticed it was not the restaurant Robert told her about. She was a bit intrigued. She looked around as Robert helped her down off the carriage.

Robert saw her gazing over the area and leaned into her ear.

"You don't see the restaurant I was telling you about, do you?"

Carrie laughed and said, "Well, now that you mention it. No, I do not. I thought you said it was called *The Bank*."

He offered his arm to escort her down the sidewalk, but not before placing her on the inside of the sidewalk away from the traffic. He thought of absolutely everything, and Carrie felt treasured, valued, and respected. It was a magnificent feeling, and one she would like to get used to.

"That, my dear, is because I wanted to stroll you down the street and give you another vantage point of Charleston. This city has so much to offer, and before we reach the restaurant, I thought we could take it all in."

"Thank you for being such a kind and a gracious host to us. This is utterly amazing. Our next vacation will never top this one. You have just upped the ante. I hope you know my excitement and appreciation is genuine. It's like I'm living out a movie! You are something else, Robert," said Carrie as she looked around the street and Robert patted her hand tucked in the crook of his arm.

The setting sun behind the various architecture was a stark contrast against the skyline. The light played off the colorful architecture and cast a rainbow of colors. It was like walking in a multi-faceted prism of light that sparkled all around them.

They stopped in a couple of boutiques to browse around and they read a few historical signs that were posted along the way. Robert was correct—the walk brought the nostalgia the city offered to life.

When they could not carry anymore shopping bags, Robert slowed his pace. Carrie looked up at the sign over a building: The Bank. The hostess took the bounty of treasures they had purchased to hold in the coatroom and escorted them to their private dining room.

The room was very chic—it was a quaint little section of the restaurant that once was a vault. The building's renovation several years ago revealed a hidden vault discovered behind a wall built in the 1950s. The room was just large enough to hold a table for four. The walls were adorned with pieces of art, currency in paper and gold and silver. Shadow boxes held vintage jewelry. Some pieces were fascinating to Carrie, as she recognized items her grandmother and mother had worn. She stopped as she looked at one display on the wall and Robert noticed it caught her attention.

"What about that display grabs your attention?" Robert asked.

"I recognize some of these pieces. They're costume jewelry from years ago. I think it's called *Sarah Coventry*. My Aunt Helen had that necklace right there, and she let me borrow it to wear to a Christmas dance one year. I think I might still have it since she let me keep it when she realized how much I liked it."

"That's interesting. You know, now that I look at it through your eyes, I think you're right. My grandmother had some necklaces that looked similar. I remember her having a jewelry party at home," Robert said, as he looked over the pieces in the shadow box.

Robert extended his arm to the small table and pulled the chair out for Carrie to sit down, then sat across from her. The candlelight in the hurricane-style lamp made Robert's eyes sparkle. She couldn't say a word for a moment as she took in how handsome he was, and the magical ambience of the room.

"Proverbial cat got your tongue?" asked Robert.

"No, I was just thinking. You mentioned your grandmother again. Tell me more about your family."

The server came into the room to open and pour Robert's favorite red wine. After she left, Robert described small bits of his life as a child and a teenager. Once they ordered appetizers, he talked about his college days. At that point, he slowed the conversation and became vague about details.

"You were on a roll there for a while, and it was truly fascinating to hear about your life. Why did you stop at college? Tell me more. Have you always lived this large or is it something you grew into?" asked Carrie.

"Let's order our meal before they kick us out of here," Robert said with a laugh, as he motioned for the server to come back to the private room. His expression grew solemn as he opened the menu.

Carrie looked over the selection of entrees. It was easy to see why he favored this restaurant. She selected her meal quickly. Mostly because she was curious about Robert's nervous laugh and his now solemn face. Was he hiding something? He did almost seem too good to be true, so of course her mind wandered. Is there something about him she didn't know or want to find out - his demeanor completely stopped on a dime and Sandra's guarded intuition might have been on to something.

The server took their orders and refreshed the wine in their glasses. There was an awkward silence at the table. Carrie was not sure if she should press the inquisition of details about Robert's college days or let it be. It was his story to tell if he wanted to do so. She fiddled with the cloth napkin and looked around the room. Robert reached out and touched her hand.

"I'm sorry. I should apologize for that last bit there. I sort of shut you down when we reached my university days."

Carrie said, "No, really, don't apologize. We said we would talk about chapters of our lives, and I know there are some you may not want to discuss, and me, likewise."

Robert continued, "No, it's just the biggest part of my college days included my wife, Beth. I met her as a sophomore, and she was a freshman. We dated throughout college and married as soon as she graduated. So, to talk of those days, would be filled with stories of Beth."

"Mercy, that's quite fine. I mean, Robert, you didn't lose your wife by choice. You lost her to death; there is a difference. I would love to hear all about your college days with her. What you did, where you went, your favorite songs. That is if you want to share, and I hope you will."

"Well, if you're sure, I don't want to overshare or bore you."

"I promise, I don't think there is anything about you that could bore me," replied Carrie.

They spent the next few moments talking about sorority and fraternity days on campus, the proposal, the wedding, and their honeymoon destination of Williamsburg, Virginia. Then Robert paused for a moment, rubbed his forehead, and took a sip of wine. He leaned back in his chair and crossed his arms with a smile on his face.

"Whew, that was a walk down memory lane I have not visited in an exceptionally long time. I forgot about the trip just down the road to Williamsburg, we barely had enough dough to afford the two-night excursion. I'm sorry. I just went on for what must have seemed like an eternity. Your interrogation and interview skills are on point, my dear."

"When you've been in the media business as long as I have, you learn to ask questions, find out what the media buyer wants, find out details about the person you are interviewing, so it is my nature to ask questions. Reporting used to thrill me, and I enjoyed writing headlines for the 6:00 news. I ask questions, sometimes too many. But I love learning about people, and I have enjoyed every bit of your story."

The server came into the room to deliver their meals. Carrie looked around the room, enjoying the pleasant ambience for a moment. To Robert, it may have seemed like she was withdrawing, but that was not the case at all. In fact, she had never felt more alive and present than she did at that very moment.

"You are very quiet. Is everything okay? Is your Tomato Pie prepared to your liking?" asked Robert.

"Oh, I'm sorry. Yes, it's delicious. This is just a lot to take in and I am enjoying it. How is the lobster piccata?"

"Quite delicious. Just wait until you try their key lime pie. Or we can stop by Carmella's for a cannoli. They are amazing."

"Oh, they both sound so delish! I just find it incredible to be on a date, at my age. And to be at this place, having arrived in this town on a yacht. Wow! Then a horse-drawn carriage ride. Life is full of surprises."

"Yes, it is, and you are one of those surprises. I would like to get to know more about you, Carrie. That may sound a bit of a stretch to ask on our first date. I said that word—*date*. That's what you said, so I just followed suit," Robert said.

Carrie clasped her hands and let her chin rest on them as she intently looked into Robert's eyes. "It sure feels like a date. Am I overstepping? I don't know how this works these days."

"That makes two of us, my dear. I don't know either," said Robert, as he offered her a croissant.

They finished dinner and decided to take a leisurely slow stroll back to the carriage Robert had waiting for them. There was a mild evening breeze, and a slightly waning moon in the night sky. During the carriage ride, Carrie thought about the last two days. She had not picked up her cell phone at all. It was a nice break, and she felt relaxed and stress-free for the first time in years. She had forgotten how this felt. She felt that her peace had been stolen from her, and she needed to claim it again. It just might be possible that Robert could be the person she needed to help her get back to a place of harmony and peace in her life.

"Robert?"

"Yes, my dear?"

Carrie leaned over and put her head on his shoulder for a quick second. "Is it okay if I rest my head on your shoulder?" she asked.

"It absolutely is," responded Robert.

"Thank you for this weekend. I think I'm finding me again."

"Well, you are welcome. I'm glad I found you."

Chapter Nineteen

After Dinner on the Yacht

The dinner Laney and Ben whipped up was impressive as it should be from two chefs. The restricted space in the galley kitchen did not impair the creativity in their culinary skills. It was a natural act of artistry to see the two in action. The kitchen cupboards were stocked well with condiments and spices. They found fresh vegetables, fruits, and seafood when they went out on their market trip. The result was a heavenly blue crab ravioli with a parmesan cream sauce alongside sauteed mushrooms and spinach. Laney served up her famous version of shrimp and grits. Her friend, Chef Scott had shared his recipe with her many years ago, and it was her tried and true favorite. For dessert, Ben concocted a decadent lemon curd parfait with fresh cream, drizzled with a sugar crystal crackle glaze. Even Sandra requested a serving of the parfait, which shocked them all.

Sandra and Leslie returned to the deck lounge so Ben and Laney could finish up in the kitchen. They both could have raised their hand to help, but it was clear the two chefs owned the kitchen. Sandra and Leslie also sensed that Ben and Laney wanted more time alone together.

As they relaxed on the deck, Sandra looked across the marina and admired the many yachts anchored there. As Leslie followed the moon rise, she imagined that Stan would be on the back porch at home looking at the same moon with their dog, Luke. A smile curled up the corner of her lips as she imagined the view of them.

Leslie looked over at Sandra. It looked like she was asleep; she didn't dare disturb her. She recognized how much she required this time to rest, unwind, and not worry about the infertility issues. She could see it was working for her, and her disposition had improved after just a couple of days away. The fact they had not touched a cell phone helped as well. Sandra regularly used the fertility app her physician recommended. But for the last couple of days, she had not looked at it once.

Just as Leslie thought Sandra was asleep, she stood up, wobbled a bit to get her sea legs working, and walked over to Leslie. "Hey, I've been speculating on something. Can I ask you a question?" asked Sandra as she leaned against the deck railing.

"Gosh, I thought you were asleep. You always concern me when you initiate a conversation like this. What's up?" asked Leslie.

"You know how we dislike secrets, right? The little white lies story from earlier has me thinking. I mean, I would not choose to keep a secret from you. But you also know that Mitch is sworn to confidentiality at the bank, right?" asked Sandra.

Leslie nodded her head, "Yes, and yes. So, what's the question?"

Sandra sat down beside Leslie. For a moment, she did not say a word. She was fidgeting with her fingers and tapping her knees.

"For mercy's sake, Sandra, spit it out! You are making me nervous."

"I'm not sure if I should say anything, but then again, you are one of my truest and best friends. But if Mitch finds out that I saw something in his study and told you, he will kill me."

"Saw what?" asked Leslie.

By this time, Sandra and Leslie were standing face to face and leaning on the railing of the deck.

"I'm going to need for you to finish what you started, Sandra. What are you rambling on about?"

"I saw something on Mitch's desk. I was in there to get some documents to file our taxes. Yes, we are late. I know, all my fault. I wasn't looking for anything, it was just there right on top. I am so excited for you!"

"What are you babbling on about? Excited about what? Out with it," said Leslie as she put a hand on her hip.

Sandra clenched her hands nervously and sat back down. Leslie sat beside her.

"Well, it looked like a blueprint and an appraisal for the family farm," said Sandra.

"What? What family farm? Our farm? Maybe Stan is getting some new equipment and it had to be appraised. So, I'm not sure what you're talking about."

"So, you did not know. Well, I'm not absolutely certain, but I'm almost positive that the farm was your family's farm, not the farm that you and Stan own now. I thought you knew."

And Sandra squinted her eyes when she realized what just happened.

Leslie was silent for a moment. "Why do you think that was on Mitch's desk? Why do you think it has anything to do with Stan?"

"Because it was clear on the blueprint and maps who ordered the appraisal. It was Stan. I thought maybe you knew about it and, well, I have a case of the curiosity that killed the cat, as you very well know," said Sandra as she rubbed her forehead.

"Are you sure it was for Stan? You are sure it was his name and our farm name: S&L Farms?"

"Yes, it was Stan. Yes, it was for S&L Farms. But the maps and the house were not your current farm and home—it was for the homeplace of your family."

Leslie threw her head back to stretch the tension out of her neck.

"Why would he have an appraisal done for a farm that we do not own, and technically never owned? We just always thought it would stay in the family."

"Leslie, is it possible that he's purchased your family's farm for you as a surprise? I just assumed you knew. Oh dear, I have really screwed up here. I can never keep my mouth shut."

"For me? What in the world for? What would we do with it? It's not that large—maybe 300 acres. We could plant some acreage there, but it would be more trouble than it's worth to go that far and keep up with the crops," said Leslie.

"Well, Stan knows how horrible it was when your family went through that entire ordeal and the homeplace sold so quickly. It was all over town how that fiasco went down. He might think it would bring closure to you if you could have the original house back in the family. I mean really Leslie – you loved your grandparents' homeplace. You still talk about it all the time," said Sandra as she put her arm around Leslie's shoulders.

Leslie pondered the thought. She wanted to call Stan and ask him. On the other hand, Sandra would be the one to pay for sharing the information. That could not happen. She could go to the bank and ask Mitch herself, but that would present him with a confidentiality issue, too. What did Stan have in mind? Leslie felt confused and frustrated, and she wished that Sandra hadn't brought up the topic.

"You know what, Sandra? We are going to table this conversation for later. We are enjoying this weekend so much, and I really don't want to think about this anymore."

As Leslie turned to walk away, she stopped and turned back around to give Sandra a hug. She knew it was difficult for Sandra to keep her nose out of other people's business sometimes. She always had the best of intentions, but she was not great on timing or choosing when to speak and when not to speak.

Sandra and Leslie heard laughter as Robert and Carrie were boarding the yacht.

"Well, what in the world is going on here? You two look like you have seen a ghost," said Carrie.

"That's more accurate than you can imagine, Carrie. Hey y'all, I think I'm going to turn in and read for a while," said Leslie, as she left to go to her cabin.

Carrie turned to look at Sandra and said, "What happened? It looks like something is troubling her."

"Me," replied Sandra.

"What does that mean? What did you say? What did you do, Sandra?" asked Carrie as she had both hands on Sandra's shoulders.

Robert felt it was best to let them discuss this matter on their own. "I'll head in now, Carrie. I'll be happy to join you on deck later."

"Okay, Robert. I won't be long," Carrie said. As Robert headed into the lounge, Carrie turned to Sandra.

"So, how was your evening?" asked Sandra with a forced grin.

Carrie stood with her hands on her hips and looked intently at Sandra. "It was magical. But we can talk about that later. What happened here just now?"

"Well, I may have brought up something about Stan getting an appraisal of her family's homeplace," said Sandra.

Carrie gasped. "Why would you mention that to her? You know how sensitive she is about that entire ordeal. The selling of the farm without a single thought as to how it would upset the rest of the family. It tore the entire family apart."

"I know, but I couldn't help it. I saw the appraisal for the farm and homeplace on Mitch's desk. I think Stan is working with Mitch on a loan to purchase it. I thought she knew something about it. But it turns out my question surprised her." Sandra sat down and rested her head in her hands. "Why do I do this? Remind me again?' asked Sandra.

Carrie sat down facing Sandra. They said nothing for a few seconds, then Carrie patted Sandra's hand and broke the silence. "Look, gosh girl, you always have the best intentions, but the most horrible methods. I'm going in and do some damage control here. You always mean well, Sandra. Leslie knows you do, so don't be so hard on yourself. Show yourself some grace."

Carrie got up and headed inside to Leslie's cabin. Sandra remained on deck, and she overheard Ben and Laney in the kitchen. Robert had joined them, and they were talking about the evening he and Carrie had enjoyed in town. Sandra smiled as she heard Robert talk about Carrie in such a kind and gentle manner. Ben and Laney recapped their dinner menu, and both agreed that it was a tie on the best dishes. Sandra laughed, because she thought Ben had Laney beat with his dish. Probably because she was used to Laney's cooking and Ben's was a new experience for her. She overheard Robert ask for the dessert leftovers, and it disappointed him to hear the dessert had been devoured.

Sandra continued to sit in the moonlight. She also felt that she was sitting in a huge pile of guilt. She always opened her mouth at the wrong time. *Focus on what is around you – ground yourself.* Her survival technique. She looked at the moonlight sparkling on the water under clear skies. Sounds of music, laughter, and the voices of children echoed throughout the marina. No matter where Sandra's daily life took her, she always heard the voices of children and the cries of infants. In the grocery store, the mall, restaurants—she always heard the children. From where she sat, she could see families lounging on decks and some returning from a day or a night in town. Sandra thought about how it would be to have little voices in her own life. But would that ever be for her and Mitch? How many children had sailed with their families on the yacht she and her friends were enjoying? For a moment she envisioned a family sitting at the breakfast table and talking about their next port of call destination. She imagined the excitement on the faces of the children, how their eyes would sparkle and dance as they anticipated their new adventure.

Robert came out and informed Sandra the yacht would be leaving soon. He startled her and interrupted her dream. She decided to call it a night. She noticed that Carrie had joined Robert in the lounge, so her talk with Leslie was over. On the way to her cabin, she saw that Laney and Ben were still talking. They were testing their bartending skills. It would be nice to share a nightcap, but her loose lips had done enough damage for one night. She should avoid everyone until morning. She would go to bed and dream of the sweet little faces she imagined sitting at the breakfast table. Perhaps those pleasant thoughts would carry her to a night of better dreams instead of the nightmares that often plagued her. By the time she reached her cabin, Leslie had turned out the lights and was asleep. Sandra slipped out of her shorts and slid into bed quietly.

"If Stan has bought the farm, I would be in heaven, but I cannot get my hopes up. I don't know anything about this, but I'm sorry if I seemed cross with you," said Leslie, in the silence of the dark room.

Sandra set up on her side and faced Leslie. "It's okay," said Sandra. "I just couldn't hold it inside any longer. I remember when I was going through treatment for my pill addiction. You used to tell me wonderful stories about your time there as a child. I loved hearing all of them. It helped me to focus on a world where everything was fine, where people were good, where you could sit in your yard and see for miles the land you owned. The pond, the path lined with oaks, and the willows planted by the pond bank. I just knew if this is something Stan has planned—it would help you heal from the years of sorrow you have had since it sold. The stories you told me when I needed healing would come to life. Those stories helped heal me, Leslie. I was just hoping that if you got the homeplace back it would heal you, too. I'm sorry. Rest well."

"I know, I know. Good night. No worries. Sweet dreams," said Leslie as she rolled over on her side.

It was quiet in the room again for a just a few seconds. Once again, Sandra could not help herself. "I guess in a way I was selfishly hoping that he was buying it. That way I would get to see the beautiful homeplace you always talked about. So, really, I'm just as anxious as you are to know."

Leslie yawned as she replied, "That's sweet. Time will tell. Now, goodnight. I feel the boat moving. Be careful if you need to get up."

"Thank you for loving me even when I don't feel very loveable."

"Always, my friend. Remember that—always."

Chapter Twenty

Sunday with Stan

Sunday was Stan Cartwright's favorite day of the week—the day the good Lord told everyone to rest. The week had been a long and busy one, and he was ready for some of that peace. The timing was excellent that Leslie would be away for a few days. It afforded him time to square up the details with the purchase of the homeplace. He prayed he was doing the wise thing. Should he go to church and have a talk with the man upstairs about it again? But he had devoted many nights praying about the matter, and there were no red flags that he would have taken as a sign to pull back.

While Leslie was out of town, he organized a visit to inspect the property with the previous owner. The place needed some repairs, but there had been an impressive start on most of the required code updates by the previous owner. Stan had crops to tend, and the timing was not conducive for him to take on a project on his own. He would require help, so he contacted a contractor that specialized in historical renovations, and he had an appointment for a consult the next week.

Stan brewed a pot of coffee, poured a cup, and went to the porch to enjoy the early morning sunrise. Luke greeted him at the door, Stan always said that dog was his best friend. But if the truth were told that dog was Leslie's baby. She found him and rescued him after they lost their lab of fourteen years. It almost killed her the day the veterinarian told her it was time to put him down. That old lab laid right down at her feet and wrapped his legs around hers as she whispered in his ear, "*Let's go home boy; it's time to go home.*" There was not a dry eye in the room as the vet and staff watched the lab hug her ankles. The tears flowed for the next few weeks every time she thought of him. Two months later she spotted a hound's face on a pet adoption website. She went to the veterinarian office to "*just look.*" Stan knew she would come home with that dog. He was right, and it turned he loved having him around for company. Luke followed him all over the farm during the day, and he followed Leslie all over the house at night. Soon as she sat down, he curled up beside her.

Stan started thinking about possibilities for the homeplace. It could be one of those venues that folks were offering all over the state for weddings. It looked to him like no one was getting married in a church anymore. They did everything on farms or country clubs. Seemed like a shame—he loved a church wedding. But that was his taste and liking; not everyone felt the same way. They could build a small covering to resemble an open-air chapel. That's a thought.

He finished his coffee, read the morning paper, then jumped in the truck and headed down the dusty path to the main road. He loved the ride out to the homeplace. It was not too far—just minutes on the other side of Willow Green. The drive gave him a chance to take the less traveled back roads that almost felt like going back in time. Small corner stores, roadside stands for produce, a few cattle farms, and one alpaca farm were located on the way to the property. The scenery made for an interesting ride down two-lane roads scattered with homes, ranches, and the occasional country church. To Stan, it was a peaceful ride that gave him a chance to relax and admire God's creation. One stop he always liked to make was at Duke's boiled peanut truck. The friendly old man always had a pot of peanuts, hot and ready. Stan liked to chat with the fellow as much as he liked the boiled peanuts. He had retained a healthy amount of knowledge about war history, and Stan learned something from him with every visit. Stan pulled into the stand located at the intersection and parked his truck.

After an hour of talking about local war history and devouring a bag of boiled peanuts, Stan said his good-byes to Duke and headed to his destination. Within minutes, he turned down the path lined with cedar trees and oaks. He glanced over at the pond and the creek lined with willow trees. The trees were dancing in the breeze and had grown quite large in recent years. He saw a truck parked in the side yard of the main house. Stan pulled his truck up.

"How are you doing, sir? I'm Stan, the one that is purchasing the property," said Stan as he tipped his hat at the driver.

The man in the other truck got out and walked over to his door. "Yes sir, Mr. Stan. I am sorry we didn't get properly introduced the last time you were here. I was out behind the house looking at the smokehouse repairs. You and the realtor were gone by the time I came back to the main house. I'm Rudy Mann. It's nice to meet you." Rudy walked up to the truck and shook Stan's hand.

Stan looked over at the smokehouse. "I hope that smoke-house is still in working order. That could come in handy. I hope everything will go through the first of this week. I'm asking for confidentially, though. It's a surprise for my wife."

"That's what I hear, sir. No worries. Your banker already told me, so I have not said a word. Plus, I don't really know anyone local, so your secret is safe with me," said Rudy.

Stan nodded and replied, "I appreciate that, and the time today to walk through the house one more time. The last time I was in a hurry, I have more time today."

"Of course. Come on up and I'll show you around," said Rudy as he started up the steps.

Stan looked up at the porch ceiling and noticed it was the original bead board. It was authentic, and he liked it. It had been sanded and repainted, and it looked as good as new.

They stepped into the main room of the house. "The story goes that the original owners had these beadboard ceilings throughout the entire house. In the 70s, they put in a tile drop ceiling in the front rooms of the house. I think they wanted a more modern look in the living room and drawing room, and it would have saved on heating, too. The rest of the house has the original high ceilings, all made of bead board, but you could remove this drop ceiling pretty easily I think," said Rudy.

Stan smiled, not wanting to give away just yet that he knew the original owners. "Is that so, you say?"

"Some rooms have the original wainscoting paneling. In a few areas, they updated and put in the paneling that was popu-lar back then, too. It's avocado green in some rooms, but as you can see, we already started painting those," said Rudy.

"The painting you all started looks good. Can we go upstairs? I want to see the bedrooms," asked Stan.

"Sure. Let's go," said Rudy, and they turned to the staircase.

The steps were about eight feet wide, and it had a nice size landing at the top. When they reached the landing, Stan counted bedroom doors. It had been a while since he walked those halls, but he could still picture all the life they once held.

"It looks like we have six bedrooms here?" asked Stan.

"There are six, and there's a room up on the third floor. You get to it through the middle room here. It could be a bedroom, but most likely from the looks of things, it was an attic turned into a playroom at one point," said Rudy.

Stan grinned. "Let's look then."

When Rudy opened the door to the stairway, he recalled the first time he went up there with Leslie. It was a Christmas dinner with her extended family. Some of them began quarreling over a ridiculous political theory or religion; he couldn't remember exactly. It was usually one or the other, and sometimes both. They always found something to argue about. Leslie hated it when they argued. She preferred to spend time alone with her grandparents. When all the aunts and uncles came together, nobody got along. Stan always wondered why. Years later, it should not have been a surprise when the same generation of children were still arguing over the property after her grandparents passed away. Leslie used to go to this room as an escape. She showed him all the things they used to do up there as kids—puzzles, books, an old rocking horse, tables, and chairs for sitting to color or draw art. He could clearly remember. When they reached the playroom, Rudy opened the door and Stan's memory was there right in front of him.

"When my family purchased this place, we got an opportunity to work on it quite a bit, but we left this room out. My mom couldn't bring herself to change too much in here – she loved children and she imagined how it was enjoyed by many kiddos. It looked like the previous owners didn't have time to clean it out before the sale. There are lots of great things in here I bet they would have wanted to pass down to generations. Some unique toys, and lots of books, as you can see," said Rudy.

Stan walked around and touched the old rocking horse that stood beside the table and chairs. The wallpaper had been scraped off the walls, but that was as far as the repairs had progressed. It was like walking into a time capsule. The shelf was there, and they had packed the books up in boxes. Stan grabbed a book and blew off the dust. He opened it and saw the name of Leslie's cousin. He grabbed another book, and it had Leslie's name on the inside cover. After all this time, he could not believe these things were still there. Her family members that sold the place never knew how important these things were to Leslie. On the shelf he noticed a Partridge Family lunchbox. When he opened it, he found it filled with colored pencils. On top of the lunchbox, Leslie's name appeared on a piece of masking tape. Stan chuckled, as he knew Leslie would love to see the old beat-up piece of tin again.

"Rudy, can I ask you a favor? Do you mind if I take this lunchbox and book with me?" asked Stan.

"Well, no. I mean, my mom never knew what to do with all of this stuff. She had hoped to contact the original owner's family members, but she came to a dead end. She had a grand vision for this house, but then she got sick. After she died, no one else had a desire to tackle the place or finish the work she started.

That's why we wanted to sell. Take the book and the lunch box if you like. It's going to be yours soon anyway," said Rudy.

"Thanks, this will be helpful," said Stan.

"Sir, I'm not sure I understand how an old copy of *Little Women* and that rusty old lunchbox is going to be helpful to anybody," said Rudy.

Stan smiled and knew it must seem ridiculous to this young man to watch a grown man eyeing an old lunchbox and book as they were treasures. But Stan knew that they were treasures to Leslie.

"Well, let me show you the name in this book," said Stan as he pointed to the name. "That's my wife. This was her grandparent's home, and this was the playroom where all the grandkids played and our boys too, when they were small."

"You're kidding, right? Really? You are buying this for your wife?" asked Rudy.

"I sure am. Some family members sold it to your mom, as you know, many years ago. There was a family dispute about property and such, and some relatives decided to sell this place. It broke Leslie's heart. When I got word it was back on the market, I jumped at it."

Rudy popped Stan on the shoulder. "Aren't you the creative one, sir! I remember mom saying that the property was a real bargain because the owners wanted to sell fast. They left a lot of furniture here. It was good stuff. We have some stored in the back-room downstairs."

"That's great! Leslie is going to be thrilled," said Stan.

They walked back downstairs to look at the kitchen and pantry. It was just as Stan remembered. The built-in shelves were still there, and the floor under his feet was the same black and white linoleum floor that was there when Leslie's grandparents owned the house.

As they entered the dining room, Stan noticed the china hutch in the corner. Underneath a layer of dust, he could see it was just as lovely as ever. Rudy noticed Stan staring at the hutch and he walked over to him.

"That piece holds a memory for you?" asked Rudy, as he helped Stan wipe away the dust.

"Yes, it does. Rumor has it, and on good authority, the only time Leslie ever heard her granddaddy curse was over this hutch."

Rudy laughed and said, "Why is that?"

"Well, they were transporting it here in the back of a pickup truck. Leslie's granddaddy didn't trust her daddy to get it here in one piece. Turns out he was right. Her granddaddy rode in the back of the truck holding the piece in place as her dad was driving and Leslie was in the truck cab. Sure enough, her dad turned a curve too quick, the piece fell over, and her grandaddy's pipe went straight through the glass," said Stan, shaking his head.

"He never let go of the pipe, funny story. I guess that explains why the glass on that side is different," said Rudy, as he pointed to the left side pane.

"Yes, it does. They could never match the glass to the others. But it made for a great conversation piece. Well, listen, thank you for this. It has been a walk down memory lane. I really appreciate it."

"Absolutely, sir. I look forward to getting everything closed this week. Mitch said he had a couple more documents to draw up, and then we would be good to go."

"It was great to see you. Thanks for everything," said Stan, as he shook Rudy's hand. "This has been great."

They both returned to their trucks and Rudy waved as he drove away. Stan sat in his truck for a while and admired the property. It was going to take some work, but it was not impossible. He was ready for some lunch and a nap. Leslie's chicken salad and deviled eggs sounded good. He drove down to the main road and headed for home. He looked over at the lunchbox and recalled the many nights Leslie had watched Partridge Family reruns. He touched the book on the seat beside him. He smiled with contentment, feeling at peace with his decision.

Chapter Twenty-One

Sunday with Karen

Karen was at the Airbnb she rented. It was not extravagant, but it was sufficient. She needed to figure out a plan that made sense to her. Life had flipped on a dime, and she needed to reorganize the framework that had just gone up in smoke. She had no family; she was an only child. She had not seen her parents in years. Truth be told, she preferred it that way. Life had been a living hell growing up with them because their parental skills were nil. Karen left when she was eighteen to make a life for herself, and she was proud of what she had created. Until now. For all she knew, her parents may not even be alive. She had not revisited the mobile home park since the day she left home. Eventually, communication fell off the grid, and she was fine with that. They never understood her. They always tried to get her to conform, and that never went well. Karen was a true rebel at heart. She would never fit in any run-of-the-mill, cookie cutter world. They had made nothing of their lives, why should she respect, honor, or conform to any advice or suggestions they provided.

The sun was high in the sky before she opened her eyes. For the first time since the accident, she could finally sleep. It took longer than it should have to reach Memphis since she didn't feel well. She made numerous stops for ginger ale and saltines. This entire ordeal had made her sick to her stomach. It was mid-afternoon, but she still had no appetite.

The owner of the home she rented was an animal lover, no doubt. There were bird feeders everywhere outside, including a feeder for squirrels. Karen could tell they had a dog. There was a doggie door and an automatic feeder in the laundry room. This was not something she normally cared for. She really did not like dogs. As far as she was concerned, they were smelly, loud, and more trouble than they were worth. Even the smell of the dog food was making her nauseas with each inhale that passed her nostrils, but this house was available and close to contacts she had in the business. It was going to be easy for her to make some connections. She would be back in the trenches in no time at all, and out of this house. If nothing else, it was going to prove to be a powerful motivator to find more permanent housing.

Karen sat down at the kitchen table and turned on her iPad. She needed to search for the ad agencies she used to work with for TV and radio commercials. She knew several media buyers. One of them had suggested that she would be a suitable fit for an agency she worked for in Memphis. So now was the time to put some substance to the suggestion.

Karen was confident in her skills and knew she was good at her work, but it would not hurt to have someone drop her name on the right desk. She always thought that living in Memphis would be a unique experience. The atmosphere was diverse with food, blues, music and hopefully it would include a fresh life for her. She had grown tired of the Southern small-town community of Greenway. Everyone knew your business, wanted to know your business, or made up something about your business. Karen smirked when she thought of the small-town issues and small-minded people in the town. Goodbye and good riddance! Her new life was going to be grand, nothing but blue skies and sunshine on the horizon. She had created a life before, and she could make a new one in Memphis.

Karen noticed she missed a call from Jerry. She didn't call him and let him know where she was. What difference did it make to him, anyway? He probably drank his way through the rest of the weekend and just sobered up. She didn't want to deal with him right now. She needed to get her plan for next week together. It would require strategically planning every part of the process. If she was going to get what she wanted, she needed to focus.

She looked at the agency's website and their portfolio of clients. She had worked with some of them before in TV and radio contracts for media outlets in the Northeast and the Midwest. This was going to be a cinch to pull off. She typed "local real estate" into her browser to seek permanent housing. She would have to look for something else to rent that could hold her over until she put down roots.

Just as she was filtering through the search, she felt sick again. She ran to the bathroom and knelt over the toilet. This bug, or bundle of nerves, was relentless. It was not giving up the fight. She needed to find a pharmacy to get some nausea medicine.

"*What the hell is wrong with me? I'm tougher than this,*" She asked herself in the mirror of the small bathroom. "*Maybe the caterer's food was bad – something must have been left out in the heat too long.*"

Then she took a long look in the mirror and said out loud, *"I look like hell warmed over, rode hard, and hung up wet."* She paused for a moment and the thought that raced through her mind made her feel even sicker.

"No, I can't be. No, no, no." Karen shook her head. She touched her breasts and noticed they felt tender. *"No, no, no!"*

Karen raced down the hallway to her purse and pulled out her phone. She pulled up an organizer calendar and looked through a chart. She kept excellent records of everything. Being vigilant about details made Karen tick like a clock, and she knew she would have a record of dates. The last three months had been crazy. The broadcasting media buying season was at its peak for new contracts for the next year. The engagement party and house hunting with Bill had kept them both terribly preoccupied.

Karen found the dates she was looking for. She did the math and counted off weeks. She set the phone down on the kitchen table as she sank into a chair.

"Oh, no,no,no. It can't be. I cannot be pregnant. Damn."

She laid her head down on her cradled arms. She saw her reflection in the glass top table and a tear drop fell and muddled the view of her face.

Chapter Twenty-Two

Sunday on the Yacht

Laney and Ben were back in the kitchen, and the smells floating about in the air had been enough to sufficiently wake the dead. Robert dressed as soon as the aroma drifted by his cabin and headed to the kitchen. While walking down the hall, he noticed Sandra and Leslie's door was closed. He peeked at Carrie's door, and it was the same, so he proceeded on to the kitchen. He heard Laney and Ben laughing and prepping for breakfast until midnight. Robert was certain it did not take that long to prepare for cooking a meal in the small kitchen. He perceived it was more about them spending time together than the actual cooking preparations. It surprised him that they were back at it, even though they had been up extremely late. It pleased him as well too since he was famished.

"Good morning chef and sous chef. You two make an awesome team. You should cook up a partnership venture. No pun intended," said Robert, as he poured a cup of coffee.

"That depends on which one of us you think is the chef and which one is the sous chef. And you know what I think about that already," said Laney.

"Yes, I think I do, but what do you think, Ben?"

Ben gave them a crooked little grin and said, "Sure, she can be the boss. That will be fine."

Maybe it was cooking together in close quarters, but it was obvious that something was taking place with those two. That's what Robert had in mind when he invited the young man along for the journey, and it turned out they were as compatible as he hoped. Laney was an awesome young lady, and she deserved happiness. Through the years, he had brokered several boat sales with her father's family, and he grew very fond of Laney during that time. He had known her since she was two years old, and he became "Uncle Robert." Once she was all grown up, he was just Robert. He was happy to see her glowing. The breakup she experienced with the last boy, while they were engaged, was something that lingered in her soul. It had been a long time since he had seen her gleaming smile.

"Listen, we are almost to the marina. I will let the ladies sleep if they like. We can take our time," said Robert, as he reached for a muffin.

"It has been incredibly refreshing to be away from social media, no Instagram, no Facebook, no news, no phone. I think I could get accustomed to this way of life. Hey Robert, thank you, this weekend has been great," said Laney.

"You are very welcome, my dear. I have loved meeting your friends and spending some time with you as well. How is your lovely mother doing? I appreciate her Christmas cards. They are always beautiful, and she writes such a genuine heartfelt note each year."

"I'll let her know they bring a bit of something special to your holiday. She is one of the last folks I know that sends out cards for all occasions—in the mail! She's doing great and loving retired life. I will tell her you asked about her. Speaking of mother, I'm sure she has blown up my phone with messages. She calls every day. But other than that, it has amazed me at how well we all coped without Wi-Fi and cell service. I mean, really, no phones turned on at all – not even when we were in port in Charleston. And Carrie leaving hers at the beach house, that surprised me. But I think she needed some time to be unplugged. You've been good for her Robert," said Laney, as she raised her coffee cup to Robert.

"Likewise—she's been good for me. Not sure where it will go, but I would like to spend more time with her. If she's obliged to do so, I would be receptive to the idea."

"Receptive, is that what you call it? From what I see, the feeling is mutual. Robert, you two are slam smitten with each other," said Laney.

Ben leaned over and whispered in Robert's ear, "It's kind of totally obvious, bro."

"Good morning, y'all!" said Carrie as she entered the kitchen.

Robert turned to see Carrie standing there in white capris and a madras plaid shirt tied at her trim waist. A straw fedora donned her head with her hair pulled back into a ponytail. The lady had a style that was all her own, and she made any outfit look elegant. Robert thought she looked lovely last night, but now he had to say that he thought she looked even lovelier this morning. Possibly because he knew more about her heart and soul today, and it matched the outside with equal beauty.

"Good morning, sunshine," said Robert, as he stood up to greet her. He offered her a seat next to him at the bar.

"Hello night owls. Good gracious, y'all talked half the night, I could hear you laughing in the wee hours of the morning," said Carrie to Ben and Laney.

"That may have had something to do with the bartending class I put Laney through last night," Ben replied.

"I slept well. I'll give you that," replied Laney.

"Something smells divine. What is it? Are those crepes I see over there?" asked Carrie.

"Why yes you do, we tag teamed here. Laney did the crepes, I whipped the cream, we have some strawberries to go on top. Along with that, we have leftover shrimp and grits and orange marmalade jam with corn bread muffins," said Ben.

"What happened? Laney's shrimp and grits are never left over," said Carrie.

"Well, that's when it's the only thing on the menu. This guy tried to steal my thunder with dinner last night," replied Laney.

"Good morning. Where is the coffee?" asked Sandra as she walked in with sunglasses on.

"Coffee is over here. Get a cup and maybe your disposition will improve a tad bit," said Carrie.

"I have to admit, you ladies have been amazing to watch. It's like watching an episode of *Designing Women*. Really, you all remind me of them—about the same variety of ages, and such distinct personalities," said Robert.

Sandra gave Robert a look over the rim of her sunglasses. "You know what, you may be on to something there. I never thought of it like that before. *Designing Women*, I loved that show. I used to watch it with my mama."

"*Designing Women*? What are you talking about?" asked Laney, with a puzzled look on her face.

Carrie laughed and said, "Honey, you are too young to remember that show. It was about four women in Atlanta, and all of them are uniquely different. Robert, you're right; there are similarities. They own an interior design firm. Google it. I'm sure one of the streaming networks probably has the series," said Carrie.

"Thank you, Laney, for reminding us how old we are. That is a better eye opener than Folgers in your cup," said Sandra.

"Hello, did someone say Folgers?" asked Leslie as she entered the lounge. "I need any black coffee in my cup. No matter the brand, hit me."

"We don't have Folgers, but try this out," said Ben as he handed Leslie a mug. "You need cream, or sugar?" he asked.

"No. A good cup of brew needs nothing," said Leslie as she reached for the cup and took a sip.

Ben waited for her response.

"This is good. I mean, this is *very* good. What brand is this coffee?" asked Leslie as she held the cup to breathe in the coffee's aroma.

"It's from a new shop – Awaken Coffee. This is one they gave me to try. I like this one the best, but there are some others that are worth trying too. It's a shop that enables the disabled to work in an atmosphere of dignity. It's quite a project, they are accepting donations to get opened now," said Ben.

"Oh, I would love to donate, do they have a website?" said Leslie.

"Yes, they do. I'll text it to you once we have cell service, but if I forget – it's Awaken Coffee." said Ben.

"That sounded funny. When we have cell services. We haven't used our phones all weekend, and I think I sort of liked it," said Leslie.

"I thought I would never agree with a statement like that. But this weekend has been a fairy tale adventure like something right out of a movie. I feel like we've been living like rock stars. The no phone issue turned out to not be an issue at all for me," said Carrie.

"I hate to see it end," said Laney, as she looked at Ben.

Robert cleared his throat and said, "Who says it has to end?"

"We can get together again, right? If we all agree that it would be a good thing. I mean that would be important, that we all agree," said Ben.

"Agree? I think it would be fantastic," said Laney. "How about we plan something next month at my house?" she added.

"Well, let's get this beauty in the marina and we can figure out the details when we all turn our cell phones back on. We should be there soon, so start trying to see if you have any reception yet," said Robert.

"Will do. Hey, we head down to our other stop tomorrow. Any chance we can all hook back up on our way back through? Maybe for lunch at the end of the week?" asked Carrie.

"I would love to, ladies. I'll see how our schedule lines up. You good for later in the week, Ben?" asked Robert.

"I have to get back to an event planned up in Raleigh. It's a cook-off and a charity thing. I do it every year with some friends. I may have to take a rain check until we meet up next month," said Ben.

"That is a very noble endeavor. Fortunate for them, but our loss. We'll miss you," said Laney.

Sandra looked up and propped her sunglasses on top of her head.

"All you folks do is talk about food and eating. Good gracious, can we do something other than eat?" she asked.

"I have an idea. How about when we get together next month, y'all come out to the farm? Carrie, you could get your neighbor, Buddy, to bring the horses over. Give it a go around the farm. The creek is a great spot for a stop, and then we can go back to the house for a bonfire. And well, um, yes, food! My husband makes the best smoked brisket," said Leslie.

"I knew it! It always comes back to food," said Sandra.

The yacht was close enough to see land, so the ladies went to gather their bags. Robert and Ben were cleaning up and packing up items from the kitchen.

"I don't know about you, Ben, but this has been an incredible weekend," said Robert.

"I totally agree with that statement. I've never met anyone like Laney. I could get into seeing her again," said Ben.

"I think the feeling is mutual. I watched the two of you; I can tell. She is an amazing woman. I wanted you to come along so you could meet her," said Robert, as he patted Ben on the back.

"I am glad you did. Much obliged," said Ben.

The yacht was almost at the marina, and the ladies had their bags on deck. They spent a few more moments lounging in the sun. Robert walked out to begin saying his goodbyes.

"I think your phones may work now, I think we are within range." said Robert.

"Who cares about phones? I think this has been the most serene weekend I've had in a long time," said Carrie.

Sandra reached into her bag and retrieved her cell phone. As she turned it on, there were several texts that came over. As she read them, she covered her mouth to keep from speaking. She looked up at Carrie and Robert sitting together on a lounge chair.

Leslie glanced Sandra's face as she turned her phone on. It dinged with messages being delivered. She smiled. "Awe, Janie Williams had her baby—a healthy baby boy. Oh my! By C-section finally after 24 hours of labor," said Leslie.

Then Leslie's face became somber, and she looked at Sandra. They made eye contact and looked at Carrie. Carrie was looking out over the marina, oblivious to them staring at her. Laney looked at Sandra and Leslie and walked over to them. She didn't have cell reception yet, and her curiosity got the best of her. They obviously had some news that she wanted to know about too.

"What's going on?" she whispered. Sandra handed her phone to Laney.

"Oh my God," said Laney.

Carrie, still fixated on the serenity in front of her, was undisturbed by their conversation. She took in the sight of a thin, dark line of deepest blue on the horizon against an open Carolina blue sky. Glistening white caps and slow ripples of water underneath created a soothing melody. She felt peaceful in heart and mind as she was captivated with the view and Robert's company.

Laney, Sandra, and Leslie were still looking at their phones, and remained silent.

"It can wait," Leslie said. "Hold your tongue for now, please. Let's get back to the beach house. We can stay one more night there, deal with this and then head home in the morning."

"That's best, I guess. Wow, I can't imagine," said Laney, turning away so Carrie wouldn't see as she wiped a tear from her eye.

Sandra was trying not to cry, but it was useless; she was crying, so she put her shades on to hide the tears. She didn't want Carrie to see and ask questions.

"Well, he was a donkey's backside and an arrogant as hell, but no one deserved that," said Sandra.

"She needs to deal with this in a safe environment with us back at the beach house. We can get her home in the morning. Dear Lord, help us get through this night," said Laney.

"Thank the good Lord she left her phone. She would have missed out on all this contentment. I love seeing her so happy right now. Just look at them; they are a great couple. I know that sounds like matchmaking, but I see it. Y'all do, too, right?" asked Leslie.

"Yes, totally. Robert is a great catch, and I would trust him with my life. I told you so the first night they met," said Laney.

Sandra shook her head as she sniffled, "I see something beautiful happening right in front of me. Look at the spark between the two of them. Yes, they would be amazing together. But now we are going back to the beach house to tell her something horrible. Monumental even, pivotal. How are we going to do this? Life is just not fair sometimes."

When they docked, the ladies said their goodbyes with promises to send out details for a time later in the month. They all exchanged cell phone numbers and promised to get Carrie in the loop and forward those contacts to her.

After a few hugs and help to the car with bags, they were off to the beach house. Not wanting to miss out on any vision of the ladies, Robert and Ben stood on the corner of the marina dock and waved to them as they drove out of the parking lot.

"What a wonderful and magical weekend! I think I am as high as you can get, without spirits, of course. But I don't think there is a drink that could ever compare. This feeling can't be bottled or replicated. It's just not possible. If I could, I would bottle it right now and make a fortune. If I could capture the sights and display them, it would be a work of fine art in the most ornate frame. The sounds would be a symphony performed by the world's most elite orchestra. The feeling would be like soft cotton, and the smell would be sweet like a honeysuckle," said Carrie as she was still watching Ben and Robert waving from the dock.

Chapter Twenty-Three

Sunday Evening
with Robert

Robert went back to his studio apartment in Atlantic Beach. It was small, but he spent most of his life on boats, so the small space suited him. He enjoyed traveling up and down the coast as much as he could, and it spared him the need of anything more extravagant. He needed little, and his motto of "less is more" was his new approach in life. Since retirement, he traveled as much as possible, visiting friends by water and land. If he was stagnant very long, he thought too much. If he thought too much, he thought of his late wife, Beth. To divert his attentions, he occupied himself by going on excursions. His many connections in the wholesale and retail yacht sales kept him engaged in travel. Friends extended invitations often, and Robert took advantage of as many as possible. When a boat needed to be moved up or down the eastern seaboard for a buyer or seller, he was always more than willing to assist in that transport.

It had been a while since Beth's death, and his friends thought he should be in a new relationship by now. He heard it often and it annoyed him. He would move on when he was ready and until now, the opportunity had not presented itself. Although he enjoyed Carrie's company and thought she was intelligent, kind, and respectful, deep down, he questioned if he was ready. How could he gauge the time? In his opinion, there was no checklist and no timeline. He thought it was more of a feeling, and he would know when it was right.

He didn't even know if Carrie felt the same way. He thought so, but it would not serve him well to assume. He was just looking forward to the lunch at the end of the week. That would help him settle his mind and confirm if the progression towards a relationship may be possible.

When Robert walked into the apartment, it occurred to him for the first time that he needed more than this in life. He had made this a cocoon, a protective shell, and he never realized he was doing so. The studio apartment was dark and small, with no personal items on display. After he sold the house, he put much of the furnishings in storage. He could not look at them. There were no children to pass things on to, so what would he do with the collection of art, furniture, trinkets, and possessions that were reminders of Beth?

Friends had suggested an estate sale. He couldn't do it. The suggestion to donate them to a women's shelter to help domestic violence victims seemed more reasonable to him, but he still couldn't bring himself to do anything with Beth's treasured heirlooms. Some of the furniture had been in her family for many years. Perhaps one day he could look at them not as reminders of her absence, but of the love they shared. Until this weekend, he thought she was the one and only love of his life. He never fathomed that he would be attracted to another woman, but Carrie had awakened in him feelings he thought were dead. He admitted it felt good, and he didn't feel guilty. He had always imagined that he may feel guilty. Like he was betraying Beth if he was attracted to someone after her death. He was thankful and relieved that this was not the case.

As he unpacked his bag, his mind wandered to thoughts of their conversations over the weekend. They agreed to discuss chapters of their lives. They hardly got past the decade of their 20s before conversation led into many areas with such ease. He could feel life, see life, and appreciate life when he was with her. She was more than a breath of fresh air—she was a cool breeze that refreshed everything around her.

It was only one weekend, but he felt like he had spent a month with Carrie. But it was a good feeling. It felt as if he knew her so well after just a weekend. From the moment they danced on Friday night, to the time on the yacht, the night in Charleston, to the moment they said goodbye, it felt like they were the only two people in the world. She had him captivated, and it was invigorating and confusing, all at the same time.

Robert poured himself a bourbon and went out to the patio to enjoy the evening. The sun was setting, and the colors were miraculous over the Sound. He had watched many sunsets alone from that patio. It was the main reason he purchased the unit. It was small, but the view was spectacular, and sunsets were Beth's favorite. Every opportunity he could sit and enjoy the sunset, he did. It helped him feel like she was near. He noticed the breeze was picking up, and a rush of wind swept across the patio. It felt refreshing after the heat of the day.

The minutes grew to an hour, and an hour to two hours, and a refill of his drink. He spent the time watching kayaks and small boats coming into the piers lined up and down the Bogue

Sound. Grills had been lit, and the smell of hot dogs, hamburgers, and shrimp boils wafted through the air. A clothesline across the way held swimsuits, beach towels, and sunhats tossing in the wind. He could hear children laughing at the house next door. He realized how in tune he was to everything around him. Had all the sights and sounds been here all along and he just never noticed? This was not the first time grills were lit, suits were drying on the line, kayakers were on the Sound. Then he realized that it was the first time since he moved to the apartment that he was not pre-occupied with loneliness and grief. Until this weekend, he never realized how lonely he was for companionship. He felt alive again.

As the sun set on the horizon, the lantern post lights came on. They startled Robert, and it broke his gaze. It was then he realized it was late, and he had not eaten. He went back into the apartment and looked in the cabinets. Slim pickings. He usually ate out and cooked very little at home. There were so many wonderful local restaurants owned by friends he had known for years. He liked to support them, and he was a horrible cook. He found a can of smoked oysters, but no crackers to put them on. Deli cheese was in the fridge drawer, but no bread to make a grilled cheese. His best option, one of his favorites—he walked down to the Shark Shack to get a shrimp burger.

As he walked down the sidewalk, he enjoyed the new awareness of life going on all around him. If Carrie had this effect on him with just one weekend, he could only imagine the way his life would be with her in it consistently. These thoughts filled his mind as he strolled to the eatery. It was unexpected; but quite often, matters of the heart are unexpected and surprising. He could not help how he felt, but he also knew Carrie might not reciprocate. Hopefully, he could slow his heart down so his brain could catch up.

Robert took his sandwich to a picnic table overlooking the ocean. The moon was waning now. Maybe his grief and loneliness would do the same. He knew that one love could not replace another, but a new love could fit into a special place in his heart. The breeze picked up again, and for a moment he took a deep breath as it passed by and rippled his shirt. He smiled as he thought of Beth and how much she would like Carrie. That thought comforted him. He sat for a while feeling the breeze rush over him. There was no hurry to rush, no one to go home to, anyway. The moon's glow mesmerized him. Even as it was subsiding, it was still quite impressive in the clear skies. Robert's phone dinged, and it he pulled it out to look at the text. He smiled when he saw it was from Laney.

"CALL ME!" texted in all caps. That looked serious. He dialed her number.

"Thank you for calling me. Listen, we have a bit of a change of plans."

"Okay, so you mean the idea of getting together later this week when you ladies come back by Atlantic Beach? Do we have to cancel?" asked Robert.

"I am so sorry, but we have to go home."

"Home? Back to Greenway? Why?" asked Robert.

"There has been an accident. Well, a crime was committed. We don't know all the details, but it's awful."

Robert was pacing on the small piece of concrete that housed the picnic shelters at the pavilion. "Well, dear, what are you talking about?" he asked.

"It's Carrie."

Robert stopped his pacing, "Carrie! What's wrong?"

"Robert, her ex-husband, was killed in a robbery at her house. The burglars robbed the safe in the master closet. They stole his Porsche, and they came back and tried to set a fire. They cleaned his clock pretty bad and knocked him out cold. They set a fire to destroy any evidence or to keep him from talking. It worked. He's not talking. He died from smoke inhalation."

"Oh, dear God. That is awful. What can I do?" he asked as he sat back down at the picnic table.

"Just pray we can get her home, figure this thing out, and find her sons. They are in Europe on vacation with their wives. This is one colossal mess."

"Well, how is she, when did this happen?" asked Robert.

"While we were on the yacht. Bill was a no show for some enormous party planned by his girlfriend. I'm learning details as we get more calls and texts. They had a shindig planned for some big announcement they were going to make, but Bill didn't show up. My bet is that it was their engagement announcement. We've been getting details from Debra, the station secretary. She made it her business to find our cell numbers and text us all this morning, including Carrie. Thank God she left her phone at the beach house. That gave us some time to get her there and tell her in a better way, if there is ever a better way to say the father of your children is dead."

"Well, where is his girlfriend now?" asked Robert. "Maybe she can shed some light on this and help make some sense of it all."

"That's the weird part. She packed up and left town. No one has a clue where she went. Bizarre."

"Yes, indeed. What about her house, can she stay there?" asked Robert.

"They think so, it was mostly minor smoke damage. They put the fire out with a fire extinguisher that was in the kitchen. Jerry, the manager at the station, went over there to look for him and found him in the closet. From what we can tell, the only thing that burned were the suits that Bill left in the closet. They just smoldered."

"Oh, my word. That is a mess. So, here is what I'll do. I will stay in town and wait to hear from you. If there is anything I can help you with ... anything at all, please call me. Let Carrie know I'm thinking of her."

"I will, thank you. So sorry we can't meet you and Ben for lunch later in the week. That just stinks. We'll plan to get together in about a month, like we said. I'll take over the planning for it and get you some details," said Laney.

"I'll wait to hear from you. I imagine Carrie will need some time, so just keep me posted."

Chapter Twenty-Four

Monday Back home to Greenway

Leslie hung up the phone with the owners of the two cottages they had reserved at the other beaches for the rest of the week. *"Best laid plans of mice and men" she said.*

She thought about the brutally long night and how Carrie was dealing with the news. Jerry, the station manager, had been helpful to some degree, but he was taking the news with a great deal of difficulty himself. They learned he stayed with Karen until she abruptly packed and left town. Karen and Bill had bought a new home together and moved in a few weeks before. For her to leave town seemed odd, with a station to run and a brand-new home. The divorce had been final for quite a while, and they were free to do whatever they wanted—get married or keep living in sin. Leslie always thought they were never concerned about appearances or sin; they were only concerned about themselves.

She loaded up more items in the Suburban and shut the door. When she looked up, she saw Carrie sitting on the deck with her head on her folded arms resting on the railing. Although Bill was horrible to her through the affair and divorce, they shared a long life together and it had yielded them two sons and a very lucrative business.

As she walked up the steps, she thought about the house they once shared. Thankfully, not much damage, according to Jerry. Thank goodness Carrie had a fire extinguisher in the kitchen. Jerry already planned for a restoration crew to come make repairs and clean up. Carrie had been relieved to hear the other part of the house was on a different circulation system, so the damage was minimal. She said that she would stay on the second floor, as usual. She had grown accustomed to staying up there, anyway. Leslie had offered to have her come and stay at her house, but Carrie insisted on staying at home.

The sun was already smoldering hot, and Leslie was feeling it on her neck as she walked over to Carrie. She had broken a sweat and was glistening.

"Hey there, want some company? But can we go inside? It's scorching out here," said Leslie.

Carrie looked up, and Leslie could see that her eyes were still red, and the dark circles under them certainly meant she had not slept at all. Carrie wiped her tears, stood up, and pressed out her sundress with her hands as she struggled to gather her composure. She walked over to Leslie, took her hand, and they walked inside together. They sat on the sofa and Leslie held her for a little while.

"Listen, you are burning up from that heat. I'm going to get you some iced tea. You want lemon?" asked Leslie.

"No lemon, I think I have enough of those right now," Carrie replied with a forced laugh.

Leslie returned with the glass of iced tea. Carrie took a sip and stared into space for a few seconds. Leslie could tell she was deep in thought, just not sure if it was a good thought or bad, anger or grief. She just looked empty.

"What's going on in that pretty little head of yours? I sure hope you're remembering something good. Try not to dwell on the bad bits," said Leslie.

Carrie shook her head as if to shake the thoughts out. She was trying to grasp all her emotions at once. It was a wave upon wave of emotions, and she felt like she was drowning.

"You know, when Bill and I were dating, I thought he was going to be the love of my life. That we would grow old together. I truly fell in love with him the moment I laid eyes on him. I think it was the same for him as me. At least I thought so. We were together maybe six months before he proposed. Then we married in three months—so soon. We probably never knew if we were compatible," said Carrie.

"Well, y'all were compatible enough for long enough. Two awesome sons and a business you grew together," said Leslie.

Carrie had to agree and patted Leslie's hand. "You're right. So why in the hell did he have to blow it all up. I mean, I knew he was acting strange for a while, then I found out about the affair. How did I not know?"

"Well, I imagine most wives don't know, Carrie. They're in denial, shock, and disbelief. Most husbands don't come home, sit down at the dinner table, and say, *"Hey Honey, I'm sleeping with the neighbor down the street."* You're not the only one to discover that secret about their husband. But I have to say the way you handled it, with such grace, is rare. You've been a true, humble, and kind person with everything you've done since the day he left," said Leslie, as she wrapped her arm around Carries shoulder.

"There were moments when I didn't want to be. There were times when I could've strangled him. But I knew my integrity was far more important than retaliation—especially for the boys. I wanted to do all I could to keep them from resenting their dad. I didn't want resentment to be an emotion that I fueled. If they hated him on their own, then so be it. But I was not going to light that fire."

"That's right, honey. You did good."

The morning was slipping away from them, but Leslie knew this time for Carrie to talk and get her feelings out was time spent wisely. It might keep her grounded when she returned home. Get everything in check now, and later she would be glad that she had.

"You know, Leslie, I remember a dance we went to when we first started dating. He was so handsome and polite. At one time, he loved to dance, and he was good at it. I'm not sure why he stopped ... or why we stopped. That dance was like our third date. We hadn't even kissed yet, since I was very shy. But that night when he walked me back to the car, he kissed me. It was not a long kiss, just a soft kiss. He asked permission to kiss me first. Then he took me home and walked me to the door. He asked if he could kiss me again, but mama turned the porch light on and scared the crap out of us. Where did that Bill go? What happened to him?" asked Carrie with a fade in her voice.

Leslie wiped a tear from her eye and tried to respond in the most genuine way without making the matter worse. "From what I knew of Bill, he was empire driven. He had a taste for success that could never be satisfied; he stayed hungry for it. Carrie, you know, we all change as we grow older. I know I have. I know Stan has. Don't read too much into that. There is nothing wrong, we just change sometimes. Sometimes two people change together, but that wasn't what happened in your case."

"Our first year of marriage was so good. We were poor as dirt, but we made it. Then we both got involved in the syndicated radio business, then came television, then came multiple stations. Within five years, we went from snail pace to running like cheetahs. We focused more on growing the business than we did on building our relationship. It's likely that was the demise and the beginning of the end of our relationship," said Carrie.

"I wouldn't say that. I think through the years, y'all took time to get away, take trips. I thought you did alright in that area," said Leslie.

"No, it looked like we did. We took the trips, yes, we took time to get away, but it was always for business. It was for something Bill had to investigate: the next franchise, the next station, a convention. It was never for us. I only went since I was the media coordinator and news editor, that just happened to be his wife. That's all. I went as an employee, Leslie."

Sandra and Laney came down the stairs with their bags, and Laney headed to the kitchen to pack up the rest of the items. Sandra joined Leslie and Carrie.

"Well, looks like you are going to have to face the music. So how are you planning on doing that, Carrie?" asked Sandra.

"Good Lord woman, give me a minute or two. I just learned about this last night. Can I take a few deep breaths?" asked Carrie.

"You can, but let's get realistic; someone has to make plans. If his girlfriend ran off, that leaves the boys. Carrie, they need for you to help them with the arrangements. When do they get back in town?" asked Sandra.

Carrie looked at her phone, "Calendar says tomorrow. Oh my gosh, Sandra, you're right. I really wish you were wrong," said Carrie as she covered her face with her hands.

Laney came into the living room. "Do they know yet, you think?" asked Laney.

"If they did, they would have called me. Where they are is very secluded. They'll have cell service when they get back to base camp at the lodge. How do I handle this, how do I get word to them? Jerry told me it is getting harder to keep this a secret. Employees are talking. It's Monday morning, and Bill and Karen aren't there. Debra, the station secretary, knows about it too, so word is going to spread."

"You're probably going to need to tell them by phone at this point. I know that's hard, but can you call the lodge?" asked Laney.

Carrie looked at her phone to find the email with the itinerary. "I have the number, but how do I do this? I really think the sooner the better," said Carrie, as tears streamed down her cheeks and her voice faltered as she dropped to the sofa. "Help me. Please help me."

They came up with a plan to call the resort and get word for the boys to call Carrie. They continued to pack up the car and grabbed some cold drinks from the refrigerator. Before leaving the house, they sat down with Carrie to make the phone call. It didn't take long to get connected to the base camp resort. The resort manager said that they were still in the countryside and would be back within the next three hours. Carrie left specific details for them to call her before they did anything else. She told the manager how important it was to reach them as soon as possible because there was a family emergency.

They headed home to Greenway to face the task before them.

Chapter Twenty-Five

Monday with Stan

Stan walked into the bank and headed to Mitch's office. He knocked three times on the door frame.

"Stan! My man, come in. How are you?" said Mitch as he reached across his desk to shake Stan's hand.

"I'm good, Mitch. How is Monday morning going for you so far?" asked Stan.

Mitch pointed to his phone and asked, "Have you heard from Leslie?"

Stan shook his head no. Then he looked puzzled by the question. The men both knew the girls were away for the rest of the week.

"Why would you ask that, Mitch? What's up? Anything wrong?"

Mitch rubbed his eyes and sat back down at his desk. "Have a seat, Stan. It appears Bill Hargrove died over the weekend, but it's hush-hush for now. Tragedy, he stumbled on a break-in at Carrie's house. They knocked him out in a struggle. Later they came back and tried to set a fire to destroy any evidence. Bill died from smoke inhalation. Stupid kids, most likely. They stole his prized possession, too, the Porsche. They ditched it in the tar river. If he was alive, that would kill him now." Mitch. said.

"My God, that's awful. How did you find out?" asked Stan.

"Sandra just called. I imagine you'll hear from Leslie soon. They're on their way back now," said Mitch.

"I left my phone in the truck most of the morning. I bet I missed her call. Well, let's get to business before she calls. So, where we are on this purchase? How much longer before we can close?"

"Do you have the last of the list I emailed you last week?"

"Yes, It's all here in this envelope."

"It'll be about one business day before we can close it up. I'll push it through as fast as I can and let you know when to come down. Expect it to be by late afternoon tomorrow. Sit tight— you are in the short rows now, my friend," said Mitch.

With business out of the way, the two turned their conversations back to Bill Hargrove.

"What an awful way to go. You know Bill and I were never friends or ran in the same circles, but still that is horrible for anyone," said Mitch.

"He was always a bit too highfalutin' for me," replied Stan.

"Come to think of it, I'm not sure he really had genuine friends, just business acquaintances. I manage his business loans, but he was so paranoid about me knowing too much that he took his checking accounts down the street to another bank."

Stan nodded and said, "Yep, sounds about right. Did they catch the guys who broke in?"

"I don't think so. I wonder if Carrie is going to want to live there now. I know if it was me, and it was Sandra that died in our house, I couldn't stay there."

"Same here. She might sell it. Leave the past behind and start fresh. Lord knows she needs a fresh start. But then again, Bill has not lived there in a while, so hard to say what she will decide."

"Well, apparently Carrie met someone over the weekend, and they hit it off pretty dang good. Sandra said fireworks were flying like it was the Fourth of July."

"Are you serious? That would be awesome. I hope it works out for her. She deserves to have someone in her life. She's an amazing person. I know my Leslie thinks the world of her. Hey, keep me posted if you hear anything. I've got some workers waiting for me to move them to another plot. Take care, and thanks for everything."

Stan left the bank and headed back to the farm. He was lost in thoughts anticipating the moment he would tell Leslie about the farm. Just as he parked the truck, his cell phone rang.

"Hey, how are you?" asked Leslie.

"I'm great, but it sounds like the trip is getting cut short. Terrible business about Bill. I was just at the bank and Mitch filled me in. How is Carrie?"

Leslie paused as she walked away from the others. "She's a mess one minute, and a rock the next. She got up with the boys. They are in Europe on one of those country hiking excursions. They have their hands full now with the business, but they can do it. But did you hear about Karen?"

"No. Mitch didn't say anything about Karen. What's up with Karen?" he asked.

"She left town. Just left town with no clue about where she was going. She told Jerry, the station manager, that she would send a moving company for her things and probably sell the house."

"My, my, my—they don't think she had anything to do with this, do they?"

"No, at least I don't think so. She was there with a house full of guests. Stan, it was supposed to be their engagement announcement. Jerry said she totally lost it."

"Well, I guess she did. What a flip on a dime change of plans there, huh? One minute you're going to get married to a man; the next minute you're going to bury him. So, who is going to take care of the arrangements? This is awkward, right?" He asked with a bit of sarcasm in his voice.

Leslie paused. She could hear Sandra calling her name, "Listen, I have to run. We are trying to get Carrie home now. But to answer your question, it looks like Carrie is going to help the boys with everything. She says she's fine with that. She can do that for them."

"Well, that's Carrie for you, always thinking of others. Listen, drive carefully—it looks like storms are popping up. How about I put a slab of ribs on the smoker, and we can enjoy that when you get home? I'll even make my famous mac and cheese. I know how you love that combination."

"Now that right there is why I married you. You know how to spoil me. Add some merlot to that combo tonight."

"You got it, babe. I love you. Be safe."

"See you soon. I love you, too," replied Leslie.

Chapter Twenty-Six

Monday with Sandra and Mitch

Sandra was glad to be home. The disaster with Bill made her more aware of how much she loved Mitch. She could not imagine life without him. It also put into perspective the work they had been putting into having a child. If it were just her and Mitch, she would be perfectly fine with that life. On the ride home, she decided to talk with him about adoption as soon as she got home. A child out there needed love just as much as they needed to love one. Adoption would relieve her of the fertility treatments but giving up on having their own child, which would take some getting used to. It was time to consider the option, and it amazed her at how a single event had aligned her perspective.

After Leslie dropped Sandra off at the side door, she looked around the yard to see if Mitch had mended any of the fence since Friday morning. To her delight, he had taken care of one side of the property line, and it looked great. He was such a skilled craftsman. He acted like he hated making repairs, but if he did, he would have hired it out to be done. She knew it was therapy for him to work with his hands, and he enjoyed being outside after being couped up inside the bank all week. He looked relaxed as he puttered around the house working on various projects. There was much to do with their historical "rambling wreck," as they often called it (affectionately, of course).

When she walked up the back porch, she noticed the water in the pool was crystal clear. He had taken care of that as well. She walked down to the wrap-around porch to find Mitch sitting there in the wicker rocking chair with a glass of tea on the table and, in his hands, the *Greenway News*.

"Hello there, handsome, how are you?" asked Sandra as she walked over to him, and he stood to his feet, "I missed you."

He picked her up in a bear hug. That was always the way he greeted her every single day. If he did not, she knew something was off.

"Miss me? Not as much as I missed you. I'm glad you won't be gone for a week, but sad to hear why. Come and sit down," he said as he took her hand and led her to the swing. He put his arm around her as they eased into a leisurely back-and-forth motion, and Sandra laid her head on his shoulder.

"Mitch, it's awful. I mean, yes Bill, was Bill—a total jerk, but nobody deserved to die like that, and the boys have lost their dad and their boss. That is going to be a monumental change in their lives. He barely gave them any control over anything. How is that supposed to work now? You're their banker. How will it work?"

"I know," said Mitch. "He really never let them in on the business plan when we would renew the operating budget. He was all hands-on, but he was letting Karen in more on some of that planning. I thought that was odd. Not your sons, your heirs, but your girlfriend?"

"Speaking of Karen, she hauled tail out of town. She told Jerry she would send a moving company for her things. What a way to show your true colors, huh?" asked Sandra.

"I heard that, too. Yes, that seems squirrelly, but giving her position, their engagement dinner debacle, I imagine she felt overwhelmed and embarrassed. Would you blame her? They had a big deal dinner party and Bill was a no-show, and they find him dead at his ex-wife's residence. What a mess."

They rocked back and forth in the swing for a while and Karen wanted to tell him what was really on her heart. *Was the time right? Shouldn't he be at work? Why was he home at this time of day?*

"Mitch, why are you home, shouldn't you be at the bank? Mondays are your busiest day, right?"

He kissed her and took her hand and said, "I wanted to be here when you got home; the bank will wait. I went in this morning and stayed most of the day. I've been online remotely, so it's fine. How are you? When you left, I was worried about you. You seemed a bit on the overcast side. I hope before all of this happened you found your sunshine again."

"I was feeling pretty down. I think the combination of these medications and the defeat of each pregnancy test is about to do me in, Mitch. We've exhausted all options, and it's getting tiresome. I'm tired. I have something to tell you or ask you, or well, discuss. I don't know how to word it," she said as she looked at him with a nervous sideways smile.

Mitch turned to her in the swing and said, "Well, here I am. Tell me, ask me, or whatever it is you need. I'm here."

Sandra didn't even realize it, but she was shaking. Mitch noticed and held both of her hands.

"Hon, you're trembling. What's wrong? You're scaring me."

"I'm scaring myself. I think I'm done with this fertility thing. Are you okay with that? Would I be letting you down? Are you disappointed in me? I'm so sorry, I just don't think I can do it anymore, Mitch. It's knocking me down a black hole. I'm surprising myself by even admitting this," said Sandra as a tear trickled down her cheek.

Mitch looked at Sandra and his eyes filled with tears. He held her until she finally stopped trembling and broke down crying. It had been building up for so long—the tug of war with the battle to conceive. She had finally surrendered, and it felt so incredible to drop the load of the burden from her soul. She said it, and she meant it. Now she would accept it.

"San, I am so proud of you. You have been a warrior through this entire process—never giving up, praying, trying, taking meds, seeing specialists. No, I am not disappointed. I am so incredibly proud of you. I have been waiting for you to come to this point on your own. You did. I'm okay with it. Really, I am."

They held each other for a while, rocking slowly in the swing. Mitch had noticed every month how heartbroken she was. It had seeped into her entire persona, and she was losing her sparkle and spirit.

"Something else I'd like to talk about, and I hope you will consider the thought since you mentioned it before," said Sandra.

Mitch looked puzzled, "Okay, what is that? You really did have a breakthrough this weekend."

"I know we've talked about this before and I have been opposed to it, but would you still be up for considering adoption?" asked Sandra. She waited for his response with her head tilted down, and her big brown eyes looking up at him.

Mitch said nothing for a moment. He put his head in his hands as he wiped the tears from his eyes. He turned to look at her. Sandra was eyeing him cautiously.

"Sandra, I would love to consider adoption, absolutely. As a matter of fact, I've already done some research, but I was waiting for the right time to come up. Gosh, this is such a good thing. Sandra, we have so much to offer a child that needs love. We could do this. We can. I just know it."

Mitch embraced her for a few moments before he picked her up and carried her over the threshold into the hallway. She laughed and Mitch grinned. They both knew where he has heading—straight to the bedroom. Anytime he was over elated with joy and feeling amorous, this was his process to their love-making. He carried her to the bedroom. This is one of the reasons she watched her weight. She always wanted him to be able to sweep her off her feet. She thought it was one of the sweetest things Mitch did, and it certainly helped to keep their love life thrilling.

As he carried her through the bedroom door, he looked at her and smiled, "Now that it doesn't seem so much like a command performance, let's have some fun."

They both laughed.

Chapter Twenty-Seven

Monday with Laney

Leslie dropped Laney off in front of her house and waved goodbye as she watched her unlock the door and go inside. She was deep in thought. She couldn't focus on anything without thinking about Ben. She needed to look at the calendar to see what was on the agenda for the week ahead. There would be time to meet with the bank and check on some locations for a suitable venue for a new restaurant. That unquestionably was going to be her focus over the next few weeks.

As she walked through the kitchen, her cell phone rang. It was Ben. Her heart skipped a beat, and then she took a deep breath to gather her composure to answer.

"Hello," she answered with her hand over her heart.

"Well, hello there! You make it back to Greenway, okay? I hope I'm not calling at a bad time. Do you have a second?" he asked as he drove down the road and smiled as he thought of her.

"I do. What's on your mind?"

"This may be forward of me, and I hope you are going to be okay with what I'm going to ask you."

"Well, if you don't ask me, you'll never find out. Fire away—what's on your mind?"

"I'm going to be heading your way later in the week. The fundraiser is being rescheduled that I was planning to attend. So, I worked out a book signing at a town near your neck of the woods, New Bern. Would it be good to stop by? We could grab some coffee, a glass of wine, or you could just show me the garden you were telling me about. Either way, would that work for you?" asked Ben. He braced himself for her reply.

Laney was bouncing around in her seat at her kitchen table, and she took another deep breath, trying to sound calm. "Oh yeah, New Bern, you're right, you won't be far away at all. What day will you be coming through here?" asked Laney.

"Most likely Saturday. The book signing is Sunday afternoon. I can get a room nearby and drive over there on Sunday morning," said Ben.

"That is exciting about the book signing. Which book—the children's book or the cookbook?"

"This is for the cookbook and a taste testing and sampling of some recipes. A book club is featuring it and they're preparing the food."

"I like that. It's sort of the concept I used with restaurants and equipment. We would cook onsite and show them how to get the most of what they purchased. That was my favorite part of the job."

"That sounds amazing, but you actually didn't answer my question. So, does that sound like a plan? I can be there on Saturday if you can do dinner. Anywhere nearby to eat that you would recommend?"

She laughed, "Yes, you goofball—here! We can cook at my house. Are you okay with that?"

There was a silence on the line. Laney thought she had might have made that sound like an overnight invitation. She quickly clarified her meaning, "Rather than going out, I thought we could cook here. As for hotels, I would try The Grand of Greenway. It's a quaint bed-and-breakfast and they turn your pillow down with gourmet chocolates. I can vouch for the breakfast buffet. I helped them create the menu. If that's not your style, the Courtyard and Hilton are a bit further down the road."

"The Grand sounds like a plan. I'll book it and let you know when I get there. Hey, how is Carrie holding up? This must be like a train wreck for her. Any idea when the funeral will be?"

"You know, one minute she's losing it, and the next it's like she finds some duct tape to hold it together. She'll be a rock for her sons, and they are going to need her right now. Carrie is from the good stuff. She will be fine. Thanks for asking about her, though. I think a private service will be held this Friday."

"Are you sure this weekend will work with the funeral being on Friday? I know Robert is looking forward to the get-together next month. For now, he just feels like he needs to give Carrie some time. You know, with all that's going on, it makes sense. However, I will have you know he is quite taken by her," said Ben.

"No, it's fine. This weekend will be great. I'll need something to brighten my life after that service dulls things up a bit. And yes, that heartbeat radar is off the charts when you see those two together. Time will tell, but I think they are adorable together," said Laney.

"I won't keep you any longer. Listen, I hope you have the best day you can, and I look forward to seeing you on Saturday."

"Same here. Bye Ben."

Laney sat down and leaned back in the kitchen chair. Did he really like her, or was she reading more into it? Or did he just want to continue to have a colleague conversation about the chef world. She needed to get her signals straight. She was off in reading men in the last couple of years. It was hard to tell when she was dealing with a friendship or something more. Her personality was the same with women and men, and some men thought she was flirting when she wasn't. Then some thought she was just a friend when she wanted it to be more.

Once her last relationship fell apart, she decided she might join the convent and swear off men for life. It was just a joke she had with herself. But at least that way she would not be the small-town spinster, the kooky old lady, affectionately called Aunt Laney by her friends' children. The godmother to cousins' babies or the single older lady at the weddings. She contemplated her future. She had played the scenario out in her head a million times.

Laney walked out to the garden and gave some thought as to what they could cook for dinner on Saturday night. Most of her vegetables were still in the early stages, so she knew she would have to go to the farmer's market. Something simple enough so they could talk and not be so occupied with a recipe. She could have a fire in the porch fireplace. Or just put candles in there. Yes, that could work—just candles. No wait, that might look like she was setting a mood. Okay, scratch the fireplace. They could eat on the screen porch and cook at the outside kitchen. It was her favorite place to cook in the spring.

The lights around the brick courtyard added a nice ambience. She really had to give this some thought. She wanted to make a suitable impression. She usually called Carrie about this type of thing, but not this time. She would rely on Leslie's advice and give her a ring later.

She pulled weeds in the garden and turned the sprinklers on. As she was walking to the front porch, she saw the newspaper delivery boy ride by. She watched him ride by each house and sling the paper to the porches. She liked the charm of her street, laced with flags on front porches, and flowerpots adorning steps. She went over to pick up the paper.

Laney sat on the front porch hammock and looked over the pages of the small paper. This paper needed a chef's highlight and a local venue to teach classes. She couldn't get that idea out of her mind. A new restaurant and Ben were the only things she was able to think about. She looked to see if there was any mention of the accident with Bill. Fortunately, it had not made the news yet. That was good. It would give Carrie and her sons a chance to catch their breath before the locals started chattering.

As she was lost in her daydreaming and planning, she reminded herself she needed to be careful and to not get too excited. She understood all things had to come together in a perfect plan. Location, right partners, loan terms, managers, staff. It may be a pipe dream, but it was her dream. It wasn't long before she drifted off to sleep in the hammock and continued to dream the same in her slumber. She was not asleep long when a horn blew in her driveway. It startled her and she jumped up when she saw a floral delivery service in the driveway. As she wiped the drool away from her chin, she walked down the steps to greet the driver.

The young man came up to the porch and met her at the bottom step, "I have a delivery for Laney Rich."

"That's me," said Laney.

"Sign here, please."

Laney jotted her name, and the deliveryman gave her an enormous bouquet of sunflowers.

"Thank you," said Laney, and she sat down to read the card.

Thank you for bringing some sunshine into my life. I look forward to seeing you this weekend. Best, Ben.

Laney smiled and thought she would put candles in the fireplace, and she might even buy a new dress.

Chapter Twenty-Eight

Tuesday with Carrie and Her Sons

Carrie left the funeral home along with her sons, John and Jason. The boys did an excellent job of preparing the details for the service. They barely needed her help, but she accompanied them for moral support. The service arrangements were private by invitation only, and later there would be a memorial service open to friends. Carrie wondered who would come. Bill had innumerable business associates, but few friends.

On the ride back home, Carrie thought the boys were unusually quiet, and that concerned her. She didn't want to try to force them to talk about their emotions, but soon the three of them needed to have a serious conversation about the future.

"Hey, listen, boys, I am so proud of how well you orchestrated everything at the funeral home. You did good," said Carrie.

She learned through the years that they could often be like their father, and it was best to approach with kind words of affirmation first, then get down to business.

"Thanks Mom, you taught us a thing or two. I told you we could manage," Jason said as he reached over and touched her gently on the shoulder.

"That you did. I really came along for emotional support, and I will be available for anything you need help in the coming weeks. I mean that—anything," she said as she turned around to look at John in the backseat of the Mercedes.

"Mom, I know this is difficult for you, but you don't have to hold our hands. For God's sake, you and dad divorced. This puts you between a rock and a hard place. You shouldn't have to go through this. We have it covered," said John.

There was a long silence, then Jason spoke up and took the plunge into the conversation he and John had on the plane trip back home. They filled the hours long flight time discussing options about the business.

"Mom, it may be too soon to have this conversation, but you know me. I'm not putting anything off – not even the hard stuff. Its business related. Are you up for hearing some thoughts?" asked Jason.

"Sure, I'm listening."

John spoke up and asked, "So, I will take the lead on this since it was me that brought the idea up to begin with. How would you feel if we sell the business?"

Carrie leaned back in her passenger seat and looked out the window. They were turning into her driveway at home. When the car reached the horse stables, Carrie said, "Pull up to the stable shelter."

Jason drove the car to the lane beside the stables and stopped under the covered shelter. He got out of the car and went to open Carrie's door for her. John joined them at the shelter, and they sat down on the wooden bench out front. Carrie put a hand on each boy's knee and opened her hand for them to hold hers. They sat quietly, holding hands for a moment, looking over the estate and the house where Bill died.

"So, are you going to say anything? I know you may not be ready to talk about it right now. But what are your thoughts?" asked Jason.

"My thoughts? Well, I didn't see that coming. Especially so soon. Why? You boys have been in the business since you were teenagers. You know it inside and out, and you are good at it, too. Why would you sell?" asked Carrie.

"Well, you know mom, John and I talked about it before now, leaving the business, we just didn't share those thoughts with anyone. We weren't growing there, and Dad left us out of the business plan for so long it would be impossible to catch up to speed now," said Jason.

"Mom, you know dad basically forced us to be in this business. It was not what I wanted, but it was clear if we didn't do things his way, we would suffer the consequences. He had us where he wanted us. He got us into the business, paid us well, set us up on the fast track, then lured us into so much debt by cosigning loans. It would have been nice to know the business plan, the goal, the projection and well, anything. I'm just over it, really," said John.

Carrie stood up and turned around and looked at Jason. He was the one that always appeared to be thriving in the media world, and he excelled in contract negotiations. He and Karen had orchestrated many impressive media buys in radio and tv syndicated shows. They traveled to various locations in each of their markets and always came home with the contracts signed. This took her by surprise, and she wondered if they were being completely honest with each other, or if Jason was keeping the peace with his brother and going along with John's idea.

"Jase, are you sure you want to consider this idea? You live and breathe Eastern Media; it's all you've ever known. John, you wanted to be in the business, ever since your dad let you DJ and host your own radio show," said Carrie.

John stood up and walked over to the car and leaned on the hood. He was choosing his words carefully. "Mom, I don't like working there. It's what I thought I would always do. But, having said that, I need to be honest with myself. It just isn't as enticing to me as it once was. I feel like I mastered it and yes, I can run that business and stay in that business, but I don't think it's in me anymore."

Carrie stood up, looked up at the house, turned around, and looked at the empty stables. She sat down and motioned for them to come back to the bench to have a seat.

"Well, now, I didn't know you felt this way. Y'all never said a word. But I understand why you did not. You didn't feel like you could. So, what is it you need from me? What do you need to hear from me to make things right for you? That's my only concern. It's up to the three of us now. We are it," said Carrie, as she wrapped her arms around both sons.

"Not right away, but as soon as we can get past the next few days, I would like for a firm to look at pricing the business to put it on the market. Dad had it appraised for banking purposes, so we should have a baseline to compare. Then we can see where we stand. I already have a buyer or two in mind to approach. The sharks have been circling for a couple of years," said John.

"Mom, what we really need from you is your blessing. You built that business, too. Although you haven't been in the business lately, we still know you have a soft spot for it in your heart. Do you want to come back and run the show? If so, maybe we can figure that out," said Jason.

"Wow, this is a lot of information to process right now. But I can tell you this—no, I do not want to come and run the business, especially without you two. If you really feel this way, I will support whatever you want. Get this funeral behind us, then let's talk with the attorneys and a firm."

John nodded as he put his sunglasses on. Jason had no comment, and that gave Carrie the confirmation that she was right. Jason was just going along with his older brother.

"It will change the trajectory of how things move forward now. Thank you for opening up and sharing your heart with me. Gosh, I just love y'all so much. But we are not rushing into this without a bit more conversation," said Carrie.

They returned to the car and drove to the house. As they entered the foyer, they saw the ozone equipment the restoration company had put in place. Carrie walked toward the kitchen. She could smell something, and it was not the smell of smoke.

"What is that smell? Is that what I think it is?" asked John.

"Oh, I would know that smell anywhere," said Jason.

They reached the kitchen, and there stood Mae over the stove. She was leaning down, trying to read the timer on the oven.

"Ma Mae!" shouted John, as he went to hug her.

"Do I smell your apple pies?" asked Jason.

"You sure do. You know I know what my boys like. Now, get over here and give Ma Mae some love."

Carrie stood back and watched in awe of how much love the boys had for Mae. She loved them like her own. She had been incredibly good at spoiling them throughout their childhood and continued to do so even though they were grown men. She made all their favorites for birthdays and holidays.

"Mae, you really shouldn't have gone through this trouble. Really, but I know the boys are glad you did," said Carrie.

"We sure are, how you been Ma Mae? I miss you. Work has kept me so busy, and that wife of mine has me even busier," said Jason as he peeked at the timer on the oven. "You have two minutes left. Alright Alright Alright now!" He rubbed his stomach to show her his anticipation of her treat.

"Busy getting y'all a baby yet?" Mae asked with a wide grin.

"No ma'am, not yet. We aren't quite ready for that just yet," replied Jason.

"You sure you know what you're doing, right? You know what I mean?" Mae said as she winked at him.

"Ma Mae, you better stop cutting up. You are a mess! And you are going to embarrass the boy," said John.

They sat down at the table and told Mae about the funeral plans. When they asked her to sit with the family, Mae broke down and cried. John gave her a hug. She was inconsolable. Her broad shoulders bounced with each sob. She had always been an emotional sort and John kept his arm around her shoulders to comfort her until she calmed down.

"I'm sorry boys, and Miss Carrie, I can't. I just can't. I can't go. I couldn't bear to see him. You understand, don't you?" said Mae as she inhaled and exhaled another round of sobs.

"We understand. We really do. Listen, how about I give you a ride home, or is Sonny coming to get you?" Asked John.

The timer on the oven buzzed and Mae nearly jumped out of her skin. She turned back to go to the oven and Carrie motioned for her to stay seated that she would get the pies.

"That would be good. Sonny said he may be late getting back. Miss Carrie, thank you for getting those pies out. Now, I folded that laundry, and I put it in them sealed bags like you asked. I know you said I could still have the week off, but I am going to be here every day for you, you hear? I finished the parlor last week as soon as I did that ironing. It's dusted, but not sure what it looks like now. I shut the door when I left though, so I hoped that helped," said Mae.

"Thank you, hon. I appreciate everything you do for us," replied Carrie.

John and Mae headed to the foyer. Jason and Carrie stayed at the table to talk for a while longer. Carrie felt like there was something more he wanted to discuss with her.

"What's up, Jason? You have something else buzzing around in the rafters. What is it?" asked Carrie.

"Mom, you do know all the details about how this went down right? It sounds like something straight out of a movie."

"I did. Various sources have filled me in. I know it was an engagement party. I know I was depending on Lee to set the alarm. I cannot imagine who he sent over here to do the work. He promised me he would do it and set the alarm. I know your dad came to set it. I know he would have gone to the closet to retrieve the firearm we kept there when he realized there were intruders. But I had it with me," said Carrie as her head fell into her hands.

"How do you feel about all of it? Are you okay?" asked Jason.

"You know, son, I felt like an engagement was imminent. No surprise there. I knew Karen would do something huge and over the top because that's her style. You know that. The part that's a mystery to me is why she left town and said she may not be back."

Jason rubbed his eyes and shook his head, "Mom, at first I thought she set him up. But then why? What would the motive be? Nothing. She had nothing to gain until after they were married. Plus, she was with her dinner party guests."

"The coroner's report was very clear. He was alive when the crooks started the fire, and he died of smoke inhalation. The report had noted a head wound. If I would have left the gun here, your dad could still be alive. I feel horrible. I'm so sorry Jase," said Carrie as she choked back tears as she reached for Jason's hand.

"Mom, we have no way of knowing that for sure. Those dumb asses could have had guns too, you know?"

"Nevertheless, I feel a tremendous amount of guilt. But to be sure he would have realized if I traveled, I would take the gun."

"Mom stop beating yourself up over it. That's what I wanted to say to you. Back to the earlier conversation. So, if we sell the business, will you be okay with that? You know we will make sure you receive a fair portion."

"I know. I'm not worried about that. I may want to sell the house too. It's time to begin life all brand new. But my intuition tells me that you are not as excited about leaving the business as John is. Am I right?"

"I will be. I mean, Karen and I were a team. I know you dislike hearing that since she was the reason for you and Dad falling apart. I could have hated her for it, but hell, she's good at what she does. Exceptionally good. But enough of this. How was your short-lived trip?"

"Well, it was incredible. Can I tell you something since we are sharing so much today?"

"Absolutely. Go."

"It's as much a surprise to me as it will be to you, I bet. Seems odd to bring it up now, but I have to tell someone that I met someone."

"Oh, like a gentleman someone, huh?" asked Jason with a grin.

Carrie nodded her head, "I don't know if anything will come of it, but he wants to see me again," she said with a reserved smile as she waited for her son's reaction.

"Mom, if it makes you happy, and if he is a good man, then I'm happy for you."

Carrie smiled. Jason gave her a hug, and she walked him to the door. She paused for a moment as a thought came to her.

"How are things with you and Brianne? Any better?"

"I think so, mom. I just can't ever gauge her mood swings. One day it's a roses and chocolate life, and the next day I'd swear she's mad at the world. But mostly, it feels like she's just mad at me. I have hope, but I'm getting tired. But the trip was good for us – I think, well at least I think so."

"I am sorry. I will keep you two in my prayers. That is enough heavy for one day. How about you go home and get some rest for a while. How about we have dinner later and top it off with Mae's pie? Is Brianne working?"

"Yes, she is working tonight, so it will just be me. I'll bring back a plate from Sam Jones BBQ. Sound good?"

Carrie gave him a hug, "Yes! You know I love some Sam Jones BBQ, but not as much as I love you. I'll see you later. Tell your brother to join us, and Cassie can come, too. But that wife of his will not want BBQ. She's on a vegan diet now." Carrie walked Jason to his car.

"I will. See you later with some BBQ. Oh, do you want to add their homemade fried chips, too?" asked Jason.

"You know it! Thanks, honey."

Chapter Twenty-Nine

The Farm at Willow Green

Leslie rolled over and rubbed her eyes as the morning sun peeked through the master bedroom window. When she glanced at the clock, she jumped up thinking she was late for work. Then she realized she was off for the week, laid back down and rolled over to go back to sleep, but the smell of bacon drifting in the room was more than she could resist. *Stan was great at cooking on the grill, but what was he doing cooking breakfast so late in the morning?* He had outdone himself on dinner the night before, with his special four cheese mac-n-cheese and cowboy baked beans to go with the ribs. Afterwards, he showed her how much he really missed her. *Carrie may be on to something—a little distance does make the heart grow fonder.*

She put on her robe and slippers and headed to the kitchen. As she walked down the hallway, she noticed that the table was set with vase of daisies in the center. There was a present sitting at her place. This was really unlike Stan, but she smiled because she kind of liked it.

"Good morning," said Leslie as she walked up and patted him on the shoulder. She headed to the coffeepot and poured a cup. "You want another cup?"

Stan was taking up bacon from an iron frying pan. "No thanks," he said as he took up the bacon and dropped four eggs in the hot grease.

"What has gotten into you? Are you planning on entering a cooking contest, or is it too wet to get in the fields after last night's rain?"

"No, on the cooking contest. I'll leave that kind of thing to Laney. Yes, it is too wet in the fields. I thought I would hang out with you today. You are still planning to take the day off, right?"

"Yes. I might as well since someone is already covering for me for the interview scheduling. What is this little something here? You have someone a gift, do you?"

"That is for you, but how about we eat breakfast first. You know I don't like cold eggs."

"Yes, I know that about you. Thank you for keeping mine in the pan a bit longer, you go ahead and eat yours. I don't know how you eat that runny stuff," said Leslie as she sipped her coffee.

After they ate, they cleaned up the kitchen. As Leslie turned from the sink, Stan handed her the gift. "Come sit down. I hope you will be as excited about this as I am. I'm a bit nervous and have some mixed emotions over it. I just hope that you. . ."

Leslie stopped him and held out her hand, "Just give it to me to open or you will never know."

She sat down at the table and unwrapped the gift. Stan was not much on presentation. He usually used newspaper to wrap gifts, and that always amused her. Once she pulled back the tape and saw what was inside, she stopped. She stared at the contents, then looked up at Stan with a puzzled expression.

"It's an old lunch box and a book. Why are you giving me an old copy of *Little Women*?"

"Look at the book ... closely," said Stan.

Leslie turned it over and looked at the front and back covers.

"I don't get it. Yes, I loved this book as a little girl. I don't know what happened to my copy."

Stan stretched over the table and opened the book to reveal the nameplate label on the inside cover. She was completely stunned. It looked like it could be her name. Stan handed it to her opened so she could see the old and tattered nameplate.

"I do - does this look familiar to you?"

She ran her hand over the inside nameplate, and it was obvious this was her copy of *Little Women*. In faded writing, she could see her name and the date that her grandmother gave it to her. As she recognized the handwriting, tears welled up in her eyes. She flipped through the pages and looked for a page in particular. Page 22 was missing because she and a cousin had an argument about who could take the next turn to read a page, and that page was ripped out in the struggle. The tears spilled over onto her cheeks. She wiped them away as she brought the book to her chest. As she embraced the book with one hand the other reached for Stan's hand.

"Stan, my gosh, where did you find this? This is mine. How did you find it?"

"Well, I have a few surprises for you. Take a closer look at the lunch box."

Leslie picked up the lunch box and giggled through her tears. "*The Partridge Family*! Gosh, I loved that show. I thought David Cassidy was *so* hot."

Stan said with a laugh, "How well I know, you have said that many times, when I have endured the pain of watching a rerun with you." He smiled and gave her a wink and waited to see her reaction when she found the colored pencils and stencils.

"Stan, this was my *Partridge Family* lunch box! Where on earth did you find this? The last place I remember seeing this was at my grandparents' house."

Stan handed her an envelope.

"What is this?" asked Leslie, holding the manilla envelope up to look at it closer.

"Well, like you said earlier, you're never going to find out unless you open it. So, go ahead. Open it."

Leslie pulled up the tabs on the clasp and reached inside. She removed documents from the envelope. When she unfolded the papers, she saw that the first page was a photo of the homeplace of her grandparents. She flipped it over to see the attachments—small shots of surveys and legal documents. She noticed the appraisal papers Sandra mentioned she saw on Mitch's desk. She wasn't sure what to do or say. She stared at the photo of her grandparents' home.

"Stan, what did you do? What are these papers about?"

Stan reached out for her hand across the table, took another sip of coffee and a deep breath.

"Well, my love, this is my gift to you for being the rock of my life, the love of my life, the mother of our sons, and my best friend. I know how upset you were when the homeplace at Willow Green sold. I know you always hoped it would stay in the family. It took me a little while, but I was finally able to make it happen. It's yours now."

Leslie began to cry. She cried so hard that Stan became concerned that he just made things worse. She cried until she could not even speak. Stan pulled her up from the chair and held her until she calmed a bit. Did he make things worse? Did this only remind her more of the nightmare she lived through so many years ago?

"Leslie, I need you to say something. What has you so upset? Did I mess up?"

She composed herself and held Stan's face in her hands. For a moment, she couldn't say anything at all. Then suddenly the simple words came out.

"Thank you," said Leslie, catching her breath. "You have no idea how liberated I feel right now. I feel like the weight of the entire world has lifted, and the baggage I've been dragging around every day has been unpacked, for good. The dark cloud that has been hanging over my head just broke away, and I can see the sun. Stan, how did you pull this off?"

"I've had it on my mind for years. I was finally able to line it up when I saw it was for sale again. I met with the owner just this weekend, we went through the house. Leslie, some of it has not changed one bit, I found this book and lunch box in the upstairs playroom."

She sat back down in the chair, looked at Stan again, and reached out for his hand.

"This is amazing. You don't know the guilt I've had for years, that the place was sold outright and there was nothing

I could do. Do you think the owners could let us see it again today?"

Stan pulled out his phone and looked at his contacts. "Here he is, Rudy Mann, the son of the lady who purchased it from your family. She had planned to make it into a venue or bed-and-breakfast, but she became sick and had a battle with dementia. But they made a good start on repairing and restoring already." He dialed Rudy's number.

"Hey, there Rudy. It's Stan. Listen, my wife is home, and we were wondering if we could meet you at the farm? Is that a problem?" asked Stan.

Leslie watched and waited for the response.

"Thank you. Sorry we will miss you though. Thanks Rudy," replied Stan and he ended the call.

Leslie squealed with excitement and within minutes, they were both out the door. Leslie was no longer in tears but smiling and laughing with sheer joy. She talked nonstop about her many memories in the house and on the farm. Some stories Stan had never heard before, and he loved hearing her describe them as they drove to Willow Green.

"Stan, there are so many things that could be done with that place. You know, Laney was just talking about wanting a quaint place for a restaurant. She met someone on the yacht that might be interested in helping partner with her in the venture. You know, I can envision this as a genuine team effort. I think Carrie would love to be involved in something like this, too."

Stan noticed Leslie's excitement. It was exactly what he hoped would happen—for Leslie to have some joy in her life with the memories of the homeplace instead of the nightmare she had lived as she fought diligently to save it and keep it in the family. The battle had involved fighting relatives that were more interested in the cash than the memories and the legacy the homeplace held. To her it was a matter of the heart. To them it was a matter of cash flow.

"I am so glad you're thrilled. I wasn't sure, but I thought, I can always flip it and put it back on the market and sell the acreage in plots for a subdivision."

Leslie's head turned to him as she said, "No, this is great! Let's make it into something wonderful. We can take some pics, then I can get with Laney and Sandra and see what they think. Later, after this business with Bill's funeral is over, we can pull Carrie in on it. I would love to see it brought back to the splendor it possessed when my grandparents owned it."

They pulled into the lane, and Leslie leaned up on the dashboard, eager to see the old homeplace. Her face lit up and her eyes filled with tears as the house came into view. She had not seen it up close in years. Stan stopped the truck and let her take it all in. The oak tree lane framed her view of the house down the path. It was just as she remembered. Down that lane there was the home once filled with laughter and the smell of her grandmother's homemade bread, jams, and jellies.

"Can we park here and walk up to the house? I want to take every moment in as slow as I can," said Leslie as she opened her door.

They walked the rest of the way down the lane, and Leslie could see the wide porch and columns. She pointed to the pond down the hill. It was a little overgrown now, but they could still see the old brick fireplace her granddaddy built on the bank.

When she spotted the weeping willow trees, she cried all over again.

"Stan, do you remember how grandaddy planted a willow tree each time a girl was born and an oak tree when there was a boy born in the family? Look at them, they have really grown through the years. Oh my, those willow trees are beautiful. I see mine on the right side of the pond next to the dock. My goodness, look how big it is!"

Stan nodded his head and said, "Well, it's been there a few years now, honey."

They continued their stroll toward the house, and Leslie veered off the path to walk over to the gazebo by the pond.

"Oh, my gracious. Grandaddy built this gazebo for holding tables and bands for the picnic balls they used to have. He called them a blend of a picnic and a ball under the moon, and he always picked a full moon twice a year to hold the ball. The one in the fall was always quite impressive under the Hunter's Moon."

As they got closer to the house, Leslie stopped to sit on the concrete bench in front of a birdbath that was now broken and had fallen over.

"This was my grandmother's favorite spot. In this little garden, she had every cutting flower you could imagine. We used many of them for the dining table, or arrangements to decorate the sanctuary altar at church. She loved to surprise friends with bouquets and would drag me all over town with her to every shut-in and make me sing. It was humiliating."

"I bet. Humiliating for the shut in. I've heard you sing," Stan said as he laughed.

"Stop it, you are incorrigible," said Leslie, as she popped him on the arm.

"Well, is it everything you imagined?" asked Stan as he reached for her hand.

"Absolutely, Stan. Oh, how much I have missed this place. I know it sounds outlandish, but sitting here, I can almost see my grandma down by the pond on the bench under the willow tree. She went down there to read her Bible. I feel closer to my granddaddy. You know, other than you, he was my favorite man ever. He was the sweetest human I have ever known. He beats you in that area, I'm afraid. Especially after you just made fun of my singing," Leslie said with a grin on her face.

"Well, honey, he was not married to you. You were his beloved and perfect granddaughter. I happen to be your husband, and I think somehow that is a little different. Are you saying I'm not sweet?"

"All I'm saying is I never heard him say a cross word. He was always kind to everyone. He never raised his voice to me but one time in the years I had him in my life. I could not say that about other family members. You know that."

"I know. Let's go inside."

"Wait what? You have the key? I thought there was one more document to sign and Rudy had already left town?"

Stan smiled at her and said, "Do you think I would drive you all the way out here and not have the key. That would be like the torture of hell."

He took her hand and lead her to her willow tree. "You didn't have to remind me which willow was yours. I can still see you sitting under that tree when you stole my heart so many years ago. That first Christmas that you brought me here when we were dating, that was it for me. I fell head over heels in love with you on that winter break," said Stan as he pointed above their heads.

Leslie was unsure what he was referring to. Then she guessed and said, "Oh yes, thank God for bringing us together."

"Yes indeed, that is true. Absolutely true. But I actually meant for you to literally look up," said Stan as he laughed and pointed up again.

When Leslie looked up, she saw something dangling from a branch just above her head. She saw the silhouette of a key in the sunlight peeking through the branches. She looked back at Stan.

Stan smiled wide as he said, "It's the key to the house. Go ahead, take it down."

"Oh my, how did it get there I wonder?" Leslie reached for the key as she gave Stan a grin.

They left the banks of the pond and her willow tree, and by now she was almost running to the front door. Suddenly she stopped and took in a deep breath and immediately recognized the smell. On the far edge of the wrap-around porch, she spotted them—her grandmother's climbing rose bush.

Leslie took a whiff of their fragrance and said, "Look, it's my grandmother's 4th of July variety given to her by Grandaddy, and he planted it for her on the 4th of July." The spicy, fragrant scent was unique, and the bright candy cane petals showed off well against the white house. It needed some taming, but that was easy enough to do.

As she walked to the door, she noticed it had been replaced. It was a set of beautifully carved wood double doors with ornate details. The glass panes were nicely beveled and etched, and

Leslie thought to herself how much her grandmother would have loved them. She would be able to see out the front door. She always said that was the one change she would make – so she could see who was at the door. Leslie took the key and unlocked the door. When she walked across the threshold she was overwhelmed and began to cry silently as Stan gave her a consoling embrace.

Going through each room, she picked up draped cloths to see what was underneath. They headed up the stairs, and Leslie raced to the playroom. Just as Stan had said, it was basically untouched.

"Wow, our boys and their cousins came up here to play. This is bringing my childhood back to life again. We should call the boys later and let them know about this. I think they will be excited too. I'm not sure if they even remember coming out here. They were very young."

"Now, I see that brain of yours already cooking up ideas. There are many things that can be done here. It could be a retail shop with consigned rooms, a wedding or event venue, a restaurant, or it could be our new place when we retire."

"No, absolutely not. I do not want this enormous house to take care of in my old age. I think we should put a business plan together for a wedding and venue place. I can imagine it could be a restaurant too, but it's kind of out of the way. But for that reason, I think it would be great for wedding events. We could use the house for holding the wedding party in bedrooms. Then we could have the dining option downstairs in the living room, sitting room, dining room, and even in the front piano parlor. We could add a dance hall, or for now just an outdoor tent with walls. We could rent floors for the tent if the customer wanted a dance floor."

Stan watched as she walked around, peeking under tarps. He enjoyed the look of surprise when she would discover another treasure. "I wonder why they kept everything. What were they going to do?" asked Leslie.

"Well, I think Rudy's mom had started the project of turning this into a bed and breakfast inn. They did quite of bit of work—electrical and plaster work. It won't take too much to get this place up to snuff and ready. She had some plan of keeping it authentic and using as many of the furnishings as possible," said Stan.

"Some of these pieces here were in the family for a couple hundred years. I know they have a history that Sandra could uncover. You know she is a natural at stuff like that."

After a couple of hours, they walked back to the truck, and sat looking over the property.

"Stan, do you think the pond is big enough to stock? It would be nice to offer cane pole fishing. That would be so nostalgic, and the kids growing up today do not do enough fishing. You know a lot of the world's problems get solved with a good fishing hole. I have heard you say that many times. If nothing else, like our youngest son says, you catch some peace."

"I would imagine it was stocked years ago because it's a nice size pond. But if not, we can stock it, that would be an awesome idea. We could hold some camps for kids out here. I thought about some farm animals too. That would be nice."

"Stan Cartwright, you want farm animals? Every time I have ever mentioned goats, you have firmly protested. And don't get me started on chickens. You know I always wanted fresh eggs. But you adamantly protested that too."

"Honey, this is different. This property totally calls for farm animals. Especially a miniature pony and a peacock. Yes, a peacock would be awesome."

"I'm not sure if I know who you are anymore. You are full of surprises."

"Well, it's about time I surprised you again. I think sometimes you believe me to be completely predictable."

"Set in your ways, yes. A creature of habit, totally. Predictable? This just proves that you are not. I'm amazed and so excited!" said Leslie, as she kissed him on the cheek. "Let's head home, we have some planning to do."

They continued to talk about the many possibilities. Stan thought Leslie would burst with excitement, so he kept cautiously advising her that Carrie, Laney, and Sandra might not share in her enthusiasm.

Leslie listened to Stan's reasoning and agreed, "I know Carrie is available and not working, but she may go back to the station with Bill passing away. As for Laney, she's used to big city lights and fine dining venues. This might not be her speed. Now for Sandra, I can see her falling right into this plan you have brewing," said Stan.

She looked out the window, and then back at Stan, "I know you are erring on the side of caution, and I thank you for that, but I really think the four of us could make something work here. I can continue to work at the hospital. Laney could still make some engagements around events we have or let this place be her hub for engagements coming to her. As for Sandra, this could be a great distraction for her right now."

"It sort of looks like to me that you had this idea cooked up in your head already. You've imagined this for a long time. Just realize that the plan may evolve into something totally different. I just know I want you to do with it what you like. I will support you totally. Except, one thing—I'm not waiting any tables," Stan said with a laugh.

Leslie popped him on the arm and said, "That's fine. I'll put that in your employee profile. I know, it's a long shot, but I think this may be perfect timing. This could be great for Laney. She is very well-known in the restaurant industry. This could work Stan. I know it. I feel it."

Leslie continued to talk nonstop all the way home. Stan was right, this was perfect. Leslie was finally viewing what once was a tragedy in a fresh light. His prayers had been answered. The spark in her eye could light fires right now, and he loved seeing her this way. She was back in her element, and he would bet the farm she was going to make this project work. He knew it would because it came to her so naturally. Those were the times Leslie got it right—when she was free to be creative. This was one of those times.

Chapter 30

Karen in Memphis

Another steamy day was in the forecast for Memphis, and Karen started the day out the same way as the last few, kneeling at the porcelain throne. She hadn't done this since her college days. But back then she knew why she was sick – too many margaritas, or too much pj. This time that was not the case. She needed to find a clinic and have a pregnancy test. The dates still confused her. She and Bill had been careful since they both decided they did not want children. She was very cognizant of her body and schedule, and this was not part of the plan, especially now.

She found a clinic that took new patients, made the appointment, and tried to eat some toast. But she really needed coffee. She popped a KPOD in the Keurig, then grabbed her iPad and sunglasses.

She walked out to the porch and immediately felt the humidity and it fogged up her shades. She took them off and sat down. She had stared at the walls of the rental for three days. She had to get outside. Maybe some sun would be beneficial. She pulled up the local news back at Greenway and paused for a moment. She had been putting off reading Bill's obituary. It was best that way, she thought, to leave that life behind. It was over. She had placed all her proverbial eggs in one basket. She had broken the adage of don't get your bread and meat from the same place, and she was paying for it. Her life was in ruins.

She decided not to look for the obituary, her day could be better spent concentrating on getting better, stronger, and ready for interviews and Zoom meetings. She had those lined up for later that day with a few of the contacts she had in Memphis. But first, a visit to the clinic. It could just be just stress. She had to find out.

She went inside and placed her phone on the kitchen counter as she headed to the bathroom to get a shower. She heard her phone ring. She looked down the hall and thought about ignoring it, but then what if it was one of her contacts? She ran down the hall to grab the phone. It was Jason Hargrove. *"I'm not talking to him"* The last interaction she had with him was a few weeks back. The night is one she was trying to forget. There had been too much drinking and too much celebrating over a new contract they landed in Baltimore, Maryland.

Karen rarely drank, but that night was an exception, and they had just acquired the highest grossing contract the business ever signed. They got caught up in the moment and both became completely inebriated. The part that Karen could not make clear in her mind was how he ended up in her room. She had no recollection of what happened the night before. He later explained he wanted to make sure she arrived in the room safely. He was afraid she had a bit too much to drink, and someone would take advantage of her. For that she was thankful, but it was quite a surprise to wake up and see him lying on the other queen bed in the room. She looked around for any evidence or indication of what happened, to see if they had slept together. Since he was fully clothed, she thought she was safe. Once that was determined, she popped him on the head and told him to get out. She barely had spoken to him since that morning and avoided him at the office. She never wanted Bill to discover that he had been in her room. There were already whispers about him and his wife, Brianne, having some marriage issues. That piece of gossip along with Jason being in her room would add fuel to the rumor mill. He never liked the idea that she was going to be his stepmother. Before he married Brie and before she was with Bill, Jason had made a pass at her once. She never told Bill, and she knew Jason should have been smart enough not to mention anything, either.

She headed back to the bathroom, and the phone rang again, "Geez, this jerk will not give up!" Karen yelled in the empty room. She looked at the phone, but it was not Jason.

"Hello, this is Karen."

"Hello, Karen, this is Liz Murphy from Multimedia Connections. How are you?"

"I'm wonderful. I hope you are staying out of this heat; it's brutal out there today."

"Yes, I am fortunate to have all meetings in the office today, so I'm not venturing out. So, listen, can you talk for a minute?" asked Liz.

"I can, indeed."

Karen could hear Liz had put the phone on speaker. "Karen, can you hear me? I have placed you on speaker and I brought in the VP of our media buying department, Andy Rowland. Is that okay?"

"Of course. Hello, Andy."

Liz gave Andy a summary of Karen's career, and they discussed a few opportunities within the organization. In just a few minutes on the phone, Karen had sold herself like an auctioneer racking up the highest bidder.

"So, Karen, we will not beat around the bush here. Your reputation in the industry speaks well of your worth. We know it's true, as we have followed up on a few areas in markets you have previously worked. We are just concerned about your location issues. You are in North Carolina, and we are in Memphis. Are you willing to relocate?" asked Liz.

"Not a problem. I'm already in Memphis. I have a temporary rental, and I'm hoping to plant some roots."

"Excellent, Karen! How about I have my assistant reach out to you on scheduling some time to bring you in, meet the crew, and see where this goes. How soon could you be available?" asked Andy.

"I can be available as early as tomorrow morning. Thank you both for the opportunity, and I look forward to learning more. It sounds intriguing," said Karen.

Karen hung up the phone, ran back down the hall, and jumped in the shower. Within twenty minutes, she was out the door and on the way to the clinic.

The visit went well. The doctor was kind and mild-mannered. She explained the test they would run and said they would call her with the results. She offered some suggestions for nausea and told her what over-the-counter remedies might be effective. Karen picked up a pregnancy test at the pharmacy for double insurance.

She went back to the rental and put a dry erase calendar on the table. She wrote out the appointments, strategy, and goals.

It was an old school method she liked, and it worked for her. She thought again about looking up the obituary. No. Absolutely not. She couldn't go there. It had to be in the past now. She had to get a process on the whiteboard so she could see her vision for the future taking shape.

For now, she would focus on getting her life back, even if it included a pregnancy. If she was pregnant, keeping the baby was not an option. She would have to figure out how and when to make some arrangements. She put her head in her hands and cried. As she was trying to make a fresh start in life, there was an irony that it might include ending a new life. Her new life was quickly becoming complicated. She hesitated to do the pregnancy test. She wanted to focus on being ready for the interview and waiting for the call from the clinic. She sat frozen in the chair with a mix of emotions and a flurry of thoughts. Suddenly she took a deep breath, exhaled, slammed her hands down on the table, and reached for the pregnancy test.

Chapter 31

Laney Hears Leslie's News

Laney was sitting at her dining room table looking at information and ideas for a restaurant. Her main challenge was location. There were few options in their small town, and she did not want to get involved in building. She could handle the business plan, but location had to be perfect, or it was going to be a bust. She was making a list of possibilities and options for locations when the doorbell rang, and Laney found Sandra and Leslie standing at her door.

"Come in, ladies. What brings you around this time of day? Leslie, you didn't go back to work?"

Leslie and Sandra walked through the door. "No, I didn't, Listen, sit down. I have an insane idea. I brought Sandra in the loop yesterday and got her feedback, and we are here to bring you in now. Gosh, that sounded bossy. Can we please just sit down and talk for a minute?" said Leslie.

Laney motioned for them to head to the kitchen, and she put a pot of coffee on as they sat down at the bar. "What has your feathers strutting, girl? You look like a peacock right now, what's up?"

"Well, you remember I said I had an idea about a location for you for a café, a culinary school, bakery, something? The original idea I had—I did not even get to thinking that one out. I was thinking Sara at The Bread Basket and you might get together on something. But Stan had a much more magnificent idea," said Leslie.

Sandra was smiling, waiting to see Laney's response when Leslie broke the good news.

"Do you remember the time we went to Emerald Isle, and I carried us down the back road by the country club over to the community called Willow Green? I took us to my grandparents' homeplace? It's been years, so you may not remember," said Leslie.

"Yes! I remember. It was a beautiful plantation style home down a long lane. There was a pond and that pretty gazebo. Of course, I remember. I had never seen a weeping willow tree before, and I thought it was the most graceful tree," said Laney.

"It's mine! Stan bought it back for me to do whatever I want with it. What I have in mind is for you to have a culinary school, us to book wedding parties, business events, dinners, reunions. It's perfect!" said Leslie.

Laney looked thoughtful. "I agree—it would be perfect. But it's an enormous place, and I'm only one person. How do you think I would pull this off? That's a high dollar threshold in real estate and remodeling up to code will cost a fortune," she said.

Sandra rolled her eyes and said, "Come on now, don't be a party pooper! We can do this together. I really think so. Plus, remember, I'm married to a business banker."

"Sand, I know, but it's a lot to run an operation like that. I would need some sous chefs and waitstaff. It is an offer that sounds good, but on paper can we make it work? I mean goodness, Stan must have already gone into debt. Are you all able to foot the remodel?" asked Laney.

"Don't worry about that just yet. The previous owners have already done an incredible job at beginning that process. I know when things roll like this, they become very fluid and have a way of working out. I want Carrie onboard, too," said Leslie.

"So, the four of us would run this place? Are you quitting the hospital, and are you going to stop being a nurse, Sandra?" asked Laney.

"No, not just yet. For now, I'll be the background partner who provides the facility," said Leslie.

Sandra chimed in, "I won't stop work right away, but I'm so excited about this I can hardly stand it. The timing is just perfection for you, Laney, and for me. Hopefully, Carrie will be interested," said Sandra.

"Why is the timing perfect for you? What's going on?" asked Laney.

Leslie nodded to Sandra to go ahead, "Sandra has some life-changing news," said Leslie.

"We have stopped infertility treatments and we are researching adoption. Mitch has some agencies lined up for us to see in a couple of weeks. So, a fresh, new start. We're both okay with the decision. In fact, I feel a bit of relief."

"Relief? How so?" asked Laney as she leaned over the counter to pour the coffee.

Sandra took a breath, "I felt like I was letting Mitch down. I know I wasn't, but it felt like I was. I didn't even realize how depressed and anxious I was becoming. I feel like I stopped fighting a battle. We feel good with this decision. It's the right one for us."

"That's great. I am glad you're at peace with it, too. That's amazing to me—some kid is going to be so lucky to have you two in their life. You are a bit on the living large side, Sandra, so you will be the mom with hype, no doubt," said Laney.

Sandra smiled, "I hope so, but we'll just take it one step at a time."

"So, y'all have news. Well, I have news, too!" said Laney. "Guess what hot hunk is coming to dinner this weekend?"

"Wait! What—Ben?" asked Sandra, giving Laney a high-five. "I knew it! You baited him like a fish."

"I did not. I may have worked my charm and batted these lashes, but mercy, did you get a good look at him? Total hotness," said Laney.

"I would agree. He's easy on the eyes. But what I was most impressed with was his personality. He is so genuine, and kind. What are y'all going to do?" asked Leslie.

"Have dinner here, out back on the patio at the outdoor kitchen maybe," said Laney.

Sandra jumped up and went to the patio

"Where is she going?" Laney asked Leslie.

"She's checking your ambience out. This is why we need her in our new venture. She's good at setting a stage, a room, a table—anything about sprucing a place up," said Leslie.

They walked out to the patio and Sandra was moving potted plants, raising the umbrella, checking the strands of patio lights, and pulling up weeds in the patio bricks.

"Would you stop? It's fine. Really," said Laney.

Sandra looked up in the umbrella, "You have a wasp nest up here. Get me some spray." When she noticed Laney was not moving, she repeated the order. "Go, now before one of them stings me!"

Laney followed orders and went back in to get wasp spray. Leslie was back inside the house, reading the card on the flowers that Ben had sent to Laney.

"My, my, my, looks like you have an official suitor, my friend. These flowers are beautiful, and the card is so sweet."

"You know something? What I felt when I met Ben does not compare to anything I've ever felt about any man on first impression. That scares me. I fall hard and fast. You know how I am," said Laney.

Leslie gave her a hug, "Take your time. If it's meant to be, it'll be. Just like this new business venture. Hey, Ben might be interested in hearing about this idea."

"I think I'm going to keep our conversation on learning more about each other, we'll see where it goes. Let's hope he's not too disappointed," said Laney.

"Never," said Leslie. "You came in here for wasp spray. Remember?"

"Oh gosh, my mind goes to mush when I talk about Ben," Laney replied, with a laugh.

They went back out to help Sandra with spraying the wasp nest. All three of them decided they would wait until later in the week to mention the new business venture to Carrie. Give her time to get through the week. She had her hands full with family and business details. Leslie's news could wait. In the meantime, they could build the plan so they could share more with her when the time was right. By the time they finished tidying up the patio, they were dying of thirst. They retreated inside for some of Laney's famous virgin mojitos.

Chapter 32

After the Memorial Service

Carrie was standing in the chapel, staring at a closed casket alongside her sons. Leslie gave them some time to be alone and she kept her distance, but it was still easy to overhear their conversation. Leslie was impressed with Carrie's elegance and grace throughout the service.

"I see the pain you two are in, and I feel that for you. Your father was immensely proud of both of you," said Carrie.

"Mom, this might be the most unthinkable thing I ever thought we would be doing this time last week. Burying our father seems surreal," said John.

Carrie was quiet for a moment and then nodded. "I know, honey."

Jason put his hand on the casket, then turned around and looked at his mother and brother, "We have to walk out of this chapel now and know that we did a respectable job of laying Dollar Bill down to rest."

"We did, son. I think considering the awkwardness of this entire scenario, we made it work out well. I was waiting any moment to see Karen show up. To tell you the truth, I really am surprised she did not."

"I'm not. It suits her style. If she can't have what she wants, she throws a childish fit. So, this fits her perfectly," replied John.

Jason shook his head and said, "Leave it to you to bring that up at a time like this. She just knew how to make things happen John, and she was damn good at it. Somehow, I think you may be a little jealous. Secretly, it may also be the reason you are ready to sell the business so fast, because she left."

"Hey, easy now," replied John.

"She got the rates she wanted, and the contracts signed. We both did. What are you afraid of since she isn't coming back? You think I can't bring in the goods?" asked Jason.

"Boys, stop! This is not the time or place to have a sibling bickering contest. I know your brides are in the hall waiting for you. Leslie is here to carry me over to Sandra's house. They have a little after thing they wanted to do to cheer me up."

"Okay fine. You're right. We'll talk to you soon, mom. Enjoy your time with your friends," said Jason.

John looked at his mother and put both of his hands on her shoulders. "You sure you're okay? This has been a real mess for all of us, but you must have feelings all over the place."

"I should feel something right now. But to be honest, I'm just numb," Carrie said.

Jason put his arm around her, "Makes sense to me, mom. It really does."

Carrie turned around to see Leslie sitting in the last row of the small chapel. Once the boys left, she went to greet her friend.

Leslie hugged Carrie and asked, "How are you doing, Carrie?"

Leslie was shocked when Carrie laughed. She pulled back and looked her in the eyes. "What is that all about?" she asked.

Carrie laughed again, and then her laughter turned to tears. She was crying relentlessly, and Leslie was beginning to look concerned.

"How many times can you bury a husband?" said Carrie through a broken whisper.

"Oh honey, come here. You held it together for as long as you could for your boys." Leslie rocked her back and forth.

"I'm sorry. I am so sorry. I feel overwhelmed with relief that this is over. But this time, this death is final; It's not just the death of a marriage by divorce. Bill is dead to me forever now."

They left the chapel and both ladies were silent on the ride to Sandra's house. Leslie pulled into Sandra's driveway and noticed the set-up of tables on the wide front porch. It was picture perfect with beautiful linen tablecloths trimmed in lace, and she had set up a couple of hurricane lamps. Tea candles were placed around the porch, and the sun was setting. Sandra came outside with a pitcher of margaritas, looking like the perfect hostess.

"Let me help you. What can I do?" asked Leslie, as she ran up the steps.

"I'm fine here, but can you get the salsa and chips? I need to mix up the guacamole and I'm heating the cheese quesadillas now. Carrie said she wanted margaritas, so I just went with the entire Mexican theme. Where is she?" asked Sandra.

"Give her a minute. She needed to make a call to Jason. Things went haywire at the funeral home with the boys. She's trying to get them to hug and make up. You know Laney is going to grade all of this, right?" said Leslie as she dipped a chip in salsa.

Sandra shook her head, and they both went back inside. "Bring it! I stand behind my salsa and cocktail skills."

Mitch greeted Leslie with a hug and said, "Well, how are you doing? I hear you are extremely excited about getting the property back in the family."

Leslie patted Mitch on the back, "Thank you so much for helping with that. It blew me away. Has Sandra told you about our thoughts for creating a venue there for events like weddings and banquets?"

"She has hardly talked about anything else. I'd be happy to help you ladies develop a business plan and run it through for processing. There is a business model we ran through a couple years back like what y'all want to do, and I would love to help."

Sandra walked by the two of them with more food, and Mitch grabbed a tortilla. Sandra smacked his hand, then kissed him on the cheek.

"I'm going to need Carrie onboard, and Laney, too. I want to bring it up to Carrie soon. Sandra and I both thought it could be a great distraction for her right now. By the way, I thought the memorial service today was nice. I think they did good," said Leslie.

Sandra came back through the door and said, "They did a fantastic job of making the backside of a mule sound like a thoroughbred prize-winning horse. That is what they did. Y'all know it's true, but I'm the only one brave enough to say it. Bill Hargrove was a self-centered, egotistical, misogynist jerk. Karen is just one affair we know of. I'm sure some loose lips could spill the beans on that man about more than just Karen."

"Stop Sandra. You know it's not nice to speak ill of the dead. My mama always said they would haunt you for sure if you did," said Mitch.

"Mitch, every time he looked at me, he always licked his lips like mama had called him to supper. It was disgusting," said Sandra as she rolled her eyes and continued to the porch with more food.

The three of them waited on the porch for Laney to arrive and for Carrie to get out of the car. Mitch was rocking on the porch swing as he waited for his card partners. Leslie watched her Suburban with an intense eye and tapped her fingers on the table. She wondered what was keeping Carrie. She had planned for them to enjoy the evening on the porch, and just let Carrie be however she needed to be. She had experienced a week of more than a few rocky days, and now she should enjoy a margarita on the rocks. It was hard to imagine that she went from such a magical weekend on a yacht to such an ordeal at home.

Leslie poured them all a sampling of the margaritas.

"Cheers," said Sandra. "Let's wash this mess down and out. May fresh new winds blow in for all of us, including Carrie. I know she has been wanting to work but could not work at the business since the divorce. She may go back now, but I hope not. It might be selfish, but I want her in on this venture with us."

Leslie tasted the drink and said, "Hmm, this is good. You did something different, and I like it. What is it?" asked Leslie.

"The something different is a splash of agave. I think it balances out some of the bitterness. Sometimes the lime can taste too bitter to me," said Sandra.

Headlights flashed across the porch. "Laney is here," said Leslie. As she jumped up from her chair to meet Laney, she noticed that Carrie had opened the door to her Suburban.

As they approached the porch, Laney smiled when she saw how Sandra had gone all out with a cozy and warm set up. As they reached the last step, all four of them embraced in a hug. It was a beautiful sight, and Mitch watched from the porch swing as the friends shared an intimate moment of support. After a few seconds, they sat down at the table and decided it was time to make a toast to new beginnings.

"To new beginnings, ladies," said Leslie as she offered the traditional raising and clinking of the glasses.

Carrie sat down first and took a sip of the margarita. "Sandra, that is so good."

"Thank you. I am glad you approve. Laney, how about you? Does it meet your discerning taste buds?" asked Sandra.

"Approved! It's almost as good as mine," Laney said with a laugh. "But I taste something else?"

"Yes," said Sandra. "Just a splash of agave syrup."

"Okay, it's creative. I'll give you that," said Laney.

The conversation went from talking about the memorial to discussing what new beginnings might look like for each of them. Mitch was still on the other side of the porch and listening in while enjoying the evening breeze. He smiled when he heard Sandra talk about their new beginning, as she brought up the matter of adoption for her and Mitch. Laney mentioned the possibility of a new business venture, but admitted she was more than hopeful about the possibility of a relationship with Ben.

Then Leslie had an opportunity to bring up her new beginning. "So, Carrie, there is something about my future you have not heard about yet. Just happened this week, and it is pivotal, it is monumental, and it is life changing. It involves my past and now my future," said Leslie.

Carrie looked at Leslie inquisitively, "Leslie Carol, what have you been keeping from me?"

"Well, you have been going through something, lady. We wanted to give you some space," replied Leslie.

"I've had enough space. So, tell me some good news please. I've had enough bad for one week," said Carrie.

"Do you remember my family's homeplace that was sold?" asked Leslie.

"You know I do. What about it?" asked Carrie.

"I own it now," said Leslie.

"What! Get out! How did that happen? When did that happen? This is so exciting!" said Carrie, as she jumped up from her seat to give Leslie a hug. "I know how much that place meant to you. Mercy, how did that happen?"

Leslie saw Stan's truck turn into the driveway, and she pointed as his lights flashed across the porch. "My husband bought it for me," Leslie said through tears. "He surprised me when we came home earlier this week, and I'm still in shock."

"I know you are. So this doesn't mean y'all are moving, does it?" asked Carrie.

"Not at all. We have some other plans. We are still working on ironing out the details," said Leslie.

Carrie smiled, "Like what, and who is the *we*?" she asked.

"Well, the four of us, we hope," said Sandra. "Would you like to know more?"

Laney joined in, "It's all up in the air to be sorted out. We can wait awhile to tell you more. No rush, Carrie. We want you to have a rest for a while."

By this time, Stan was standing by the table and gave Carrie a hug from behind. "What are you ladies up to?"

"That is what I want to know," said Carrie. "I hear you surprised your bride with the gift of her family's homeplace. They were just going to tell me about the plans they have for the place. Well, Sandra was, but Laney and Leslie have not. So what is going on?"

"Oh yeah, so what do you think about being a part of it? I mean, I know you just went through something life changing this past week. You may not want to jump into anything like this right now," said Stan.

Carrie looked up at him, "Well, for me to answer that question, I need to know what we are talking about. I'm going to need some more details."

"Oops, sorry about that, Leslie. That's my clue to exit. Mitch are you ready for me to beat you in blackjack?" asked Stan.

"No but come on anyway and beat me again. The boys from the bank are already out back."

"So, men folk are out of here, lay it out. What are we talking about here?" asked Carrie.

Leslie and Sandra spent the next few minutes describing the plans, and with every word, they drew Carrie into the idea. Laney noticed Carrie asked all the right questions, and Leslie did a wonderful job of laying out the possibilities. Sandra was brilliant in hoisting the idea up with just the right amount of enthusiasm. Once Leslie had the total spill out on the table and they were halfway through the pitcher of margaritas, they realized they had been talking for well over an hour.

"Well, what do you think?" asked Leslie. "We know you have so much going on in your life right now and you might want to get back in the media business, but we would love to include you in this project. I think you would be a tremendous asset. I mean, hospitality is your gift from God. There's no one better at it than you."

Carrie nodded her head, "Well, thank you for that. I'm certainly very interested. Now, I have some news to share with you that could determine how I answer you. Believe it or not, the boys told me they want to sale the business. They want out. They said they have for a while but felt pressured by their dad. So, we've decided to get an appraisal to get the business ready to sale."

Laney, Sandra, and Leslie were stunned into silence. Carrie poured another margarita and sat back in her chair.

"Y'all need to say something. Close your mouths before a fly goes in there," Carrie said with a laugh.

"Wow, I didn't see that coming. You don't want to go back and run the business? I know Karen flew the coop, but Jerry is there to help," said Sandra.

"No, I'm not going back without the boys. We all agreed we need a change. Obviously, you all might make that happen right now. You know what? I'm all in. Count me in. Why not?" said Carrie.

The squeals from the porch made the neighbor's dog bark. When the sound traveled to the garage out back, Mitch and Stan came running to the porch.

"What the hell happened here? Which one of you saw a snake?" asked Mitch. "Y'all are going to make the neighbors call the cops."

"She's in! Carrie agrees it's a perfect idea! The magnificent four will be a talented team," said Leslie.

It relieved the men to see that was the reason for the squealing, and they shook their heads as they headed back to the garage.

"We have some major hurdles—a business plan and financing for one. Sandra said Mitch is ready and willing to help with that process. But that means our finances will be scrutinized, and there will be loans that all four of us will be responsible for with our signatures. If it's going to be a team effort, we all should be equally paid and equally in debt," said Laney.

The table became quiet, and all of them looked at each other. Pondering these thoughts brought a bit of heaviness to the conversation. The silence was deafening and put a damper on the fire they had been stoking.

"I think we can work that out, I have an idea. I know this may be crazy – it's just a thought," she said as she stood up.

"Well, we are just waiting for your idea," asked Leslie.

Carrie stood up and walked around the table twice, then she paced back and forth. All of them recognized this behavior as Carrie's thinking mode. She was in deep thought and consideration. When she had a great thought that required full discernment, she paced. In a few seconds, they could see she had gathered her words and composure, and she sat back down at the table.

"Okay, Jesus and I needed to talk that out for a second there. So here is my thought—I haven't made this common knowledge. In the divorce settlement, Bill had to give me a healthy sum of money to buy me out of the business. It also required him to have a life insurance policy with me as the beneficiary, and it's very substantial. I am not bragging or being boastful, I'm just letting you know where this idea is coming from. If I'm going to do anything positive here to take this mess and turn it into a message, I must change my way of thinking. I need to make something great out of something bad. I can't think of a better way than to bank roll this project. Ladies, I can be your bank," said Carrie.

Silence fell upon them again. Laney poured the last of the margarita in the pitcher into her glass, "I'll go inside and make another batch."

Immediately Sandra jumped up, "I'll help. You'll forget the agave syrup."

As they left the table, Carrie asked Leslie, "Did I say something wrong?" They both watched Laney and Sandra walk down the hall to the kitchen.

"No, I just think they feel like that might be something we need to talk through. Me being the property owner and you proposing to fund the project. They may feel like that is a discussion we should have in private since they would not be capital partners, but operating partners. They may think it leaves them as less important partners in the venture. Carrie, really, this is too much for you right now. It's too fast. Let's wait a bit before we get into the actual planning," said Leslie.

Carrie shook her head no, "No, it's not. This is a new beginning for me, and the timing really could not be more perfect. Let me do this please. It will give me purpose again, and we can partner on this together and hire Laney and Sandra. We could film culinary school episodes. We can have cooking classes, weddings, reunions, seminars, and retreats. But I have one question."

"What's that?" asked Leslie.

"When I sell the business, I'm selling the house. I tell you; the boys and I have decided it's time for change. Is it possible, just an idea, that we could build a small cottage on the property or breakout a piece of land to build something simple but nice for me? I'll purchase the land from you. Is that too much to process? I also want to look after Mae. I would want her to come with me. I'm sorry. Is that too much to ask?" asked Carrie, and she waited for Leslie's response.

Leslie looked at her with her hands on her hips and was silent for a moment. "Stop apologizing. But do you think you could be happy out there, as active and on the go as you are? It's in the sticks, Carrie. It's perfect for a venue, and there is a hotel just a short Uber drive away. But you might feel isolated. And yes, of course I know you want to look after Mae. She has been your Godsend for years, and frankly I think we could use her help. She is still pretty agile."

"Well, I wouldn't live there all the time. I have another plan up my sleeve, too. I stumbled across a property in Atlantic Beach on a real estate site last night. It's small, but all I would need. Enough room to have you girls come down too. I talked to a realtor, and I'm going down to see it tomorrow," said Carrie.

Leslie looked shocked and was about to speak, but Laney and Sandra came back out with a second pitcher of margaritas.

"Sorry that we bolted, but it just seemed like that conversation might be best between the two of you. I mean, we would be working partners, not owners, and we respect that situation. We just had a little talk about it in the kitchen. It's all fine," said Laney.

"No worries. We all will be work partners. It could be a great venture for you Laney. You can really show off in an environment like that. The boys can help with cooking shows you could host," said Carrie.

"Well Carrie just laid another card on the table. Tell 'em," said Leslie, as she motioned to Carrie.

"I'm going to look at a house at Atlantic Beach tomorrow, and If I like it, I'm making an offer," said Carrie.

"You are something else, lady," said Sandra. "You really are having a total remodel of your life. I love it! You are taking something that is broken and turning it into something new and exciting in your life. That takes skill," she said as she sipped her margarita.

They spent the rest of the night writing down ideas, googling and researching, talking about names for the venue, and dreaming of the changes ahead of them. Before midnight, the margarita pitcher was empty again, but coffee mugs were full of strong brew as the four went inside to sit around the kitchen table and Sandra brought out a day planner.

Mitch and Stan came in from the garage, and Mitch helped explain some ways they could create the partnership. His proposal would protect Leslie's investment, guard Carrie from losing her investment, and include Laney and Sandra as the working partners of the business. By one in the morning, they agreed they could talk until dawn, but decided it would be best to begin again with fresh minds in a couple of days. They said their good nights finally around 2:00 a.m. Laney and Carrie stayed with Sandra in their spare room. Stan drove Leslie home, and he was sure his wife would be up until dawn, unable to sleep from excitement as she talked about ideas all the way to the farm. Even through sleepy eyes and with her voice growing hoarse, the electricity was still high voltage, and it made him smile.

Chapter 33

Laney's Date

Laney yawned as she shielded her eyes from the sun coming through the windshield. She was kicking her own behind for staying out so late, and now she was running late in getting her day started.

Once she arrived home, she walked through the living room and noticed the sunflowers still looked lovely. If Ben was anything like the first impression she had of him, she was done for. She wanted to guard her heart, but she couldn't stop the feeling that came over her when she thought of him. Often. She liked how it felt, but she reminded herself how it felt to have a broken heart, too. The last heartbreak taught her that a broken heart never beats the same again, and it can change a person forever. That change in her heart became her internal alarm that kept her in check. But with Ben, it was proving impossible. But she did not feel any alarms going off. He felt like a soft and comfortable place to land her heart.

She went to the bedroom and started laying out dresses. One choice, she thought made her look fat, the other would be too hot, the other one looked more like she was going to attend a funeral, not a first date. She went back to the closet and found a linen pantsuit she had never worn. It was simple, but she could jazz it up with accessories. It had clean lines and the pants had a ruffle at the hem. The lavender color looked nice with her dark hair. It seemed like a good possibility, but she was not good at these things. She snapped a few pictures of each of the outfits and sent them over to Leslie.

Within seconds, her phone dinged. Leslie responded: "Pantsuit, wear a long necklace and those slides you bought at the beach." Laney looked back at the outfit and knew she didn't have a long necklace. Most of her days were spent in a chef's attire.

Laney texted Leslie back: "I don't have a necklace that will work."

Leslie texted: "I do. Hang on. Will run it over when I go into town."

Laney trusted her judgment, so the problem was solved. Now to the butcher, and other errands. She needed to get everything done and back home to shower and tame her hair. Maybe she would wear it up. But would that look too formal? She decided to decide once she got dressed.

Laney laughed at herself, "*You are making a planet out of a pebble! It really is just a dinner. I'm acting like I'm going to the prom for the first time. Or the first episode of The Batchelor or something. Stop it.*"

After picking up everything she needed, she headed back home to get everything ready for dinner so that she and Ben would have more time to talk. Going through her list of ingredients and checking everything off, she realized she needed to look in the wine cooler for the perfect pairing, then she thought better, let Ben pick.

The doorbell rang, and Laney saw Leslie's car in the driveway.

"Hello, special delivery for your hot date. I think this necklace will work. What do you think?" asked Leslie.

Laney and Leslie walked to the bedroom and looked at the necklace with the pantsuit. Leslie gave it her approval.

"Go get dressed. I'll dress things up a bit. Although Sandra did well already, but I will get some candles lit and set your table. You go get dolled up now, you hear?" said Leslie.

"Really? Are you sure? That will help so much. And can you come do that shadow thing with my eyes; the contour thing you do so well? You know I'm horrible with eye shadow," said Laney.

Leslie replied, "Yes, I can, but you don't need it. You are beautiful just like you are, but if it gives you a little confidence, I am happy to do your makeup."

Laney laughed, "Confidence? Do I need some? Do I look nervous?"

"Well, you are wound up a little tight. So, get on in there and unwind, and I'll finish up in the kitchen. I know your routine. I got it."

Leslie headed to the kitchen, found candles, and lit them at the dining table and in the living room. She went outside and lit the citronella candles on the patio. Everything looked lovely. Laney's place had an eclectic atmosphere, and when she paired her food with the ambience, it had an amazing vibe. The only way she could describe it was by calling it "happy."

Just as Leslie was finishing up, Laney walked into the kitchen. Leslie gave her a head-to-toe inspection while Laney waited with a forced smile.

"You look so glamorous in that pantsuit. It flows so softly and looks comfortable, but elegant. The lavender is an excellent color on you. Why have you never worn it?"

Laney shrugged and said, "I don't really know. I just never had an occasion come up, I guess. Do you think it looks like I'm trying too hard?"

"No, I do not. Now you really do not need that eye shadow contour. I think it would be too much. You'll be fine with just a touch of blush and lip gloss and a stroke of mascara," said Leslie.

"Thanks Leslie. I really appreciate it."

"No worries. I'm out of here. Have fun, relax, and just get to know each other."

Laney nodded, "Now cross your fingers."

Leslie walked out with her fingers crossed and gave her a salute goodbye. Just as she was pulling out of the driveway, a strange car pulled into her place. Laney saw Leslie wave to the other driver like she knew them. It was Ben, he was early. Leslie struck up a conversation with him and that gave her enough time to quickly add some blush and lip gloss and a touch of mascara, and she ran back before the doorbell rang.

Laney opened the door, and there stood Ben. He looked different. He was clean shaven, in a pressed white shirt, khakis, and Bass loafers. He was a traditionalist in the southern gentleman dress code book, and she thought he sure cleaned up well.

Ben looked at her for a moment and then shuffled his feet, he was frozen in place with his hand up to press the doorbell, "Hello! I didn't ring the doorbell yet. Were you heading out somewhere?"

"Um no, no. Yes, I mean - yes. I was just going to my car. I think I left something out there," said Laney, knowing it was a little white lie. She couldn't believe she didn't even wait for the doorbell to ring.

Ben turned to look at Laney's car, "Well, I can get it for you if you like? You look amazing by the way."

"Oh, thank you. Heaven's no, you come on into the A/C and cool off, the afternoon sun can be brutal on this porch. Go on in. I can get it. You're early, must have made good time on the drive. Not too hard to find me, huh? One road into town and one road out. There are some subdivisions off the main road that you can't see from here, so this small town is growing. Go on in and have a seat. I'll be right back."

On the way down the sidewalk, Laney realized she had not even given Ben time to answer her back. She was rambling on. She was nervous and it showed. Once she reached the car, she took a moment to look around for something she could take in the house since she had declared there was something in the car. She found the copy of his cookbook she had picked up earlier in the week, and her backpack in the back seat. That would have to do, especially since she wanted him to sign her copy. Laney was afraid that Ben was watching her from the window. When she walked in, she found him standing in front of the sunflowers he sent her. He was smiling, and she quietly walked up and stood behind him.

"They make me smile, too, when I look at them. Thank you again. I have really enjoyed them this week," said Laney.

"I'm glad," replied Ben.

Laney motioned for Ben to join her in the kitchen, and she showed him what was on the menu for the evening. She had listed everything on a small chalk board on the refrigerator. Ben looked at the menu and nodded his head in approval.

"A girl after my heart, right there. That's my kind of eating. You know it's amusing to get in the kitchen and at the bar and concoct the best cocktails, the savory appetizers, the perfect pastries for dessert. But when it's just me – I like it just like this. Simple," said Ben.

"Thank goodness. I was afraid I was going to disappoint you. But I will have you know this is the best filet mignon you will ever taste. I have it shipped direct to the local butcher. The bacon I wrap it comes from our local Piggly Wiggly, I have them slice it just like I like it. The asparagus, carrots, and new potatoes all came from the farmer's market down the street. The wine is from a local vineyard down in Duplin County, and the beer is brewed local at a place over in the next town called Uptown Brewing Company. Every once in a while, I get lucky and they will bottle some for me. I tried to make simple extra special," said Laney.

Ben smiled and replied, "I love it. Can we start off with a beer?"

Laney turned to the galvanized bucket on the counter filled with ice and beer, "You choose one. My favorite is the Five Points, here's a koozie."

He reached in and grabbed one and so did Laney. She extended her hand to the patio, and Ben followed her as he looked around the kitchen.

"That is one heck of a kitchen. I look forward to seeing you cook in there."

"Wait until you see my other kitchen," said Laney, as she stepped out through the French doors to the patio.

"My, my, my! You 're killing me. This is amazing. You have a full outdoor kitchen. You want to cook out here?" asked Ben.

"That's the plan. I'll turn the fans on. I already lit the citronella candles so the dang mosquitos should not be too bad. If they are, we'll start a fire."

"Start a fire. What did you have in mind?" Ben asked, with a raised eyebrow.

Laney's eyebrows raised just as high as she replied, "In the fireplace behind you, silly."

"Oh, of course. I knew that's what you meant. Really, I did. I was just messing with you."

Laney believed him. He was a genuine person, and she didn't feel like he was advancing toward her improperly in any way. But she had to admit, it was on her mind.

They sat down and started chatting about timelines of careers, school, travels, and thoughts for the future. Laney told Ben all about the idea for the new venue on Leslie's property, and he was more than excited to learn more. He contributed some ideas and thoughts as well. Before either of them realized it, they were on beer two, and well into a great evening. They went back in to get the food to cook and started with an appetizer of pimento cheese dip with homemade chips. As they were preparing to get the food started, Ben asked her if she would sit down for a moment.

"Laney, here's the thing. I wanted to come here to see you alone. I know we talked about everyone getting together in a month. But I have to be honest with you—I couldn't wait that long. I'm hoping that I'm reading this situation here correctly, but I sense the same. Maybe? Possibly?" Ben asked with a sideways smile while biting his lip.

Laney didn't know what to say. She knew he had to see that she was blushing. She was sure her forehead was glistening with perspiration. She could feel it. She took a moment, and that made matters even worse.

"I'm sorry, forgive me. It's just, I have . . ." said Ben.

Laney quickly interrupted him.

"Stop! No, I'm sorry. You wouldn't be wrong. I didn't want last weekend to end, and when you sent the flowers this week, my heart stopped. That's when I knew I felt something, too."

"Great! Wow, whew! I thought I just made a huge mistake. Really? Seriously? Do you think it's too soon to think or talk about this? I have to tell you; this has never happened to me before. The moment I laid eyes on you—when you talked, the time we spent cooking together, made drinks, every single second—I felt like I was living a dream. I didn't want it to end."

Laney replied, "It's not too soon if it's how we both feel, right? But I'm a fan of taking things slow. Does that make sense? I would like to know everything about you, but in small doses so I can take it all in."

"Are you saying you think I'm too much to handle? Really, I'm just an ordinary guy that wears his heart on his sleeve. I don't mind speaking how I feel. Sometimes that gets me in trouble, but it looks like in this case it didn't. That is, unless *you* are one hot mess of trouble. Are you?" asked Ben with his head tilted to the side as he waited for her response.

"Depends on who you talk to," Laney said with a grin. "Now Robert, he can tell you some tales. He has known me since I wobbled as a tot. But don't talk to Sandra about me. She thinks I am insanely obsessive over my cooking and not enough over my wardrobe. And she's right. Leslie would tell you everything about me in a guarded manner. Carrie, well, she's just going to tell you that I'm perfect, because that's how she is."

"I don't care what they have to say. I want to hear what you have to say. Who is Laney?"

"At this moment, she is enjoying the company of a wonderful guy, but her stomach is growling. So, are we going to get this dinner started, or what?" Laney said, laughing uncontrollably.

Ben stepped back with his hands on his hips, "Just what is so funny?" he asked.

"You don't know how anxious I've been about tonight. Now I feel relieved."

Ben took her hands and held them in his as they stood face to face and said, "See, this right here, is what I'm talking about. You are like a burst of energy rolled up in the best package. It immediately drew me to you. Let's get these veggies on, and then you just sit back and let me do all the cooking tonight. My treat. Point me to your spice cabinet."

Laney went inside to open the pantry door, "Have at it. I'm a lucky girl to be spoiled like this tonight."

Throughout dinner, the conversation continued to lead into ways the venue could be an opportunity for the two of them to work together. Ben was ready to learn as much as possible and offer any help he could. Laney was glad to hear it. The idea of the venue now just reached another level if it meant they could get to know each other better. Laney suggested Ben come back through town to meet with Leslie, and he seemed eager to do so.

It was getting late, and Ben had to get going. It had been a long day, and he had a book signing the next day. He helped Laney clean up in the kitchen, and they finished the last of dessert. Laney suggested they sit outside for a few more minutes, so they walked out to the porch and sat down beside each other in the swing. Ben had been a gentleman all evening and not one time did Laney feel uncomfortable. It was like there was a natural familiarity between them. Laney wondered if this was what it felt like when you found your soul mate.

After a few moments of sitting in the swing, Ben stood up and said, "Well, I don't want to say good night, but I must. You sure make it tough. I think I could talk to you forever."

"Wait! You didn't sign my copy of the book. Sit tight," said Laney as she dashed to the front door.

Ben waited for her to return, and he laughed to himself as he heard her running back out the door.

"Here's a pen, may I have the honor of acquiring your signature sir?"

Ben jotted his signature on the book and gave it back to her. Laney led him down the steps to the driveway. As they walked side by side, Ben's hand brushed hers, and she almost grabbed it. Ben noticed the closeness, as there was very little air between them. He wrapped his arm around her waist, and it proved to be the right move. Laney followed his lead and wrapped her arm around his waist.

Once they reached the car, Ben held her hands and he leaned up against the driver's door. Neither one of them wanted to say good night, and neither one of them felt comfortable enough to make the first move.

"Hey," Ben said, "One more question for you. Would it be alright if I kissed you?"

Before he could get an answer, Laney kissed him. Afterwards she asked, "So, did you get your answer?"

"No. You kissed me. I asked if I could kiss you."

"Yes."

Ben leaned over and put his hands on her cheeks and kissed her softly, slowly, and with great passion. Just as he pulled away, he gave her a hug. Laney smiled and then she kissed him again. He leaned in and wrapped his arms around her.

"I look forward to doing that again real soon. Good night," said Ben, as he opened his car door.

"Good night. Rest well," said Laney as she waved good-bye from the driveway. She watched his car drive away until she could no longer see his taillights when he turned off Main Street.

Chapter 34

Carrie visits
Atlantic Beach

Carrie rolled back into town a little later than planned. Her late start was induced by her late night, but it turned out to be fine. She found a pleasant surprise waiting for her at the Shark Shack. So her timing turned out to be perfect.

As she walked in the door, her cell phone was ringing but she couldn't get to it in time. She stopped to put her keys in the tray on the credenza and looked at the plastic zipped curtain over the other end of the hall. For a brief second, you could get a whiff of smoke, but it wasn't too bad. The ozone equipment was working, and hopefully it would be over soon. She really wanted to get the house on the market.

Carrie sat down in the gallery room and looked at the family portraits on the wall. She had avoided this entrance since the accident and made her way upstairs from the garage back entrance. As she sat in the quiet, she took in the sight of the portraits through the years. She had never taken them down after the divorce out of respect for her sons. Caught up in a sleepy gaze, it startled her when her phone alerted her to the missed call. Checking her cell phone, the call she missed was from Laney.

She dialed Laney's number and sat down on the sofa in the gallery. "Hey girl, how was your date?"

"Well, I have to tell you, it was amazing. Ben made a confession to me," said Laney.

"Oh really, how intriguing? What was it?"

"He told me he was so excited about tonight that he could hardly think of anything else all week."

"I hope you told him you felt the same way. Go on—tell me more."

"We both admitted that there was a little spark there. We laughed, we talked about our past, and our dreams. I told him about the new venue, and he is ready to help anyway he can."

"That would be incredible! It would give you two a way to spend more time together."

"So, I have to tell you something. He kissed me."

"Get out of town! Really?"

"Yes—after I kissed him first."

"Girl, you are a mess. I'm glad it went well. I told you on the way home from the beach you could see the sparks flying when y'all were together on the yacht."

"It was a wonderful night. Hey, enough about my night. Did you like the house at Atlantic Beach?" asked Laney.

"I did. I think it is perfect. It needs some work, but the realtor showed me a house that had just been completely remodeled that is about the same age. The price is steep, so I went in with a lower offer than the listing price. But that was not the biggest news of the day."

"Well, don't keep me in suspense."

"I saw Robert."

"What? How did that happen? Did he know you were going?" asked Laney.

"No, he didn't, and I was not even sure if he was in town. After I finished looking at the properties, I was starving. I remember him talking about a little joint called The Shark Shack nearby, so I drove around until I found it. I placed my order and was on the way back to the car when he called my name."

"He loves that place. He walks there all the time to eat. You two are destined to be together! That was Heaven's work right there. You know I'm right. God doesn't make any mistakes in how he lines these things up, Carrie Ann."

"It was so good to see him. He was having dinner outside on a picnic bench. He asked me to join him, and we talked for three hours. Funny thing is, I had my day all out of sorts by leaving so late, but I guess that was the end goal—my delightful surprise at the end."

"He is a wonderful man. I keep telling you that, but I think you are seeing it for yourself," said Laney.

"I am. This week I had been struggling with the guilt of knowing that Bill thought the gun was in the closet. I mean, it always was there, until I took it. If the gun had been there, he may still be alive."

"Carrie, it's not your fault. You will get past that," said Laney.

"Well, that's where Robert was so helpful. He pointed things out in a different light. It's almost like he put it under a microscope, so I could view it better and really examine the situation. It really helped when he reminded me that Bill should have called 911 when he first saw them here, instead of taking matters into his own hands. At least that way, the officials would have shown up before he would have died of a head injury or smoke inhalation."

"Robert is a wise man. I hope that piece of insight is sinking in some."

"It really is. I never thought of it that way. I was just so consumed in my guilt and grief that I couldn't make sense of some facts. Bill was responsible for his own demise. If only he had just left well enough alone."

"That's right. Well, you sound exhausted, and I think you should get some rest. Call me in the morning. If you need me now, I'm happy to come stay with you tonight."

"No, honey, I just need some quiet time to think. But thank you for being such a sweet friend. I love you," replied Carrie.

"I love you bigger. Night."

Carrie put the phone down and gazed back up at the portraits. One had always been her favorite. They took it in their backyard when the boys were young. A photographer came over and set up several props. The boys were on rocking horses, and Carrie and Bill saddled up on their horses. It was quite a sight to see the difference in the size of the small rocking horse compared to the stature of the horses. She always thought the portrait was a bit humorous. As she touched it on the wall, it slipped and fell, crashing to the floor. Glass shattered everywhere, and she stared at the mess laying before her. How ironic because that is exactly what had happened—that life, that time, those days, Bill's life shattered and broken. Something in him changed, and she could never figure out what triggered that change. It began before Karen came along, but she played into the situation very well and helped him complete his transformation. She became his coach, and he followed her playbook rule for rule. She always suspected that Karen was not the only one. Not long after they divorced, Carrie had received an anonymous letter in the mail. It stated that Bill was having an affair with his wife. The writer said he would do them both a favor one day and take care of it. Carrie never told Bill or anyone else. To be honest, it embarrassed her. She often wondered who it was. There were whispers when they went to dinner at the country club as she and Bill walked by tables. Carrie knew they were talking about them, but never realized it may have been about Bill's affairs. She eventually figured it out. Then she wanted life to be normal and had attempted to keep up appearances for the last two years of a good marriage. Until the day he told her he was leaving. It became real at that moment, and she no longer had to pretend that everything was a state of marital bliss.

As she sat in the room, she looked over at the draped plastic. On the other side of that plastic wall, Bill had died. Just steps away from where she was sitting, he took his last breath. Carrie realized tears were streaming down her face, but she was not even sure why. Her emotions were all over the map and she needed to navigate herself back to today's reality. Just then, her phone rang again. She looked at the caller identification. She smiled. It was Robert.

"Hello, I am so sorry. I forgot to call," said Carrie, as she wiped her tears away and sat up straight.

"Well, yes, you did, and I was getting concerned. Did you make good time, are you okay?"

"Sort of, I think. I just got caught up in some thoughts. They are overwhelming me right now, but I need to process this and move on."

"Can I help? I'm a rather good listener. I hope you know that by now."

"You are that, indeed. I think today helped me so much; you really brought perspective to Bill's accident. There were things I had not even thought of. I'm sitting here staring at a plastic draped over our master bedroom door and knowing that he died just steps away from where I'm sitting. In my heart I remember the good days, and that makes me cry, then my mind remembers the horrible way things ended, and then I'm mad as hell. He doesn't even deserve these tears I'm crying, but he was the father of my sons. It's such a mess to sort out," said Carrie with a trembled voice.

"Good, that's good right there. You are processing your emotions, and you have to do that eventually. It is perfectly fine to feel angry, sad, mad, scared, and even sorrowful. It's all a part of the process."

"I think I'm tired, and all of this is settling in my heart and mind kind of heavy right now. I just need to go upstairs and get some sleep. But not off the phone until I tell you one thing."

"What is that my dear?"

"You were right about the grouper bites at the The Shark Shack. They were scrumptious, and the conversation while enjoying them was on point," said Carrie.

Robert replied, "I'm glad you liked them; it totally blew me away that chance had us both in the same place. Or maybe ... maybe we should say fate?"

"I would go with fate. Good night. Can we talk tomorrow?"

"For sure. Rest well. Call me if you need me. No hour is too early or too late. Good night."

"Thank you, Robert; you have been a breath of fresh air in my life. Good night."

Carrie took another look around the gallery hall, stood up, turned off the lights, and headed upstairs.

Chapter 35

Then Came September

The contractors did not deviate from their schedule. Leslie didn't allow it, they worked diligently onsite every day with a project manager moving the efforts to the finish line. It was a restoration that would keep the home looking like the era when it was in its glory, but with some new and contemporary touches. The only major difference to the property would be the cottage at the end of the back path. Leslie and Carrie decided it would have several uses. Carrie would stay there when events were being held. Her main residence would be the beach house she purchased at Atlantic Beach. The cottage had two bedrooms, so if Leslie wanted to stay the night, she could as well. It would be ready soon, and Carrie was excited about moving there. They had even discussed building some more cabins on the other side of the creek. It could prove to be a larger concept in renting spaces for corporate and family events and offer more rooms for wedding parties for overnight stays.

As promised, they had designated a section of the backfield for Mae. It was a small mobile home, and it thrilled her to get out of her government housing apartment and have a place of her very own. Carrie purchased it for her as a gift for being so good to her family for so many years.

It was a monumental day for all of them. The four ladies would celebrate the project with an on the ground's reception. A tent was on the front lawn, and Laney acquired a few smokers and pig cookers, and the yard smelled of hickory and oak wood as the cookers rolled smoke from beef ribs, pork ribs, beef brisket, and smoked hams. The cooking was being attended to by a crew that Laney and Ben were managing. The two of them were great at organizing the event all the way down to the port-a-john location, which was behind the house and out of sight. The tent looked lovely in the front yard, down near the gazebo and pond. It was filled with white wooden tables and chairs, and the color scheme was lavender and green. It was a fresh look against the bright blue skies and up against the slope of the bank of the pond lined with oak and willow trees. Stan had done some research and the pond was his favorite part of the project. It was now stocked with fish, but he did add an extra-special touch—a gaggle of geese and a brood of ducklings. The last few days he worked on an additional dock for sitting or fishing. He also had a peacock in transit to the farm.

Carrie and Sandra had selected all the fixtures, furniture, colors, artwork, for the main dining room, banquet room, and hall and that was still a work in progress. Leslie worked on designing the bedrooms with a special intent for each room to represent one of her family members. Those rooms would hold special treasures and once the furniture was placed in each room, they would be complete. She had a room called The Eileen, named for her grandmother, and The Beulah was named after her great-grandmother. The Caroline was a tribute to her mother, and The Peony, was named after her mother's favorite flower. The Helen was in honor of her aunt. Each room represented each one of their lives and held keepsakes and trinkets that belonged to each one of them. It was a labor of love for Leslie and brought her a healing that she had been lacking for many years. Rudy Mann's mother had saved some items, and they found them in a trunk in the pantry. It was such a gift that Leslie treasured, and she wrote a note to the Mann family to thank them for how well they had respected each broach, picture, frame, and linen keepsake. She found some of her grandmother's books stored in the buffet in the dining room. One book contained some tried and treasured recipes, and Laney and Ben had worked on incorporating those items into the menus for the venue.

The other rooms downstairs were decorated by Ben and Laney and included a groomsmen room, and two rooms with a more masculine design. The groomsmen room was called The Red Room as a nod to Leslie's grandfather's nickname, his favorite color, and his alma mater's North Carolina State University school colors. The adjacent rooms were for groomsmen that could stay on sight or just as well for any guests. They would not limit it to weddings only. The last room was the Pirate Room, in honor of her children's graduation from East Carolina University. The other two rooms downstairs had a classic golf décor with memorabilia from several of the best courses in the Carolinas. The only thing left to place in the rooms was the furniture and beds.

Leslie had kept the naming of the rooms a closely guarded secret, and they would reveal it at the reception. For every relative that was honored, she had contacted the closest next of kin she could locate. She wanted them to be there to see the house being restored to its former glory. She had not even told Stan about her plans, and the excitement was overwhelming. She had a speech prepared that included some emotional memories about the house along with information about the new journey they were embarking.

The name of the venue had also been decided. It had taken the four of them a bit of deliberating to agree. Then one night while enjoying dinner at Laney's, Carrie brought up how all their lives were changing so quickly, and it was one pivotal moment in time, one weekend, and one event that brought on the change. She said that despite the storms, they had remained standing—strong as oak trees. Within seconds Leslie mumbled, "Four Oaks Hall." For a moment, there was silence, then Laney was the first to speak up to approve and Ben agreed. For lack of an argument to not use it, they agreed it would work. They were incredibly rooted, grounded, and strong women. It was a creative way to reference their strength by the comparison to the strength of an oak.

Leslie loved how the venture of Four Oaks Hall brought back an excitement that she did not even realize she had lost. Stan saw something she did not for several years—losing the family homeplace had deeply damaged her. Other relatives never grasped the complexity of the heartache Leslie had experienced. They had no emotional connection to it like she had, so it did not matter to them if it was sold. But for Leslie it was a lifetime of memories that she cherished. Thanks to Stan, she had a future that was filled with a project she could have only dreamed of, and her best friends to create a new legacy along with her. The restoration was restoring more than just the house—it was restoring all their brokenness and it was as beautiful as a four-part harmony melody.

One of the unexpected ideas that excited Leslie, was the television series that Carrie's sons had created—it was genius. They were going to rent the facility to Carrie's sons and their new company, Media Marketing Innovation. The filming would be done at Four Oaks Hall and aired on syndicated networks all over the United States. The idea was already in progress, and they lined the clients up to begin as soon as they opened. Ben and Laney would have their own cooking show, and the boys were marketing the location to networks across the country. There was plenty of room on the property for it to be a destination for filming television shows and movies on location. They even had a few inquiries from local churches to film Bible studies to broadcast to their congregation and air podcasts. The possibilities were endless, and Leslie was eager to see how that would all shape up as a secondary venture under the principal business. The more they touched this project, the more it grew.

Leslie walked out to sit under the veranda her grandfather built many years ago. A few repairs were made, and they changed the flooring to a composite decking to avoid any future wood rot. The benches had been replaced, and the veranda looked as good as new.

She looked around the yard and the house and saw all the life and positive energy it had today. She felt tears well up in her eyes. The yard was filled with the smells of great food, the laughter of people, and music. For a moment, she smiled and cried at the same time. She finally felt like she was doing her grandparents proud. They would have loved this. It was almost a carbon copy of the events her grandaddy would plan. The only difference was the type of bands he would hire to play. The bands her grandaddy favored looked like something from an old country western movie with one band member blowing on a jug, another playing spoons, and a harmonica player to round out the sound. When she was a child, they went to Disney World. When her grandaddy saw the Country Bear Jamboree, he loved it and he aimed to make sure all their events had a band that could "play like them bears." It was a special occasion when he had a violin added to the mix. They did not play classical - they fiddled. Granddaddy liked his music lively and always said that opera music was for the more sophisticated. He preferred to be unsophisticated in the most sophisticated way that he could. That sentiment always made everyone laugh.

As the sunlight peeked through the branches of the willows, it formed a lace pattern in the contrast of light. Leslie could see guests were driving down the lane of trees. It was a bucolic sight to behold. From where she was sitting, she could see through the willow trees to the parking attendant motioning the cars into spaces. It was time to change clothes and go over her speech again. She turned to take one more look at the pond to see the breeze creating a dance through the willow branches. She glimpsed a car coming down the lane. It stopped and the attendant spoke to the driver for a moment, then motioned for them to turn around on a path. The car turned around and left. Must have been someone who made a wrong turn and needed directions.

When Leslie walked into the main room at the Inn, a familiar smell immediately caught her attention. She would know that smell anywhere, any day, anytime—peonies. But where did anyone find peonies this time of year? It was early fall. Just as she turned the corner, she saw Stan waiting in the large room by a table with an enormous bouquet.

"Stan, what are you doing?" asked Leslie, as she walked across the room to join him.

"Waiting for my bride to finally come in the room. What were you staring at for so long?" asked Stan.

Leslie looked back at the window to the drive. "Oh nothing, I just saw one of the parking attendants turn someone away. But never mind that, what is all of this here?"

"Your mother's favorite. I'm positive she would be proud of you, and I know she's here with you today in spirit," said Stan, as he kissed her on the forehead.

"Where did you find peonies this time of year?" asked Leslie. "Just the scent of them reminds me of her."

Stan looked at the peonies and winked at Leslie, "It was difficult. It took a couple of calls, but I am a resourceful guy."

"Yes, you are," replied Leslie as she noticed another table filled with red roses.

"Who are these from? They are beautiful!"

"Go read the card," said Stan, as he motioned to the table.

Leslie read the card out loud, "*Congratulations, I know your grandfather loved red, so here is a little something red to let you know he would be proud. Love, Aunt Susan.*"

"Oh, she is really the only living relative left that would have known he loved red. That is so sweet of her. I guess her health isn't good since she's not coming in person."

"No, she's fine and she's already here. She's outside, sitting in the tent. Said she wouldn't miss it for the world. She was just talking about her original homeplace down the other road. She had her daughter drive her by there on the way here. Seemed to bring back some wonderful memories for her."

"That's great! I cannot wait to see her. Let's take these arrangements out to the tent."

Leslie looked out on the lawn and noticed that Sandra, Laney, Carrie, and Ben were already under the tent putting food out on tables. Laney had it worked out to a science, almost military precision. The menu contained ambrosia salad, carrot and raisin slaw, collard greens, orange and pine-apple fluff, deviled egg potato salad, baked beans, creamed potatoes, and gravy and topped with cheddar cheese, cucumber salad, and of course, fried green tomatoes. She and Ben were cooking them under the tent and delivering them to the tables with a slice of mozzarella and a remoulade sauce that was Ben's mother's recipe. Ben had chosen the selection of desserts: Red Velvet Cake, Pig picking Cake, and Strawberry Shortcake. There was a cordial bar located beside the dessert bar of samples. They had schooled the staff on making their signature drinks: mimosas, margaritas, and Ben's famous Bloody Mary. His Bloody Mary was more of a meal with a celery stick, a skewer of olives, mushrooms, jalapeno cheese, a slice of bacon and a skewer of shrimp. The other offerings were straight up whiskey and bourbon alongside a wine bar featuring Duplin County wines. Uptown Brewery provided beverages for the draft beer connoisseurs.

Stan stood behind Leslie as she gazed at the hustle and bustle outside on the greens. He leaned in and gave her a kiss on the cheek.

"You know something, when I worked out the deal to purchase this property and get it back to you, I had no idea this is what you would come up with. You never cease to amaze me. I am looking at the Leslie I once knew, but somehow grief and family turmoil dirtied her all up and dimmed her sparkle. But honey, you are shining bright right now. I'm enormously proud of what you and your girls have put together here. It's spectacular," said Stan as he wrapped his arms around her.

Leslie wiped tears away, "The smoke from the grill must be getting my eyes teary."

"Nonsense. I know you and your tender heart. I also know you cry equally hard when you are happy as when you are sad, so I know you are happy right now. That is all I ever wanted."

"You, my husband, are more that I could have ever imagined. For the first time in a long time, I feel like me again. Carrie has a new lease on life, Laney is ecstatic, and Sandra has a purpose. You did more than restore me. Your gift to me is also a gift to them, and it's restoring all of us. Thank you from me and all of them. Who knew the day I pulled that key down from my willow tree that it would lead us to this?"

"You owe me no gratitude. I receive it by watching you all at work here. Now get out there and mingle and sell this place to those guests. You will have bookings for weeks on end, I just know it," said Stan.

Stan and Leslie walked out to the tent. Ben and Laney were finishing up details with the bartenders, and Carrie and Sandra were adding the last of the food to the tables. Laney was helping them, and her smile and enthusiasm was enough to light up the tent.

Leslie saw one of the parking attendants and recognized that he was the one she saw with the car that he turned around.

"Hello, I'm Leslie. How are you?" asked Leslie, as she approached the gentleman.

"Ma'am I'm good, really good. Nice place you have here. It's going to be grand, just grand," he said.

"Thank you so much. I did not catch your name," said Leslie.

The older gentlemen laughed and looked at her with a grin. Then he looked over at Stan and laughed.

"You don't recognize me, do you, girl?" said the older gentlemen.

"I'm afraid I do not. I didn't work with hiring the staff for tonight, my husband did. I'm sorry. What is your name, sir?" Leslie asked.

Stan stood beside Leslie and seemed amused. This irritated her because she was beginning to feel embarrassed.

The older man laughed again and replied, "Try it one more time. I bet you'll remember."

Leslie looked at the older gentlemen and sized him up. She felt like her face had turned beet red. It was obvious he knew her, and she felt ashamed that she could not place him. She looked at his weathered brown face and silver hair and beard. She came up with nothing. All the while Stan standing there with his smirky grin made her even more uncomfortable.

"Well sir, you have me guessing, that's for sure. But I am at a total loss. I am afraid and ashamed to admit that since you obviously know me," said Leslie.

"Well, it's been an awfully long time, so I forgive you. It's me—Duke," said the older man with a big grin on his face.

Leslie's mouth flew open, and her arms opened wide as she hugged her old friend. He was older, but that didn't prevent him from picking her up and spinning her around.

"Duke! Oh, my goodness! How would I have ever guessed with all that white hair on your face?" asked Leslie, as she stepped back to inspect him further.

"When the wrinkles set in, it helped cover them up," he said with a raspy laugh.

Leslie looked at him closer, and she could see the age on him, but he was still as strong and strapping as he was when he worked for her grandfather.

"Why didn't you tell me you were still around when we put that article in the paper about fixing the place up?" asked Leslie.

"Well, I wasn't sure how you feel about an old farm hand coming around and ruining the fancy appeal."

"Nonsense, you are welcome anytime. Wouldn't granddaddy be proud, Duke?' asked Leslie as she surveyed the property.

Duke put his arm around her shoulder and looked out over the view with her. "Yes ma'am, he sure would. Well, I came up for some water. It's warm out there in the parking lot, but I can handle it. I better get back out there and park some cars."

"Well, my work here is done. I just wanted to see your reaction when you found out it was Duke – your Duke," said Stan.

Leslie turned around to see Stan's halfway grin turn to a smile. "Wait a minute here, you knew it was Duke, you hired him, and you kept this all a secret?"

"Well, missy when he kept coming around to my boiled peanut truck more often, I asked him why. Then he told me what he was working on, I told him I used to work that land myself," said Duke.

"I've been going to Duke's peanut truck every time I came over here. Plus, I love hearing his knowledge of war times that his family has passed down to generations. When I learned that he was the Duke you always talked about, I thought it would be a nice surprise. I remembered how much he meant to your family," said Stan.

"Oh yes! It's so glad to have you Duke. I look forward to having you around here more often. Duke, listen, before you go, I have a question. I saw you turn someone away earlier. What was that all about?" asked Leslie.

"Yea, some lady wanted to come up and talk to a lady named Sandra. She didn't have an invitation ticket. I told her kindly, but boldly, that no one can get through here without that ticket. The man down there in charge said everyone had to have a ticket that came through. She said she wasn't planning on staying. I wondered why she even wanted to come up here. She seemed a little frustrated with me, but I was nice, really nice."

Leslie looked around for Sandra and saw she was greeting some guests. She would not disturb her now, but it seemed strange that one of her acquaintances listed would not have a ticket.

"You're sure they asked specifically for Sandra, right?" asked Leslie.

"Yep. Sandra is who they asked for, or Mitch, they did say Mitch would be okay. I told her she would just have to get up with Sandra or Mitch another time. Without an invitation, I could not let her in. I bet she was trying to peddle them something."

"You did right, Duke. It's fine, did you get her name?"

"No, I didn't ask that, but I guess I should have. I'm sorry."

"No Duke, that is fine. No worries at all. Thank you."

"I look forward to seeing you more now that you will be back around, Miss Leslie. Gosh, you were always a pretty little thing, running around this farm. It's good to see you back. Real good. I best be getting back down to the parking lot. I don't want to fall down on my duties," said Duke as he gave Leslie a pat on the shoulder.

Leslie had to wonder why would someone be asking for Sandra or Mitch with no ticket? She knew that wondering would have to take up some brain space later. For now, she needed to focus on a seamless and perfect event that would make folks want to book and come back to for their weddings, celebrations, and dinners. It was time to present Four Oaks Hall and let others see the vision the four ladies held in their hearts and minds.

The band was taking requests, and a few attendees were enjoying the dance floor. Leslie was admiring the sight and sounds when Carrie tapped her on the shoulder.

"Look who's here. It's Robert!" said Carrie.

"Robert, I am so glad you made it. I never had a doubt, but Carrie said you had some issues with your work schedule. I thought you retired. What's up with all that?" asked Leslie.

"Just piddling, as they say. Once you get the yacht and boat wholesale business in your wheelhouse, it's difficult to get out of it. But it keeps me out of trouble. This is looking first class. Carrie said it was coming along faster than you girls thought, and it's absolutely incredible here," said Robert.

Laney spotted Robert and motioned to Ben, "Robert, you made it. So glad you are here. Listen, can you get the attention of the crowd? It's time for Leslie to make her announcement." said Laney.

"Absolutely," said Robert. "Listen, I may have a proposition for you all. I have some furniture in air-controlled storage. Some marvelous pieces. In looking over this place, I think I may have just found a suitable home for them if you will consider them."

"Really, oh wow! Are they new or vintage?" asked Sandra.

"They are most definitely vintage. But in excellent condition. I can send you some pictures when I get back to Atlantic Beach."

"Oh, I am excited about that, Robert. But we must purchase them. Okay?" said Leslie.

"No worries. I was planning on donating them to charity for auction. They just need the perfect home where they are admired, and this will be the perfect place for them to rest," said Robert.

Laney looked at Leslie as she fidgeted with the notes in her hands. She knew she was nervous about speaking to such a large audience. The attendees were business owners, friends, wedding planners, and family. It was quite a menagerie from many levels of society.

"Come on Leslie, you'll be fine. Just speak from your heart about what this place meant to you, the events your grandparents held here, the memories, and how you hope everyone that attends an event at this venue will feel as welcome and at home as you did for years," said Laney.

"I know, but there are a lot of folks out there. How many did you all narrow it down to?" asked Leslie.

"200," said Laney through a forced smile.

"What? 200? I thought we agreed on 100 tops. Oh, my word! What caused us to go over?" asked Leslie.

"Um, you. You kept adding more. It's fine, really. It will produce bookings. We already have several weddings penciled in for spring, and two engagement parties after we open. That happened just a few minutes ago. Sandra took the bookings and a credit card deposit. So, it's all good. The more the merrier," said Laney.

"Wow, that's great! So let me get to this speech," said Leslie.

Robert took his glass, raised it in the air, and tapped on the side with a spoon to get attention. Leslie greeted everyone from the small podium and microphone.

"Good evening, Welcome to Four Oaks Hall. We are so pleased that you all are here," Leslie stopped dead in the middle of her sentence. She looked to the back of the tent and past the guests. At the edge of where the light and dark met, she saw a woman standing in the shadows.

"Excuse me, but I was just distracted by this awesome looking crowd and a bit overwhelmed. So, let me tell you all about the legacy of this land. My grandparents would have loved to see you here and would want to celebrate every event with you."

Her speech went on for a few minutes as she described the many services and the event planning that would be available. All the while, she kept her eye on the woman in the back. The woman was a distraction, especially when she saw her approach Mitch and they walked away down the path into the darkness. Sandra was so intent on every word that Leslie said that she had not even noticed that Mitch left. Leslie had the advantage with her view, as she was the only one looking in that direction.

Everyone else was watching and listening to her speak and no one had seen Mitch walk away with a strange woman.

"Ladies and gentlemen, I trust you will enjoy the sophisticated Southern meal we planned for you. We will build our reputation on taking Southern classics and adding a new contemporary element to jazz them up a bit. As an example, how about that gouda pimento cheese? We added some last-minute items to the menu to show you our truly creative side, and we are not afraid of straying off the traditional Southern cookbook at all. I love traditional Southern collards but wait until y'all try those stir-fried collard greens. And my favorite—our creamed potatoes mixed with sour cream, cream cheese, bacon, and brown gravy with mushrooms. Mercy, that will do me in for sure. Be sure to get a mini sampling of Ben's famous Bloody Mary. So, enjoy and don't forget the dessert bar and the cordial samplings. So, ladies of Four Oaks Hall, please join me up here to thank our guests for coming. Laney, Sandra, Carrie—come on up here girls! And Ben—you, too."

As they were making their way to the podium, Leslie spotted Mitch coming back to the tent. He made it back just in time to see them thank the guests and join in on the applause. He seemed changed. Leslie could not describe it, but it was as though he was in shock. She was not sure what he was up to, but she would find out.

The night ended well, and it was a successful christening of the new birth of Four Oaks Hall. While the help was cleaning up, Leslie spotted Mitch and Sandra in an intense conversation. Mitch was waving his hands in the air and Sandra was asking him questions. It appeared to be more of an interrogation than an argument.

Leslie walked over and said, "Hey, what's going on here? Is everything okay?"

"Leslie, would you mind too much if we just sort of split, like right now. There is something we have to attend to, and it cannot wait," said Sandra.

"Sure. There is nothing more to do here. That's why we hired people to clean up and tear down. So run on," said Leslie.

Mitch looked at her and mouthed the words *thank you*. When Sandra left to get her things, Leslie grabbed him by the arm.

"Do you want to tell me who that was you slipped away with earlier tonight? What are you up to, Mitch?" asked Leslie.

"Don't worry. It's fine. It's not what it must have looked like to you, and I can see how you may have gotten the wrong idea. Trust me, Leslie. Please."

"Okay, let's go. I have everything," said Sandra, as she grabbed Mitch by the arm.

"We'll talk tomorrow, right?" asked Leslie as she hugged her.

"Of course," said Sandra.

Leslie watched them leave, and she locked her eyes in a trance of watching their car. By the time they reached the end of the path, Mitch paused, and a car parked at the bottom lot pulled out behind them. Something was odd about this situation. Who was that woman? It was the same car Duke turned away earlier. She shook her head and returned to the tent to wrap up a few details for the evening. Stan was paying the band. Duke was waiting for Leslie at a table and motioned for her to come over.

"Hello there, how many cars do you reckon you parked tonight, Duke?" asked Leslie.

Duke pulled out a small pocket notebook and pen from his shirt pocket. It reminded her of her grandaddy—he always carried the same thing. She imagined that under his wings, he must have instilled the same technique to Duke.

"By my count, we parked almost 141 cars down there in the fields. Nice crowd. You know that woman I turned away? She came back. I thought you would want to know. She parked down by the road and walked up here to the house. I kept my eye on her and she must have known one of the folks here cause I saw 'em talking, I guess that she found Mitch."

"Thanks Duke. I saw that myself. Not sure who she was, but no harm done. It's fine," said Leslie.

"Okay. I just wanted to be sure and let you know before I headed home. You have a real good evening and I look forward to working around here again. It's not farming, but it's still like home to me," said Duke.

"Thank you, Duke. You are always welcome here. Say, how's your baby sister Lydia? She was the youngest out of all your lot, right? I loved to play with her as a child."

"Oh, little Lydia did good. She's the baby of eight, and she did real good. She's a fancy lawyer in Atlanta now. She writes up contracts for sports teams and athletes. You should see some of the people she knows, like celebrities."

Leslie smiled, "Well, that is wonderful. Please tell her I asked about her and I would love for her to come visit when we open. She's welcome to stay here at the house."

"I'll get you her telephone number, and you can tell her yourself. She would love to hear from you. She always thought you were something special."

"Oh, I would like that. Thank you. Good night, Duke."

Leslie watched him walk to his old blue pick up truck. She laughed out loud when she saw the sign on the side door, "Duke's Boiled Peanuts."

She took a moment to sit down at a table and thought about what both witnessed and what Mitch said. Sandra and Mitch had some explaining to do in the morning.

Chapter 36

The Day After the Reception

Carrie woke up early, made a cup of coffee, and walked out to the balcony of her hotel room. She was glad she had stayed nearby; she needed a good night's rest. The reception, while an amazing success, it was exhausting work. The hotel was just a short drive, and she needed some time to finish up some orders before she headed back over to the Inn.

The sun was up, but Carrie could hear the distant sound of thunder; she thought she better enjoy the sun while she could; that storm was heading her way. Just as she sat down, she noticed someone on the balcony on the lower floor. She stopped to watch as she thought she recognized something familiar about the woman. Something about her mannerisms. It seemed like she reminded Carrie of someone, but the fiery red mane of curls did not fit anyone she knew. She would remember those locks for sure; it looked fake.

She continued to enjoy the sunrise and sipped her coffee as she went over spreadsheets of inventory and supplies. Robert recently brought her around to his way of thinking, and she was embracing early morning sunrises. Their relationship had grown over the last few months, and she was elated about that development. He had been talking her into getting up early to meet for a walk on the beach. Usually, it was followed with breakfast at Four Corners Diner. Carrie smiled when she thought of those morning walks and realized he could probably talk her into almost anything.

Carrie knew she was in love, but she also knew she needed to move slowly to guard her heart. She was concise and clear when she shared her heart with him. Robert shared that the feeling was mutual, and his love for her was patient enough to let her lead them with where they belonged on the journey.

Carrie's mind drifted back to the conversation. Robert had arrived to pick her up for dinner with a single red rose and a note attached: *"One rose for one of a kind—you."* After she read the card, she reached up to embrace him and she kissed him on the cheek. As they held each other, he whispered in her ear, "Carrie, I think you should know that I completely adore you." In response, Carrie had kissed him passionately, and he eagerly reciprocated. Just thinking about it now made Carrie a bit flushed. *"Back to details, Carrie. Mercy, girl!"* she mumbled, as she finished her coffee. She would go back inside and get ready to face the day, then head back to Four Oaks Hall. There was much planning to do, and Carrie did not want to miss the interior designer delivering the last of items they ordered.

She was almost to the door of the balcony, when she noticed the woman on the balcony below her was on the phone, and Carrie watched as she paced back and forth. Carrie stopped and analyzed the stranger. There was something about her that seemed so familiar. But that hair! Carrie had never seen such red hair on anyone she knew. *That was it,* she thought. *Could it be someone I know, but they dyed their hair?* She was intrigued, so she looked back again as she could faintly hear the woman's voice. She tried to make out what she was saying, but then the stranger turned around and Carrie was afraid she would see her, so she turned her head and went inside. She did not want to appear to be nosey.

In a few minutes, she was packed and ready to check out. She made her way down to the lobby, fixed a cup of coffee for the ride, and was adding her cream when the redheaded mystery lady made her way through the lobby. Carrie watched her as she walked to the parking lot. Carrie moved closer to the window to watch her go to her car. That walk, Carrie knew that walk, and she recognized the way she flipped her hair. Carrie walked down the side of the hotel lobby to get a view from the other window. She watched as the woman put luggage in the back seat. She could not get a good look at the vehicle, so she moved to the lobby's front doors. The car was backing out, and the hedges and trees in the landscaping were hiding her view of the car. When the car came around the corner and sped out of the drive, Carrie could see the car and the driver. She gasped and stepped back so as not to be seen. She dropped her coffee as she leaned against the lobby door for support. No wonder she seemed familiar to Carrie. It was Karen.

Chapter 37

Baby Maybe

Sandra sat on the front porch, sipping a protein shake as she watched a storm making its way across town. The shocking news that an expectant mother had an adoption agency seek them out was beyond comprehension. As she watched the storm, she realized she felt like one was brewing in her. The agency offered detailed paperwork and information about the process. The only part that concerned Sandra, was how fast they were pushing for a decision. The representative was nice and polite, but rigid about a deadline for an answer.

Mitch came outside with a coffee mug in one hand and a doughnut in the other. Sandra waved her hand no to a bite Mitch offered her.

"If I was ever tempted to indulge in a doughnut, this morning would be the time. Mitch, did I dream all this last night? How is it an expectant mother has sought us out with this adoption agency? It makes me wonder who it is and if she will come back and want this baby. I have too many questions," said Sandra as her straw caught air as she finished the last of her shake.

Mitch took Sandra's hand in his and said, "Honey, I'm not sure, either. However, the paperwork on this thing is airtight. In all the agencies we have investigated, I've never seen such professional work."

"Mitch, what do we do? I mean, I'm excited. But on the other hand, my brain is telling me to think, think, think. You know me, I over-think everything. Help me here, Mitch. What do we do? It seems like they won't give us much time."

"My guess is that if we don't agree, the mother will move on to other options fairly soon. That makes sense to me because it takes a while for all this paperwork to be completed. I get that part. The agency knew exactly where to find us, and the paperwork was ready for our review. Sandra, this is a God given thing. Maybe we shouldn't scrutinize so much and just accept this blessing that is literally being brought to our front door."

Sandra began to cry, and Mitch was not sure what that meant. He held her close, and they rocked back and forth in the porch swing. He knew his wife was struggling with the decision, and he wanted some quiet time to let her gather the thought of having a new baby very soon. It had been so long in coming that she seemed almost in shock at the possibility of it happening. Even though they had talked about it and done some research, neither of them thought it would happen so fast.

"Mitch, I'm tired. We were up so late last night reading that information. Would it be okay if I just laid back down for a bit? When I wake up, we can talk this through and try to call the representative."

Mitch nodded his head and said, "Get some rest. You go shut your beautiful eyes and rest. We'll figure this out."

Sandra went inside and Mitch remained on the porch swing. This was a fast track to what they had wanted for an exceptionally long time—a baby. It was almost surreal, and he could not help but imagine what it would be like to have a newborn baby in their home. He tried his best to hide his excitement from Sandra, because ultimately, they both had to be in total agreement. He could envision them in the swing, with Sandra holding a sweet baby in her arms.

As he continued to dream and finish his coffee, Sandra's cell phone rang in the swing beside him. It was Leslie.

"Good morning, Leslie. How are you after such a big night?" said Mitch, as he closed his eyes to brace for what he knew she really wanted to talk about.

"Good Mitch, and you? Really, Mitch, what the heck was going on last night? Who was that woman and what did she want with you and Sandra? Duke told me he turned her away, and she came back, parked the car down the path and walked up in the dark. Then I see the same car follow y'all out of here. Who was she and what was going on? Where is Sandra, and why didn't she answer?"

"Leslie, I know it seems odd, but as I asked last night, trust me on this. I can't say a word right now, but it's nothing bad. Please trust me. Sandra is lying down for a while. She's exhausted. Can I get her to call you when she gets up?" asked Mitch.

"Exhausted and laid back down? Mitch, it is 9:00 in the morning, she is supposed to be back here at the Hall in thirty minutes. I drove back over here to meet the contractor and she was supposed to join me, then I am headed over to the restaurant warehouse while Sandra worked with the details here. This is not like her at all. You need to come clean and tell me what's going on. I swear you can tar and feather me and hang me at the town square if I say a word. What is going on?"

"Leslie, keep this to yourself. Not a word to anyone, not even Stan, okay?"

"Honor promise, I promise to honor," replied Leslie.

"We may be adopting. The lady last night was from an adoption agency. She says an expectant mother has hand-chosen us for the first option for adopting her baby. It's due in about 10 weeks and we have to decide now so she can move on to other options if we decline."

"Oh, my word! That is wonderful news! So, what is keeping you from saying yes?"

"It's overwhelming. I mean, who picked us? Will they come back into our lives and cause problems? Will they renege on the agreement? We feel elation, confusion, hope, apprehension, and scared as hell, to be honest with you. I mean, we just started investigating adoption and now here it is coming to our door."

"Well, it just might mean that the man upstairs is working on your behalf, and you had years of prayers answered when you leaned into letting go of conceiving. God has given you a gift. We should just go with the flow of the blessings upon us. Who knows how He is working in our lives? It's not our job to question it. But it's not my decision. That's just my two cents worth."

"You make a good point. Listen, keep this between me and you. Not a word to Sandra that I told you or anyone else for that matter. I will let her know we talked after it's all over, okay? We are hoping to meet the representative again this morning. She is staying nearby until we give an answer, so we can sign the paperwork right away."

"Absolutely, no worries. Listen, prayers to y'all. I know you'll make the right decision; y'all always do. I wonder how the representative knew to come to The Hall. It was a publicized event. Maybe that's the only way they knew how to pin you down."

"Possibly—I'm not sure."

"Listen, I'll let you go. Prayers to you both. I love y'all."

"Thank you. We'll talk soon. Goodbye," said Mitch, and he sat back down in the swing. Going out to the Hall would not work for Sandra today, and the bank – he knew he would not make it in. For now, they needed to make the best decision about the baby.

Chapter 38

Who Did Carrie See?

Laney had a breakfast spread for the supervisor and the crew. Her thoughts were to keep them fed and happy in hopes that they would stay on schedule. She was finishing up her coffee when Leslie and Carrie both pulled up at about the same time. When they got out of their cars, neither one of them had their hard hats on, so Laney grabbed a couple of them and met them at the door.

Laney handed them the hard hats, "You hard-headed knuckle heads, if you don't put a hard hat on, we'll be in a world of trouble with the project manager."

Carrie and Leslie went straight to the table with Laney where she had the blueprints, furniture, wallpapers, colors, fabrics pulled up on the computer and spread out all over the table. Laney and Leslie were looking at the items on their order, when Carrie realized Sandra was late.

"Where is Sandra?" asked Carrie.

Leslie jumped a bit and attempted to conceal her nervousness. "Yeah, about that, listen, she and Mitch have something going on right now and she will not be here today. A family thing came up, and not sure what it involves just yet, but we'll carry on. She will be fine since she picked all of this out with me already. No worries," she said.

"Wow, that doesn't sound good. Is everything okay?" asked Laney.

"I think so. There's something they need to work through today, and I didn't ask too many questions. Mitch was holding his cards close the to the vest, so I did not press," said Leslie.

They heard the front door shut, and the interior designer walked into the foyer.

They went to work, and in just a while they selected the final paint colors and fabric for the curtain panels. The furniture had already been delivered that morning and placed in a back storage room. Robert's antique treasures found their new home at Four Oaks Hall as well.

Leslie went to find Carrie. She had walked out of the room; she had left the table a few minutes before they wrapped everything up.

Leslie found Carrie in the kitchen at the sink, "Hey you! What's up? You alright?"

"Oh yes, I'm fine. Really. Just needed some water," said Carrie, with her hand over her forehead. "No wait, I'm not fine."

"Sit down. Let's talk," said Leslie.

"No, not now. Ben and Laney are leaving soon, and we can have some privacy. Meet me down by the willow trees when you get done," said Carrie.

"Okay, I'll wait then."

Laney and Ben came back through with boxes and a cart filled with supplies.

"Well, ladies, Ben and I are heading back to Greenway. We have that cooking class to start tonight, and we need to get ready and be at The Bread Basket to help Sara set up. Thank you for hooking us up with her, Leslie. It was a perfect setup for her and for us," said Laney.

"Most welcome. I'm glad it worked out. But don't let her have any of our secret recipes now, you hear?" said Leslie.

"Pinky promise and scout's honor," said Laney with a grin.

They said their goodbyes and Leslie stood in front of the house, looking down the lane as they drove away. Carrie walked out to the bench by the pond, and Leslie went to meet her there. The weather was nice, and the breeze felt good, so it was a quiet place to talk in private. This was the second issue that had come up in less than one day. She sure prayed this was not building up to be a trilogy.

"So, are you going to tell me what's on your mind?" asked Leslie, as she sat beside Carrie on the bench.

Carrie stared at the lily pads floating in front of her in the pond. Leslie put her arm around her friend's shoulders. In a while, the words came to her lips. Then she was telling Leslie the entire story, but it came out as babbling nonsense.

Leslie stopped her, "Carrie, I'm not understanding a word of this. Who where you watching at the hotel? What about seeing her in the lobby? I'm not following you. Did you think you were in danger? Do you think it was a stalker?"

"I'm sorry. I don't mean to scare you. I'm just; it's just I'm confused right now," said Carrie as she took a deep breath. "So ... I was having coffee on my hotel balcony, and I saw a woman on the lower balcony and something about her looked familiar. I couldn't put my finger on it, but I couldn't brush it off. I kept watching her."

"So, why did you follow her to the lobby? And why does this have you so upset?"

"I didn't follow her. I was getting ready to leave and I saw her walking through the lobby. I had the same feeling again—that I knew her. By then she had on a sun hat and shades. She had the reddest hair I have ever seen, and that threw me off. It clearly came from a bottle."

"Why did that throw you off?"

"The red hair and a little weight gain—she didn't even look like herself. But her car was the same Jaguar and plates, but she definitely has fallen off the work-out wagon."

"Who was it?" Leslie asked.

"It was Karen. Can you believe it? What are the odds of me staying in the same hotel, at the same time, when no one has seen hide nor hair of her since Bill died? I wish you had been there as my witness. You think I'm crazy right now, don't you?"

"No, I don't. But are you sure? Were there just similarities? Karen always had a figure to die for. You said red hair?" asked Leslie while she was deep in thought about the description.

"I know it's insane, right? She was always a slave to that body in the gym, but she looked a bit on the pudgy side to me," said Carrie.

Leslie was suddenly silent.

Carrie tapped her on the knee and said, "Earth to Leslie, where did you go?"

"She was thicker? Like body building, maybe?"

"Oh no. She looked like she had put some weight on. It was quite shocking. I didn't understand the red hair. What could be up with the hair color?

"Not sure, but this is interesting. Maybe she didn't want to be recognized? So how did it feel seeing her?" asked Leslie.

"I didn't realize it was her until she pulled out of the parking lot. I still can't understand why she bolted after Bill died, and never came back. And what is she doing out here in the boondocks in a hotel? I thought she was living in Memphis."

"Carrie, are you absolutely sure it was Karen? This seems odd."

"Yes, for God's sake - I think I know the woman. I worked with her, and she had an affair with my husband. I know what she looks like."

"Okay, easy now. Let's think. She could be traveling again with media sales. You know that's her thing, and that takes you all over the place. She may be tying up loose ends on the house sale and didn't want to stay in Greenway," said Leslie.

"Possibly, but it's just an odd coincidence that we were in the same hotel, out here in the middle of nowhere. Don't you think?"

"I do. But stranger things have happened. I know that had to be shocking to see her. You seem a bit rattled, are you okay?"

"I am. It just threw me off. I dropped my coffee and almost took out the lobby door when I nearly fainted. I'm sorry I was so distracted when we met with the designer. Hey, I'm worried about Sandra. What's up with her? Is she pregnant? Oh my, is she? Is that it?" asked Carrie as she squealed with excitement, hoping that she guessed correctly.

"I'm not sure about that. I just know that Mitch asked us to give her some time," said Leslie, being careful to avoid specific details about her conversation with Mitch.

"Wouldn't it be great if that is it? Oh, I hope so!" said Carrie.

"Time will tell. So, let's focus on the task at hand, put that nonsense about the red headed mystery girl, Karen or not out of your head. You left that life, it's behind you now," said Leslie.

"You are absolutely right, not another word about it. Let's get to work, we have some finalizing to do."

Chapter 39

Ribbon Cutting

Leslie was in the office working on a software installation. Such a mundane task in her thoughts, but it had to be done. Ben had stayed overnight at the Inn and was working with the contractors on the last details. He heard Leslie in the office and went to see if he could lend her a hand. He found Leslie reading the software manual with a puzzled look on her face. He was right—she might need his help.

"Good morning, early riser. Are we on schedule?" asked Leslie, looking up from the manual.

"I'm great, but nervous—maybe a little. Well, no, maybe a lot, to be honest," said Ben.

"Uh oh, did we hit a snag on our opening day? Everything is still on schedule, right? You didn't really answer my question. I mean, we have four events straight out of the gate to make perfect," said Leslie.

"Oh that. No, I mean yes. Everything is wonderful—even ahead of schedule," replied Ben.

"Is this where I ask what has you so tangled, or do you want to keep it to yourself? I'm all ears if you need a pair. But you can tell me to leave well enough alone, too. But you started it, so finish. What's up?"

Ben reached below his desk drawer and pulled out a box that was a shipping container. As he handed it to her, Leslie thought it may be his proof of his next book from the publisher.

"What's this? Your new cookbook?" asked Leslie.

"No, it's not my cookbook."

"Did you pack your desk? You're not resigning, are you? Please say no."

"No, it's not that. It's quite the opposite. I hope I'll be staying around for a while," Ben said with his famous sideways smile.

Leslie opened the box to see a smaller box that was surrounded by Styrofoam and packaging paper. She removed the Styrofoam case to see a small jewelry box. She took the box out and looked at Ben.

"Is this what I think it is? Are you proposing to Laney?"

"I am if this ring meets your blessing. As one of her nearest and dearest friends, I would like your blessing. So, look and see what you think."

Leslie opened the box, and the beauty of the ring was so breath-taking. She placed her hand over her heart and looked up at Ben. She lifted the ring out of the jewelry box and held it up to the light. It was magnificent—a round, flat cut suspension diamond with smaller diamonds surrounding the lower band to halo the ring. The bridge of the ring featured small diamonds wrapping around the ring and throughout the entire band.

"My word! This is beautiful, Ben. I have never seen a ring quite like it. Where did you find it? It is stunning."

Ben smiled and let out a sigh of relief, "It was my mother's ring. Some mothers leave their rings to their daughters. In our case, my sisters had rings of their own when my mom passed away. My sister has been keeping this one in her safe for me for a very long time. My mother told me she wanted me to have it to give to the perfect lady one day. Who knew it would take so long to find her?"

"Well, that is a sweet story, I love how it has sentimental value too. Now as for you—I think you'll do," said Leslie with a laugh.

"Oh thanks."

"When are you planning to do this proposal?"

"Tonight. We have dinner planned at her house. I wanted to recreate the night we first had dinner together. Same sunflowers, same meal, same wine, same everything. Because that is when I knew she would be the one to wear this ring," said Ben.

"Oh, your love story is so cute. I just love you two! Congratulations! I know the answer will be yes."

"Keeping my fingers crossed. She really is perfect for me. You know that, right?"

"Absolutely. I love that girl."

Leslie's cell phone rang, and she saw that it was Sandra.

"Oh, it's Sandra, Ben."

Leslie answered the phone, "Hey Sandra, how are you? Ok, slow down. Yes, I' at the Hall. Where are you? Oh great, then I will see you soon."

"She's on her way? I bet she has some news too on the final paperwork for the adoption – she is so excited. Weren't they wrapping up paperwork with the adoption agency this week?" he asked.

"Yes, they were. I hope she has news; they have had their hands full with this process."

"Maybe we'll have good news all around today. Well, I will see you tomorrow. I'm heading over to town now to get everything for dinner while Laney is out. I'm pretty stoked about this. You good here to get this software up and running?" asked Ben.

Leslie looked at the manual and knew she could and should do this on her own. Ben had more pressing things to take care of. "Good luck. But you don't need it. And yes, I think I can manage."

Ben left with the little ring box in his pocket and an enormous smile on his face. Leslie could not help but think how sweet young love is when it's brand new and exciting, and every day another mystery is revealed about each other. Leslie went back to working the software installation. She was having difficulty concentrating, and she caught herself staring out the window. She recalled the memory just as if it were happening in real time. She thought of it several times and the thought about the coincidence of Carrie seeing Karen the same weekend a mystery woman appeared at the reception. It seemed strange that the mystery woman asked for Sandra but ended up speaking with Mitch. She didn't want to jump to conclusions, but that meant something, and she had not figured out what just yet. It was all too coincidental that the timing of the adoption agency contact was also at the same time.

Leslie stared out the window at the reflection of sunlight on the pond. She recalled her conversation with Carrie as they sat on the bench by the pond. Carrie was certain it was Karen. She certainly knew Karen's mannerisms. They had worked together for a long time. The part that was challenging Leslie was the description Carrie gave about Karen being on the thick side.

Suddenly, the puzzle pieces all fell together in Leslie's mind. Karen was pregnant. But really, would she reach out to Mitch and Sandra to adopt? She would have to know how tricky that would be. Leslie thought about the hair color. It was obvious that Karen was disguising her identity. She didn't count on Carrie's clever perception, and that she would stay at the same hotel.

If the baby for adoption was Karen's baby, and if Karen wanted to give it a life with Mitch and Sandra, then that was her decision. But what if they didn't know it was Bill and Karen's baby?

It was no secret that Mitch and Sandra had been trying for a long time to have a child. Small towns hold big mouths, and gossip travels at the speed of light. Whenever Sandra was asked about it, she always told the truth, saying *"if you don't tell them, they will just make up something, anyway."* It was entirely possible that Karen knew about their struggle. Leslie couldn't imagine that Karen would be careless enough to get pregnant. She had always stated that she would never be a parent. Leslie always wondered if it had to do with her upbringing. Rumor mill through town told of a horrible childhood she was dealt. Even Carrie talked about some of her stories, and it sounded like she didn't have a stable relationship with her parents.

The sudden honk of a horn startled her out of her thoughts, and she jumped from the interruption. The delivery truck was at the back door and Leslie went to let them in. Just as they unloaded, Sandra pulled up and parked her car. Leslie saw her face and at once recognized that her disposition was one of elation. They walked inside and sat down in the office. Sandra was smiling. Leslie studied her face closely. For a few seconds, they just stared at each other.

"Are we going to talk or are we going to have a staring competition?" asked Leslie.

Sandra started laughing, and the laughter turned to tears, "We're going to be parents! We're adopting! It's all final. It took some tweaking for a bit there, but now it's a done deal!"

Leslie jumped up from her desk, ran to Sandra, and hugged her.

"I am so excited for you. God answers prayers, doesn't He?" said Leslie.

Sandra wiped the tears from her face, "Yes, indeed. Parents!"

"Wow, that is amazing. Soon, huh?"

"Yes, soon. We need to get busy and get everything set up. I don't know anything about what I need. Can you help me, please?" asked Sandra.

"Certainly. We can do most of it online and have it here in no time. Do you know if it's a girl or boy?"

Sandra was ecstatic with excitement, "It's a girl!"

"Mercy, you are so going to be the perfect girl mom! I'm guessing, if I know you like I think I do, it's going to be all pink and bows and monograms, right?"

"Yes. Absolutely. I envision pink and white stripes, with mint green, and soft watercolor florals, with a touch of metallic gold in the nursery. Oh, and pink gingham, I have to have that."

"Beautiful. So, what is left to put in place? I don't want to throw cold water on your joy, but it is an ironclad deal?"

"It is. Mitch made sure of it. The mother is extremely specific about this adoption. She had an awful childhood and never thought she would be good mother material. She's not married, the best we can understand is that her fiancé passed away before they could get married. We don't know what happened, maybe he was sick? She found out about us from a friend that lives in Greenway. I just wonder if anyone of you were a part of this?"

"Well, not from me, and really, let's not look the proverbial gift horse in the mouth, right? Just enjoy the moment. You have a baby girl coming to you soon. I'm so happy for you and Mitch. My goodness, he is going to be smitten with that baby girl. You know that, right? You just lost rank."

"I know and I wouldn't want it any other way. He's already talking about a swing set for the yard. I had to tell him that would be awhile down the road. He has managed the entire process so well. I have had little involvement, other than agreeing to move forward. How many couples get a baby delivered to them? Who are we to question the fate of that? I certainly won't. I'm just embracing the moment."

"I have an idea—let's have the baby shower here!"

"Oh yes! Thank you! You are always right on time with everything."

"We may have a baby shower *and* an engagement shower in the books real soon, too."

"Really? Is Ben proposing?"

"He is! But our lips are sealed, you hear? It's happening tonight."

"Absolutely sealed. I can't wait to hear from Laney tonight. You know she's not waiting until morning," said Sandra.

They turned the lights out in the office and headed to the kitchen to do an inventory check. Leslie wanted to be sure they were fully stocked and ready for their first event this week—their ribbon cutting.

"Let's get started," said Leslie. Sandra grabbed the clipboard, and they started checking off the list.

Chapter 40

Marry me?

Laney finished up at the cooking event and packed up the car to head home. She was looking forward to the next series at Four Oaks Hall, she wouldn't have to worry about packing up. That was the best part, aside from the fact that Ben was joining her in the lessons. That was secretly what she was looking forward to the most. She tried not to let on how excited she was about that venture. She felt like she needed to pinch herself every day. Ben was a dream come true, and she didn't want to read too much into what might or may not be happening. It was usually at this point in the relationship timeline when the wheels fell off for her in these matters of the heart. Most of the men she dated lost their patience with her about now, not because she was intolerable, it's just restraining from sex until marriage was not in their plan. Along about this time, they lost interest in her not having any interest in sex.

She pulled into the driveway at her cottage and noticed Ben's car was there. They had dinner plans, but he was early. Laney went in the side door, took one look at her kitchen, and was quite surprised. She found Ben standing around the corner, leaning against the wall watching her.

"So, did I pull it off?"

Laney walked over to him and gave him a kiss, "Well, let's see—something about all this seems familiar to me."

"It should. Did I get it right, did I replicate our first date? All the way down to the beer and wine, the cut of steak, and the sunflowers. Although this time we really need that fireplace going out there. It's getting chilly."

"Yes, you have done a ditto, that's for sure. What exactly is the point of all of this?"

Ben took her by the hand and they walked into the living room. When Laney saw the sunflowers in the vase on the sideboard, she smiled and kissed him on the cheek.

"You are spoiling me, but I'm not complaining," said Laney, as she kissed him again.

Ben began meal prepping, and Laney went to go freshen up and change clothes. Where had he been all her life? Why couldn't she just believe this was real and not have the feeling that it would all go away at the drop of a hat? If history repeated itself, that's what would happen. But this felt different—it felt genuine and comfortable. It flowed easily without effort and without hesitation. What if she was reading this all wrong, and he was seducing her for sex? Tonight?

"*Oh no, what is this really about?*" she said to herself in the bedroom mirror. "*I mean, I am definitely ready, but I made a commitment to myself. After all these years, I think you can stick to it, Laney.*"

She picked out a pair of jeans and grabbed a flannel shirt that Ben had left there a couple of weeks ago. She pulled her hair back in a ponytail, got dressed, and went back to the kitchen. Ben had taken a bottle of wine and an ice bucket to the porch.

He had the fire going and he was sitting there with a beer in hand, staring at the fire. He was so handsome. He had a little of that young George Strait look about him, especially when he wore his cowboy boots like he had tonight. Laney stopped in the doorway to admire the view before going to the patio. *"Gosh, I sure hope we aren't getting our signals crossed tonight."*

A piece of wood in the fireplace snapped, popped, and rolled. Ben got up to poke it around and level the logs out. Laney snuck up behind him and wrapped her arms around his waist. Ben turned around and gave her a long, slow kiss. She melted like she did every time they touched. The fire between them was warming her, they didn't really need the fireplace.

Ben walked over and poured her a glass of wine and offered a tray of savories he had prepared. Laney took a sip of the wine and immediately knew the brand.

"Oh, the Duplin Magnolia! I love it. Thank you. So why all the re-creation here? I like it, but I'm simply curious, that's all."

As they sat on the sofa by the fire, Ben turned and faced her. He took both of her hands and brought them to his lips. Laney took her hand to his cheek and stroked his face. She noticed a tension that had come over him, and she was getting concerned. His jaw line was tight, and the silence was deafening. Laney braced herself to hear the words, *"I'm sorry, but I can't do this anymore."* Was she right, was it at that point in the timeline?

"Ben, is everything okay?"

"Laney, I wanted to go back to that first date. That was the first night that I knew I loved you. The first time we kissed, the first time we were alone together to share and talk and get to know each other. What I'm trying to say is that I would like to spend the rest of my life experiencing every first in life with you. Laney, you know I get straight to the point, so I'm going to right now," said Ben as he knelt before her.

"Laney, will you do me the honor of being my wife and my first, my last, my everything, forever? Will you marry me?" asked Ben, as he held her hands.

There was silence for a moment, and Ben was looking into her eyes as she burst into tears. He wasn't sure if that was good or bad. Laney was speechless. She fell into his arms and her tears spilled onto Ben's shoulders. Once she regained her composure, she responded.

"Yes, yes, yes. For now, and forever, the answer is yes! But Ben, you caught me by surprise. Oh, my gosh!"

Ben stood up and took the small box out of his pocket and opened it to show Laney the ring. Once again, her tears spilled over her cheeks, and she could hardly speak. Ben took her left hand and placed the ring on her finger.

"This was my mother's ring. She gave it to me when she got sick. She told me to find the right lady to wear it one day. The first dinner we had here, I knew I had found her. That is why I wanted to recreate our first date—to show you how long I have loved you and how I will love you forever."

Laney embraced Ben and was looking at her left hand over his shoulder. She leaned back, looked at him, then kissed him. Ben was getting concerned because there seemed to be a sudden shift in her disposition. He held her hands and looked at the ring sparkling in the light on her left hand.

"It looks lovely on you, mama was right. She said when I found the perfect one, the ring and her would look just right. It would be perfect, and it is. She would have loved you. But I will tell you, she would have outcooked you any day of the week with her Cajun cooking. Some of it I can't even duplicate."

Laney took Ben's hand and pulled him to sit down with her. He knew right away that meant she had something on her mind. Did she say yes in the excitement and was having second thoughts about her quick response?

"This ring is beautiful. I don't think I have ever seen anything like it, Ben. It is so unique," said Laney as she held her hand up admiring the ring.

"It is as unique as you are. It's a perfect match."

"Ben, I need to ask you something. If you love me, you need to know everything about me. And I about you. Right? Do you agree?"

"I do, well ... I'll say *agree*, we will say *I do* at another date," said Ben with a laugh.

"I'm kind of concerned that I haven't met your family and you haven't met any of mine. I think meeting family is important. I mean, Robert is like my dad, so you know him. After dad died, he stepped up into the role model of a father figure. But you haven't met my mother. She could tell you a thing or two about me that might change your mind. I warn you now – she is a force to be reckoned with in a clever way though."

Ben nodded his head and said, "Here is how I see it—I love you; I'm marrying you, not your family. I hope to learn to love them when we meet. If that doesn't happen, I will always be hospitable and show them great kindness, no matter how difficult they can be."

"Wait until you meet Aunt Pearl! She'll tell you more than my mother. I never knew she really wasn't my aunt. She just helped mom raise me and looked after the house. I thought everyone had an aunt like that at their house. I was 12 years old before I learned the truth."

"I would love to meet her. Let's make a pact. A simple one. I love you for you. You love me for me, and we will tolerate any family members that are difficult."

"Well, mine are not necessarily difficult, and you won't see them often. They are all over the country. But I think you know how important family is to me. Mine and yours. It would help if we could meet soon," said Laney.

"Why, are you thinking my crazy family is going to help you change your mind? Never! You are mine for the rest of my days. But I will say this—let's have an engagement party at the Inn, say in three weeks," said Ben.

"You want to pull off an engagement party in less than three weeks? You are insane."

"Not insane, just resourceful. I will look at your Facebook family, you look at mine, we will create a group and send invites that way. Simple and sweet. Electronic invitations are not warm and fuzzy, but fast."

Laney sat back down, deep in thought, "You know what? You're right. Let's do this. I want to tell everyone!"

Ben looked at her and smiled, "I really have got to learn how to gauge your sudden thought surges. Sometimes you scare me. Really, you think too hard sometimes, but that is why I love you. You know I'm not an overthinker at all. You balance me."

Laney looked at Ben and put her arms around his neck. "There is one more thing I have to tell you about family. I want children. I know we have not really talked about that at all. But

I want a family."

"Girl, I am looking forward to trying for that—a lot, as a matter of fact. But I know you have been clear from the beginning that you didn't want that to be a part of our relationship just yet. Don't read me wrong—I have so respected that about you. However, I have one last thing to ask of you."

Laney got the eleven wrinkles in her forehead. She was in deep thought and anticipating his question. *What's next? He just said he respected that in me.* Ben took his finger and smoothed over the two vertical wrinkles and kissed her on the forehead.

"What do you need to ask?" asked Laney, still with concern on her face.

"Can we have the shortest of engagements ... please?" he laughed, and she joined him.

Laney felt a sigh of relief. It had been important to her to be sure she waited for her husband. While she knew some thought it to be old-fashioned, she just wanted to know that she had loved only one man in her life.

"I will make you a deal. You do the engagement party details while I plan a wedding. I am as anxious as you are, so would it be too soon to say about three months from now?"

Ben threw his hands up in the air and said, "You're killing me! I was thinking like two weeks after the engagement party. Really, I am. Why not? We can pull it off. We have the venue already, and we have Leslie and Sandra to plan. We can do this, I know it. Then we can spend all the chilly winter together keeping each other warm. Very warm if you know what I mean."

"Okay, I'll talk to them. But first, I have to call my mom," said Laney, as she pulled away to get her phone, but Ben pulled her back to him instead.

"Seriously, if anyone had told me at the beginning of this year that I would marry the woman of my dreams by the end of the year, I would have laughed in their face. You have made me the happiest man alive. I will spend all my days doing my best to make you a happy lady. I love you."

"I love you more. Now let's call my mom!"

Chapter 41

Engagement Party at Four Oaks Hall and Inn

Ben delivered on the coordination and the food preparation for the engagement party. He called in family members to be there early to help cook some of his mother's favorite Louisiana style Cajun dishes. Laney found her relatives, and many of them came to celebrate with her. Her mother, Edna, quickly became smitten with Ben, and Laney could tell the feeling was mutual. That made her incredibly happy.

Laney noticed that one of Ben's uncles seemed to take a shine to her mom. It was quite the surprise to see her mother returning attention to him. She had not heard of her mother having any love interest since her father passed away. Laney had taken her mother's advice to heart: marry once and marry for life was her words of wisdom. She was proud that she could look her mother in the eye and let her know she had done just that to honor herself and her parents. She recalled the day she made her purity pledge and she looked over at her mother and smiled. Now she could let her mother know she had kept her vow.

Laney looked around at all the guests. She couldn't wait to see their surprise when they opened a wedding invitation for just two weeks away. The sudden date might shock some of the guests, but not Laney's mom, she had told her about the date.

Her mother had leaned in and whispered behind the shield of her hand in Laney's ear, "I think I know why there is a rush, don't I?"

"Mom, cut it out. But yes, we both are eager to get to know each other better. *Really* better," Laney said with a laugh and a blushing in her face.

"Your father would be so proud of you, honey. But don't let that be the driving reason for the rush. The wait will make it all that much better, trust me on that piece of advice," said Edna as she winked at Laney.

"It's not, mom. Ben is everything I have ever dreamed of. As for walking me down the aisle. You probably have already thought of it as well. I want to ask Robert—with your blessing, of course."

"I cannot think of a more suitable choice. Thank God, for a minute I thought you were going to ask me. Thank you for sparing me and knowing I would be a mess. With Robert, it will be like having a part of your daddy there. They were so close and so much alike. I know he stepped in and has really kept up with you through the years. He's a good man, and I am so happy to see him so in love with your friend, Carrie. They are adorable together," said Edna as she looked over at Carrie and Robert dancing cheek to cheek.

"Yes, they are. But mom, I must be honest, I always thought you and Robert would have made a try at romance. With him being so much like dad, I always wondered about that," said

Laney, as she tipped her flute to her lips and finished the last of her champagne.

"Laney, there will never be another man for me. It will always be just your father. I am okay with that. He was the love of my life, and I'll be forever grateful for the time we had."

"You and dad taught me well. From what I have learned from Ben, he cherished his mother, and I have always heard that was a great attribute to look for in a man."

Ben was standing behind Laney as she was talking, and Laney's mom laughed.

"Mom, what is so funny about what I just said?" asked Laney, with a bit of frustration in her tone.

Ben slipped up beside her, "Absolutely nothing. I loved my mama, that's for sure. But my sisters can tell you that all three of them spoiled me since I was the only boy. I was lucky."

Leslie tapped her champagne glass and asked everyone to join them for a toast. Ben and Laney watched from the back of the room as the guests gathered around, Carrie had motioned for Robert to come up front.

"Good evening. We are so glad you are here for this engagement party. May I ask the lovely couple to come up front please?" Leslie motion for Ben and Laney to come to the front of the room. "Come on down. Let's give them a hand, ladies and gentlemen." Leslie cued the disc jockey to play, "You're the First, The Last, My Everything" by Barry White.

Laney took Ben's hand and they walked up to the front together. Robert was beaming and applauding enthusiastically as he watched them come forward. He always thought of Laney as a daughter and Ben had become as close to him as a son. Robert radiated joy. His plan of bringing them together on the yacht that summer weekend had worked exceptionally well.

When they reached Robert and Leslie, Ben spun Laney around in a smooth dance move, dipped her, and brought her back up for a kiss. Leslie cued the music to be lowered as Robert nodded his head that he was ready to give the toast.

"Well now, my dear Laney, this man has asked you to be his bride. Do we all need to ask his family to give full disclosure right now and spill the details about Ben?" Robert said with a grin. His question elicited laughter from the guests.

"I think we're good. We'll figure it out as we go," Ben said.

"So, Ben," Leslie said, "have I told you about all of Laney's quirky issues with shopping for clothes? Since most of her days are spent in chef's attire, I trust that you will have many dinner parties where she can get all dolled up and, of course, invite us over."

Laney popped Leslie on the arm, "You will be invited over – but don't expect me to be dolled up – most likely it will still be my work clothes or a t-shirt and jeans"

Leslie raised her glass, "I will be there no matter what you wear. To the most precious couple. When they met on that yacht just a few months ago, it was obvious that sparks were there. These two have been inseparable since that weekend. I love you, Laney, you know that. I have grown to love your guy Ben here. What a beautiful life you two are going to have. To Ben and Laney!"

Leslie motioned for Laney's mom to come up, "Now it's time to hear from the mother of the bride-to-be. Mrs. Edna

Rich, please come down. Everyone—a round of applause for the mother of the bride."

Edna took the microphone from Leslie, "My daughter, my baby girl, all grown up and marrying your Prince Charming. I'm so proud of you. You have always been my ray of sunshine. Your father would be so proud of the young woman you have become. I do have a few words to share that I hope the two of you will take to heart. I know that for your father and I, this was something that helped keep us grounded in our marriage. So here goes. You and Ben—focus on cherishing and treasuring each other like you are gold. Be solid as gold, but soft as cotton with love. You see those oak trees out there? Be strong as an oak, when need be, but bend like the willow does over that pond when you forgive. Sometimes we bend, and sometimes we stand firm. Take a lesson from the oaks and the willows. Just remember when you master how and when to do both well, you will be fine."

The room was silent as everyone listened to the knowledge and wisdom as Laney's mother spoke with such love and eloquence. Robert walked over to Edna and embraced her as Edna closed out her speech.

Edna continued, "So, my lovely princess and your dashing prince, love softly, boldly, strong, and long. Be deeply rooted in love and be kind enough to bend when you can. You will find that a life together grows best that way. There may be tears—let them water the soil to help your garden grow. To Laney and Ben. Cheers!"

The tears were already flowing from the newly engaged couple. Carrie noticed that Robert quickly wiped away a couple of tears. She wondered if they were tears of joy, or in remembrance of his late wife, Beth.

It was time for Robert to make a toast. As Robert was getting ready to toast, Leslie looked for Sandra. She spotted her in the back of the room on the phone on one ear and her hand over her other ear to drown out the noise. Within seconds, she left the main room and headed toward the office. Leslie didn't see Mitch, either. She looked out the window and saw the two of them getting in their car. Leslie watched as they left a trail of dust as they sped down the lane. Leslie gathered her composure as Robert raised his glass, but suddenly she wondered: *Was the birth mother in labor?*

"If I can please have everyone's attention now," Robert said, clearing his throat. "Edna, my friend, that has a hard toast to follow, but I will give it an old college try here. This little lady here has been in my life since she was knee high to a grasshopper. Her dad was a great friend, and we got to know each other through the boat business. He traded boats about like some people change their undies. I was pleased that he did—it kept us in touch, and I could watch Laney grow up. Ben, you have caught yourself a good one. Keep her for the rest of your life, and you will not regret it. Laney, I think you will find that this young man will bend over backwards to see your bright smile and your eyes light up. Always appreciate it when he does, he has a gift for knowing what makes people happy and I know you will find that to be true for many years. To Ben and Laney!" said Robert, as he raised his flute, and the guests echoed his toast.

Laney leaned over to give Robert a hug, and she wiped away a tear as she thought of her father and how Robert would stand in for him. Laney motioned for Ben to come to the side of the room. Ben was quick to thank the guests for coming, then he walked over to chat with Robert and Edna.

Laney took Robert's hand, "Robert, I have a question for you. You know we're not having a long engagement. In fact, the wedding is just two weeks away right here at Four Oaks Hall. Are you busy that weekend?"

"Well, I won't be busy if there is a wedding to attend. Yes, I'll be there. I wouldn't miss your wedding for the world."

"I want you to be more than be here," said Laney as she looked over at her mom. They smiled, and Edna nodded her head for Laney to continue.

Robert rubbed his chin, as he customarily did when he encountered a perplexing situation, "You have my curiosity piqued. What's going on in your pretty little head? You know I can't sing a lick, right?"

"Yes, I know that about you—I've suffered through some of your karaoke. Simply put: will you give me away?"

To this question, Ben's head spun around, and he looked at Laney, at first with disappointment, and then with a smile. Laney didn't know that Ben had thought of asking Robert to be his best man. But after a split second, he realized Laney needed him more. Laney read Ben's face like the page of a book and realized she must have beaten him to the ask.

"Laney, it would delight me to honor your father and step into that role for him. You have just warmed my heart. You know I've always thought the world of you, and I cannot think of anything more honorable than to be asked to do this. Thank you," said Robert, as he kissed her on the cheek.

Laney and Robert gave each other a hug. Ben was grinning and looking a bit bemused, "You know, I think that is an outstanding idea. But it leaves me in a bit of a pickle. You can't be the best man *and* give the bride away. Or wait, can you? Who is to say that rule can't be broken?" he asked.

Laney said, "I could tell by watching your reaction when I asked Robert, that you had planned to ask him to be the best man. I'm sorry."

"Leave it to us to be quite unconventional. But in this case, it makes sense. Without Robert, we would have never met. So why not be both? Once he walks you down the aisle and gives you away, he can stand by my side as the best man. What's wrong with that? I think it's a novel idea."

"I knew you two were right for each other. This right here proves that to me. Look at the teamwork and ingenuity you have! You two are going places, and I can't wait to watch where it leads. Heck, yeah! Why not? Put me down for both!" said Robert.

The night was winding down, and some guests were preparing to depart to the local hotel. Ben and Laney knew now was the opportunity to give the invitations out with a take-home dessert for their departure. It was all in the kitchen and ready to be rolled out on a cart.

Ben made an announcement, "Everyone, we have a parting treat for you. So, hang tight here just a second. We did not want you to go home without something sweet to remember the night, so we have prepared a slice of cake to go for each of you. Take careful notice of the note attached to your cake box, it has specific instructions."

Laney entered the hall with the rolling cart filled with elaborately decorated cakes that Ben had coordinated with Sarah at the Bread Basket. Laney had individually boxed each cake with a note tied around with the invitation and a stamp of Four Oaks Hall in gold to secure the box. It was a lovely presentation.

Leslie was excited to see everyone's reaction when they opened the note that read:

Join us for a wedding and more cake in two weeks.
It's a date.

Everyone was shocked by the sudden turnaround for the wedding date, but Ben and Laney had already worked those details out with the family that needed to attend from far away. Ben graciously agreed to pay for the airfare and, of course, those guests were going to stay at the Inn.

Gradually, the guests departed down the two-lane dirt road under a star-covered sky. Ben and Laney finally sat down to reflect on the night's festivities. They were enjoying the crisp air on the wrap-around porch and the glow of the moonlight reflecting off the pond through the willows and oaks.

Laney sat on the deacon's bench and looked out over the parking area. "Ben, something is off. Where did Sandra get off to? I saw her and Mitch slip out when the toast was going on. I hope nothing is wrong. But her timing is impeccable for leaving an event," said Laney.

"I'm sure it must have been necessary, or she would not have just left like that. She was so looking forward to seeing everyone open their invitations. Has anyone tried to call her?" asked Ben, as he sat down beside Laney

"I'm not sure. Where is Leslie? Now she is missing too?" asked Laney.

Laney and Ben headed to the office to check the schedule board and their desks. There was a note from Sandra that read: "So sorry. Emergency. Have to leave. Will call soon. Did not want to interrupt the toast."

Laney sat down on the sofa in the office and looked at Ben. "Can you find Leslie? I'm going to call Sandra."

Ben headed out the office door and ran down the hallway. Carrie and Robert were in the kitchen helping some of the staff take care of kitchen detail when he passed by. Ben stopped when he saw Leslie in the banquet room.

"Hey, what's up with Sandra?" asked Ben.

"Not here, not right now. Come down to the office," said Leslie as they both left the room. "Our voices will echo in that huge room."

They hurried down the hall to find Laney on the phone with Sandra. Laney had tears in her eyes and was consoling Sandra. Leslie quickly shut the door behind her and Ben.

"Ok, it's fine. It's fine. Stop apologizing. I understand, I really do. Keep us posted on the baby, please, and the birth mother. How tragic—a car accident is bad enough, but when you are pregnant, that's awful," said Laney, as she wiped away a tear.

Laney hung up the phone and Leslie was sitting at her desk. She looked at both Ben and Laney. The two of them could see the concern in her eyes.

"We never lack for excitement around here. Oh, my word, this is unreal," said Laney.

"What happened? Where was the accident?" asked Ben.

"Ironically, just down the road, between here and Greenway. Sandra thinks it's the intersection where the peanut truck always sits. Someone t-boned her. She is in critical condition from what they can tell. Now, the baby seems to be fine, but they are planning to do a C-section soon. The adoption agency got up with Sandra and Mitch because they would need to step in right away as per their agreement. Plus, the baby is premature, but I don't think by too much I don't think," said Leslie.

"But what was she doing around here?" asked Laney. "I thought she lived out of state."

"She does, but apparently she travels here often. It seems she may do some type of business here. I think she might even have lived here before. Ben, are you good to finish up here? I want to head over to the hospital to be with Sandra. One more thing—do not let Carrie and Robert know about this. I have my reasons. I do not want them worried, and I do not want them at the hospital. Get creative and keep them here to wrap up details or send them on their way for the night. Or let them know we need them to handle the delivery in the morning. Just let them know the birth mother is in labor, but everything is handled," said Leslie.

"What do you mean it's handled? That's an odd thing to say. Why don't you want them at the hospital? Leslie, what do you know that you are obviously not sharing?" asked Laney as she looked her straight in the eye.

"I don't know if I know anything at all, but my gut tells me I do. I just can't talk about it yet. Just trust me on this one. Please. I think Robert and Carrie plan to stay here for the night or grab a couple of rooms at the hotel down the road. Carrie has stayed there before, it's decent," said Leslie.

"Okay, we promise. But you're making me nervous. We'll meet you there once we close here. What about Stan? Where is he? He'll be looking for you," said Laney.

"He's going to take me to the hospital on the way back home, he's waiting for me now. I'll see you there later," said Leslie, as she headed out the door.

Chapter 42

The Sun Will Rise and the Sun Sets

The hospital lobby café was not open, so Leslie could only drink coffee that came from the hospitality stand. It was awful, but it provided the needed caffeine. Laney, Ben, and Leslie had been up all night with Sandra and Mitch in the waiting room. They waited, and it exhausted their patience, as things did not seem to move as quickly as they had hoped. It was the birth mother's request for Mitch and Sandra to be present in case something happened. It was unorthodox, but a reasonable request in this situation.

Sandra paced the floor most of the night, while Mitch would doze in and out of naps. Leslie tried to gather as much information as they would allow to be given out, but until the adoption agency arrived, it was extremely limited. All they could gather was that it was touch and go, and most likely would not have a favorable outcome. The agency arrived, and the representative had talked with the mother. The nurse had given them that much information and the mother was stable for now.

The minutes seemed like hours. The representative said she would be in the lobby to talk with Mitch and Sandra by 6:00 a.m. Leslie looked at the clock. It was 6:05. Sandra had been staring at the clock for over an hour. The chaplain came by the waiting room and offered her counseling and prayer. He told her he would go in and check on the patient and pray over her. Sandra was most appreciative, and it eased her mind for a while. But that was at 2:00 in the morning—four hours earlier.

The chaplain finally came out at 6:09. He asked Mitch and Sandra to go with him to a counseling room. The three of them headed down the hall. Sandra looked back at them as she walked down the corridor. She looked so afraid. Leslie gave her wink and a head nod and mouthed the words: *It will be fine.*" They were gone for about five minutes, then Mitch came out alone.

"What is it Mitch?" asked Leslie, as she jumped to her feet to meet him at the double doors.

Mitch rubbed his eyes, walked over to a chair, and sat down, "They have her stable. They wanted to give her every chance to recover before jumping into anything rash. But it has become critical for the baby, so they are preparing for a C-section now. The adoption agency is here, and they just presented us with a very unusual request. That is why the chaplain is back in. You will not believe this—the mother wants to meet us, and she wants us present for the delivery."

Leslie gasped, "What? I would say that it does seem highly unusual. I don't know what I think about that, Mitch."

Mitch nodded, "It's unusual, but they rarely have their birth mothers facing death. This is a different circumstance."

"I would say yes—it sure is, but I'm not sure about this, Mitch. I really am not. What are y'all going to do? Are you even considering this?"

Mitch looked at Leslie with a frown, he shook his head with frustration at Leslie's negativity about the idea.

"Of course we are, Leslie. For God's sake, she's giving us her child, and she is most likely going to die. She may not survive the C-section. I think that calls for a bit of allowance for the untraditional, and maybe a healthy dose of compassion. She is choosing to go through with the C-section to save our baby. I think that's pretty brave and admirable, and we will honor her request."

"I'm so sorry. I'm just worried," said Leslie, knowing that she had angered Mitch. "Just forget I said anything. Maybe I'm worried about nothing," said Leslie, not wanting to speak about her suspicions. What if she was wrong?

Mitch looked back at the doors and turned to Ben, Laney, and Leslie. He cracked his knuckles and rubbed his head. It was obvious that he was nervous.

"Listen, you two have an emotional hurricane going on right now. Just hold steady. It's going to blow over. Focus on the fact that you are going to be parents—soon," said Ben, as he patted Mitch on the back.

"Thanks Ben. Thank you for that. I appreciate it," said Mitch.

Leslie went to Mitch and gave him a hug, "Forgive me. I just have Sandra's best interest at heart. When you go in there, if you need me, just come, and get me. Promise?"

"Will do. Say a prayer; it always helps. Sandra is scrubbing up now, and I'm next. Be back out soon," said Mitch, as he left through the double doors.

Ben, Laney, and Leslie sat down, and there was silence for a few seconds, then Laney spoke up, "Leslie, I will ask you again. What do you know that you aren't telling us? What the hell was that all about, and why don't you want Carrie to know? What's really going on?"

Leslie covered her mouth with one hand as if she was holding back on voicing her suspicions. She took a deep breath, "I'm sorry. I'm just being overly emotional about this whole thing. I'm worried that something will go wrong."

"Like what? The mother might not make it? Are you afraid the father will come back into the picture now?" asked Laney.

"No. The father is dead," said Leslie then she realized she slipped up and said the wrong thing, she quickly tried to correct her statement," I mean he must be dead. Why would she be giving her child up?"

Laney looked at Ben, and they both stared at Leslie. Leslie was not telling the entire story, and they were sure of it.

"Leslie, mothers give their babies up for many reasons—not just because the father is dead. You know who the birth mother is, and the father, don't you?" asked Ben.

Laney started pacing with her head in her hands, and Ben stood there silently waiting for an answer.

Laney turned to Leslie, "You do, don't you?"

Leslie was quiet for a few seconds before she spoke, "I may be wrong. I don't know. I just stumbled upon some information about her, and it may be all wrong. I'm just worried that if I'm right, it may change everything on the adoption."

"Oh dear Lord, you know you're right, or you wouldn't be saying it. You never gamble with information unless you know it is solid. Mercy! Who is it? Why would it change anything?" asked Laney.

"It may not. I'm just sure it will come as a surprise. Let's wait and see how things go," said Leslie.

"You have got to be kidding me. You *do* know something," said Ben.

"I'm sorry. It shouldn't be long now. Let's wait until Mitch and Sandra come out after the C-section. I may not have accurate information," said Leslie.

As the three of them sat down, Leslie's phone rang. She looked at the phone—it was Carrie. She took a deep breath, put a smile on her face, and answered the phone.

"Hey, we're still here at the hospital. Everything is fine, and we should have a baby real soon," said Leslie as she looked up at the ceiling to avoid eye contact with Ben or Laney. She didn't even say hello to Carrie before she spilled out details. "I will call you as soon as I know anything. Thank you so much for taking over last night and finishing up everything. When Laney told me you guys were covering it, I knew the job was in good hands. And thank you for going to meet the delivery truck this morning. So, can you and Robert check out the delivery and be sure we received everything we ordered? Oh, thank you so much," said Leslie as she shrugged her shoulders, while looking at Ben and Laney.

Leslie hung up and said, "I'm sorry, I just think it may be best if she stays away."

"You're not making any sense at all, Leslie, and you are worrying me," said Laney.

"Well, if it's any comfort to you, I'm worrying me right now, too. So, we both can agree on that," said Leslie.

Minutes ticked by on the clock, and it had turned into a waiting game. Watch the clock. Watch the door. Watch the clock. Watch the door.

Suddenly, the doors swung open, and Sandra was standing with Mitch in the doorway. They looked shell shocked.

Leslie ran up to them, "Well, do we have a baby?"

Mitch pulled out his phone and showed them the snapshots he took of the newborn.

Leslie embraced Sandra. Sandra began to sob, and Leslie held her tightly.

"Honey, you're going to be fine. You are going to be an exceptional mother. You have all of us to help you out. It's going to be fine," said Leslie as she rocked Sandra back and forth to comfort her.

"Yes, count me in on the baby spoiling. Ben and I need some practice," said Laney, as she gave Mitch a hug.

Mitch and Sandra were silent. They all paused for a moment and waited. Mitch looked at Leslie with compassion.

"Leslie, I now understand the concern you had. It was quite a shock for Sandra. You were right. It's all going to be fine. We have a baby girl, and she is perfect," said Mitch.

Laney and Ben looked at Mitch and then at Leslie.

Sandra smiled, and tears flowed again, "She's beautiful, but tiny. As far as they can tell, she is fine. It's a miracle she is okay, most of the injuries totally missed her. She will still have to stay here for a little while. She's a living breathing miracle," said Sandra trying to get words out, but her voice was shaking, and she was trembling.

"How is the mother?" asked Leslie, with a guarded hesitation in her voice.

Sandra began to cry again and couldn't speak, so Mitch answered, "She's gone. She didn't make it through the operation. It was touch and go for a while, and drastic measures were taken to get the baby delivered quickly. They tried everything. She wanted to put the baby first, and she was clear about it. The chaplain walked her through her last rites and prayers. I've never seen anything like it and I hope I never do again."

Sandra showed them another photo of the newborn. Through her tears she said, "The most bizarre thing I will ever experience is watching one life end as another comes into the world. I don't think I'll ever be affected by anything quite like this ever again. We talked with her and made her the promise that we would guard this child for the rest of her life. We were able to thank her for this beautiful gift. She was able to live long enough to meet us. I was able to hold her hand while we all prayed. I held the hand of my baby's mother," said Sandra as she looked at the picture of the baby and broke down sobbing again.

"I'm so sorry you had to go through that Sandra—just meeting her and then she dies. I am so thankful the baby is okay. Thank God," said Laney.

Sandra was choking back tears. She gathered her composure as she watched Mitch looking at Leslie. Mitch reached out to Leslie and gently took her hand.

Sandra managed to get the words out, but her voice trembled, her tears flowed and still in her moment of weakness, she was able to mouth the words, "It was Karen! The mother was Bill's Karen. This is Bill and Karen's baby girl!"

Chapter 43

Mae

The news traveled fast by local town criers about Sandra and Mitch's baby being born. Mae thought it was wonderful. Every family needed a baby to love, and adopting one was mighty special in her opinion. Mae loved mothering Carrie's boys, and she treated them as well as her own. Her son said she treated Carrie's kids better. She knew she did because they behaved better, in her opinion. But then again, Mae had to raise Sonny on her own without a husband and father figure, he had really struggled. But his difficulties seemed to be behind him. Thanks to Duke, he was getting his life turned around. That man was a godsend for Mae. When Carrie moved to the country and took Mae on staff at the Inn, that was the best thing that ever happened to her.

Mae's mobile home at the back of the farm sat next to a lane of cedar trees, close to where Duke lived. They would often share a cup of coffee on the porch and discuss what was coming up at the Inn for the day or week. Miss Carrie had been nice enough to hire her son, and he took care of the grounds. On the extra acreage, Miss Leslie let Duke have a vegetable, fruit, and flower farm. With the help of Mr. Stan, Duke was farming again, and Sonny helped him. They sold produce in town and provided the food, fruit, and flowers for the Inn. Miss Carrie had called it "farm to table." The farm provided for them all, and Mae was grateful.

Duke never married, and Mae often wondered why. He was always so gentlemanly to her. That was always a pleasant quality in a man, and she couldn't believe he had never snagged a lady. Miss Leslie told her that his first love died from a terrible sickness the doctors could not cure. Mae thought Miss Leslie might try to do some matchmaking between the two of them. Mae was alright with that. It was sad to Mae that he had lost his only love so young. Duke had been alone for a very long time. They both had that in common.

As Mae sat on her porch, she could make out someone coming down the lane. She had undergone eye surgery before they moved and it helped, but her vision still was not completely clear. She leaned over the rail on the steps and looked down the path. It looked like Duke walking toward her, and she sat back down with a pleasant grin on her face.

As she watched Duke make his way to her, she thought about how much life had changed in the last year. Certain events had a way of making life turn on a dime, and this last year had surprised them all. They all could see a better future. It was a nice life, and she could live with what she did not do and what she should have done. There was no use in her worrying over it now. No one even knew she was still at the house when those robbers came through. No one knew she was in the front parlor taking a nap. No one was there to see her slip out that night. No one knew but her and the good Lord, and she reckoned she would deal with that when she reached the gates of heaven.

Mae wiped a tear from her eye, as she remembered how frightened she had been. She was taking a nap like Miss Carrie always said for her to do if she got tired. She didn't know who was coming in the house when Mr. Bill arrived. When she realized it was him, she remained quiet in the parlor so she wouldn't have to talk to him.

Mae often relived the night in her sleep. The nightmares eased up some, but some nights it haunted her from the rise of the moon to the dawn of the sun. She could still hear the struggle between Mr. Bill and the boys that broke in. Mr. Bill wakened her as he came through the hall, cussing Miss Carrie out for leaving the alarm off. He didn't think anyone heard him saying such terrible things. She did, and it made her madder than a wet sitting hen. It woke her up from her nap and she thought he might cuss at her for still being there. One day, when she was supposed to be gone, he came in with a lady friend and cussed her out up one side and down the other. She messed up his afternoon delight, and he was mad as a badger.

She always thought he was a strong and smart man who could handle his own. She never understood why he hid in the closet. Mae heard those boys come in but remained quiet as a church mouse. After all, she was an old woman—what was she going to do? But he was a strapping stud of a man, or at least he thought he was. Hiding in that closet seemed like a cowardly thing to do. After the noise settled down and she heard the crooks speed away in Mr. Bill's car, she ventured out of the parlor. She made her way down the hall and searched the bedroom. She found him lying in the closet. She got close enough to tell if he was breathing, and he was. She thought he would be fine. Her next thought was that she wished it had been her to knock him on the head. He deserved it.

To stop the memories from flooding her mind, she went in the trailer to get a cup of coffee ready for Duke. He would be thankful that she had one ready for him. She looked out the kitchen window as she stirred in the creamer. She admired the hanging basket Miss Carrie had put on the front porch for her. It brightened the place up. She picked out red petunias since she knew Mae could see those the best. The cool fall had not bothered them yet, since her porch had plenty of sunlight.

Making Duke a cup of coffee did not stop her mind from wandering straight back to that night. When she walked out of the house that day, she looked back just once. As she stopped in front of the stables, she thought about going back to help him. But then she remembered all the women he would entertain down at the stables when Miss Carrie would be at the office. Mr. Bill didn't think she knew, but Mae was smarter than he ever gave her credit for. Then she remembered the day she caught him in bed with that woman from the office. She never let on she saw them.

He had always ignored Mae and treated her poorly. She looked at the stables where he would hide with his lady friends, then back at the house. She decided it served him right. Maybe those intruders knocked some sense into him. She began the walk toward the main road, hoping her son would see her along the way. Sonny picked her up where the path met the highway, and Mae went home that day with a secret. She didn't realize it at the time, but it was a secret she would have to carry to her grave. How could she regret it now when things were so much better for Miss Carrie? She loved seeing her so happy with Mr. Robert and working with the ladies at the Inn.

About that time, Duke tapped on her front door. It startled Mae, and she almost spilled his coffee. Duke walked into the kitchen to find Mae standing at the sink.

"Duke, don't you go sneaking up on lady folk like that. You just scared the pee out of me, and I bout spilt your coffee," said Mae, as she handed him the newspaper.

"Now Mae, I saw you looking at me coming up the path. You knew I was coming. What's got you so jumpy this morning?" asked Duke.

Mae walked to the porch and Duke followed her and they sat down in the rocking chairs. Mae rocked for a few seconds and avoided Duke's question.

"I am waiting for my answer," Duke said.

Mae shook her head. Duke stared at her intently for a moment.

"Mae, have you been crying? Your eyes look all whelped up to me."

Mae turned to look at him, "I just heard about Sandra's baby getting here. Babies make me cry, that's all."

"Are you sure that's all?"

"I am. Now stop your fussing and drink your coffee before it gets cold."

They sat there in the morning's silence, watching the steam from the coffee cups float into the chill of the morning air. Mae looked at Duke and realized he was one of the things that went right in the last year. He had become a good friend and someone her son could respect.

It seemed like everyone's lives were in a better place. If she had it to do all over again and knew what she knew now, she would do the same thing. She just had to convince her mind to tell her heart to stop giving her so much trouble.

"Well Mae, you ready to head up to the Inn? I hear we have our work cut out for us today. There's that festival this weekend for those beach music folks. I love it when we have those festivals, it reminds me of Miss Leslie's grandfather and the balls he would throw. Whoop, we would throw down like we were in high cotton even if we weren't!" said Duke, as he laughed and walked down the steps.

"Well, I hope they don't keep us up all night. I need my beauty rest, you know," said Mae, as she winked at Duke.

He folded his arms and turned his head to the side as he looked at Mae, "No, you don't. You look just fine ... mighty fine. I know you said you're okay, but you know if anything is worrying you, I want you to know you can talk to me. You do know that don't you?"

"I do know that, and I am very appreciative to you for your kindness towards me and my Sonny."

They began the walk down the lane to the Inn and Duke let her place her hand in the bend of his arm. Mae liked it when he let her do that, like she was being escorted to a safe place. She wanted to remember moments like this for always and forget the nagging visions that appeared in her sleep and woke her up in a cold sweat. This is what she wanted to remember. If she could keep her mind on these moments, she felt that her world would be fine. If she could always have his arm to steady her, she would be fine.

Chapter 44

Baby you are Home

The sun beamed through the bedroom window, casting light across the bed. The new day was bright and clear with no haze of humid air lingering. The clear blue sky was a beautiful sight for Sandra. This was her favorite time of year. She stayed in bed for a while, staring out the window, taking in the view, then she rolled over to see the bassinet at her bedside. She smiled as she reached over and touched the white eyelet trim and the pink ribbon that ran through it. Today was the day they dreamed of for so long—bringing a baby home.

Sandra walked down the wide hall and into the kitchen where she found Mitch toasting bagels and squeezing oranges for juice.

"Good morning. You finally slept well. I know you did because you snored," said Mitch, as he poured juice in a glass.

"Mitch, I do *not* snore."

"You do when you're exhausted, and several nights of no sleep did you in, sweetie."

Sandra kissed him on the cheek as she walked to the coffeepot, "Are you ready to do this, Mitch? We are going to be parents. I can't believe I am hearing those words come out of my mouth. I am so ready to bring her home. I'm glad we met her mother. I would have never guessed in a million years that it would have been Karen. Sometimes I didn't speak very highly of her, but I sure feel differently now. We saw a side of her that not many people knew. I still can't get over it."

"You know Leslie's instincts are impeccable. How she kept that suspicion to herself is beyond me," said Mitch, shaking his head.

"I know. But I think when she was born and I told them it was Karen and Bill's, I should have just stayed quiet. But I was in shock, joy, and disbelief all at the same time."

"I know you were. But you know the vow we took at that moment to never breath word of that again is solid. Laney, Ben, and Leslie are good at keeping their word. I have faith in them to keep everyone's best interest at heart. Don't you?" asked Mitch.

Sandra nodded her head yes, "Leslie would do anything for Carrie. I trust Ben and Laney to keep their promise. I feel comfortable with our promise. That's what it is. It's a promise, not a secret. A secret sounds scandalous. It is a promise. Promises are better. I can't think of it as a secret, and I can't even think of anyone in this town finding out. Everyone would talk, and I do not want any blemish of the past to mark our baby girl. Gosh Mitch, we are making the best decision, right?"

"Absolutely. You already sound like a protective mother. I love it. Yes, it is best this way."

They sat down to hold hands and say grace. Mitch prayed for their baby girl and for the next few days to go smoothly. A tear slipped from the corner of Sandra's eye as his sweet words touched her heart.

"Mitch, you're always so attentive to my every need. I know you will have this fatherhood thing down pat in no time."

"I hope so, because whether we are ready or not—it's happening. Did you think more about a name for her?"

"I'm at a loss. I know it's tradition for mama to name girls and daddy will name the boys and dogs, but I am really struggling."

"Well, it needs to come to you on the way to the hospital, because it has to happen before we leave. Get that pretty head of yours in gear and name that baby. They have asked us every day this week," said Mitch, as he kissed her on the forehead.

Sandra was about to answer when the doorbell rang. Mitch backed up from the table to look out toward the circle drive, and he could see it was Carrie.

"It's Carrie. You good? You still feel comfortable keeping this to ourselves? It is a secret, sorry, a promise we will have to carry to our graves, so you are good, right?"

"Yes. It's just for the best. Karen was kind enough to give us this gift, and in her last moments, I could see a very tender side of her that she hid from most. I really think she wanted us there so she wouldn't die alone. That's sad to me. Under her tough as nails exterior, she had a heart. We did promise Karen, remember? But then I go and blurt it out in the waiting room, like a fool."

"Honey, it's going to be fine. You were shocked. Look, I'm going to get the door. Don't worry your head anymore."

Carrie came in with several bags of gifts and plenty of take-away meals from Ben and Laney.

"Hey parents! I just love saying that—you are parents!" said Carrie, as she put the gifts down in the hall and took the goodies to the kitchen. "There are some great smelling muffins in this box from Laney for Mitch. For Sandra, the picky eater, Ben fixed a fresh vegetable and fruit bento box—it's the cutest. He put some of that low-fat cheese in there you like so much."

"Thank you. That is so thoughtful, and we can't wait for you to meet her. We need to ask you something first. Can you sit down?" Sandra asked, as she sat down on the sofa.

"Sure, but you have me concerned. Is everything okay? The baby is fine, right?" asked Carrie.

"She is perfect. A little on the tiny size, but healthy enough to come home now," said Mitch.

"However, she needs a little something in her life that only you can do," said Sandra.

"What on earth is that?" asked Carrie.

"A godmother. Will you be her godmother? And for your first official duty, will you help me name her?" asked Sandra.

"I am honored. My goodness, what a pleasure! Thank you for thinking of me. I am going to be the best godmother anyone has ever seen," said Carrie, as she gave Sandra a hug.

"You will be, indeed. We know you will spoil her rotten," said Mitch.

"What is this about name troubles? How about your mother's name or Mitch's? That's always a sweet sentimental name to me, naming after the grandparents," said Carrie.

Sandra shook her head, "Nope. A Dorlina or Eunice is not happening."

"Can't say as I blame you there. An aunt or a woman from the Bible? Are you thinking traditional or trendy? Unisex or specifically a feminine name?" asked Carrie.

Mitch looked at them both and cleared his throat, "I *am* in the room, you know. Maybe I have a thought about a name."

"Well, why haven't you said something?" asked Sandra.

"You two have not given me an opportunity."

"Well, give it to us, then. What are you thinking?" asked Carrie.

Mitch smiled and looked at Sandra, "My grandmother's name was Opal."

"Oh Mitch, I like Opal. How about Opal Grace? My grandmother and your grandmother combined," said Sandra.

"Now that wasn't hard! That's beautiful, and we are in October. Isn't that October's birthstone. It's Opal, right?" exclaimed Carrie.

"There you are, being the perfect godmother already in your knowledge of her birthstone. Hey, go eat some breakfast with Mitch while I get dressed. As godmother, would you like to come along to meet your goddaughter Opal Grace and bring her home?" asked Sandra.

"You know I would love it! Thank you! I cannot wait to tell Robert!"

Sandra went to get dressed, and Mitch and Carrie went back to the kitchen. When they sat down, Carrie touched Mitch on the hand.

"Listen, the next few days are going to rock your world. You know I have no problem staying here and helping. I'm raising my hand up as a volunteer. I'm happy to do so. It would be my duty as godmother to insist."

"We will leave that option up to Sandra."

"Well, you know she can be stubborn, so you call me if things get overwhelming, okay?"

"Will do. I promise."

Sandra yelled out from the bedroom, "Almost ready! Mitch, you double-checked that infant seat in the car, right? But humor me and check it again, okay? Don't make me have you stop by the fire department to get them to inspect your installation."

Carrie laughed, "She's going to be fine. She's already being a mama bear."

Mitch went out to check the car seat while Carrie cleaned up the kitchen. Sandra came into the kitchen with the baby bag. Sandra stopped dead in her tracks and suddenly put her hand over her heart as she sat down at the kitchen table. Carrie was quick to notice that she was feeling overwhelmed.

"Let's go get your girl. It's all going to be fine. I promise," said Carrie.

Sandra looked at Carrie realizing that her friend really had no inkling as to why she was nervous. It may have had a little bit to do with bringing their daughter home, but more to do with the fact that Carrie didn't know whose child she was going to meet. Sandra knew it should stay that way. It was their chance to have a baby, and if it meant keeping a secret from Carrie, then it would have to be. She just prayed that everyone would keep their promise. It was a prayer she would whisper every day.

Chapter 45

Our Lips Are Sealed

The phone rang at the front desk of the Inn and Leslie answered, "Four Oaks Hall & Inn."

"Hey, it's Sandra. We are home from the hospital. Carrie came with us, and you were right—she said yes to the godmother role."

"I knew she would and trust me, she will be the best! Is it okay if we stop by tomorrow? You'll have your hands full today, and we have that reception tonight and a planning meeting for the festival this weekend, remember?" said Leslie.

"Sure, tomorrow night is fine—on one condition. Ben needs to bring his chicken marsala and I'm placing an order for Laney's marinated asparagus."

"I will work on that order for you. Let Carrie help all you can now," said Leslie.

Leslie stared out the window to the geese on the pond and the ripples they created across the surface. She remembered the moment when she first thought the baby was Karen's, when she was sitting with Carrie on the bench at the edge of the pond.

"We are going to try and manage the best we can on our own," replied Sandra.

Leslie shook her head, "Now listen—now isn't the time to put up that independent gate and lock everyone out. Trust me, in about three days, you are going to want to tap out and call one of us so you can get an hour of sleep. And when you do, one of us will be there. Always."

"Thank you, Leslie. You are truly a dear friend. See you tomorrow night," said Sandra.

When Leslie hung up the phone, she went down to the banquet room to see Ben and Laney. They were a couple of work horses in motion and were running on full throttle.

"Hey, you two, got a minute? We need to clear some things up."

"Like what?" Ben asked.

"I'm sorry, that might have sounded a bit bossy. I mean, we need to sit down, and for lack of a better word, get our stories straight. This could blow up in our faces. Remember, we promised Sandra it would be a secret for life," said Leslie.

"So, tell me again how you put this all together? I'm still foggy on the timeline of events and we have not been alone together long enough to talk about it," said Laney

"Well, Carrie's description of the lady she saw at the motel sounded like Karen, but Carrie said she had put on weight. Then it all sort of came to me, but it was only a hunch," said Leslie.

"It was a good one. I wondered why she left so fast and never came back. Maybe this was why," said Ben, as he pulled out two chairs for Laney and Sandra, then pulled one up for himself.

"Maybe, but I think it embarrassed her in some way about the engagement party. Imagine if Ben had not shown up for yours? You would want to hide as well, right?" asked Leslie.

"No, I would find him and kill him," Laney gasped. "Oh my gosh, do you think Karen had something to do with it?"

"No, no, no, not a chance. She never left the engagement party," said Leslie.

"Now—as for Karen being the birth mother, we never mention this again. We never talk about it, write about it, give any indication that we know anything about the baby's birth parents. This is Sandra and Mitch's baby girl, and that is that," said Leslie.

"I know it shocked Sandra when she saw her. It was good on Karen's part to let them know why she specifically chose them. That bit of assurance from her had to be encouraging, knowing that the birth mom handpicked them. I wonder what else they talked about?" asked Ben.

"It really was a good thing for them to know. Now both of the baby's birth parents are dead. On the good side of this, they don't have to worry about either of them returning," said Laney.

"Laney, that was cold, but it's the truth. From what I have gathered, Karen worked with Mitch some on the operating loans for the business and she knew Sandra from her work as a nurse at the clinic. She told them before she passed away that she knew exactly who she wanted to have the baby when she found out she was pregnant. Although at first, she considered an abortion. Thankfully, Karen showed us she did have a heart," said Leslie.

"That is something else right there. This is mind blowing to me. As I said the other night: my lips are sealed. All I would ever want is for that baby to have the best life with two great parents. Now she will," said Ben.

Laney agreed by shaking her head.

"So, we are all square on this and God help us, I hope we have made the right decision," said Leslie.

Chapter 46

Thankfulness Abounds

The autumn leaves tumbled across the tan and green carpet of grass. The fall evening produced an early nightfall, and Laney went out to the courtyard to light candles and turn on the heating lanterns. It was a chilly evening, and Ben started a fire in the outdoor fireplace. Married life suited them well, and they had turned into home bodies. If not at the Inn or in cooking school, they were home enjoying their newlywed life.

Ben and Laney's swift and simple wedding was just their style. That was how their romance started, like a rushing wave guided by strong gales. For them, it was just as well to leave off all the formalities of an elaborate day, otherwise it would seem like work, not their wedding.

Leslie decided they should take an intermission before the holiday hustle and have a work-free dinner to celebrate all the positive events that had happened. It was not every year you created a new partnership with friends and one of them marries, one brings home a new baby, and one has discovered a new love. They had earned a celebration, and they all had so much to be thankful for. The year began with its share of troubles for all of them, but together with a little care and devotion, it was going out in a blaze of glory.

Ben and Laney were eager to host the celebration since they had not entertained in their own home as a married couple yet. Sandra and Mitch arrived, and Laney was delighted to see the new baby. She could envision her and Ben starting their family soon. She expected it would not be long for them to plunge into parenthood. Laney smiled as she thought about how often they were working on the effort. Laney loved holding Opal and always claimed dibs on holding her. Everyone let her because they realized she needed the practice for the future.

Robert and Carrie arrived with a cornucopia bouquet wicker basket filled with flowers and fall leaves. Robert never showed up empty-handed or without his favorite bottle of red wine. Carrie had a takeaway box from The Bread Basket. It was Mitch's favorite—Sara's squash casserole.

Leslie and Stan brought Stan's famous ribs, and Leslie made her pound cake that never disappointed. It was her grandmother's recipe and it had graced many tables when someone lost a loved one or they needed a special treat when recuperating from an illness.

Ben was busy in the kitchen, and he enjoyed watching the gathering of the crew in their little home. He put together a charcuterie board and was finishing up with placing all the finishing touches.

Carrie had the larger home and thought about hosting the dinner. She decided against it because it held unpleasant memories of Bill's death, and boxes were packed up for the move. She had accepted an offer on the house, and she rarely stayed there anymore, anyway. She spent most of her time at the Inn or at Atlantic Beach. Mitch and Sandra's house was a good size, but it had been totally baby-proofed, and there was baby paraphernalia in every room. You couldn't walk through the living room without encountering some contraption that Carrie had obtained to spoil Opal Grace. Leslie and Stan's house was in renovations to sell so she and Stan could move to a new house to be built at Four Oaks for them. The change of mind came about when Stan realized he liked what they were accomplishing so much with the Inn, that he would take early retirement. Leslie decided that if he was retiring, she would take an early out as well, and they amped up projects for the Inn to serve the corporate world with day retreats during the work week. It was flourishing with dates booked through Spring. Hopefully, the house and farm would sell soon, and Four Oaks Hall and Inn Estate would be their new home.

Leslie set up the outdoor bar for champagne and drinks, and Stan called everyone out to the fireplace. It was time to give her friends a good "attaboy" pat on the back. What started with her became an adventure when the ensemble pulled their resources together, and she wanted them to know how much value they brought to the table.

She poured everyone champagne and topped each glass with a strawberry slice on the rim. Laney gave her an eye roll because she constantly claimed that was a cheesy thing to do. Leslie smirked and that made Laney laugh. She knew Leslie did it just to get a rise out of her.

"Well, my crew, what a year we've had! This will be a bit long-winded, but I want to tell you how proud I am of what we have accomplished in a short period of time. I'm not sure if I can express in words the love and gratitude I have in my heart. Carrie, thank you for believing in the dream and putting your money where your mouth is. Laney and Ben—your cooking skills are already establishing a mark in these parts. Nobody does it better. Sandra—you are the "hostess with the mostest," and your skillful decorating and coordinating details are unmatchable. Last, but not least, Stan and Mitch. Thank you, Stan, for making my dream come true, and thank you, Mitch, for being the banker that knew a good thing to take a risk on when we went into produce farming at the Inn. Then we had a marriage. Ben and Laney—we look forward to seeing your relationship grow for years to come. Oh, last but certainly not least, and the sweetest of all occasions this year, baby Opal Grace for Sandra and Mitch. Oh, and Carrie—you and Robert are adorable together, and you have the cottage at the Inn and one at Atlantic Beach. Raise a glass! Here's to my friends, my partners in good times and troubled times, and in all things. What a sensational year. Cheers to you all. I love you!"

Ben raised his glass with one hand and his other arm around Laney, "Cheers to you, Leslie. Your dream became our dream, and all our lives changed because of you. Never in a million years would I have ever guessed that my life would end up being this amazing. To Leslie!"

"I think we can all agree that this crew makes a fabulous team. I could see it the moment I took you out on the yacht. I knew there was something special about you ladies and Ben—you are just icing on the cake, my man!" said Robert, as he laughed and raised his glass.

"To an outstanding year and another on the way! Cheers!" said Laney.

"Thank you all for the help and patience through our adoption. We couldn't have done it without all of you," said Sandra, as she swayed baby Opal back and forth in her arms by the warmth of the lantern.

"This year has been pivotal. That's the only way I know how to describe it. Or should I say - monumental. It's been a roller coaster for me. But right now, cheers to the trade winds continuing to steer us in the right direction," said Carrie, as she raised her glass.

"Well said, my dear, well said. A little of me may wear off on you after all. You could prove to be my first mate yet," said Robert as he gave her a salute and Carrie reciprocated with the same gesture.

The future was all that was discussed, and no one dwelled in the past. They envisioned years of success at Four Oaks Hall & Inn. Their evening was a celebration of the restoration to many lives. They held the key to the future now and they also held on to each other.

As for the secret of Mitch and Sandra's baby, the future would tell if it stayed a treasured secret locked away. Carrie had really taken to little Opal and even kept her a couple of days a week for Sandra to get out and have a break. The other days, you could find Opal Grace in her bassinet located in the office at Fork Oaks. She was never lacking for attention, and Mitch and Sandra appreciated the help.

As for Mae, she would carry her secret to the grave as well. That was her plan if her conscience would leave her alone. Her self-preservation was a powerful strength she possessed. It was almost as strong as her love for the family she had cared for all those years. What happened to Bill was his own fault, she reckoned. Served him right after the way he treated her. What Bill didn't know is that her sight and hearing were not as bad as he thought. She heard more and saw more than she ever let on. Being loyal to Carrie was her intention. She never told her about the floosies she had seen him with over the years because she could not bear to hurt her. Mae figured that Bill could not keep up the lies forever, and the truth would be revealed in its own good time. Eventually, Mae's thoughts proved to be right.

The winds of change came upon them all and rearranged their lives like a Carolina hurricane changed a landscape. But after every hurricane, clean up and restoration brings a newness to life, and that is exactly what happened for all of them. The pages of their stories became filled with revised endings, leaving them in a landscape of renewal and growth with deeper roots to strengthen their lives.

The years ahead would surely bring additional storms, with some being as fierce as a Carolina Category Five hurricane. Winds might blow, and changes were certain to come along the way, but the melody of their lives would continue to be woven together in a tetradic song.

Just like the willows, their inner grace will allow them to bend. As the oak grows deeper roots to anchor itself, their roots were firmly established and nourished by continual love and devotion to each other.

Most days right before sunset—no matter the weather, except for rain—Leslie would go to sit on the bench by the pond. If the Inn was hosting an event, she would slip away to take a moment to stop, meditate, and reflect on her blessings. To her, the bench had a therapeutic effect. It was where she spent her inner devotional time as her grandmother had done for many years. In this place, she felt her grandmother's spirit as she whispered prayers for family and friends. From her perspective on the bench, she could see the pond and the Inn. Beyond that you could see the many acres of land that Stan, with the help of Duke and Sonny now farmed. She could see the framing of their new home just beyond the creek at the tree line. From that spot, she could relive the fond memories of her childhood and see all the dreams she had ever wanted in living color. She could see life again.

Stan usually watched from the porch as she made her journey to the bench. His smile demonstrated the contentment in his heart as he sipped his evening coffee and admired the view against the backdrop of the sunset. Every evening as he watched the willows dance around her in the breeze, it was if they were welcoming her to join them with her company.

In the evening breeze, the oaks and willows swayed as she sat quietly and listened to their song. The rustling and swish of the branches soothed her soul. She would close her eyes and recall a treasured memory. While the willows danced on the bank of the pond, she would sit and take in the last of the light through their leaves. Before she left her seat on the bench, she always looked up to the branch that held the key that changed so many lives. The thought brought a smile of peace to her face. She was finally home.

THE END

A Word from the Author

I cannot have you depart from these pages without a personal thank you. Thank you for investing your time to read *The Key in the Willow Tree*.

This was truly a labor of love. I became invested in these ladies and their struggles and their joy. I hope you felt the same. It was also simultaneously one of the most difficult and rewarding projects I have ever experienced. From the first moment that I typed the first line, to the night that I finally typed the last, I was determined to get to the last.

I learned so much in the process and had the help of friends, beta readers, editors, publisher, and businesses. I thank you all. My husband demonstrated a great deal of patience as he listened to theories, plots, and heard the keys clicking at night.

As I did research with technical issues (although fiction, I want it to at least be believable) and listened to feedback from readers, I was humbled, educated, anxious, excited, and scared. Each time the editor corrected my run on sentences, like the one preceding this one, a bit of anxiousness would creep in. After the editing process we were able to keep the bones of the novel intact, just a better version. I also knew that my work would be a "PG" version and did not want to deviate from that rating. It would be nice if all works of literature came with the ratings like our favorite movies or tv series.

To keep up with details about book signings, updates, visit our blog spot. It is located at The Journey of an Independent Author (soidecidedtowrite.blogspot.com) or follow us on Facebook at our page *The Key in the Willow Tree*.

When you visit these locations, you will find more details about the recipes these ladies loved and the locations they liked to visit. You can also find details about the possibility of a sequel – I don't think their story ends here . . . do you? Drop me a personal note at lisaallen@thekeyinthewillowtree.com and let me know your thoughts. I look forward to hearing from you.

Thanks for reading!

Lisa C. Allen

About the Author

Lisa C. Allen is a writer with roots in Eastern North Carolina. Much of her career has been spent in publishing and the multimedia arena. She was the publisher and editor, of The Winterville Resident News for several years. *The Key in the Willow Tree* is her debut novel.

She enjoys the occasional visit to the mountains and the beaches she mentions in her book, as well as painting those two landscapes. She lives in Winterville, NC with her husband, Sam and she enjoys spending time with her children and granddaughters.

Please visit her at The Journey of an Independent Author (soidecidedtowrite.blogspot.com) or email her at lisaallen@ thekeyinthewillowtree.com. You can follow her on Facebook on her page The Key in the Willow Tree.

visit thekeyinthewillowtree.com